THE
ANTAGONISTS

By Ernest K. Gann

A SIGNET BOOK from
NEW AMERICAN LIBRARY
TIMES MIRROR

SIGNET TRADEMARK REG. U.S. PAT. OFF. AND FOREIGN COUNTRIES
REGISTERED TRADEMARK—MARCA REGISTRADA
HECHO EN CHICAGO, U.S.A.

SIGNET, SIGNET CLASSICS, SIGNETTE, MENTOR, AND PLUME BOOKS
are published by The New American Library, Inc.,
1301 Avenue of the Americas, New York, New York 10019

FIRST PRINTING, JANUARY, 1972

PRINTED IN THE UNITED STATES OF AMERICA

The Most Passionately Praised Historical Novel of the Decade!

"This is beyond question Ernest Gann's finest book, and with *Fate Is the Hunter* and *The High and the Mighty* to his credit, it makes *The Antagonists* quite a book indeed . . . one of those full, rich novels that becomes engraved in the reader's mind, and will not be forgotten."
—*Seattle Times*

"Wonderful! The most convincing historical novel I have read in years! A triumphant parable of human freedom . . . spirited, lusty, cinematic detail in storytelling . . . sheer grandeur of theme . . . Ernest Gann's most successful, emotional, and mature work."
—*San Francisco Chronicle*

"A remarkably vivid and absorbing achievement! Gann builds breathless suspense."
—*Washington Star*

"An exuberant historical novel! A return to the days of heroes larger than life silhouetted against the desert sky above the rock of Masada."
—*Kirkus Service*

This . . . for my dear Polly

Author's Note

In these days of patriotic cynicism some readers may be inclined to disbelieve the behavior of the zealots of Masada. I direct the doubts of such unfortunates to more contemporary martyrs, say those of Hungary who defied Russian tanks with rocks, and those like the Czech Jan Palach, who chose to welcome the Russian invaders by self-immolation. Also present at the barricades have been the many wildly courageous North and South Vietnamese, Cubans, Africans, Russians, Frenchmen, Germans, Chinese, Greeks, Bulgars, and Japanese, who in one fashion or another decided life was not worth living without what they personally conceived as freedom. These are the true Now people and there will unquestionably be more of them tomorrow.

In the loosely employed name of freedom man remains the only creature on earth to make war on his own species. Anyone who has convinced himself patriotism is dead has learned nothing from ancient history and does not know contemporary history.

I have been meticulously careful to insure authenticity throughout this book. Many facts were available, although nowhere near the quantity found in the usual research of a historical event. So if I have erred, it is not for want of trying. The works of Josephus were of course of inestimable value, but unfortunately he was not personally present to report the siege of Masada. The magnificent works and archeological research, plus the vicarious inspiration of Yigael Yadin, affected this writing more than any other single force. From his discoveries I have contrived a story.

Both Eleazar ben Yair and General Flavius Silva existed and were the actual antagonists at Masada. However, Eleazar ben Yair's career was terminated as described on Masada, and Silva seems to have simultaneously disappeared from history.

Friday Harbor   ERNEST K. GANN
San Juan Island

FLAVIUS SILVA
General of the Legions

One

DURING THE FOURTH YEAR OF VESPASIAN . . .
A.D. 73

"It is like this," said the Centurion Rosianus Geminus. "Your putrefying helmet is your home and it will be until you are too crippled to fight, or you are killed, or you are pensioned off. This putrefying desert is no paradise, but it is not so bad when you remember what it is like in the northern lands this time of year. . . ."

He scratched at his black spade beard and heaved a ponderous sigh to indicate how thoroughly he understood his listener's misery. "We are all together in this putrefying shithouse and I don't pretend to know how long it will last, but there's no sense mooning about where you came from or why. You're here. I'm just as tired as you are of looking at that putrefying rock and watching it dance when the sun gets high. One thing only will I promise you. This putrefying situation won't last. Our putrefying General may have his snoot in the jug more than is good for him, but he'll bring the Jews down from this rock if he has to give up the grape to do it. I have known Flavius Silva a long time, soldier."

Having spoken, Geminus, the many-scarred veteran who knew all things, moved his bulk off through the starlight.

When the stars began to dissolve in the ashen light the sentry murmured his gratitude. It was nearly the end of his patrol and no matter where you stood a post an empty belly sounded the same. Condescending remarks from putrefying officers about how things could be much worse did not fill your grain bin any more than they soothed this maddening eruption of heat rash wherever metal, leather and flesh met, or the most powerful irritation which was not in the belly but in the groin. The old-timers jeered and spat and mimed copulation with an imaginary female if you mentioned the yearning, but some of the better-natured said they were old men of eighteen before they realized they had married the Legion.

He looked up at the black mass that obliterated most of the eastern sky. It was there forever and ever. Like the people on it ... and the stars. Here was another morning staring up at the hated rock of Masada which was more a mountain than a rock. You were supposed to watch the chasm between you and the rock, as if the Jews could pass unseen beneath the stars. The officers knew it was impossible and the putrefying General should know it was impossible.

The sentry pushed back his helmet until the rim tormented the pustules and volcanoes on the back of his neck. He sighed. All of this was so far from home.

He turned to look west toward the center of the camp and his own tent, which was at least more of a home than a helmet. It stood not far from the much larger tent which was the General's and which probably *was* like a home. No common soldier entered there except Praetorian guards and they were so anxious to keep cushions under their putrefying asses they would never speak of the wonders within that tent. So every man had his own idea, and some said it was full of booty all shining and some said the whole world east of Brundisium was ruled right in there, and others said the General was drunk all the time, especially at night.

He was called Shem, the son of Ishmael, that same Ishmael who along with thirty other captives had been used as a human torch during the celebrations after Jerusalem. Shem's father had been set afire because Titus wished to celebrate the birthday of his brother Domitian— or so he declared. Those close to Titus recognized the burning as a matter of dual purpose, not only would it add spice to the routine slaughter of some two thousand other Jews, it would also serve notice on all who might witness the show even by hearsay that the war was over and the Romans would not tolerate the slightest opposition.

Although many of Titus's staff considered the burning distasteful and urged that all those selected be allowed to kill each other or prove they were mortals against the wild beasts assembled for the purpose, the majority were more unhappy about the site. Instead of a proper amphitheater to accommodate their number, the shadeless, fly-infested valley Titus had chosen for the occasion offered little comfort, and those who crimped their rumps sitting on stones said the choice was probably a true reflection of Titus's secret contempt for his brother.

Shem, the son of Ishmael, drawn irresistibly to the vicinity along with more than a hundred other boys, crept to the edge of a thicket which rimmed the valley and from that distance watched his father expire. At fourteen he had reached the *naar* stage in life and he knew then that he would spend the rest of it killing Romans. Now, having survived for seventeen years and therefore having ripened into a *bachur*, he was entrusted with one of the thirty-eight towers along the ramparts. Thus far he had struck down eleven careless Romans with only fifteen bolts.

There were times, as on this morning, when Shem thought of himself as a bird. For his perch was so lofty and commanded such a view that he experienced, before the dawn light revealed the horizon, a soaring sensation. It was as if he had been lifted among the stars and there supplied with a pair of wings to drift as he pleased over his friends and enemies. Just below his tower slept the people of Masada, then in the void all around lay the soft-lit desert. He had but to glance downward to see Romans. The lights in their camps twinkled like the stars above and they appeared to be in the same number. And along the west side, where the Romans drove their captives night and day to labor on the great ramp, the torches of the overseers moved about unceasingly.

The Romans had learned their lesson. Even at night they now kept their distance and if work had to be done close beneath the walls of Masada, they sent their captive Jews. Or, Shem suspected, they disguised themselves as such.

The possibility troubled him greatly and he had spent many nights trying to think of a way to identify the targets he so desired. It had been much too long, nearly a month since Shem, son of Ishmael, had killed a Roman.

General Flavius Silva lay flat on his back watching a thin crescent of light appear above the middle of his tent and slowly gather intensity. Its very presence caused him to reflect unhappily upon the thickness of his head, and alternately, upon his house in Praeneste. By all the gods, it was the same frustration everywhere whether you tried to accomplish something in that lovely rose-scented region so convenient to Rome or here in the wilderness of Judea. A new house or a siege—to have things properly done required more than an order. You must see after whatever it was yourself, letters from architects notwithstanding.

For a moment he reviewed the latest post from a correspondent he had decided was not only a scoundrel but inept as well—Antoninus Mamilianus, who presumed to call himself an architect.

> To Flavius Silva, General of the Legions, Procurator of Judea, from Antoninus Mamilianus, greeting:
> . . . I am confident you would approve all the latest work done during the past month, though the cost has exceeded the original estimate by a considerable sum. Most of the excess is due to changes in plans made by your esteemed self . . . in particular the addition of a bathing pool and the six statues which will grace the peristylium. The columns are of Etruscan marble and the heads of obsidian, which I was fortunate to obtain. I tried very hard to persuade the great Sextus Cerealius to do the sculpting, but he is so much in demand these days he could not promise delivery in less than three years. Consequently I have split the work between Drusus Balbus, whose reputation may be known to you, and Colpurnius Fobatus, a Greek freedman from Syracuse who has recently produced some interesting basalts.
> Both of these men are expensive to say the least, the former demanding sixty thousand sesterces and the latter forty thousand with an additional bonus of ten thousand if he delivers before the close of this year. You may obtain some satisfaction in the knowledge

that when the flower boxes are in place and the grape
arbor and shade trees are all flourishing, then the
whole must certainly fulfill your original desires. When
all is done the villa should be a place of great
tranquility.

Silva tried to remember what Vitruvius had written in
his *Training of the Architect*. Something about practice
and theory. Something like, Those who rely only on theory . . . were hunting shadow, not substance?
Mamilianus would do well to reread his Vitruvius.

. . . there has been a great deal of unrest among the
building trades recently. First the plasterers refused to
whitewash their own work, which required calling in a
second group whose monetary demands were such that
I myself was stunned. However there was no individual
workman who could even come near the villa until
this matter was settled, so I could only surrender to
their extortions and take comfort in the assurance that
my principal value to you as a creative watchdog is to
keep harmony among the laborers, and thus we may
progress steadily. Then just last week the plumbers
refused to install the ornamental bronze stopcocks
without payment for the extra labor involved fitting to
the present lead ducts . . .

Et cetera!
The crescent of light now above was caused by some
clod who had set the tent ropes too taut, therefore causing
a breach between the cloth itself and the supporting pole
and therefore betraying Rosianus Geminus, who was not
only Captain of the Praetorian Guard but was also responsible for details concerning his General's comfort.
Ergo, Geminus would soon hear harsh words from his
supreme commander on the subject of military perfection
in the Tenth Legion and he in turn would pass his embarrassment on to the clod who had caused the crescent. Via
the end of his most eloquent whip, no doubt. And the clod
would protest that it never rains in Judea and so what was
all the fuss about a little gap in the General's tent, and he
would be right—and he would still suffer the lash. Because
the Roman army was too small for the world it must rule,

it existed on discipline, not only for the people it conquered but for itself. The bleeding flesh of the clod would remind the entire camp that so small an oversight as a tent rope set incorrectly found punishment.

Silva decided it was his own head that must be made of obsidian and during the night someone had certainly sprinkled his eyes with cinders. He half rose on the couch to look down upon the woman beside him. She appeared to be sleeping. Doubtless, he thought, she is faking, as she has done with varied success during the more aroused moments of yet another night oversoaked in wine and now lost forever. She had squirmed at the appropriate times, grunted and moaned as if by military drill numbers, but there had been no inner heat to her flesh or emission of her life juice during their writhings. She had submitted once more with sullen willingness, complying with every physical instruction, and had thus once more made a mockery of their union.

He regretted the night. It was as if he had again lost a skirmish he should not have lost. A woman armed only with a skin of polished amber, he thought, has caused me to taste the bitterness of retreat and is so careless of her victory she dares make me wait upon her awakening—as if I were some poor courtier standing attendance upon a queen.

Watching her, amused at his patience with her, he wondered how he could make absolute conquest of this female who was like an old and acid woman masquerading in a youthful body, a sorceress who had managed to case her first spell from a distance and then close it upon him like a net. It was a unique relation, he thought, the result of some barbaric necromancy he could not recognize. Preposterous! Why should he trouble himself with this one female when he had only to clap his hands for a multitude? Yet a multitude of what? What relief was to be found in wrestling with the filthy local cows, those diseased camp followers of skin, gristle, hair and bone left over from the long campaign? They were hardly solace for the Lowest Legionary. During all this time in Judea which had now been over three years, he had not before seen one woman he had considered worthy to receive his sperm.

Have I been so long from Rome, he thought, that this girl-woman now beside me seems a prize? How, if I am so stubborn and foolish as to keep her near me until she becomes habit, will she appear on the Capitoline Hill? How will she behave in the theater of Marcellus, the shops about the Forum, or, say, strolling beneath Pompeii's portico? If I take this country bumpkin to the games, will I introduce her to my friends . . . to be laughed at? Will the dear sweet absolutely merciless ladies of Rome perceive her history at a glance? "Regard the blind General," they might say, "he who lost both his vision and his mind in Palestine and so brought home a trophy he thought was a baboon. Another Jewess! Have you heard that on the sight of her every last one of his household gods jumped into the Tiber? Do you suppose she will one day insist poor addled Flavius Silva have himself circumcised?" Ouch!

What a spectacle, he mused. Apparently I am just another stallion thrusting myself at something I have told myself is, or should be, in heat. And the owner of the something looks so very tempting because she has no real competition. Am I so taken with her simply because she speaks Greek as if it were her native tongue, Hebrew so that it does not sound like a throat irritation and Aramaic so that even I can comprehend it? Does she drop her final consonants in the latest vulgarian fashion? No indeed! Not once have I caught her softening her W's or otherwise chewing on our national tongue. Then why?

Do I snort and paw the ground in her presence simply because she is fearless or is such a clever mime she convinces me she is not afraid? How hungry must I be, and lonely, to find myself preening for her arrival and then posing with chin in hand like some eager youth while I listen to her as if she had some immortal message to convey! And of all the manifestations doubled and redoubled in absurdity, I must play the game of seduction, actually cooperate in petty flirtation while we survey each other and she so coldly measures the force of my desire. When the heat and pressure is sufficient then we must toy with each other, experimenting and very cautiously exploring as if she were the most innocent virgin, and then at last when my eyes are dazed and I have been reduced to a whinnying stud, then at last, depending upon the time of day, the weather, the consumption of wine with our meal of assignation, coupled with what the soothsayer confided in her yesterday, then after an overture of laughter or tears, and

testing the velocity and direction of the wind whether it be
north or south or east or west, matched against the
existence of any possible noise, musical or otherwise, then
and only then can we embark on one variety of fornication ... unless at the very last moment she changes her
mind.

For which activity, he reminded himself, there is nothing worse than an indifferent partner.

Now he was certain that she was feigning sleep and he
saw that she had even contrived to fix an appearance of
contentment about her rather heavily featured face. She is
too large of mouth, he told himself, as he had so many
times before. On any other female her mouth might be
considered outrageous, yet her lips formed such a seductive frame they caught all attention. Her cheekbones and
nose and brow were also molded with definite force, and
still each was in such harmony with its neighboring feature
the whole visage became a subtle masterpiece. Was it not,
blind man? After all, a true masterpiece dared not be
perfect in all its parts.

He suddenly remembered the first time he had noticed
her eyes staring at him defiantly from an ocean of other
eyes, mostly beseeching. That day, less than a month ago,
he had left this interminable business in the wilderness and
traveled with all speed to Jericho, where the garrison was
reported to have mutinied. The report proved to be an
exaggeration although the troops were certainly out of
control, and no wonder, since they were all auxiliaries, a
mixed bag of Syrians, Numidians, Greeks, and Arabians
without a true Roman among them. The chief fault lay
with their weakspined commander, who called himself by
the normally honored Roman name of Quadratus although
by birth the man was an Egyptian. The poor wretch had
been so terrified of his troops he had allowed them to
rampage as they willed simply because their pay had been
delayed. Among other activities they thought to solve their
greed by rounding up all able-bodied inhabitants of Jericho and selling them off as slaves. Just who would buy
during these days when the markets from Rome to Byzan-
tium were glutted, they had not bothered to consider.

It pleased Silva to recall that it had taken only himself,
ten of his Praetorians and forty mounted Legionaries to
bring that rabble to their senses. He had plunged into the
turmoil driving his finest chariot, the one presented to him

after the fall of Jerusalem by Titus himself—a glorious vehicle with bronze heads of Medusa decorating the wheels and a golden satyr as the finial on the end of the draw-pole. Surrounded by his Praetorians, wearing his finest cuirass with the breastplate embossed with the four seasons, a bull, an eagle and two standards against a sky background, he had driven through the rebellious troops as if they were beneath contempt. He had commanded them to release the Jews at once and their answer had been shouts of derision. Then he had raised his right hand signifying his Roman word was Roman bond and assured them their pay was newly minted and en route from Rome—which was the truth or he would not have given his right hand. It pleased him now to think that in his thirty-seven years he had not once pledged his word to deceive. His predecessor Lucilius Bassus had been expert at the double tongue, but there was a different sort of Procurator of Judea now, a true Cornelli on his mother's side, hers being the last womb in the Empire to produce bearers of that famous and most honored name.

After some grumbling all but a handful of the auxiliaries released their captives, but one group of a hundred or so hesitated too long. As their protests continued Silva had simply opened his left fist in their direction and instantly his escort charged into their midst. Nine of the hesitants were run through and left to die in the street before the lesson in military protocol was thoroughly understood. When order had been restored Silva had patiently explained to the survivors that looting, raping and killing were to be done by order—Roman order—or not at all. And he had advised them to pass on his proclamation to their comrades. *All* Jews were now part of the Empire's wealth and as a consequence not available for casual distribution among those who depended for their very life upon that supreme authority.

When he had first arrived in Jericho several hundred of the more resourceful Jews had sought protection from the marauding auxiliaries in Quadratus's own courtyard. It was a pathetic refuge had they really known the man, but at least they were spared the perils and indignities occurring in the streets. It was then that he had first found her eyes among so many others.

Silva remembered how Quadratus had managed to host a reasonably decent meal on the upper terrace of his quarters, albeit the man was so distressed about his own safety he could hardly drink his wine. The quail had been tough and the olives mediocre, but there had been an excellent mullet fresh from the Sea of Galilee, and for a cracked-lipped, dried out, desert soldier that fish had been enough to make a feast of the occasion.

Afterward they had stepped to the parapet surrounding the terrace and looked down upon the Jews. They had been confined in the courtyard for three days and of course were milling and fighting among themselves as Jews always did when their hands were idle. It was astonishing how much mischief these people could get themselves into if they were not gainfully employed. It seemed to be one of their eternal curses not to know what was good for them.

Quite by accident Silva had noticed one group of Jews who remained a little apart from the others. They were quiet and only the female among them looked up. After a moment he had realized that she was challenging him. He found himself wishing she would forsake her boldness and look away, but instead she seemed to defy him in a way no other Jew had ever dared. Finally it was he, Flavius Silva, master of Judea, who had broken off the staring.

"Do you know that girl?" he had asked Quadratus.

"Yes. She is of a family from Alexandria. I understand they were rather prosperous shippers—mostly grain to Rome."

"Is that the father beside her?"

"Yes. He seems reasonably intelligent for a Jew. Actually the entire family affects an educated manner which I find rather amusing."

"What are they doing in Palestine?"

"They claim they had merely planned a pilgrimage to Jerusalem and their temple, and to visit relatives. But of course Jews are incapable of purely exalted intentions or even simple affairs. One must always seek for their hidden motives. They also came to arrange for the export of wheat, oil and balsam, because they are, or were, members of an association we in Egypt called the Naviculari."

"Who is the other man?"

"He is brother to the father and a native of Jericho. It was he who urged his relatives to come, three years ago. Rather bad timing, wouldn't you say, General?"

That pompous ass Quadratus had then laughed so

uproariously all eyes both far away and near had turned upon him.

Silva could still hear his laughter becoming thin and then ceasing altogether when he had decided he had endured more than enough Egyptian snobbery. Why did that decayed race persist in behaving as if they were all descendants of Cleopatra?

"You laugh too easily, Quadratus, which is perhaps the reason your troops are so unruly. I will solve your present troubles, but if they get out of hand again I warn you that it will be *your* head on a pike."

The girl could not possibly have heard the reprimand yet she seemed pleased when Quadratus had nearly gone down on his knees. "I am deeply grateful, Sire. You may be sure I shall find some way to enrich your life in return for mine."

How such a craven goat could enrich anyone's life remained a mystery until more than a week had passed and once more the desert seemed all of life and all there had ever been of life. Then a small caravan was reported approaching Masada from the oasis of Ein Gedi in the north.

With typical Egyptian deviousness and admittedly some imagination Quadratus had attempted to repay his debt. He had sent "the eyes" to the wilderness, accompanied by her father, her uncle and his wife, three alleged cousins, as many servants and an armed escort to assure their safe delivery. And with unmitigated impudence he had revealed his *modus operandi,* having also sent a message of such flowering phrase and obvious scent, the long dead Cleopatra must have wept in her tomb. Worse, an Egyptian had presumed the Roman form in his communication.

To Flavius Silva, Procurator of Judea, General commanding the Xth Legion, from Ptolemaeus Quadratus, Military Governor pro tem of Jericho, greeting:

All those acquainted with your location inform me it is one of the most desolate and uncomfortable places on earth. Thus do I even more admire your noble perseverance and utter dedication to the task at hand. In such a place I can only assume that even a Roman of your well-deserved power and resourcefulness cannot but lack for certain fundamental amenities of life, and for that want be troubled, which as I think of you robs me of what little sleep this minor command permits. . . .

The vision of Quadratus losing sleep over his command-er-in-chief's discomfort was touching, but as nothing compared to his subsequent gesture.

As he reviewed the heart of the message Silva found himself smiling.

. . . forgive me, distinguished General, if I presume to send you a present which may at first be difficult to open and may even try your patience. With your very great charm I have a notion this gift may soon become more reasonable and afford you some hours of amusement and soothing relief from your arduous duties.

. . . though my gift comes to you amply supplied with tents and all manner of goods, I apologize for the size, the truth being that the most important part resolutely refused to leave without the others. I would not, of course, be surprised or in the slightest offended if you disposed of the excess at your pleasure.

. . . inspiration for this gift came to me as I watched your face during the recent troubles here and particularly when you stood on my parapet observing the courtyard. It is said that we Egyptians are possessed of a special sense which permits us to detect human affinities even at a distance. I shall make a sacrifice to Venus in the hope that in this case my senses were functioning at their peak and that my selecion pleases you.

May the great Vespasian rule us forever!

Quadratus, you conniving bastard! While you should have been inspiring more discipline in your troops you were scheming in your Oriental fashion to cover your faults with a perfumed gift. Very well, Quadratus, you have indeed pleased me, though I refuse to become so lost in this strange creature as to forget your shortcomings. Yes, your gift was to the mark, for I have been yearning for some trifling of softness in this present environment. We are surrounded by rocks each harder than the other, and the people we oppose are harder than the rocks and that greatest rock of all, Masada, appears more formidable every day. Hence, as you hoped, Quadratus, I am disposed to smile upon your name whether it falls from the lips of others or merely passes through my mind. And I do salute your acute perception, for you have chosen to my taste exactly; were your choice any other I must certainly have refused. But I am not at all certain I can ever excuse your propagandizing this girl and her family with tales of the fabled Bernice and what she has done for herself, let alone what that extraordinary Jewess has done to Titus and, so the gossip goes, to Vespasian himself. Oh you have planned with the utmost cunning, my fine Quadratus, for if such a consummation were the result, if indeed this creature could drain my wits as well as my testicles and make of me another Titus granting her every whim and favor, then where would *you* be, my good fellow? Directly under the sun. As her original sponsor it would be quite natural for you to become her confidant and as her confidant become my secret sovereign, nicely positioned to maneuver all manner of affairs to suit yourself. And so in time there would be a new Procurator for Judea, oddly enough an Egyptian by birth and talents, one who calls himself Quadratus in the Roman fashion. As a dividend you would have early revenge for whatever humiliation my presence in Jericho may have brought you, for you would have the exquisite pleasure of observing me trapped in that most ancient of snares, that unenviable bypass in which a man wonders if his woman serves him for himself or because of what he can do for her.

But no, Quadratus. As a career soldier I can promise you that it is the unexpected factors in any campaign that spill our best-laid plans as messily as an overturned cup of wine. My father used to advise me against worrying about what might happen, because he said what you worry about doesn't happen—it is the unborn thought that matures unseen and then very suddenly explodes before us. You failed to consider one element in this elaborate cabal and that is the *nature* of the female you sent as a gift. I am certain that it never occurred to you that in order for her to please me sufficiently to lose my reason, then I must please *her*—a development I regret to report has not been accomplished.

I suspect the trouble lies in your anxiety to launch her on this expedition without resorting to torture or threats

of death, both of which you must have known would be
the undoing of your final purpose. If you did not actually
promise, then you at least suggested that if she obliged me
I would no doubt proclaim her free, and possibly the
members of her family now accompanying her. This is the
treaty she is really after and she will think of nothing else
until it is agreed. In some ways it is a pity you cannot be
here to witness her tender regard for me.

He pressed his hand against her cheek and called her
name.

"Sheva! The morning is here."

She groaned, then opened her eyes and stared at him as
if he were a total stranger.

"Can I go now?" Her voice was flat.

"No. I have been thinking about you, which is amusing,
and these days with your insane compatriots perched
above my head like so many defecating pigeons I find too
little cause for laughter."

"They are not my compatriots. I have told you a
hundred times I am not a native of this Godforsaken
land."

"How you blaspheme the soil your perpetually invisible
God is said to prefer! If you were a proper Jew your
home would be anywhere. Sometimes I think we have
more Jews living in Rome than Romans."

She started to rise, but he caught her arm and pulled
her down to the couch again. "I have a notion to have
another go at you." He spoke more in jest than intent, yet
he was vaguely disappointed that his words caused her to
twist quickly from his grasp. After she had broken away
she stood looking down at him and he could find no hint
of encouragement in her eyes. Suddenly she reached
down, pulled back the silken coverlet and seized his penis.

"There is one power even General Silva does not have,"
she sneered. "Behold the glory of Rome reduced to a
worm!"

For a moment not a sound passed between them. An
instant flush of rage sent the blood stinging through his
body. Then as suddenly as her hand had closed upon him
he became limp. He put back his head and began to
chuckle softly.

"Alas, Sheva, you speak the truth." When she released
him he looked down at his nakedness and grunted. "But if

you ever try that again I recommend you be more gentle. Otherwise I shall most certainly have you crucified."

She shrugged her shoulders and stepped to the opposite side of the tent. There she raised her arms and slipped into a heavily embroidered linen robe. What a pity, he thought. Now that amber skin is hidden again.

As she tied her sandals she spoke angrily in Greek. "I was promised that if I did not resist your loathsome paws and jaws, if I tolerated contact with your reptilian skin, then I would be free."

"Who made such promises?"

"You."

"Nonsense. I had a little wine but I never lost my balance, mental or otherwise."

He pushed himself to a sitting position and instantly found that his head was like a great marble stone. He decided that he knew why statues carved so that they appeared to be holding up the roof of a temple were always bent forward. He had indeed drunk a great deal of wine. It was happening too often and he must stop it. If Vespasian knew a man was seriously courting the grape he was soon relieved—and sooner or later Vespasian knew everything.

Holding his forehead he said, "I think you poisoned me last night."

"My God, who is the one and only God, blessed me with leprosy and instructed me to share it with you."

Slowly and very cautiously he stretched his arms and legs. He took his time. Then he yawned. "If that be true I know of a certain Greek surgeon attached to the Tenth Legion who for the carelessness of his examination will be impaled butt-up on a rusty javelin." He groaned and added, "Come rub the back of my neck."

He was mildly surprised that she obeyed without hesitation; that was the spell of this female—she had so many inherent surprises. You kept wanting to see what happened next.

He noticed that she manipulated her fingers in such a way that their movements could not possibly be mistaken for a caress, but the effect was still soothing so he twisted his head far enough around to smile at her. "I have wasted some time this morning trying to decide what it is about you that intrigues me. I finally decided I have been so long in this noxious land that I can no longer differenti-

ate between a she-goat and a woman. I even wondered if
it could be that when I lie with you my normally discrimi-
nating penis discovers something rare, or is it that he has
lost communication with my brain and neither cares what
the other does?"

"Perhaps it's the way I smell? All Jews stink, do they
not, great Caesar?"

"Oh come now, let us not spoil these intriguing excur-
sions by preoccupation with facts. I prefer to ignore your
unfortunate ancestry."

He noticed that her moving fingers had not lost a beat.
They could have been talking about the weather. I must
therefore be certain to maintain my own composure as
well, no matter what the provocation, he thought. The
game is amusing because my opponent is alert to my
every weakness and thus forces me to remain on the
defensive. Even so, she cannot possibly win unless I permit
her to rattle me, in which event I might do or say
something very foolish. If once I allow her to wheedle
through my defense then that will be the beginning of
the end. It is I who will be made captive, and what is
more rare than a truly merciful female?

For a time they were silent and Silva listened to the
grinding hum that never ceased outside his tent. It was
like living in the center of a rock quarry, he thought, yet it
was a great deal more endurable than if the sound
stopped, which could only mean something was wrong
with the great work at hand, a military engineering feat
all men on earth, foe or friend, must soon admire. Or, he
had often considered, laugh at. Flavius Silva's great ramp!
Ho! Ho! Dare give the man six cubits on his chains and no
more and do not forget to remove his teeth lest he bite his
keeper. Can't you see he is insane?

It was unfortunate that Vespasian had never seen
Masada. Then he might better understand how its conquest could not be simply a matter of attack in force. If
Vespasian were here he could only agree that the Jews on
top were maniacs, and he could also hear them declare
themselves as to how they would not come down from
Masada at any persuasion, and how all Romans were the
obvious result of mass fornication between baboons and
hyenas. What a satisfaction it would be to point at the
summit of the rock after the Jews had dumped their daily

quota of insults and say to Vespasian, "As you may easily observe, Sire, there is no way to scale the heights unless you are a lizard. Therefore we must bring these heights down to our level, which means moving a good part of that mountain to that mountain, which is of course expensive. But when the ramp is finished you can see how we will move our machines up the ramp, break through the wall, and finish this very last nuisance in Judea. . . ." And of course Vespasian would smile approvingly and announce loudly enough for all his staff to hear that Flavius Silva had created something of a military marvel which, after all, one might expect from a genius. Ah? He would *not* so speak unless there had been a vast change in his philosophy since last seen—when was it?—on the very day he had announced the construction of a forum. The most parsimonious Roman in history would complain bitterly of the expense involved in building an absolutely necessary military tool and demand to know why the job couldn't be done with one hundred donkeys instead of five hundred. And if the ramp proved a failure? For a certainty General Flavius Silva would soon find himself a Procurator of the 5 per cent tax on inheritances somewhere in the frozen wilds of Britannia. At best.

Listening, Silva tried to separate the grinding sounds of great stones being moved from the constant echoes and reverberations of pick and hammer, the squeal of sledges, and the snapping of whips. There were counterpoint cries of pain and anger, the honk of pigs and the bray of donkeys from outside the camp wall, and the occasional shouts of complaint and derision of his soldiers. All this in the middle of a desert wilderness. All this, he thought, for less than a thousand stubborn Jews! He listened for a shout from the heights, but all sound from above seemed to be lost in the general bedlam.

He tipped back his head and sighed. "Bacchus has covered my tongue with fungus. I will not touch another drop of wine until your friends up there surrender."

Her fingers did not pause as she answered. "Congratulations. You have just ordered yourself to abstain forever."

"The ramp will be finished soon. The grapes can wait so long."

"Ho!" she said contemptuously although her fingers continued rhythmically, "You haven't the will."

Now the fingers stopped and she moved around to face him. "Now what about your promise? You said I would be free. You said no harm will come to me unless I commit a civil crime. Those were your own words, great and benign Governor of Judea."

"Then I *was* drunk."

"So? It is as I thought." She stood before him, her eyes unwavering.

He looked away. Vaguely now he did recall some discussion about her status, but when wine commanded who was not inclined to become overly sympathetic to the woes of others? Yes, once in Gaul he had presented a fine horse to a passing beggar simply because the man's feet were bare and it was snowing. And because in the fort he had just left, which was near Chardonay, he had drunk a skinful. Ah, my dear poor brain! It is so mired in remorse it can only cope with the most routine matters this morning. It tells me I must smell like a camel and the sooner I refresh with a bath the better. It also tells me this Sheva has me pinned to something I said when out of my wits.

"*What* is as you thought?" he asked. He looked up to meet her searching eyes and found it so uncomfortable that he looked above her head and studied the crescent of light. "What did you think? Come tell me what is gnawing at you. I am in good temper."

"I have been thinking that your word is as weak as your will—*and* your loins," she said flatly.

He rose quickly and flinging back his arm struck her across the mouth. The blow propelled her far from the couch and brought blood to her lips.

His voice rang out so hysterically when he called for the guard he could not believe it was his own. When they appeared he waited for his heavy breathing to subside. "Take this female—" he began. Take her and do what? How could this little slut be best repaid? I must show her the mercy of wine is not a permanent affliction and I must show myself now before it is forever too late that I can be rid of her.

From now on, he resolved, he would treat all Jews as Jews, as a treacherous race of barbarians. Furthermore he would not touch so much as a drop of wine until he was relieved in Judea and was safely established in the new house near Praeneste. And he would most of all not waste any more of his precious time on this vindictive little animal or her relatives.

He deliberately kept his voice soft and controlled when he motioned to the guards. "Take this woman to the Centurion Rosianus Geminus. Say that I wish her given her freedom. He will release her in the camp of the third cohort to run at will—after he has called for fifty volunteers to achieve the following reward. The first man to catch and mount her will receive fifty shekels. Once he is done she is to be free again so that a second man may win forty-nine shekels. The last man, who I doubt need be very fleet of foot—perhaps old Galineus who was somewhat crippled in Macedonia might be the final one to pin her down—will receive one shekel. . . ."

He inclined his head slightly toward her and thought, At last I have seen dread in Sheva's eyes. "By that time one shekel is about what she will be worth."

He was determined to appear indifferent as the guards took her arms and urged her toward the exit. Paternus and Severns, peasant lads from Spain, very strong and not very bright, he thought. Look at them, Sheva—can't you see from their stone faces that the best of your wiles will not alter their orders? Can't you see they are iron men with iron heads and unless you have the good sense to beg my mercy they will indeed take you to the camp of the third cohort? Can't you see, little Jewess, that I am a very lonely man and can't you remember how only a short time ago we were locked in such pleasure—and perhaps, could there not be even more for both of us, given time and understanding? Would it astound you to know, little Jewess, that I too am frightened of what might become of me and that I need you?

He searched her face for the slightest hint of compromise and finding none halted the guards with his raised hand.

"Sheva. Do you understand you can never return? Do you understand what will happen to you?

She stared at him in exactly the same way she had from the courtyard in Jericho.

"Yes," she said quietly. "And I understand the word of a noble Roman General. Like all other Romans you speak with your mouth and promise with your anus!"

She cleared her throat carefully and spat directly into his face.

LATER, General Flavius Silva sat in his oval-shaped campaign bath, which was of bronze and lavishly ornamented at both ends with ram's heads. It had been given to him by his godfather, Sejanus Piso, a name revered in Roman military society, and the occasion had been Silva's original assignment as a Tribune with the Seventh Legion in Dalmatia. He had not then intended to serve more than the customary six months after which he would strive for a senatorial career. Alas, he thought, such a divergence was now highly unlikely. I may be a Procurator newly appointed, but for more than fifteen years I have been the world's most dedicated procrastinator! Witness how I have contrived to postpone every separation from the army, using the limp excuse that it was in its way its own guarantee of the gods' favor. The same life, the same bath, the same sword and personal equipage through all of my travels and wars. Regard this tub! It has become a reflection of myself, a much-used thing, prematurely aged, quite unnaturally beaten and dented and scarred in performance of its duty. There, at the foot, is a crumpling left as a memorial of that clumsy donkey responsible for its transport across Macedonia. The beast fell over a cliff and it took half a cohort of men to retrieve the tub. Yes, as am I ... dilapidated. So many dents and scratches acquired banging around on camels in Africa, horses in Aquitania, barges, sleds, quinquiremes, caïques, and the backs of slaves in Thrace, Dalmatia, Britannia and Lusitania.

Silva wondered idly if he should give the tub a rank and medal for service and perhaps promote it once a year?

He looked down at his body. Ah, it matched the bath all too well, even to the bronzing provided by the Judean sun. There was the molded crater in his right thigh, the souvenir of a Thracian javelin which the surgeon, a rather clever Greek, had thought better to dig out rather than pull through.

The fellow had first soaked a sponge in Mandragora juice, then placed it in your mouth. As he had predicted, the juice slipped down to your digestive tract and its soporific effect at least partially eased the pain when he cut away and tied off the blood vessels and finally cauterized their orifices with a hot iron. The result was a well-healed blemish now sharing an originally well-formed body with a rather full complement of others.

"I had better do all I can to sharpen my wit," he said to Epos, his Numidian, "because this overabused carcass is becoming a thing of very little value." It pleased him to make a confidant of the Numidian since the man was deaf and dumb, yet not as a consequence of nature, which would have left him merely another uninteresting slave. His former master had been a magistrate and tax farmer in Cyprus and it seemed Epos had observed him seduce a Cypriot boy and had been so unwise as to confirm the fact when the consul's hopelessly narrow-minded wife began to ask questions. While it was intriguing to reflect on what might have been Epos's fate had he refused to testify before the wife, the magistrate's fury was forever recorded. Determined that Epos would pass on no more gossip concerning himself or anyone else, he had ordered his eardrums destroyed with repeated and prolonged head-slapping, and then had one half of his tongue removed. Soon after, the jealous wife killed the magistrate over a subsequent affair, again with a boy, and eventually Epos, as part of the estate, was sent off to the Antioc market where Silva had bought him. And why not? He was a bargain at a mere one thousand sesterces, hardly a week's salary for a Procurator. Few people wanted a mute hovering about, but for a General of the Legions who must have his own secrets, how could there be a better attendant?

As Epos oiled his body, Silva wryly inspected his own powerful chest, noting with pleasure the absence of fat about his middle, and with casual regret his legs, which were much too long for the bath. The right leg with its scar of Thracian revenge was muscular and as fine a limb as ever, but the left without a scratch on it was now almost a third less in diameter and visibly shorter by almost two inches. Procrastination again. During the attack on Jerusalem, Sextus Cerealius, Commander of the Fifth Legion, had maneuvered himself into a tight spot. He should have known better than to arrange a parley with the Jews; the dunce had convinced himself that for a few thousand shekels he would be told of some easy entrance to the city. He had agreed to take only four men as escort and of course was ambushed. Cerealius, who was a much better politician than a soldier, would never have orated again if you had not chanced along the same gully with a troop of horses. The Jews fled and you swung down from your horse very much the haughty fellow. Too quickly. Instead of Cerealius's thanks you soon received his sympathy, for in your hasty dismounting you had landed on a rock instead of solid earth, sprawled face down in the dust in a most undignified manner, and somehow managed to part most of your Achilles tendon.

The pain was endurable when diluted with wine, so it had been nearly a week before you had summoned the Greek surgeons. They had contrived poultices of elaterium without favorable result so they had filled you with poppy-tear pills and once again they had cut and tied. They said the leg would always be short and you would limp forever. A gimpy old man at thirty-seven! Zeus! You could not catch a turtle. As a final and bitter reminder of the event, Cerealius had managed to have his cipher of a son assigned to your staff. Now *there* was a lad to make a man grateful he had remained childless!

The warmth of the bath and the oiling of his body eased Silva's wine depression, yet he found it impossible to avoid brooding about the Jewess. "I have marched across the world," he said to Epos, "and never have I known such aggravation with a female. . . ."

Moments after Sheva had been taken from his tent he had bellowed for Attius his aide and dispatched him to the camp of the third cohort with a new order. "A counterorder to my original order, Epos. Confusion at headquarters. Counterorder my counterorder! Another way of confessing I want to stall until I can think of something else. Master procrastinator that I am, she is now back in her comfortable tent enjoying a morning laugh with her conniving relatives."

When the Numidian began to scrape the oil from his back and arms with a bronze strigil Silva warned him to be gentle even though he knew he would not be heard. "I am in a delicate condition this morning and the coming heat is going to make me whimper."

The anticipation of yet another day in the desert suddenly seemed to multiply his loneliness so that even the rumble of his own voice became reassuring. "When I was a young boy, Epos, a Greek nurse bathed me and I can remember her taking an extra long time to wash my jewels. I could not understand why she would be grinning all the time she was at it until one day I found out the pleasant way, and I've been trying to find a home for my staff ever since."

He splashed his hands in the tepid water and studying them said, "If I have one claim to fame, Epos, it is that there is not a single ring on my fingers. I believe I am the only Roman in the world who refuses to wear one or a dozen. My wife Livia, whom I loved more than my very breath, bought me all sorts of rings and I refused to wear them. After she perished I took a concubine who vowed she would not be seen in public with me unless I wore at least two rings. And I refused. It was the same with playing the flute. Both my Livia and the concubine insisted I tootle away because it was the thing being done and nothing I could say would convince them I had no ear for music. Once to please the concubine I did pack a flute to Lusitania intending to practice, but after ten minutes' insult to the instrument I knew I had been right in the first place, so I threw it in the Tagus. When I returned after a year and a half my concubine asked me to blow her a tune and I said, Would you rather have a tune or a romp on the couch with me? She said she would rather have a tune first so I handed her an ivory phallus I had bought in a market in Valentia and told her to go play a tune for herself. And that was the last I ever saw of her."

While the Numidian massaged the remaining film of oil into his shoulders Silva tried dutifully to exercise the lid of his left eye, which drooped until the eyeball itself was barely visible. The deep cut extending from his chin diagonally across his lips and terminating at the helmet line had severed the orbicularis muscle. With exercise the surgeons had promised he might some day regain use of the lid. Nonsense. Six years had gone by since that Gaullic brute had left his mark and if anything the lid was drooping ever lower. Well enough! At least if it closed completely sleep would come easier.

"Quite a story about my fluting, is it not, Epos? But somewhat afar from the truth. I invented it to cover my real trouble, for I did not present the phallus to my concubine with any such carefree dash. I sent it to her by messenger who also carried my deep apologies. She was a woman of great humor and I hoped the symbol would cause her at least to smile if and when she ever thought of me again. I hoped by bringing mirth to her lips that admirable woman would forgive my total failure to successfully consummate our partnership even so much as once.

"Give me credit for trying, Epos, as indeed I tried later with so many others. Believe me, Epos, I called upon every god to help me, and I called in every quack, every priest I could find, every sorcerer and adviser. In the way of aphrodisiacs I tried hot and cold mud baths, I drank the urine of a bull mixed according to a secret formula with goat hooves crushed at dawn . . . I ran around the Circus Maximus at midnight, starting once on my left foot and once on my right . . . I dipped my thumbs into the springs of Clitumnus, kissed the snout of a boar, drank a daily portion of egg whites, cinnamon and hot mead until I retched at the thought of another, and I made a special pilgrimage to the Alps so I could stand naked before the summer thunderbolts. I hired harlots and their pimps to perform for me while with another more than willing partner I worked up the most awesome sweats attempting to duplicate their feats. And all, Epos, was a failure. No sensation, visual or auditory, no touch or odor could erect my standard. . . .

"For reasons I cannot comprehend he has absolutely refused to stand duty since the loss of my wife. And that was a long time ago, Epos, so long there have been periods when I thought I should lose my reason because of it—times of such despair I seriously considered cutting my veins. . . .

"This Jewess has made him stand again. She has but to pass through my line of vision and I feel the blood coursing toward my formerly retired friend—he pulsates as if he were a youth, he stands again as my spear. . . .

"What should I do, Epos? Is this Jewess the only woman in the world of appeal to him or has there been some internal change which would not enable me to satisfy any woman? Should I keep the Jewess or send her on her way? Should I test him against another female . . . ah, I am afraid of that. Supposing I should fail?

"Epos, what shall I do with this Jewess who hates me?"

Silva bent forward and arched his shoulders so the Numidian could better scrape down his back. How he longed for a real Roman bath with its laconicum to draw the soreness from his muscles and a tepidarium where he could meet with other men of like status and discuss how the Empire was being ruined by sycophants, fools and opportunists. They must agree that the youth of Rome had grown soft and inexcusably spoiled—the doing of over-indulgent Roman mothers who owned an alarming proportion of the national wealth.

"Epos, my silent friend, can you imagine that it used to be against the law to leave any part of your estate to a woman if it amounted to over a hundred thousand sesterces? But they got around that by persuading their husbands to leave it to a friend who had guaranteed to pass it on to the wife, so that now they own a part or all of everything in sight and Vespasian will have to do something about it or we'll all soon be their slaves."

Silva pushed himself to his feet so the Numidian could scrape his legs, and while he waited he thought how much better he would feel if he could take this wine of remorse through a frigidarium, shouting and slapping his backsides as the steam rose from his body. I am out of touch, he thought, out of touch with Rome which means out of touch with life. With the imperial post taking from thirty to fifty days, how could anyone even hope to sense the trends in the capital of the world? I drown myself in wine because I have no other friend, no person on this earth who will care about my troubles, nor seek me out for myself. "And furthermore," he said aloud as he stepped from his bath, "I, Flavius Silva, am sick of Flavius Silva and his endless sorrows for himself!"

Epos held a mirror before Silva while he carelessly shoved at the curls about his head. "Balding," he murmured, "and the rest might do for an actor's mask providing he must represent a long-neglected jar of wine pickled in the sun and torn by the winds—and badly cracked down one side." He passed a finger along the deep scar left by the Gaul. "You are exceptionally pretty this morning," he said to the mirror. "Who else bears a cut that changes with the color of last night's wine?

Silva preferred to shave himself, and when he had finished he brushed his teeth with a powdered mixture of calcined bones, oyster shells, and a scripulum of nitre, which was said to be an aid toward strengthening the gums. He reached out for his short pantaloons which the Numidian held out to him and when he had pulled them on he sat on a chest so Epos could tie his sandals which were of chamois and adorned with a miniature fox's head at the upper limit of the lacings, but hobnailed along the sole in the same style as any Legionary's.

Epos held a tunic before him with the bottom end open. He dived into it and when his head emerged through the neck he was astonished to see a stranger standing just inside the tent entrance. No, he thought, he is not a stranger at all! Beneath that ridiculous getup was Pomponius Falco, the one man in the great city of Rome, Silva decided instantly, whom he was least interested in seeing. And with him, of course, standing shyly just inside the entrance, was one of his pretty boys.

"By the gods, Falco, how did you get here?"

"A most arduous journey I assure you, dear fellow, and after such effort I had rather expected a warmer welcome." He touched the hand of the youth beside him. "I present Cornelius Tertullus, also formerly of Ravenna."

"I am not particularly honored," Silva said, ignoring the youth. He was watching Falco's cruel eyes dart about the tent and he knew they would be inquiring into every detail of his personal life. The scoundrel was wearing a wig or had his hair curled—it mattered not which—and he reeked of nard and perfume as always. His fingers were cluttered with rings, and Silva now remembered his very bad complexion. Instead of treating it with galls, or horehound, or bitter vetch in the normal manner of those so afflicted, Pomponius Falco was known to travel with a herd of asses so he could make a dough of their milk and smear his face with it before he retired. How cheering it was now to observe how the ceremony had not remedied his appearance in the slightest. But careful! Whatever the stories about Pomponius Falco and however much the urge to express your loathing, it is best to bear in mind that he can be an exceedingly dangerous man. He has an accountant's mind with a nearly incredible memory for people's affairs, gossip, and deeds—a very feminine mind, Silva thought. He was one of those quick and shrewd men who these days so infested the capital. Like so many others he had become rich by participating in stock companies which bought the revenues of a province at public auction. By some fluke, or more likely by deliberate connivance, Silva thought, Pomponius Falco had managed to become chairman of his company. During the five years of exclusive rights enjoyed by the winning bid he had squeezed enough income to buy other rights and companies. Now he was supported by his flow of dividends and no one knew his true wealth.

Three years had passed since he had seen Falco, but if the rumors were true then he had managed to endear himself with Bernice who in turn must have persuaded Titus that he should be proclaimed Vir Perfectissimus, a most excellent man. As a dutiful son Titus would naturally pass on that impression to Vespasian who some day might be so ill-advised as to name him Vir Clarissimus—a most illustrious man.

"If you had sent word ahead of your coming I might have been better prepared," Silva said carefully. "As it is I am afflicted with a monstrous head, my gizzard is stiff with verdigris and my liver frothing with bile. While I officially welcome you to Judea, I will remind you that entrance to my tent, particularly at this ungodly hour of the morning, is subject to announcement and prior appointment regardless of the supplicant's rank. I suggest you return later in the day when I have done with my pressing business."

The Numidian was holding out Silva's skirt of leather studded with brass. He buckled it around his waist and pretended that he had lost interest in Falco. "I will call one of my Tribunes who will see to it that you and your party are made as comfortable as the limited resources of this outpost permit."

When Falco replied Silva heard a touch of deep anger in his normally thin voice. How satisfying! With what dreadful affectation did the man embroider his Latin!

"I am not supplicating anything. I have come a long way, endured considerable expense, and suffered outrageous hardships to bring you word straight from the Emperor. Here is his word."

Silva accepted the short roll of heavy paper and forced

himself at least to appear indifferent. But I am a poor actor, he thought, while this peacock has made a career of it. No matter what display crosses my face he must realize it is not every day the hand of Vespasian reaches out so far across the world to touch my own.

He broke the seal and read, "The Emperor Titus Flavius Vespasianus, Pontifex maximus, holding the Tribunician power for the fourth year, acclaimed Imperator twelve times, father of his country, Consul four times and designate for a fifth, Censor—to Flavius Silva, General of the Tenth Legion, Procurator of Judea, greeting:

"I declare that Pomponius Falco journeys to Judea as our approved envoy. He is to communicate certain vital matters to you and render such assistance as he can to alleviate your situation.

"I, the Emperor Caesar Vespasian, have signed this."

Silva noted the scribbled signature and muttered involuntarily, "Blah-blah-bub-blub-bah." He caught himself and took a moment to compose his thoughts. "Well, well—it seems you are on some quasi-official mission. However, I am sure Vespasian would understand the routine demands which obligate every soldier at the beginning of the day. When you have delivered his message will you have the consideration to let me relieve my eyes and organs?

"Vespasian is annoyed with you."

"Indeed? Well, I am annoyed with Vespasian."

"You would not dare speak those words before him."

"Wouldn't I? I will put it in writing. Do you suppose I consider this a reward—after the battles I have fought for Rome? I am given the most wretched land in the Empire and told to bring it back to life after we have gone to endless trouble killing it. I assure you this is the only tolerable hour of the Judean day and very soon even the lizards will complain of the heat. If you can discover any amenity to please either mind or spirit in this desert I will appreciate you informing me promptly so that I may rush to it before it melts. Thus far I have been unable to arrange any opportunity to increase my purse by service in this wasteland, and the natives are filthier and more irascible than any other we have conquered."

"We have Jews in Rome. Many of them. They are no problem."

"Not Jews like these. These are all crazy. The large majority of these people are so devoted to squabbling among themselves they have no time or interest in anything else. Some of them actually took off after a beggar they call the Christ, despite the fact the man is supposed to have died something like forty years ago. The only industry or agriculture I have so far been able to encourage has been as a consequence of the lash and I assure you the sight of a Roman to these people is an open invitation to their daggers. Of this wilderness, populated by people who would rather fight than eat, I am supposed to make a Roman republic. And with very little assistance from Rome, I might add."

Silva thrust his arms forward with his fists closed. With practiced ease the Numidian moved around him strapping on his brass epaulettes and armored jacket.

Falco raised a jeweled hand to his ear and toyed with the lobe. He glanced at Tertullus as if he wanted to be assured of his full attention and said, "But, General, certainly we cannot deny that Judea is conquered? Triumphs have been celebrated and arches erected to commemorate our victory. Coins have been minted—"

"So I understand," Silva growled. "And all is well in Judea save for some nine hundred individuals perched just above this tent who stubbornly refuse to admit they are conquered."

"That is precisely why I am here. Both Vespasian and Titus are displeased with the situation."

"Now at least I have some clue why you have come so far. Next I shall be fascinated to learn what you are going to do about it."

"Vespasian finds it embarrassing that a handful of miserable Jews can so long resist Roman arms. It is difficult to explain in the Senate. You are his Legatus—"

"Our esteemed Emperor's triumphs were somewhat premature."

"Are you suggesting this rabble can hold out indefinitely?"

Silva took a long deep breath and told himself to chain his patience. "A long time ago a certain Jew called Herod fortified the top of Masada. For his personal comfort he built two palaces up there. He also had a strong sense of the practical and some very clever engineers. He filled warehouses with food enough for thousands of people and preserved it so carefully it is keeping the present occupants of his ruins very healthy. And the soil is such they grow the greens they need. The same Herod built enormous cisterns and took water to them from this very hillside via a system of rock channels."

"If you are trying to confuse the issue, General, I assure you I know very well that it never rains in the desert."

"Do you, now? Well I will augment your education to the extent of assuring you that it does, at least enough for Herod to have troubled constructing two major aqueducts. We have destroyed both of them, but we are quite unable to do anything about the water already in the reservoirs, which I am informed is in sufficient supply to last them several more years. As for so-called rabble, by which you so conveniently identify the people up there, you may better appreciate their stubborn and recalcitrant nature if you also understand they are fighting side by side with their families and are led by one Eleazar ben Yair who happens to be a very clever and resourceful commander. A sword will not cut stone."

"I did not come all this way to hear platitudes."

"You will suffer more than platitudes if you annoy me further."

There was a moment's silence in the tent broken only by metallic clicks as Silva buckled his sword to his right side Legion style. Then Falco said slowly, "Nor did I expect to find our Emperor's deputy whoring with Jewish women."

Silva lowered his head and pressed his lips tightly together. He thought, I am not going to tiptoe around this fawn with fangs any longer. He baits me on the wrong morning so I am going to kill the bastard in my own tent.

He half drew his sword, then slowly slipped it back in its scabbard. Keep your temper, winehead! Pomponius Falco does not venture anything without the most careful preparation. More than full protection will be standing by just outside the entrance, and his fancy boy remains within a cubit of the flap. He will certainly scream for aid and the regrettable death of Flavius Silva along with his Numidian could easily be explained by so grand a personage as Pomponius Falco.

Poor fellow—discouraged over his inability to conquer Masada, he has fallen on his sword! And there was no use in denying Sheva. Falco undoubtedly knew all about her long before he came to the desert. Mails to Rome might take over a month in transit, but word of mouth flew on wings of a falcon.

"She is not a whore," Silva said deliberately.

"Ah then? Just a naughty lady I suppose? Privy to the secrets of our military commander in Judea and therefore able to pass them on to her own people. How convenient."

"That's ridiculous! You assume there *are* any secrets in Judea, Roman or otherwise."

"Nor did I expect to find the man Rome has entrusted with such grave responsibility so sodden with wine he either is incapable or unwilling to properly welcome his Emperor's envoy."

Silva took a step toward Falco, then another, until he could almost touch him. At last he halted, knowing that if he approached closer he would be unable to resist reaching for his throat. His voice trembled with his anger. "I do not welcome parvenus to my camp. I do not welcome advisers and schemers who come to see a few of my soldiers die so they can return to Rome as experts on the situation. I do not value military advice from those whose battles have been fought in the marketplace. The longest journey you ever made started on the day your uncle reached into the bowels of his second family, plucked you from the slums of Ravenna, chewed on you for a while and then spat you out into the sewers of Roman society. I will concede you are a fast traveler, but nothing you have ever done recommends you as a soldier."

The Numidian held his helmet. Silva reached for it as Falco said, "You are an uncouth ... military ... *beast!*"

"Right. Now you will excuse me for my duties. Get some rest and take your little friend with you. He must be weary."

I must hide my uneasiness, Silva warned himself. He is waiting for the slightest hint I fear him.

Silva blew some imaginary dust from the plume of his helmet, tucked it under his arm, and stepped around his two guests. He drew back the tent flap and congratulated himself, for there stood Falco's preparations for any serious opposition. Waiting just outside the entrance, barely a javelin's length away from his own Praetorian guards, was a solid block of perhaps twenty auxilia, Germans from the looks of them. It was now becoming fashionable among men of influence in Rome to employ such barbarians as bodyguards, as well they might, Silva remembered, since they were loyal to their nearest superior and utterly fearless.

Silva managed a smile as he turned back to Falco. He spoke with a deliberate Sicilian inflection to his Latin so his own men would be certain to understand him. "I must say you do travel in style." He glanced contemptuously at the Germans. "I hope you brought enough feed for these animals."

He stepped into the scorching sun and was about to advise Falco that he would send an officer with instructions about suitable quarters when he suddenly changed his mind. The great noise had ceased. How long had it been so? He remembered the volume had been normal during his bath, then there had been a little time while he started his dressing. If it had stopped before Falco's arrival then most certainly he would have noticed it. Silence in this place meant only one thing. Eleazar ben Yair was on the wall!

Silva clapped his hands in anticipation. He turned his bad eye toward Falco and smiling, reached for his arm. "Come, Pomponius Falco! I shall demonstrate how thoroughly we have conquered Judea. I will show you something you can take back to amuse bored Senators. If the deserts of Judea offer nothing else, you will see that we cannot complain of the acoustics."

In spite of his limp Silva set such a rapid pace that all of the procession following him were obliged to break step frequently and half run until they caught up. It was exactly as Silva had hoped, for all eyes in the encampment were on his visitors as they passed along the Via Principalis and he saw no reason to enhance their dignity. Once, unable to resist the temptation, he had glanced over his shoulders and had seen how they were already panting and dripping with perspiration. The sight was so pleasing that for a moment he was able to ignore the effect of the searing sun on his own wretchedness. It was true—each day it seemed hotter.

He tried to concentrate on more agreeable matters. Here now, he reminded himself, who has the present honor of commanding the celebrated Tenth Legion? Trajan had led them at Jotapata, Vespasian himself had depended heavily upon them all through the campaign in

Palestine. Not bad company! Look at them, regard the special spirit in their very faces—everywhere in this throng packing both sides of the roadway, familiar faces. More than five thousand men in the Tenth, two thousand in this camp alone, archers, slingers, pikemen, artillerymen, Syrians, Arabians, levies from every province welded into one indomitable Legion. Scattered everywhere throughout their mass were comrades in battle, names you took pains to call out and whose raised hands you returned. . . .Pedanius! . . . Longus! . . . Fabius! . . . Valens! . . . Maesius! . . . Ummidus! . . . Matarus Arrianus! . . . and Silvius, your blood brother! Old Plinius—by what indulgence of Mars are you still alive? Vettenius Severns, what mischief are you into now and what name do you call her? . . . Attius, how is your wound, and Lupercus how goes yours? Calpurnius Cilix! How about sharing your secret with me? They tell me you gamble so cunningly you now own the Tenth! Valerius Paulinus, your scheme for conserving water—well done!

Quickening his pace even more, Silva thought, *This* is Rome! *This* is the Empire, not the exotic softness of the capital where men are judged as much for their beauty and words as their might. *This* is Rome as it is on this morning all over the world, everywhere other generals, other legions, other thousands upon thousands of men bear the arms of Rome to keep the Empire supreme. The capital is sick, it is afflicted with parasites like those now trotting behind me. They suck at our Roman blood and transform it to pus. There is not a man in this camp, be he the lowest and youngest of trumpeters, who is not more noble than this master vampire at my heels.

Silva eased his step because here on a slight promontory he could view most of his own camp as well as three of the eight others surrounding Masada. And as always, he found a sense of accomplishment both in the arrangement and efficiency of his master scheme.

In planning the camps he had followed the standard army pattern which he had employed so many times elsewhere. There was no reason to argue with it. The soldiers of Rome long ago had learned how confusion alone can defeat the finest of troops. Hence an identical camp design had been developed and was followed by units wherever they were in the Empire. A freshly arrived recruit knew exactly his place of duty though an attack might come on his first night; and somehow, though a unit might be camped in the most distant and barbarous land, the very familiarity of the design proved reassuring to officers and men alike.

Still carrying his helmet under his arm, Silva halted for a moment to speak with Rosianus Geminus who was waiting as he did every morning near the Tribunal. Here on every fourth day Silva mounted the raised dais and reviewed the troops of his own and the adjacent western camp. Here awards were made, principal punishments assigned, the auspices consulted before battles, and duty orders passed on to the ranks by their immediate commanders.

Now he was reminded how frequently he had been censored by more aloof commanders for his easy liaison with the troops. Humph! The quickest way to silence such stiff necks was to evoke the democratic field custom of a long-gone soldier, one Julius Caesar. A pox on those commanders who waited until the final hours before battle, then mounted the dais in grandeur and delivered an oration they hoped would arouse the fighting spirit of their men. The clever haranguers might succeed, but the system was too tricky for Flavius Silva and too vulnerable to unforeseen developments. If you would ask a man to spill his blood in your name then let him know you are his brother as well as his father. Right, good solid Geminus? And right that this butterfly Falco and his fluttering companions will prove to be an unmitigated nuisance? Could they not at least send us some agreeable company from home? Do our eyes agree there must be a hundred people in his retinue, all of whom will have to be fed and given access to our precious water?

"Geminus," he said aloud, "we will have to do something for our valued guest, Pomponius Falco. You will find a place for him and his people."

Geminus eyed the assembly with the utmost distaste. "We might squeeze one tent in the central court near the command post," he grumbled. "But I cannot think where to put the rest of them."

Oh ever-perceptive Geminus! How instantly you recognize a sticky situation without being given so much as a hint of its true nature. Geminus, veteran of veterans, Centurion of the first class of the most honored cohort, the first, in the most honored Legion, the Tenth. Captain of my Praetorians, secret salutes!

Geminus blew out his cheeks and exhaled as a man much overtried. Where, Silva wondered suddenly, had the resourceful rascal obtained the garlic? I can smell you from afar, dear Geminus. Have you stolen the precious stuff from our medics who prescribe it mixed with rue and pounded up with oil for scorpion stings? Beware, Geminus! Be prudent of our supply, for it seems we are suddenly host to such a creature.

"You will have to think of something," Silva said without the slightest suggestion of urgency in his voice. He was watching Geminus's eyes roving through the company behind Falco and he pretended to be concerned when Geminus pulled on his beard and snorted, "The rest might have to make do outside the walls. I suppose I could chase away some of the Nabatean tradesmen—pack of thieves anyway. . . ."

Each of the camps surrounding Masada had its quota of followers who nestled as close to the Roman soldiers as terrain or the temper of the camp commander allowed. Silva had found them to be much the same in every land, an unwashed mixture of thieves, harlots, mendicants, fakirs, merchants whose avarice was no match for their petty wares, and professional beggars who scoured the refuse dumped by the Romans. He had ever been amazed at their ability to survive the most rigorous campaign conditions entirely on their own quite invisible resources, and it was said in the legions that if your camp followers suddenly disappeared then you were in very serious trouble, but if they remained as spectators near the field of battle then a victory was assured.

Eyeing Falco's Germans with open suspicion, Geminus asked, "And what am I to do with those northern aborigines, Sire, when we have no trees for them to sleep in?"

Silva told him to mind his tongue since they might understand Latin. Geminus shook his great head unhappily, but touched his helmet in obedience. "Where are their tails?" he growled. "I have lived with some vile people in my time, but *never* with Germans!"

Silva smiled dryly at the small force now gathered near Geminus. It was becoming a routine assembly, he thought, triggered each time at his pleasure by a Jew with a viper's tongue. There stood young Attius, his aide, obviously shocked at the gaudy spectacle presented by Falco and his darling Cornelius displaying themselves like courtesans before their ensemble of hairy savages. Poor young Attius! A six-months Tribune, away from his patrician home for the first time in his life, he had so much to learn he was nearly useless. Technically he was Geminus's superior officer, but he would no more dare give him an order than Geminus would consider obeying it.

With Attius were ten Arabian archers with their bows at the ready, picked men whose incredible skill was wasted on these affairs. But at least, Silva thought, the Jews knew of their reputation and would keep their distance.

There were three standard bearers, one holding the sanctified staff of the Legion which was surmounted by a golden eagle. Instead of a helmet the bearer wore the skin of a leopard, its jaws open above his head and the body hanging down his back. Next to him stood a Legionary wearing the skin of a wolf in the same fashion. He held a standard with a gilded statue of Victory surmounting small portraits of Vespasian and Titus—rather poor likenesses in Silva's opinion. Next to the imperial standard was the Tenth Legion's staff surmounted by its symbolic wild boar mascot and then his own standard with an outstretched hand extending from the tip and his principal medals set in vertical order of merit. Silva noticed the gilt was chipped on all three standards and his own highest honor, the Corona Civica, was cracked down the center. Alas, he thought, it has been a long campaign and it is well the Jews must view us from a distance else they might perceive how their besiegers are gradually decaying.

He put on his helmet and turned to Falco. "Do not concern yourself. My armor is like this menagerie, simply to impress the Jews. There is no danger. At these times Eleazar ben Yair fires much deadlier weapons than arrows."

He set off again for the camp's Praetorian gate which in accordance with army tradition faced the east. During the taking of auspices, omens favorable to victory were best received from that direction. The procession passed through the gate and turned toward a smaller camp which served as a control point in the great circumvallation that Silva had built around Masada. Here on the western mountain slopes the wall was relatively simple, but on the eastern side he had caused to be erected twelve towers as lookouts against any possible escape. The wall had done its job; so far as he knew not a single Jew had managed to escape from Masada, but it had been too costly and before it had been completed he told himself that he would never build another. The loss of more than a thousand Jews in its construction was unimportant, but heat, accident, and disease had cost him forty-three valuable Legionaries. He did not like to think what it had cost in effort and time. Another of Rome's ideas, he remembered bitterly. Long-distance wise men insisting that not a single Jew escape, as if there were any place for them to escape except to death in the desert.

Now as he strode alone, well ahead of the others, Silva looked up and frowned at the great rock that had thwarted him for so long. I will give it my bad eye, he thought, and maybe this morning it will fall down. Ah yes! As soon as the earth stop turning! There it stood like a gigantic anvil waiting for the hammer of the desert sun. Beyond it lay the Dead Sea and the parched mystery of Moab. This accursed rock had been designed by all the evil gods in company and with Vulcan as the master architect. It was an enemy you could not blood with spear, bolt or arrow, it was more impregnable than any castle, camp or fortified city in the world. It is my personal adversary over and above all others. When I defeat Masada, then and only then do I defeat Eleazar ben Yair and his band of Jews.

Now, Silva saw, as he had on so many mornings, how the base of Masada rose out of deep wadis on the western side and then projected at a steep slant to about half its altitude, then abruptly the sides became vertical and continued straight upward to the rim. Now, as he had since he first beheld Masada, Silva secretly saluted the Jew king, Herod. What a perfect refuge he had chosen if, as he feared, Cleopatra might have persuaded Antony to gift her with Judea! He would also be safe here from the multitude of enemies he had reason to believe were determined to dethrone him. All dead, long gone, but the monuments to Herod's fears were at last employed.

There was now only one route to the summit, a narrow, tortuous niching on the eastern face of Masada known as the Serpent's Path. And for snakes it might do, Silva swore, since no more than one man could pass at a time. Thus ten men with a few handy stones could hold off a thousand.

From his own camp Silva could see the small palace Herod had built against the face of the northern extremity. There of course would be the coolest breezes, an almost total absence of the merciless sun, plus what must be a superb view of the Dead Sea and the Judean desert. Silva had thought he might even be able to see the oasis of Ein Gedi from such a height and, he had vowed, there I will take my very best wine and cool my skin once the rock is mine. And Sheva as well? Why not?

He knew the general scheme of the rest of Masada all too well. Any time he pleased he need only visit the small camp which he had caused to be built facing the southern tip. It was perched on a high plateau at the very edge of the deepest wadi. So steep were the sides of the chasm that it always made Silva slightly dizzy to look down, but if he ignored the awesome wound in the earth and looked across it to the top of Masada he could tantalize himself with an eagle's view of the defenders. There, on the level, Herod had built a larger palace and many storehouses. There were lanes leading from one part of the rampart to another, to the reservoirs and numerous outbuildings, with gates and towers to defend it all. Recently Silva had resisted any temptation to visit the southern camp. It was too frustrating to watch your enemy still well fed and well watered after over two years, walking about as unconcerned as if they had nothing to fear. Looking down upon them he had once found himself sighing "Well done"— which he knew to be a dangerous admission when applied to any enemy.

Nor would the rock leave his mind after darkness came to the desert. Those ever more frequent nights when his loneliness became unbearable and he took solace in wine he would sometimes stand outside his tent holding his cup toward the great mass as if it lived and was then only slumbering beneath the stars. Drunk and bemused at its enormous dimensions he would mumble words at it, reaching out as if he could touch it. "Hail, you sleeping elephant—what would happen if you farted? Roll over, mighty carbuncle on the face of the earth, and dump the Jews in the sea of salt. I will live to crown you, Masada, with a wreath of my urine."

Weaving unsteadily in the starlight, his fuddled mind found strange pleasure in remembering that the grandeur and luxury atop Masada, intended for a despot to wait out a revolution, was now occupied by the very sort of revolutionary rabble he had intended to keep out.

Silva passed quickly through the small western camp and then its eastern gate that formed part of the circumvallation. His head was clearing now, but he was grateful to cross into the shadow of the great rock that stood between the western slopes and the sun. He promised himself that the moment the sun broke over the crest of Masada he would break off the parley, for he would not on this wine-soaked morning, or any other morning, stand there squinting up at Eleazar while he enjoyed the sun at his back. It was of course no accident that Eleazar never initiated these exchanges during the afternoon when the sun would be in *his* eyes.

The parleys were a problem Silva had thus far been

unable to solve although he had spent long hours discussing ways and means with his staff. In effect, they were minor battles at which he rarely came away the victor, and if they accomplished nothing else for Eleazar they held up work on the ramp long before and after their exchange was done. *Everything* stopped. Before an audience of twenty thousand-odd slaves and soldiers a Roman General was obliged to duel in words with a Jewish criminal who had spent his lifetime in rebellion. There was, Silva had reluctantly admitted, no choice. Eleazar had taken full advantage of the peculiarities of Masada, and as the great ramp rose toward him, he pressed harder and harder. His words were his artillery; because of the remarkable acoustics of his words could bridge the distance between his people and his besiegers and fall where his arrows and stones could not. By his carefully planned speeches he accomplished the encouragement of his own people and very obviously affected the morale of those thousands of Jews employed on the ramp. Before, during, and long after Eleazar appeared on the heights and shouted his first challenge the laboring Jews would lie down between the great stones where a whip could not touch them or scramble to the top of the ramp where no Roman as yet dared venture. The Legionary overseers had given up and now stood with everyone else, whips quiet while they listened spellbound to Eleazar ben Yair, the Sicarius and Flavius Silva, Procurator of Judea.

Silva hesitated to estimate how much actual damage these parleys had caused in the morale of his troops.

He crossed a dusty wadi then passed on to terrain which was mostly shale and sand and red boulders scattered across iron-hard earth. How much things of little consequence had come to mean! Now it was like viewing the gardens of Rome to discover a few pitiful wisps of vegetation.

He came to the base of the great ramp which was being built of crushed white stone and rose each day a little farther toward the summit of Masada. The engineers claimed it would be another month before it would extend high enough to erect the assault tower. Another month will take us into April, he mused. That was cutting things very fine. There were always delays and mistakes in any army, if only because rank so rarely matched talent. There was just no time for error here.

He found Rubrius Gallus, the Tribune responsible for all the engineering work, on the ramp. I could find him, Silva thought, among a hundred thousand people simply by searching for a lateen sail of a nose. There he stood, all the great height of him, his eyes displaying that permanently injured look as if all the world conspired against him and he welcomed it and was determined not to be thwarted regardless of insults to his spirit. There was Gallus hovering over every detail of his enormous project like some finicky pelican searching despondently for something to please him, Gallus the clever and dedicated road builder who yearned to build for all time while the present need was only for speed.

Silva remembered the doleful expression on Gallus's face when he had been instructed to build the ramp in a hurry and had been told it made little difference if it fell down the day after Masada was captured. "Just let me deliver machines at the top, provide a tower sixty feet high and armed with plate. Inside, give us a ram and we will support it with a brace of catapults to keep Hebrew heads down. Give me that, dear friend, and I'll have us all on our way out of this desert the very next day."

Dear friend? Ah indeed. What better and more trustworthy friend could any General have than Rubrius Gallus whose wisdom and heart were perfectly matched by his enormous physique? Who else would listen so sympathetically while you told him of the Jewess Sheva? Who else would not once look down the length of such a great proboscis and proclaim the affair as disgraceful or even ridiculous? Gallus, the one true friend left in all the world to Flavius Silva.

Now Gallus was fretting at the delay. He pointed up at the ramparts of Masada and said, "There he stands, Sire. I can accomplish nothing until he is gone."

Silva looked up at the diminutive figure high above him. He raised his voice only slightly above normal conversation. He spoke in Greek, which most Jews understood, but his own soldiers would not. Hopefully then, they would not discover what a weak word-warrior he was. But Eleazar of course would carefully frame his declarations in Latin, to make very sure they *would* understand.

"Hail, Eleazar ben Yair! What would you have of me this morning? Have you at last come to your senses about the matter of surrender?"

There was, as Silva had expected, only laughter from the heights. Then he heard Eleazar's voice, like his own unstrained and yet easily heard. "Last night my usually peaceful slumbers were uneasy because my belly was over-full! I became worried about poor Flavius Silva and his miserable soldiers scratching in the dust of our desert. And a great sense of pity overwhelmed me because I envisioned you down there when the true heat of summer arrives. All night I could think of nothing save how your eyes will fry and how innumerable insects will feast upon your heat sores and open wounds. How goes the dysentery? Do you wonder if you still have intestines? Let me remind you how the coming heat will set your bowels on fire. Have you all carefully examined your skin lately? Do so, I beg you. For it should be coming now with the heat—the curse of our land which you will all have if you remain in Judea. Leprosy! Even the wind carries it to the valleys of our desert. Look now at your hands and limbs, the smallest lesion is the first sign. If you are alert and go at once to cooler air then you may be cured. Otherwise you will wear the bell for the rest of your days. . . ."

Pomponius Falco and his company had caught up at last. Behind him Silva heard them exclaiming over the ease with which they could hear the Jew on Masada. They cluck like women spectators discussing a chariot race, he thought with disgust, but he was determined Falco should understand why he consented to such parleys.

"He calls down a challenge every few days. He asks for me by name and if I send a subordinate then he proclaims I am afraid to face his message. He knows very well we must be out by summer or go mad, hence he repeatedly reminds us of passing time, which makes the heat worse. He has my troops feeling half sick whether they are or not. They spend all their spare time pawing themselves looking for diseases they never heard of and at the slightest sign of a pimple off they run for the surgeons. By repetition, by constantly striking the heat theme, he intends to make his threats a fact, and it is now very possible he may succeed."

Pomponius Falco waved his hand limply at the flies about his face. "How long must you listen to this vermin-infested orator?"

"Would you have me retreat before his words? I do not

like fighting battles with my tongue, but until the ramp is finished I have no other choice."

Silva turned his back on Falco and addressed himself once more to the diminutive figure on top of Masada.

"Listen to me, Jew, more carefully than you have in the past, when there might have been some petty reason to build false hope in your people. I command you bring them all to the ramparts now—all of your men, women, children. Let them see how close the ramp approaches and judge for themselves how long it will be before my Legionaries soak their blades in your blood. Then will your people know how you have given them the cruelest of lies, how you have held up false words as shields against the might of your benefactors. They will call you Eleazar the Deceiver for generations, each one telling the next how you were the only cause of their calamity. Surrender now—while there is still time! In the name of Vespasian I command you to give up your arms and descend. I promise the milk of your mothers will flow again!"

While Silva held out his right hand to finalize his vow he glanced over his shoulder at Falco. "Listen now, how he will pound away on the same old subject."

Silva was almost pleased when Eleazar's voice came down to them, the tonality unchanged, the same easy and relaxed cadence of words, the suggestion of benign uncle advising a difficult nephew. Perhaps now even Falco would understand that Eleazar ben Yair was no ordinary antagonist.

"My people are on the walls now, looking down upon your wretched little soldiers in their fancy dress. O Flavius Silva, poor little General, are you by chance pleading with the true proprietors of this land to spare you at least another thousand deaths from the coming heat of summer? Beware of it! There is still time for you to strike your tents and go down to the sea where the air is fresh and cool, where our loathsome diseases will not chew on your bones. Go down to the cool sea to satisfy your lusts, where there is wine and all variety of food. Leave us our parched desert and nothing more. Go now, while there is still time. We will send down food and cool water for your journey. . . ."

While the voice droned on, repeating passages in Latin that were first spoken in Greek so that all would understand, Falco moved to Silva's side. "This is disgraceful," he hissed. "How can you tolerate such humiliation? As long as he makes you listen, he is insulting Rome."

"If I refuse to hear him, you may be sure my troops will listen all the more attentively."

"My provident arrival makes the solution quite simple. You have merely to inform the ruffian that I have arrived bearing an order from Vespasian. The Emperor has ordained that if they surrender immediately they will be granted *complete* amnesty."

"Is that true?" For a moment Silva found himself hoping.

"Of course not. Once they have given up their arms you have simply to crucify every one of them and the matter is done with."

Silva looked into Falco's eyes and for the first time noticed how he had outlined them with some sort of cosmetic. Now he saw that his lips were strangely colored with purple and he thought, Since all else is a lie about this man, how can I trust him out of my sight? Yet I most certainly cannot share a tent with him!

"Falco, I have underestimated you," he said slowly. "They should send more such clever representatives from Rome and perhaps my many other problems might be solved. Would you prefer to make the offer yourself?"

"I will consent to do so if you will understand that I am not here to demean you but to help."

Silva thought, I am being forced by circumstance to give up the grape! Otherwise how can I keep up with this chameleon?

He pinched at the ache between his eyes and said, "Perhaps it will be more impressive if you go up the ramp some distance so that you are separated from the rest of us and appear to function as a new authority. The distance between us and your lack of armor will make your offer more credible." He saw hesitation in Falco's eyes, but before he could find objection he called out to the ramparts.

"The gods have been kind to you, Eleazar! Two great Romans have arrived with the dawn. They are Pomponius Falco the Emperor's deputy, and his aide, Cornelius Tertullus. Vespasian has taken a fatherly interest in your fate. If these men come forward to give you a message, will you guarantee their safety?"

There was a moment's silence on the mountaintop, then

Eleazar's voice came without change. "Let them come as far as they wish. They will not be harmed."

For a moment Silva thought Falco was about to balk, but then he saw his expression settle into such a serious mien he hardly seemed of the same face. He straightened his blouse and touched at his hair, yet somehow the gestures were not particularly feminine, and when he beckoned to Cornelius he seemed to have passed his transformation on to the boy. Both of them started up the ramp as if they were on parade. They halted erect and proud, some thirty paces up the ramp. Silva found himself entertaining an instant of regret for what he was certain would happen. Then he smiled at his own weakness. Regret for a man you despise? Better spend these precious moments making your own preparations.

Keeping his voice just above a whisper he ordered the archers to fall back and the standard bearers to accompany them. To Attius and Gallus he said, "Let us count to twenty and then stroll slowly for that large rock over there."

As Falco's high voice rang out Attius and Gallus solemnly nodded their understanding.

"Jews of Masada! Hear the word of Vespasian!"

Falco paused dramatically. There was no sound in the desert except the harsh plaint of the soaring crows.

"If you will abandon Masada at once and pledge all of your people to our useful purpose, then all of you will be granted *complete* amnesty. All of your past crimes will be forgiven. So what have you to fight and die for now? Ask Eleazar. Ask the men who are your leaders. I await your answer!"

He does have style, Silva admitted to himself as he moved toward the large rock. And he was fearless in his way. There he stood, quite alone except for the frail boy beside him, chin high, feet spread wide apart, arms folded as if waiting in judgment on the very mountain itself.

Once behind the rock Silva peered up at the ramparts. Then he said quietly to Attius and Gallus, "Here comes their answer—as foreseen."

They watched a small shape arc over the ramparts, and appear to hang for an instant against the morning sky. It enlarged and while descending almost straight down fragmented into a collection of odd-shaped objects. Then it rained down upon Pomponius Falco and Cornelius Tertullus until they were deluged in garbage, offal, and animal bladders filled with human urine and excrement. Such was the force and volume of the collection they were knocked off their feet. They picked themselves up and crying out their dismay, screaming as they discovered each new filth, ran blindly down the ramp.

Silva kept his voice perfectly flat when he turned to Attius and Gallus. He shook his head. "Pity about this sort of thing, very bad for Roman status."

Two

OF THE BESIEGED . . .

LIKE some last exhalation of a body in death the laughter terminated and a dreadful silence again ruled the top of Masada. Eleazar ben Yair was beginning to find the silence that fell upon his people something he could hear—it was as if he stood among a sea of ears, all poised, all turning slowly around and around seeking to detect the slightest interruption in the conspiracy of listening. And as the ramp climbed even higher he noticed how the silences were becoming more prolonged, and even when they were finally broken by some individual who refused to mute his voice, the melancholy lingered for increasingly longer spans of time. My people, Eleazar thought, are as wavelets in the wind; they respond to every influence however slight and the effect remains long after the force has passed. I must comfort myself in believing that like the sea they show a different face to the sun than lies beneath.

Eleazar ben Yair preferred to consider his major perplexities in nautical terms for prior to the great war, a time he often thought of as another life enjoyed by another man, he had been a native of Bethsaida, a town known as "the house of fishes," on the western shore of the Lake of Galilee. There he had been a fisherman of more than ordinary repute, yet he took delight in warning others that if all the lies concerning the size of his catch could be believed, then he must certainly be the greatest fisherman since the exodus from Egypt, which would now be one thousand and sixty-five years.

"And maybe even longer," he would add with his inviting smile. "You understand of course that all Galileans are fighters from the cradle, and this peculiar endowment applies to the fish as well as to those of us who dwell on dry land. It is for this simple reason that only a Galilean can catch Galilean fish—all others need not trouble themselves."

Eleazar's Hebrew, with its slurred gutturals, more closely resembled Syrian, but there were few on Masada who found it offensive. Even the Judeans, who were so inclined to snobbishness about the purity of their words, easily forgave Eleazar his dictional transgressions, and after moments, if they heeded him well, became lost in his message.

There were many reasons for the almost immediate creation of this spell, whether Eleazar spoke to a multitude or simply to an individual. He was in the first place blessed with a splendid physique, being taller than most men by a palm or even two and yet of heft and proportion to match. Like so many Galileans he was of fair complexion and his eyes were blue-green as if forever stained with the colors of his sea. His strength was not unusual among the fishermen of Galilee or any other waters, and his great-fingered hands might be equally exchanged with any true mariner. Some said it was his movements that were responsible for the impression that he was a man of extraordinary beauty, although even those most under his influence knew he was not. All were agreed there was something different about his use of body and limb, for even a turn or step became a maneuver of leopard grace. He knew how to put the total of his force into a pull or a push, he knew how to gesture with his big hands so they seemed to encompass the world, and he knew instinctively how best to make his stand whether opposed by word or weapon. Even his most faithful followers admitted that his air of controlled majesty had much to do with his sometimes being called a demagogue, but they would recommend his critics ask Eleazar ben Yair himself how it was that he came to be the chosen leader of the people on Masada. Then he would tell them the truth.

"None of these people trust each other. We Galileans are chronic rebels against the Romans, yet I am a Zealot because there is nothing else in Palestine left to be. I am neither a Sicarius nor a Pharisee nor a Sadducee nor an Essene nor even a man of strict devotion to God. I sometimes even doubt the very existence of God. He seems careless and permits me to live very temporarily while others die all around me, so I can only suppose he wants it that way. I have with my own hand killed more Jews than most Romans—because they refused to fight. I am a fighter and the others know it and that is why I am their leader."

The face of Eleazar ben Yair contributed greatly to the spell which seemed to emanate from him even when he was most at ease. In the manner of his people he was unshaven, but he kept his beard well trimmed. His skin had been so tormented by wind and sun that at times it appeared metallic in texture and it seemed that if a sword struck his cheek it would only blunt its edge; yet as if to reaffirm his equality with more vulnerable men, his nose had been so badly broken it seemed to spread half across his face and his teeth were also broken and irregular. For so young a man his eyebrows were very heavy, a feature which sometimes lent him the look of a bleached Satan, and which, with full realization of the effect, he would sometimes mischievously employ to relieve the tensions on Masada. His voice was normally soft as is so often the case with men of the sea, although when addressing his Zealots it took on a special resonance as if to capture the ear of the most indifferent listener.

The people of Masada found it nearly impossible to long ignore Eleazar ben Yair whether he kept his peace or not. They were influenced by his very history, knowing that he was the last survivor of a family of fighters and martyrs, his father, who was called Josiah, having been slain by the Romans, and his grandfather, who was called Josiah, having been killed by Herod; and during the siege of Jerusalem where Eleazar himself had fought under Simon bar Giora, three of his brothers had been crucified by the Romans. Though he was careful not to seem overly influenced by the savage Sicarii he had adopted much of their thinking, and over the door of his quarters he had fixed a Sicarius banner with its defiant wording, "God alone is the Lord. Death does not matter. Freedom is all!"

Secretly Eleazar cursed all the sects of Palestine. What had they brought to the Jews but division and hatred, and now chaos and agony? There were clusters of every sect on Masada and there were many times when he despaired of uniting them. "Listen, my dear dear friends," he had so often admonished them. "I am nothing. I am only a sandstone in God's eye! I do not *care* how you worship God and I beg you now in our time of peril not to care how others do. I do not care if you live by the written or oral law or know both by heart. Be like me or we must all die of our own quarreling. Be like me—a Jew, and *only* a Jew!"

All of this contributed to his spell.

There was also the attribute of Eleazar's education, which he had obtained in his naturally zestful manner. As in most of Palestine before the war, excellent schooling was available to any youth at a price, so Eleazar satisfied his yearning by saving a fish from each catch. The fish went to his teacher, and yet even when the catch had been so light it might better have gone to his stomach, he said, "My belly can shrink and expand with my luck, but my brain cannot be preserved like a dried fig."

Therefore Eleazar ben Yair was not only renowned as a fisherman, but before he was two and twenty he was known as a "litterator," which implied that he had a smattering of letters. And all of this was also before the war.

Eleazar had brought Miriam his wife with him to Masada. And she was also of a fishing family although there was no similar record of rebellion in her blood. Though the Zealots had originated in Galilee she had never heard of them until after her marriage, and when told of their intentions, how they would drive the Romans out of all Palestine, she simply said it sounded foolish and unrealistic.

Miriam was, in the style of her people, a woman of considerable strength and large of bone and feature, which embarrassed her. Rather would she have been dainty and even fragile in appearance, and it was true that whenever she was in proximity with such a woman she became unaccountably shy and meek as if by assuming such a pose she might make it an actuality. She was fair, even for a

Galilean, and her hair so neatly braided caused much comment because it was the color of sand.

It had been ten years since Miriam had worn the veil over her eyes and crowned it with a wreath of myrtle and been given in marriage to Eleazar ben Yair, the fisherman. Since those three days of rejoicing she had known only total devotion to her husband and he to her, the same whether they fought the Romans or other Jews for survival, or lived in peace, a condition they had nearly forgotten. While her husband often expressed his doubts, Miriam would allow no influence to cloud her traditional relation with God. It was she who had frowned at the Sicarius banner over their door and quietly fixed a mesusah below it. And she had made sure it contained the longitudinally folded squares of parchment with the two passages from Deuteronomy written on twenty-two lines. Miriam was always deeply pleased when visitors touched the shining metal case and then kissed their fingers.

Eleazar had this to say of his marriage. "My Miriam was created just as were all other women, not from man's eye, which would have made her envious of nature, nor from his ear, which would have made her a gossip, nor from his mouth, which might have made her a magpie. God created her from man's rib, and I searched everywhere for the one missing from my own cage until I found Miriam." At times when he chose to tease her he would say, "Then who should be surprised that a man who is made of soft stuff is the more agreeable, while a woman made of bone is naturally so much harder?"

Now standing on the outermost rampart, Eleazar ben Yair, the son of a rebel and the grandson of a rebel, surveyed his domain with the reborn hope of every new day. He squinted at the sun and whispered a prayer that it would become an intolerable torch by midday. The sun was hope; hurling refuse at the Romans, he thought, was only a secret signal of despair.

He looked down upon the great desert which stretched to all the horizons. There beyond the plateaus to the south was the valley of Sodom and Gomorrah which he had first considered as an area of refuge but finally decided against. Long ago it had been a rich land, but now it was all wasted and burned. Those who believed in such things explained how the wickedness of the inhabitants had sucked a divine fire from the sky, and even to this day fruit plucked from the few remaining trees dissolved into smoke and ashes. At least, Eleazar thought, here on Masada we are victualed for many more years. The last of our fat-tailed sheep was slaughtered only yesterday and we have only his left horn to serve as a trumpet and a memory. But we have oil and grain and dates and wine in abundance, and we have also weapons for men ten times our number and water sufficient even for the joy of bathing. What other besieged have ever known such luxuries?

He looked down upon the wilderness surrounding Masada and saw the long line of bearers bringing supplies to the Romans from the north. They were always there, night and day, and how well he knew the route. He had come the same way from Jerusalem with a thousand men, women, and children, dragging themselves across the labyrinths of ravines, crumbled rocks, flint-hard earth and everlasting thorns, sand and swirling dust. *There* was delirium, O leader of innocents, and pure madness to suppose the Romans would not pursue, yet for some strange reason they had not followed, and certainly that had been a miracle so why was it unreasonable to expect another? Think, Eleazar ben Yair. Think how it is already the third and twentieth day of Adar and how next month will assuredly bring the heat pounding mercilessly upon the heads of the Romans and how they will never withstand the hell of summer. Save thy breath. Let the sun scream at them. They will dissolve in their own sweat.

He felt the feather touch of a small moist hand against his own and looked down upon his son, Reuben. Well now, little one, what are thy plans for this day? A run along the beach perhaps? A stop to investigate a tiny crab? Or will you capsize a shell and after examining the marvelous pattern of its sworls be forced to make that great decision—will you take it home to thy mother or throw it back into the sea? Whatever you decide, remember that next year I will expect you to start helping me about the boat and I will begin to teach you how a mullet must be caught and show you the very best place to net fingerlings. And then the following year . . .

Eleazar looked away to the east and north where he could observe a portion of Lake Asphaltitis, which some called the Dead Sea. It was already shimmering in the heat and he thought how strange it was that even such a lifeless patch of water could bring him visions of living things. For from that same water came the bitumen with which he had once calked his boat.

He looked down again at his son and wondered if Reuben would ever leave this desert tomb and sail upon the sea. How so very small he was, and still so fragile. Nor does he understand how any other human being can bear him the slightest malice. All that he has seen here is meaningless to him. He thinks the Romans build the ramp so they may come for a visit. Lord God, if you exist for all Jews, then spare him. Show me the miracle that will spare him. . . .

"His face is dirty," he said softly to Miriam.

"I know," she said. "He fell running to hear his father frighten the Romans. You had him feeling very sorry for them."

She was silent for a moment, then looked down upon the ramp. The Legionaries were rounding up their charges and driving them back to work.

"How much longer?" she asked.

"Thirty days at the most."

"And then? There are many who believe we should surrender now."

"Not so many. There are a few worms in every keel."

Her eyes told him that she was afraid and he knew she was not afraid for herself but for Reuben. He wondered if all husbands and wives could communicate with such silent ease. He picked the boy up and held him high against the sun. And while Reuben shouted his delight he said to her, "How could so happy a boy have such a gloom for a mother?"

"Once," she said mischievously, "you called me your tower of joy."

Laughing, he set the boy down. "Take warning, son. Though you may learn to reeve a net which will hold almost anything you will never equal the mesh of a woman's memory."

Holding hands, with the boy between them, they descended from the ramparts. At the side of the Western Palace, which had been Herod's principal residence, Eleazar left them and walked around the building toward the north. It was the route he followed every morning, the closing of his post-dawn tour which normally commenced at the serpent path gate on the eastern side of Masada and then continued southward along the casemates where many people had made homes between the walls. Along the way he would question the lookouts at every station, of which there were thirty and two between the gate and the southernmost tip of Masada, and he would greet those people and their children who had come with him out of Jerusalem and across the wilderness. And he knew most of them by now so that he could call them by name and he knew many of their children down to the several born on Masada.

It was important, Eleazar reasoned, for him to listen at least shortly to every lament and complaint, of which there were invariably a great number, because if he did not there were only the priests to give counsel and he mistrusted them mightily. Even in this extremity a tenth of the jars of food, wine, and oil were marked for their consumption, and every family gave challah from their daily batch of dough. Yet the priests contributed so very little. They were too busy reading the word of God to prepare their own food, and too busy arguing in the *mikveh* about the scheme of yet another ritual bath to work on the walls. They were so preoccupied praising God for things he had done long ago they could not beseech him for help at what must be done now. Nor could their overburdened attentions be held long enough to make of them good lookouts, and not one of them had the slightest skill at arms. In a moment of anger he had once said to them, "*I* am God's whip—here, *now*. I can help you if you will heed me. I cannot if we spend our time arguing about dimensions of temples!"

He had been somewhat shocked at his own words until later when he had time to think about it. Aye, in a sense it was true. He was daily obliged to play God, and when he failed to behave accordingly those who accused him of despotism were the first to whirl around and call him lax in his duty. Aye, though objections to his policies were never-ending and he had offered to step down many times, no other man on Masada disputed his leadership. Very well then, let the objections continue if they provided relief for frightened tongues and meant no more, and let the praying and scripture-reading prevail if it would keep terror from their minds. Now, in moments of desperation or even exasperation, he found himself repeating to them, "Give me your strength as you would to God, each one of you—or you will certainly perish on this rock."

Here now, he thought, was pure blasphemy if anyone dared accuse him. Let them. He would remind his accusers of the greatest general the Romans had on their side at Jerusalem. And he was God himself who allowed the Jews to fight among themselves.

During his tour he would descend to the cistern at the southern end of Masada and there solemnly examine the water level. It was a ceremony intended to impress all who watched and he was careful to conceal his true reactions. Actually there was water enough for a thousand more people on Masada and it was merely the sight of it, dropping ever so slowly in volume, that cheered him. Like our food, he mused, water was one of the very few things the God of Masada had no cause to worry about.

On the southern limits of the ramparts he would pause and study the Roman camp which stood across the chasm. It was a small camp compared to the others and he was certain it could be overwhelmed by a determined band of men. It would be possible for such a group to descend into the chasm from this tip of Masada and then make their way up the opposite side to the camp. And then what? Aye, there was the hole in the sail! Even if it were physically possible to lower the balance of the people on Masada to the bottom of the chasm and then hoist them up to the conquered camp and a possible escape route, the endeavor would take too long. Once daylight had come the Romans would be more than poised for a massacre.

In spite of his convictions Eleazar ben Yair had never been able to leave the southern citadel without again trying to envision a new route of escape. He knew that he must not permit even a moment of hopelessness to enter his mind, and lately, as the ramp mounted closer to the western gate, he noticed how many more impossible schemes he devised to cover his growing despair.

From the southernmost citadel Eleazar's inspection route took him along the western wall to the old palace, in which three hundred men, women and children now lived. They were cramped, but each family occupied one corner of a room and most had managed to construct some kind of privacy.

The beehive of activity about Herod's buildings amused Eleazar. How the old villain would rave if he could watch his present guests! He would hardly approve of their scrawling on his frescoes, or their mud stoves on his tiles, or their defecating on his terraces. What kind of a God spared such people? These survivors of Jerusalem were mostly the ignobles, the connivers, and the cunning who had determined from the very beginning to let the other man be the hero. Except for a minority of dedicated Zealots these were the people who had cowered in the ruins of Jerusalem, never to be seen during the fighting and cunning enough to eat during the famine. They had shifted from side to side, from Simon to John, before the burning of the temple, being one day a Zealot and the next a conservative—whatever seemed most likely to endure. Many would have become Romans had the chance been offered them.

"You are like so many grains of sand," he had told them when they had at last arrived safely at Masada. "To survive this time you must become mortar."

Now, as on every morning after his inspection, Eleazar walked to the building that had once housed Herod's officials and administrators. There would be gathered his own leaders and advisers for the daily council of war. They would review the latest accounts of stores and adjust the rationing accordingly. Disputes between sects or even individual families would be exposed and usually solved to no one's complete satisfaction. Plans were laid for new eventualities created by the Romans, and the progress of the ramp discussed endlessly. If there were any new reports from outside Masada, be they rumor or otherwise, they would be heard, and if the wine tithe for the priests had turned out to be sour then that was heard. Eleazar had noticed that as the ramp approached nearer there was less and less discussion of resistance strategy. Instead the ramp and all it portended slipped behind the shadow of domestic problems which seemed to multiply with the general tension. Judas, son of Merto, was tormenting his wife again and her screams were keeping everyone who lived in the east wall awake. Jacob, son of Belgas, and his whole family were sick with some mysterious ailment and would it not be wise to forbid them contact with all others? The daughter of Ardalas, son of Matthias, had been raped by Shimeon, son of Ezra, according to her family, and Shimeon had been seduced by the daughter according to *his* family, and the question was not whether they would marry or not, but the size and time of delivery of her dowry. And on and on, thought Eleazar. How could you convince people their entire life span was in imminent danger of terminating when they preoccupied themselves with petty futures?

While the building was sometimes referred to by the sour-natured at "Eleazar's pavilion," the inference that he enjoyed its relative comfort alone was unfair. Fifteen families shared the structure with his own, and if they happened to be his most trusted leaders it was because there had to be some central place where the constant problems of the community could be exposed, and the closer his aides lived the quicker they could act. The families occupied small rooms situated about a central court and here amid the sounds of children playing and wives gossiping the morning conferences were held.

When Eleazar entered the courtyard it still echoed with the laughter of his comrades. There was old Ezra, a fierce walnut of a man in spite of his threescore years. He was one of the very last Sadducee survivors, formerly a wealthy importer from Joppa whose defiant independence predated the destruction of his native city by Vespasian. For then dissatisfied with the translations of the holy scriptures into Greek he had become a student of Philo in Alexandria and set about writing his own version of the Pentateuch. Even now he vowed to finish the work as soon as the Romans were defeated and driven from Palestine.

Ezra was holding his sides and chuckling, ". . . it took twenty years off my life to see those Romans run! They will stink for a week."

Eleazar had long ago decided he would not trade Ezra for a hundred men. Not only was he wise and learned, but a fighter to the very last breath. He often said that he never thought about the future since it would come soon enough. He had fathered eight sons and three daughters, all save one killed by the Romans, and yet he kept his balance. Ezra's surviving son Heth, a powerful youth of twenty, now stood beside him. The pair often provided great amusement in the evenings when they wrestled with each other in marksmanship, a contest the father always won.

In the courtyard there also awaited Alexas, a flinty, grizzled man who had been one of the very last to escape Jerusalem. He had been captured almost immediately and forced to fight in the gladiatorial games at Berytus, whence he had again managed to escape. He had been once more caught and was scheduled to fight at Caesarea Philippi and yet, incredibly, while he was being dragged to the chains, once more escaped. This time he managed to join the Zealots and ever since had been fondly known as the "slippery one." Eleazar valued Alexas as his most resourceful leader.

There waited also Zidon, the leader of the Pharisees, an indecisive man who could be very long of wind when engaged in avoiding facts. Like most Pharisees he momentarily expected an apocalypse, and some said he looked forward to it as a final cessation of his nerve-wracking facial tic. As always these days he was wearing his phylactery and his talith, the blue fringes placed at the corners according to the law of Moses, and it being very broad and long in the style of the Pharisees.

There also waited Esau, a Sicarius who would as soon slay a man as spit. He was one of the few holdovers from John of Gischala's original band of Zealots in Jerusalem, and was such a sworn revolutionary that Eleazar wondered if he would ever be satisfied regardless of his success in creating turmoil. He had been one of those involved in the mock trials held in Jerusalem where Jew tried Jew and killed his brother for the slightest deviation from the party line. Eleazar found it difficult to trust Esau and there were times when he thought his own death might have pleased the man, but he was a skilled fighter and a fearless example to the others. So, thought Eleazar, I will continue to sleep with one eye open and throw him over the wall at the first sign of his treachery. At least Esau seemed to have mellowed a trifle since coming to Masada. Only recently he had announced his intention of taking a bride from one of the Essene families. Had the proposal been made by any other man, Eleazar thought, he might have advised him to reconsider, but with Esau involved he could only think such a mating must bring about the greatest contrast in the entire history of the Jewish people. Here was a villain from the streets of Jerusalem taking a bride from a tribe of ascetics who abstained from wine, meat, and oil and appeared content with their bread and salt spiced on gay occasions with a condiment of hyssop. No wonder they ate in silence! Esau, the former thief, would join a tribe of such moral purity they suffered agonies rather than relieve themselves on the Sabbath.

Ah, Esau! How the final days of your life will be changed!

There waited Javan and Kittim, sons of Tema. There waited Asshur, son of Joktan, and Nimrod, son of Abram. All of these were Eleazar's councillors and to each of them he gave a greeting. Then they gathered around him and sat on the steps of the courtyard as was their custom. Hillel, the young priest, blessed their meeting and even before he had finished Alexas rose to speak.

"O, we have had a good laugh at the expense of the Romans. O yes! But I say we would have done better to drop the pair of them with as many arrows. Our dung will not destroy Romans or make them go away." He turned to Eleazar and shook his fist at him. "If you had given me leave, two important Romans would be dead this moment."

Ezra interrupted by waving his hand lazily. He asked, "How do we know they were important? They could have been some kind of a trap conceived by Silva. If they were really important he would not expose them so."

"I could have put a bolt through Silva himself," Alexas grumbled. "At that distance, I'm sure of it."

Eleazar decided against rising because he wanted to save physical dominance for later challenges that might be more serious. He simply raised his hand for attention, then took his time. "Very well, Alexas. We kill Silva and a few of his aides. Do you believe the Romans would not replace Silva with another man, who would then have good reason to refuse to listen to our words? For a moment's satisfaction we would have lost our opportunity to send down dread. Very important, dread—will you not agree to that, old Ezra? Dread is the beginning of fear, and if God will grant us a truly hot day soon and augment it with a torching wind, then Silva may have a mutiny on his hands. It would not be the first time it has happened in the Legions. Do you agree that is all so, Alexas?"

"I may agree there have been mutinies, but not in the Tenth Legion. We are cursed with elite troops, and I know them better than any of you. O, I say that we do too much talking and not enough fighting. I say we sit up here like a gaggle of geese and wait for the farmers to come wring our necks."

"What exactly would you have us do?" Eleazar asked. Here of course was the snarl in the line. If you would keep a weapon sharp you must occasionally put it to the stone, and if you would keep a fighter keen then you must occasionally let him smell blood. The Romans had provided no such opportunity.

"Silva, may he roast in hell after he has fried here, keeps his Legionaries in check and out of range," Eleazar said patiently. "Obviously they are not permitted even minor forays, or night raids. They are concentrated on the circumvallation with the ramp. Nothing else counts."

When Alexas had been recaptured the second time one of the Romans beat him with the very chain intended to restrain him. The action had cost Alexas most of his teeth, which gave him an aged look far beyond his years, yet he had been able to make light of the physical blemish ever since he discovered that by pursing his lips in a certain way he could make a whistling sound that was exactly like the hoot of an owl. Alexas made this sound now as he frequently did when impatient with himself or others. Then he said, "I, for one, do not intend to wait here like an old woman for the Romans to slit my throat." He scratched at the folds of skin that hung like a lizard's beneath his throat and Eleazar saw several others instinctively repeat the gesture. "O, I say to all of you, we should slip down the serpent path at night. Ten good men are all I need and by morning I will deliver the heads of fifty Romans."

Esau the Sicarius laughed and said, "Then we could heave them back down to rejoin their carcasses."

Asshur, son of Joktan, said, "Why bother hauling them all the way up? Heads are heavy."

Hillel the priest said, "God does not like thy savage words." No one paid him the slightest heed.

Eleazar studied the palms of his great hands and sighed. "Sometimes I feel I am sailing a boat before a very strong wind and the boat is moving much too fast. If I keep all the sail then we will soon pile up on the reef ahead, but if I lower the sail a wave will overcome us and sink the boat. Now ..." He paused to be assured of their full attention. "Let us suppose, Alexas, that you are extremely lucky and manage to enter one of their camps without alarming the guard. What then?"

"Slip into one of the tents and use our Sicarii knives as they were intended."

"And then you slip quickly away and run back up here? Is that the idea?"

"Yes. O, you are beginning to see things my way."

"Alexas. I have seen things thy way all along. I also find this waiting intolerable ... but not quite when I remember how badly I need you and the men who would go with you on such an expedition. The Romans sleep six men to a tent. Do you suppose all six are going to lie quietly while you find their throats in the dark? It takes only one to give the alarm and there you are, all of you, spread out on crosses the next morning and we have to look at you and smell you until you finally rot away. O, I say *no!* I intend to preserve you for the day the Romans stand at the top of the ramp, and you may die then quite as readily as the rest of us."

Alexas considered Eleazar's words for a moment and then made his owl whistle to indicate that he was still dissatisfied.

"Well then what about the ramp? We watch it grow and do absolutely nothing."

"What would you have us do?" Eleazar asked carefully. Now then, he thought, it might as well be spoken at last. It is better Alexas should say it than yourself, better if any of the others speak out, because once the fateful words find their way down to the very last family, as always happens, it cannot be said that Eleazar ben Yair had fathered the action just to save his little kingdom.

"What would you have us do, Alexas?" he repeated very deliberately. "We are all listening."

He watched Alexas's growing discomfort and wondered if he would find the courage to speak out. With his eyes he begged Alexas to say what they had all been thinking, yet he saw only a man trapped and squirming for release. He saw him scratch at his head and then discover a demanding irritation about his crotch, and while his hands were busy not a word passed his lips.

"*What* were you going to suggest?" Eleazar pressed. "Do you need all morning to find your tongue?"

He saw Alexas's eyes frantically searching the faces around him. Suddenly now he was not Alexas the fierce and slippery one, but only a badly battered little Jew seeking some near place to hide.

At last old Ezra broke the tension with a mighty grunting and clearing of his throat. He pushed himself to his feet and stood caressing his beard for so long Eleazar wondered if he too had found it impossible to speak his mind. "Praise be to God," he said finally, and Eleazar thought Moses must have carried the same air of unconquerable dignity about him. "We must now all emerge from our rat holes and face the truth. The ramp is not being built by Romans but by Jews. We are all related to someone down there. We have oil aplenty to boil them and stones to crush them. It must be done. Even the Romans cannot force the dead to work."

During the long silence that followed, Ezra gathered his robe about his legs and sat down. He closed his eyes and muttered a prayer and seemed to have forgotten the others.

Zidon, leader of the Pharisees, said uncertainly, "The Romans have brought more than fifteen thousand Jews for the labor. Let us be practical about this. We cannot kill them all."

"We can and we should," Alexas snorted.

Hillel the priest shook his head emphatically. "You would kill fifteen thousand to protect less than one thousand? May God help you!"

"Stop begging God for help!" Alexas answered. He held his arms wide and announced. "God is our trouble and always has been. Pray, be good, love thy neighbor, kill not, covet not—be meek, let thy camels shit on you! If God cared he would stop the noise we hear right now, the same noise we hear every night and every day—stone against stone grinding and thumping and every day louder. O, I say we stop that sound. Today!"

Now Zidon rose and toyed with the great wart that blossomed from his eyelid and in so doing nearly covered his eyes with his hand so that he could easily avoid looking directly at the others. And he said in his plodding way, "I listened to the Romans and while they spoke I considered my children and your children and how they will be killed if we continue to fight and how they might live if we just give ourselves up to Silva—"

Esau jumped to his feet and seized Zidon by the neck. "You bilious old windbag!" he screamed. "You squat when you piss!"

Ezra and his son Heth pulled Esau away while there was still breath in Zidon. They held him firmly until his rage subsided.

"Let Zidon speak," Eleazar said as coolly as he could

manage. Now he would know for the first time how many of his council held secret to the thought of surrender.

Zidon's eyes darted fearfully from one man to another as he moved farther away from Esau and rubbed at his neck. Eleazar watched him in fascination, uncertain whether it would be better to cut him down now, wait until he could be caught alone, or simply hope that his own words would crucify him. He reached instinctively for the short Sicarius dagger at his side. His impulse was to rush Zidon now.

"Well Zidon, we are listening."

"If we go down to the Romans—"

"Kill him!" Esau cried lunging forward again. But Ezra and Heth restrained him.

"If we go down to the Romans we can avoid another Mount Tabor, another Gamala. Need I remind you how Vespasian and also Titus offered the defenders their lives if they would surrender? And they would not. And the Romans hurled the children of those people from the walls. Are you prepared to see this? Titus offered to spare the temple and we would not listen. And the temple is no more. The Romans want us. They will put us in slavery, but we will *live,* and our children will *live.*"

"Cut out his tongue!" Esau shouted and the plea set all the others talking at once. Esau and Javan and Kittim seemed undecided, while Asshur, Nimrod, and Hillel the priest said in various ways that perhaps Zidon was taking the sensible view.

Then Eleazar's voice rang out above all the others.

"Silence!" It was a voice that had defied so many storms it cut through the babble like a shaft of lightning. And for a moment there was not a sound in the court-yard—even the women and children were affected by Eleazar's single word. There was a ghostly quiet while Eleazar regained his patience.

He placed his big fists against his sword belt and his stance was that of a seaman balancing himself against a hard wind. "How very servile are your memories to fear. Some of you have apparently forgotten the forgiving ways of Titus when Jerusalem fell. Let me remind you how all of the aged and infirm were the first to be butchered. Let me remind you how all of our leaders who were caught were first scourged and then crucified. Have you really forgotten how all under seventeen years of age were taken to Rome as decorations for Titus's triumph? We can only guess what has happened to them. Some of you whose memories do not leak so badly may remember how all Jews over seventeen left alive were put in chains and shipped off to the mines in Egypt. I wonder how many of those people are alive this morning. Repeat to yourselves, if you dare, the names Lydda and Jamnia and what Vespasian did to those places. And Emmaus and Bethletephon, and Betaris and Caphaitobas in Idumea where Vespasian slew ten thousand of our kind. Tell me now, do you deny such deeds show the sweetness of Roman mercy?"

Eleazar paused and studied his listeners. Their mood was obviously changing. I must anchor this down now, he thought, so that it will never rise again.

"But let us suppose that certain individuals are very lucky and some Roman fancies you as a personal slave. And suppose someday you band together with the intention of killing your master and escaping. Are you aware it is Roman *law* that if one slave should kill his master, *all* his slaves, obedient or not, must die?"

Zidon said, "I still believe, as long as they need us they will not kill us. And I think of our children. Eleazar speaks of the long ago. The war has been over more than two years. We are the only people who do not know it. O, I say we must not let fanatics lead what is left of us to unnecessary death as did Simon bar Giora and John of Gischala, who would not listen to the Romans or even to each other. Believe me there are those who will make easy sacrifice to their hunger for power, and that offering is our blood. O, I ask you if we go down peacefully to the Romans, then why should they kill us or our children when they already have countless thousands of Jews easy to hand, any of whom they could kill if they pleased? These are, or should be, days of peace. Let us tell ourselves that though the state may end the spirit continues for a thousand years. Let us accept peace . . . and live."

Now, thought Eleazar, it is too late. I should have slipped my blade into his robes or let Esau at him. Now that tricky moment when anything I might do would be approved has passed and Zidon stands there pulling at his wart and making himself the image of wisdom by his visions of security. He spreads his poison with every gesture and word and I must be rid of him before he has all of us kneeling to Silva.

"Very well, Zidon. Go. Take those who would go with you of your own family and other Pharisees who are without faith in us to the number of forty and no more. I bid you farewell now because I never expect to see you alive again."

Eleazar turned and started toward his quarters. I must remove myself from the presence of that man before he destroys my own faith, he thought. A revolutionary who listens to opponents is like a sailor becalmed. He may begin to drift in any direction without recognizing what is happening and sooner or later he becomes lost.

Old Ezra moved quickly after him and came to his side. "You are discouraged, son," he said. "Do not let Zidon quench your fire."

"The man is a dangerous fool. We cannot tolerate his kind."

"I am going with him."

"*You?*" Eleazar halted abruptly. "But—you are my iron fist. I cannot fight without you. Surely you don't believe that vomit about the Romans needing you?"

"Of course not. But I am an old man and quite ready to die. Here I can only fight as one more man and I promise you my appearance of strength is a fraud. I am rotten inside and my bones are nearly petrified. I tire so quickly that minutes after the first assault I would be useless to you. But now I have thought of a scheme that suits me as it does no other on Masada. I will complement our strongest weapon, in my opinion our only one, our only chance to survive."

"The heat?"

"And mutiny. The Romans must be told what it is like to live below the level of the sea when the heat comes, how the heavy atmosphere will press them into the sand. I will make some terrible prophecies. . . ."

"Why should they listen to you?"

"Because I am old and look wise even if I am not. I speak fluent Latin and know their superstitions, of which they have even more than we have. We will not pass between two dogs, pigs or women, or eat two eggs. Ashmedai, the prince of spirits, rules by the number two. Crazy? How would you like to be a Roman General with your decision whether or not to fight a battle dependent on how the entrails of a chicken fall out when the bird is sacrificed?"

"They will kill you the moment you enter the first camp."

"I doubt it. Not for a time at least, because I will start them off with my first lie and ask to be taken to Silva himself. I will tell them that we are only the advance party of surrender. We have simply come down to reaffirm the details of Vespasian's offer as presented by his messengers—an offer, incidentally, which I doubt was ever made. But I will seem to take it most seriously, which will give me time to make certain dreadful predictions before Silva."

"And then when we do *not* come down, what then of you, dear friend?"

Ezra shrugged his shoulders. "As I told you, I'm getting old."

Three

IMPERIUM ROMANUM . . .

❖ ❖ ❖

ON yet another night the stars shone upon the Empire. In Britannia the cities of Eboracum and Londinium and Verulamium were still bathed in twilight and so it was in Gallaecia, Lusitania, Hispania and Mauretania.

The stars were taking over from the very last of the day in Cordoba, Scallabis, Gades, and the Punic cities of Timgad and Lambaesis. In each of these locations various occupying units of the Roman army prepared for the night along with the natives of the land.

In Gaul the university city of Massilia was already lost to the darkness as were Lugdunum, Narbo, Burdigala, and Lutetia. And Vindobona was also in darkness.

In Thrace there were Adrianople and Marcianoplis to be guarded and Thessalonica, Aenus, Maronea and Abdulla.

In Greece there was Athens, Sparta and gay Corinth.

In Egypt there was of course Alexandria, the more seemingly valuable because there was no regional establishment to compare with it, and in Asia there was Pergamum, Smyrna, and the rival cities of Nicomedia and Nicaea along the Black Sea. There were Ephesus, Cappadocia, Galatia and Tarsus in Silicia, and Antioc in Pisidia. There was Tyre-Sidon, Bostra, Petra, Palmyra and

Damascus, each a demanding acquisition under the stars, and in each there were garrisoned from five to five thousand Roman soldiers according to the urgency of local demands.

Scattered over all of this and much more were the stars above and the glint of Roman armor below.

In Judea the night had long arrived, and beneath the brooding shadow of Masada, Pomponius Falco dictated a highly confidential communication. In the morning the regular post would depart for Rome and he was anxious his thoughts should find transport with it. He spoke very rapidly and in bunches of words, which made it extremely difficult for the scribe to keep pace with him. When he requested a repetition Falco would frown and then speak as if to an infant, cutting each Latin word with exaggerated preciseness. Sometimes to soothe his own impatience he would reach out to caress the cheek of his young friend Cornelius, who responded each time with an automatic smile.

Falco was intrigued with the ironic relation between his present address and the recipient of his letter. Bernice—a Jewess! How convenient for Titus to have become so ridiculously enamored of the woman he would carry her slightest suggestion to his father as if her words were cut in stone. And how thoughtful of you to befriend such a remarkable bitch who was no less than twelve years older than the heir apparent, had already been married three times and mothered two children! It was a stunning example of foresight combined with an appreciation of the feminine ultimate. To approach Vespasian directly was always difficult and the results totally unpredictable if only because he was the dullest of soldiers at heart and his mind was that of a petty bureaucrat like his own father. Yet even he, so the gossip went, behaved like a rutting stag in Bernice's presence. Most certainly it was not because of any attributes with which Juno might have endowed her! She was overplump, indifferent to her dress, and careless of her hair. Yet everyone admitted she had an extraordinarily stimulating imagination, as what woman would not who had so often in her youth fornicated with her brother? She was a true Oriental, sensuous and careful to exploit an air of the mystic. She was also sufficiently realistic to recognize the constant dangers surrounding her spell and she was shrewd enough to know the more friends she had at court the longer might be her residence on the Palatine Hill.

And I, dear woman, am pleased to be counted among your trusted friends, Falco mused. I am particularly appreciative of your efforts to obtain this present commission and I shall continue to admire and adore you if you can manage to convey at least the essence of this letter to our Emperor. I shall dictate the message in our sterile Latin rather than in the Greek we would both prefer since it would be a pity if you did persuade Vespasian to glance at it and then the uneducated boor would be unable to comprehend it.

At first Falco had opened his letter with un-Roman terms of endearment for Bernice, and then remembering what had happened to so powerful a man as Caecina, who had only been *suspected* of enjoying her sexual partnership, he told the scribe to strike out the flowers and leave only the vase. "Besides, dear boy," he said to Cornelius, "verbal pawing of any female, let alone that ghastly Jewess, is as repugnant to me as actual physical contact. Why should I even slightly risk my neck for something I detest?"

So the message began with simply her name followed by his own.

". . . I am in haste to dispatch this because I am informed the next post from this wretched place will not be for two weeks. For the sake of brevity I shall omit the hardships of my long journey, hoping to relate them surrounded by comforts suitable to a Roman patriot while beholding a certain great and enchanting woman whom I have the temerity to believe is my friend. Therefore I will first to the situation, which you will recognize as extraordinary. . . .

"We are camped below a rugged mountain on top of which are a band of thieves and murderers who have terrified this region for years and utterly prevented the orderly restoration of peace and plenty to the surrounding territory. I am told, and I must warn you that it is most difficult to believe anything I am told here, that there are approximately one thousand of these brigands, including their women, who are harlots torn from the streets of Jerusalem and other cities of Judea. . . .

"You may well ask why it is that so famous a unit as our Tenth Legion has not long ago made an end of this

embarrassing situation. While I am certain numerous reports have been sent back, which unquestionably would
include military laments on the difficulties involved, the
true facts cannot be appreciated until one is on the
scene. . . .

"The scribe who cuts this letter is my trusted retainer of
many years and you may be sure will not reveal a word of
the following. . . ."

Falco paused and studied the scribe for a moment. He
had taken the name of Albinus when Falco had bought
him and had proved an expensive disappointment. His
Greek lettering was positively archaic and his Latin infuri-
atingly slow. Against these handicaps Falco remembered
that he had paid so much money for him because of his
superb physique—a dividend he had not collected because
of the almost simultaneous attachment to his household of
the lovely Cornelius Tertullus. There was now jealousy
between the two, which would be more amusing, he
thought, if it would blossom into mutual hatred.

"How long *have* you been with me, dear Albinus?" he
asked.

"Three years and seventeen days."

"And how do you know so exactly?"

"You promised I would be a freedman after five years."

"Quite right. So I did. Well, well—you will be."

Behind his half-hearted smile Falco thought that he
must have been mad to have entertained such a thought.
"Of course, dear Albinus, you represent a considerable
investment and I recommend the utmost discretion in your
behavior if you expect me to bid you a fond farewell—on
schedule? For example, if word concerned with this present
communication ever reaches outside ears you will lose
yours—among other vital parts."

"Cornelius also has a tongue." Albinus pouted.

"Indeed he has." Falco smiled. "But you must remember he is not really here. Officially, you and I plus our
immediate retainers are the only persons authorized for
this expedition." He reached for Cornelius's cheek and
passed his fingers gently across it.

"I understand," said Albinus.

"Very well then—let us resume. Now," he said, completely changing his tone of voice, "I must also beg you,
dear lady, to treat this information with your usual
discreetness."

Falco turned to Cornelius and said, "And a woman's usual discreetness is to limit the telling of any confidence to four people."

He hesitated, pursed his lips and waved his hand limply as he dictated again: "It is with a sense of profound shock that I must tell you of the hopeless inadequacy of the Tenth's present commander who is, most unfortunately, also Procurator of this land. Actually the troops are leaderless, since Flavius Silva is drunk day and night. Only this morning I followed him from his tent to the base of Masada where at enormous expense he is constructing a gigantic ramp by which he intends somehow to capture the handful of renegades now defying him. Only a mind utterly lost in the cup could have conceived of such a preposterous nostrum and, I assure you, Roman dignity, as well as our honor, suffers grievously every day. Who can blame the motley gang atop Masada if they laugh at the sight of some twenty thousand slaves and five thousand of our finest Legionaries piling rock upon rock for what appears to be a staircase to the moon? The ramp must be seen to be believed, it rivals the pyramids in extravagance, yet it pales compared to the sight of a supposedly great Roman General staggering from his tent and then proceeding drunkenly before both his own troops and the enemy alike to view his imposing folly. I pity the man. He is worn out, perhaps the victim of too many battles. Certainly he should be replaced before he pins a medal on Bacchus and brings about a military disaster that could greatly damage our prestige throughout the East. . . ."

Falco paused and wondered if he should bring up the matter of Silva's dalliance with Sheva. He decided against it. After all, his affair was strikingly similar to that of Titus and Bernice herself and any comments thereon might be taken amiss. And Bernice, though totally won over to Rome and Roman ways, was still a Jewess. Who knew what retrogression she might make in defense of a tribal sister? No, he thought, there would be other ways to use the lever of Sheva when necessary.

"You both saw him?" he said to Albinus and Cornelius. "You saw him limping along, ready to fall down any moment. Would you say I have been unjust?"

"No," said Albinus. Cornelius simply shook his head.

"Very well then, take this down." Falco cleared his throat thoughtfully because now he must be certain to express himself with delicacy and yet be equally certain his ultimate impression was achieved. Bernice, Titus, and finally Vespasian must be led carefully into the resolve that a better Procurator for Judea was already at hand, a Roman who would not consider it exile to govern such a state, but an honor. It was unnecessary, he thought, to suggest that a proper executive, say Pomponius Falco, would find ways to make these people a profitable acquisition.

"Forgive me if I seem presumptuous in feeling the gods were smiling on Roman fortune in Judea by arranging my timely arrival. Not only does our befuddled General Silva toy with moving mountains, he has also been in the habit of communicating directly with his enemies. I cannot adequately describe the sense of shame I knew and all my party knew when we were obliged to witness our hapless repesentative deigning to argue with a vermin-infested bandit. There stood our General, or I should say there reeled our General, *pleading* with these wretches to surrender! After agonizing moments I decided it was my duty to ignore protocol and take charge of the situation. It should be some indication of the General's condition to realize that he made not the slightest objection."

Again Falco looked at Albinus and Cornelius. "True? I did not hear him make any objection. Did you?"

Both young men shook their heads.

"Well then—in company with my aide and scribe Albinus, I addressed those people in a manner calculated to achieve results—"

"It was not Albinus, it was I!" Cornelius whined.

"I will not remind you again that you are not here. You were not officially authorized therefore you do not presently exist."

"Then I just imagined all that shit on my face?"

Falco reached for Cornelius's cheek again. He caught the flesh firmly between his thumb and forefingers and twisted it slowly.

"Sometimes you are worse than a child. Your peevish interruptions might be more amusing if we were merely passing time, but you will be finding your way back to Rome on foot if you continue to vex me—"

Falco twisted the flesh so viciously Cornelius was tumbled from his stool. When he began to pick himself up, Falco saw that he was weeping. At once he bent down to him and caressed the crimson welt on his cheek. Then he took him in his arms and wiping at his tears, kissed him again and again.

"Leave us," he said to Albinus. "Wait outside until I send for you."

WITH Zidon during the descent were all of his family excepting Onam, a nephew, and Ishmael, another nephew, and Jetur, his third son, each having chosen to remain on Masada in spite of their leader's pleas. There were also eleven other Pharisees who came partly out of fear for their future if they remained on the mountain and partly because Zidon was a Ben Hacheneseth, a station so high in the Pharisees any decision he would make would probably be right. Also choosing to join him was Ezra the learned one, and this puzzled Zidon very much because they had never before agreed on anything.

There were altogether thirty-eight in the party, two fewer than Eleazar ben Yair had specified.

The descent in the darkness was frightening to all because of the treacherous footing on the serpent's path and time and again the women had to be rescued when the loose shale slipped from beneath their feet. When at last they reached the base of the mountain Zidon started eagerly toward the nearest Roman camp, which was to the east. But Ezra caught his arm and said such a way led only to disaster since the eastern camps were garrisoned with auxiliaries with whom there could be no reasoning and most certainly their officers were of like caliber. Therefore, Ezra insisted, they must make their way along the wadi at the northern side of Masada and thence turn southward until they made contact with the Romans guarding Silva's camp.

"Now," Ezra explained in a voice loud enough for all to hear, "we are committed. Our only hope is boldness. We must not throw ourselves on the mercy of some petty officer whose thirst for Hebrew blood may never be satiated. We have chosen to go the Roman way. Therefore we must drive fear from our hearts, or at least from our faces. We must believe the Romans will take care of us.

We must let them know we are depending on their honor for our protection."

These were the things Ezra said to them in the starlight and after vacillating for a time Zidon agreed the flaring torches on the ramp better illuminated the western side of Masada and might help to avoid a dangerous surprise. "We will call out to them and then show ourselves. You women will let them hear your lamenting."

They trudged around the northern extremity of Masada, winding between the black shadows of tumbled rocks. As they progressed the tiny bells worn by the women chinked with their movements, and there were continuous warnings and protests as one after the other stumbled or was caught in a bush of thorns. Later the way smoothed and their silence was broken only by their panting and the fearful whimpering of the children.

More than six hours after their departure from the heights of Masada, Ezra said to them, "There it is." And they saw from an entirely different angle the great ramp of the Romans. It as now illuminated to them by a thousand moving torches and they whispered to each other that it reached to the heavens. Soon afterward, as they approached the circumvallation, they were challenged by a voice clearly audible in spite of the noise from the ramp.

"Who are you? Signify instantly or you are dead!"

Zidon replied gently. "We are Jews come down from Masada at the invitation of Vespasian!"

And Ezra added, "We will speak with your General Silva! We have words of importance for him!"

There followed a long silence from the other side of the circumvallation. As they waited, Ezra watched Zidon's tic become even more active in the torchlight. "Do not so concern yourself with the future," he said. "It comes soon enough."

Ezra saw the coins that adorned the veil of Zidon's wife reflect the torches and he said, "If you hope to keep those adornments I suggest you remove them now." Neither Zidon nor his wife heard him. They were both so locked in awe by the nearness of the Romans and the proportions of the ramp they seemed incapable of movement. Even Zidon's tick had subsided and his eyes were dead.

There was the voice from beyond the wall again. "Come to the gate one at a time. Keep your arms at your sides and your mouths at rest or they will never utter a sound again."

So it was that Zidon and all of his family together with eleven other Pharisees and Ezra who was a Sadducee gave themselves into the hands of the Romans. The first to greet them with the point of a spear was Plinius Severns, the Legionary whose guard post they had approached. Behind him had gathered the balance of the guard, some twenty men and Artorius, a Centurion, and Cerealius, a young Tribune. They listened in amazement as Ezra promptly violated the order of silence.

"O," he said to Cerealius in the lilting Latin characteristic of Sicily, "I would wager ten denarii a young man with a splendid face like yours must come from Messana."

"Wrong, Jew. I come from a far better place. Give me the denarii now or I will take them from you."

"Alas, I took a gamble and lost. But would you be willing to double the amount or cancel our wager? In spite of your esteemed Emperor's promise for our safety I have a notion that once we have left this wall any treasure we may have will be confiscated—in which event you who just met us will see nothing of it."

My dear God, Ezra thought. May the predilection of all Romans for gambling hold now. This doughy-faced young man who is a Tribune though he has barely left his mother's tits reveals a glottic stop in his enunciation of the word give. He *must* be from Sicily then.

"We are agreed," Cerealius said. "Double if you are wrong."

"Then you are from Lilybaeum, a most pleasant place. I spent a lovely month of April there and am well acquainted with the bouquet of your western grape."

Ezra knew he had won when the Tribune pushed him back among the others. Now I must plant the seeds, he thought. And there was so little time, with Zidon already shepherding us about as if he were an officially appointed Roman overseer. O, how that miserable man will soon learn the utmost authority!

Most of the Legionaries were ordered back to their posts and Zidon's band was formed into a compact column. At last, when the group took on some appearance of order, they were escorted toward the camp by ten Legionaries under the command of a Decurion and with the Tribune Cerealius leading the way. They had not proceeded ten paces up the rocky slope before Ezra's voice rang out in the most colloquial Sicilian. "I suppose all of you Romans know this place called Masada is accursed? Of course. Your officers would have told you that. But have you been told how you are now living below the level of the sea?"

The Decurion, who was a giant of a man, turned to look over his shoulder. He said, "I warn you, Jew. Keep your silence or I will spill your guts in the sand."

"And why not? I personally have changed my mind. I have decided it is better to die now rather than to have the juice that floats my testicles boiling with the heat. Do you otherwise intelligent Romans have any conception what it means to exist below the level of the sea during the coming heat? I for one welcome any quick death you may wish to administer. Crucify me, I beg you. How easy that will be compared to the horrible torture which I shall have to endure along with you if you insist on being merciful. Kill us! Do not spare us! We Jews who know this land understand what awaits those who insist on dwelling below the level of the sea where the weight of the air presses a man into the ground."

"Close your mouth, Jew!"

"That will be done soon enough. Because if my life continues for another month then I along with every human being in this desert, Roman and Jew alike, will be forced to dig a hole in the ground and place my face down in it so I can breathe. And every day I must dig deeper and deeper to match the increasing heat until finally I am digging my own grave. If you will all think how we have more air above our heads than any other people in the world then you will understand how we must soon be baked in a great pot. . . ."

Ezra allowed his voice to fall away. He marched in silence, listening to the faint tinkling of the women's bells, the sluffing of sandals along the path toward the camp and the heavy sound of greased metal against leather which came from the Legionary beside him. The man has asthma, he thought. His breathing is too heavy for so young a man. I must try to help him toward an early death. "Your breathing betrays you," he said confidentially. "Haven't you noticed how bad it is since you came to the desert?"

Ezra was not certain whether the man's grunt was an affirmation or denial. It made little difference. Wherever he went in the world the man would be sure some other place was better for his breathing. "You should go to the heights in northern Palestine. There could not be a worse place for any of you than below the level of the sea."

Just before they came to the eastern entrance of the camp Ezra raised his voice so that all might hear him. "All of you Romans should observe the old skinful of bones who leads us. His name is Zidon and he is a good man if rather naïve. He believes your great General is going to leave his tent and welcome him! Can you imagine anyone in this desert who does not know your General Silva is so full of wine at this time of the night he cannot even talk to himself? I am grateful to all your gods and my own that I am not a soldier whose fate will be decided by such a confused mind. How is it that men like yourselves will suffer such a certain and horrible death in this desert— for a *drunkard*? Please inform this old Jew the reason for this and then I can die content. Go on, run me through, but have the goodness to tell me why intelligent men will follow this drunken buffoon who left his ability somewhere in Gaul and his devotion between the legs of one of our women? How we Jews could have used such a military genius—one who would move one mountain to the side of another and walk up it over the bodies of his troops!"

The back of his escort's hand struck Ezra across the mouth and for a time there was only the sound of his choking.

SILVA noticed with satisfaction how all of his staff had thought to bring their cloaks in spite of the hot night. The scarlet overgarments edged with purple were carefully folded across their bare knees or held casually draped over an arm. Well enough, he thought. As long as there was still pride in his officers then there would be pride among the troops. Tonight, with each officer groomed for the occasion, their cuirasses glittering in the lamplight, his tent seemed to have taken on a festive air.

Silva sat in a U-shaped chair which had once been a splendid piece, but now much of the ivory inlay had fallen out and its general appearance was as battered as his tub. It squeaked with each of his movements and he wondered how soon it would collapse entirely. Hopefully, he thought, such a catastrophe will not occur in front of my officers.

His aide, Attius, now stood near the chair and half a pace behind. Seated on a wooden couch to his left were Longus Julianus, his Finance Tribune, and Larcus Liberalius, his Intelligence Tribune. Next to them stood the Tribune Metilius Nepos, a hopelessly dull man in Silva's opinion, yet invaluable for his skill at assault-weapon construction. Just beyond him stood the Centurion Lupercus Clemens, responsible for military discipline throughout the Tenth Legion. He was a gaunt man whose frightening ugliness was only enhanced by the several wens that cursed his face. He had risen from the ranks and was thus rather shy when in company with so many of equestrian rank, but Silva knew him to be totally dependable when it came to battle or family troubles within the Legion.

On Silva's opposite hand sat Maturus Arvianus, a Tribune newly arrived from Rome. He was of good family, Silva knew, although too much of a dandy for his taste. Whether he had any dedication other than fashion was still to be proven. Since his arrival he had been charged with maintaining communications to the sea coast, the handling of the imperial post and the exchange of messages by carrier pigeon among the eight camps surrounding Masada. It should be an easy job, Silva thought, yet he had recently become aware of numerous complaints and he intended to inquire the reasons this night.

Next to Arvianus, lounging with the arrogance of a man who knew his job and also knew he was appreciated, sat Ummidus Fabatus. Silva had long admired his cunning and resourcefulness and had many times openly praised his ability as a supply officer. "What Fabatus can't buy, he steals, what he can't steal he appropriates, and when all is lost—he makes it." Fabatus was a great eater, which Silva considered an absolute prerequisite for an efficient supply officer.

Rubrius Gallus brooded in the next chair and Silva was certain he was thinking about his ramp, which had obviously become an obsession with him. Silva wondered if he should spend more time worrying about Gallus. Perhaps the ramp was twisting his mind. There had been nights when Gallus had sat silently watching the continuous parade of torches up and down the ramp and no one knew when he slept, for at dawn he would be watching from the same place. Tonight, Silva thought, he looks like a cadaver with one foot in his tomb. The Jews are killing us all, slowly, by degrees, by just waiting. What a subtle people—or were they merely cunning? Gallus understood them. Remember how he stroked that great sun-burned nose and pulled thoughtfully at the tatters of dead skin when you asked him about Sheva?

"What are you going to do with her? No man *does* anything with a woman during the first verses of infatuation. *She* does things to you. Therefore you have no choice but to become reconciled to your servitude, bearing in mind, as you may be sure she does, that every passing day is in her disfavor. Nearly all women are so aware of this time element they instinctively rush to establish customs and certain intimate relations between you *now,* while the juices of your desire are bubbling so merrily. Be assured your Jewess like females of all origins is anticipating the time when you will act and appear unbelievably younger in comparison with her. This accelerated aging is a phenomenon that nature seems to have arranged as a sort of compensation for those gullible years when we trot obediently about trying to satisfy some female's various whims. She knows this, and also knowing men are prone to habit, is laying the foundation for her survival long before her magic starts to fade."

Now Silva remembered how he had then asked Gallus what he would do about Sheva if she were his affair. Would he take her to Rome? And Gallus had replied with a smile, "I am not you, hence my answer can have little true merit. Apparently, however, you have convinced yourself life might prove intolerably empty without her, which means you are in the very last stages of capitulation. So, before it is too late may I suggest you test her?"

And you had asked Gallus how, if the wisest men in the world often seemed plagued by marital troubles, how could you discover the real Sheva? And there had followed some of Gallus's basic engineering logic. He had yawned over his wine and said, "Try her sincerity. Is she simply an extremely fortunate Jewess who would exploit any Roman to the utmost, or is she perhaps actually enamored of you—a situation I daresay would be most unusual in this desert. The surest proof would be to give her a chance at your life. If she cannot bring herself to harm you, then you can be certain you have found a prize for a wife. If she kills you, then you will at least know you avoided a serious mistake."

Ah Gallus, you great nose leading a man! Here in this tent so far from home you are the true prize among all my officers!

Near the entrance stood the Centurion Rosianus Geminus with his hirsute hands clasped around the vine staff, symbol of his office. He was the farthest from the row of lamps set along a low table in the center of the tent, and the light lost in the shadows and his black beard left little to be seen about his face except his eyes. Geminus was also irreplaceable, Silva thought. There stood a soldier's soldier.

Thus far the meeting had gone so agreeably it had occurred to Silva a cup of his best wine might be in order all around. At once he changed his mind. If his officers had a cup, which they would be obliged to accept if offered, he must join them and the inevitable must happen—he would be outside in the starlight talking to the mountain of Masada again. No! This night there is too much work to be done. And because you are lonely does not mean they are. They can, if nothing better, find companionship in mutual complaint about you. Their private situation is quite different from your own, and with the post leaving in the morning they will be anxious to conclude this meeting and get off their letters home. Then there is your own report to be completed in time, and a reply to that fool of fools, Antoninus Mamilianus the architect. No, not a drop for anyone.

The auspices seemed favorable this night even without wine. Timoleon, chief surgeon of the Tenth, now reported only thirty-one Legionaries unfit for full duty. Of these a rock slide at the ramp had injured eight and the same day a cavalryman had been kicked by a horse. One Legionary had developed a goiter and was being treated with white hellebore. Timoleon also reported eleven cases of fever and four of erysipelas—the same as the previous week. There had been some increase in the prevalence of epynictis all through the cohorts. Timoleon explained the angry pustules were doubtless due to the extreme heat and he had recommended faithful treatment first with a lentil meal application and then Polygonum or green coriander. As long as the supply lasted each man was advised to treat his own suffering. There was only one new case of leprosy and six of dysentery—all camps combined. One lad from Syracuse had been stabbed in the groin by a camp follower with whom he had only moments before been copulating.

"What was she trying to do, circumcise him?" Silva inquired with a smile.

"If she was trying to make a Jew of him, she failed, Sire." The physician bowed slightly and returned Silva's smile. "We used all our skill to be sure he would breed future Romans. I am pleased to report we succeeded."

Since Timoleon, like all of the surgeons, was a Greek and hence could not become privy to Roman councils, Silva dismissed him with a smile of commendation.

When Timoleon had departed, Tribune Julianus rose to report on the provincial purse. He estimated the stipendium for Judea would amount to four million shekels, which translated into the Legionaries' annual pay of two hundred and fifty denarii per man, left the Tenth with a comfortable margin for the rest of the year.

"This would be in addition to the tributum levied on Samaria and Galilee?"

"It would be, Sire. And as the trade along the coast improves we may anticipate a direct tax upon land and businesses. If we can keep the peace we may also expect considerable sums from indirect taxes of various nature— fees through auctions, perhaps a head tax when we are ready to take a census. . . ."

"We will keep the peace," Silva replied and then wondered how he could be so positive. Was he willing to believe the old Jew made captive this very night, who had said the people on the mountain would never come down? "Julianus, as soon as we are finished with this fellow Eleazar I want you to set up a proper customs service. We should not neglect that source of revenue."

" I have already prepared the following rates, Sire, which of course would be ad valorem."

Julianus read from his notes in such a monotone Silva could not resist yawning. "Slaves each, one and one-half denarii. Horse one and one-half, mule the same . . . suckling pig one-half sesterce, dressed hide one-half denarius . . . glue, per ten pounds, one-half sesterce . . . sponges per ten pounds one-half sesterce. Wine, per amphora, one sesterce—perhaps that is a bit low?"

Silva held up his hand and said, "Thank you, good Julianus. I hardly think it necessary to go through your whole list item by item. I am certain such a meticulous man as yourself has fixed the tolls so that our revenues are substantial without killing the goose?"

Silva was pleased to note the murmur of appreciation that floated among his staff. Would this human calculating machine *ever* sit down?

"However," Julianus droned on, "I must warn you not to become overly optimistic since sea trade with this land—"

"I have always entertained more hopes for the land trade, the former caravan routes perhaps?"

"Of course, Sire. I have estimated twenty-five per cent at the frontiers and five per cent between districts. Both would be ad valorem. There again, only if we can keep the peace and thus encourage traders to pass this way may we expect to profit."

Silva next queried Metilius Nepos concerning the machines he was constructing for the final attack on Masada. The assault tower had been constructed near the base of the ramp and now stood on its great wheels. It was ready for action except for the iron plating which would armor the entire forward side and three sides of the top two levels.

"And when will plating arrive, Nepos?"

"It was brought by ship to Caesarea with forwarding orders for Jerusalem—"

"We are no longer fighting in Jerusalem," Silva said as acidly as he could manage. As much as he admired Nepos's way with the machines of war, he was not going to endure another of his excruciatingly dull orations which were always, in sum, excuses for not having things done on schedule. "We require the plating here in the desert and we are going to need it very soon."

Nepos's face remained placid in spite of his General's obvious displeasure. "I was assured by Tribune Fabatus all of the plates would be here ten days ago."

Fabatus grunted and pointed a fat finger at Nepos. "Now don't you go blaming me for your difficulties! I advised you the plates *could* have been here ten days ago, not *would* be. I told you a convoy was leaving Jerusalem and it would have sufficient capacity for your plates. You replied you were not ready yet, and that was the last I heard of the matter."

"He twists words, Sire."

"By the gods I do not!" Fabatus snorted. He turned sidewise to lift his fat from the chair and his jowls shook with the violence of his movement. "I will not be insulted by a mere Centurion! My people have brought him everything but the vestal virgins and still he complains!"

"Sit down," Silva commanded. He rubbed wearily at his bad eye and thought, The last thing I need is dissension between my two best officers. "We require the plates and we require them now. They are not here. Let us try to find out why they are not here. Fabatus, you advised the plates could be here on a certain date. On what did you base your statement?"

"I received word a caravan bearing iron plates consigned to Nepos had left Caesarea over a month ago. The plates were extremely heavy and the bearers were able to make only a few miles each day. They proceeded down the coast as far as Joppa where the Centurion in charge managed to commandeer some donkeys. Even so he lost some fifty bearers before he reached Jerusalem."

"Lost them?"

"Some died on the way, some ran away. They always do. We make provision for a thirty per cent loss along the coast. In practice it works out approximately the same in the desert; more Jews die under their loads, but not so many run away."

"You knew, then, that the plates were in Jerusalem?"

"I did, Sire. That is how I reached the date of ten days. It was only necessary to unite what was left of the original caravan with the next regular convoy."

"And where are the plates now?"

"Tonight?"

"Yes. Right this very hour. I want to know exactly where they are."

Fabatus hesitated and squirmed uncomfortably in his chair. He picked up a corner of his cloak, examined it as if he might there find an answer, then slapped it back down on his knee again. He worked his fat lips one over the other as if he had just tasted something rancid and said, "Sire, I do not know."

"*Why* should the whereabouts of a convey bound for Masada be a mystery? It is hardly forty miles to Jerusalem. Even with my bad eye I can see nearly half the way."

"Once a convoy leaves Jerusalem it is more or less on its own."

"More or less—meaning there is no communication with it whatsoever?"

"Precisely, Sire."

"Then that is wrong."

Silva turned to Arvianus and frowned. "And that is your affair, Arvianus. Why haven't you remedied it?"

"If you will forgive me, Sire. Good communications demand horses and messengers. I am short on both and decent remounts are impossible to find in this land. For example I have barely enough to carry the post in the morning beyond Tyre."

"What happens then? Does the imperial post just sit there, two thousand miles from Rome?"

"No, Sire. There is one night lost for the messenger to rest then he carries on to Sidon where he hands it over to a new messenger who comes down from Antioc with the Rome post."

"It has always seemed to me it would be faster to send dispatches by sea."

"Not at this time of year, Sire. And it is not a reliable way at any time."

Silva leaned back in his chair and beckoned to young Attius. "You will go at once to Centurion Lupus of the first cohort. He will detail eight men as messengers and sixteen of his finest mounts to the service of Tribune Arvianus. Tell him I know he is not going to like it, but we have little employment for cavalry here and he had best accept the fact with his usual good nature."

Silva turned back to Arvianus. "You will find those iron plates by no later than noon tomorrow and report to me. From this night forward I will expect a sharp improvement in all our communications, particularly between here and the seacoast."

His voice hardly pausing, Silva addressed Tribune Liberalius, a tall swarthy man without a trace of hair on his face or head. His skin shone with perspiration in the soft light, and the dampness so exaggerated the heavy lines and indentures about his face Silva thought he appeared to be sculptured in polished marble. "Have you learned anything more from the Jews who came down, Liberalius?"

"Not directly, Sire. However, two of the men now guarding them are fluent in both Hebrew and Aramaic, of which I am sure the Jews are not aware. Hopefully they will pick up something of value."

"What have you done with them?"

"For the time being they are confined in the southwest corner of the lower camp. They show no signs of wanting to escape and are heavily guarded. I rather believe they are glad to be here."

"Have you attempted to draw further information from them?"

"Not as yet, Sire. It would be my recommendation to scourge a few of them and see if there was not something they would care to add beyond what they have already offered."

"We will wait a day or two on that. That addle-headed young Cerealius had them knocked about enough. Now— this elderly man who denies he is their leader and calls himself Ezra. I was rather taken with his manner. He seems . . . quite different from the others."

"He is still a Jew, Sire, and therefore not to be trusted."

Silva massaged his crippled leg pensively. For a moment he seemed to have forgotten he was not alone. Then suddenly he studied the faces bordering the shadows as if hoping to discover some confirmation of his thoughts. But he found only an uncomfortable silence. Finally he said, "What I am hoping for, of course, is a Jewish surrender *before* we have to go after them. I don't mind so much the trouble and expense involved in completing the ramp, but I am distressed to count the number of Legionaries we will lose during the actual assault. We will need those men for the later policing of Judea, and Rome has already indicated they will not furnish replacements."

He paused and wiped the perspiration from his eyes. Dare he mention the heat? No, the less said about it the better. By some ancient military magic the secret fears of officers dripped right down through the men. "Now there is another very important factor we must weigh most carefully. When we take Masada we will make certain very few Jews survive, if any." He paused again and smiled at his listeners. "Unless some of you would care to take one home as a souvenir . . . but in my opinion there are quite enough Jews in Rome."

There was another murmur of amused appreciation, then Silva continued. "I am thinking of our future in Judea. If the Jews on Masada fight to the last, which they will probably do or I mistake Eleazar, they could possibly became a symbol for all other Jews in Palestine, and such a development might easily become a potentially dangerous rallying point for a very long time. This was not the case with Jerusalem or any other of our engagements with these people. It is something we can live with well enough, but I envision a productive land here in the future, as self-governing as the Jews can ever govern themselves, and of course with us as their supreme rulers. We must remember that while we can eliminate most troublemakers we cannot reach them all. If he has a symbol, it takes very little more for a dedicated man to set an already restless people once more at our throats, or their own, for that matter. For a profitable peace, which is the reason we are here, we must have people working instead of fighting. For this reason I believe we should explore every possibility of taking Masada without actual conflict. I will listen to any recommendations."

There followed a long and uncomfortable silence. Silva watched his staff look at one another and work their mouths and pinch their eyes as if each were on the very point of a momentous declaration. He gave them time to fold and refold their cloaks and to wipe the perspiration from their brows, until finally more amused than disappointed he said softly to himself, "Brilliant."

Their response had been no less than he had expected. Here were six Tribunes, each entitled to wear the golden ring, and in the Tenth there were altogether fifty Centurions and one hundred Optiones and one hundred Ensigns, all of whom could be classified as officers. And yet, nothing. All obedient, all willing as children if their father spoke. And who was the father?

Silva sighed, and quite suddenly there was the taste of wine on his tongue. And a voice in the shadows of his tent seemed to whisper, "There is your answer. If no man will call you friend, if no man will challenge you because of fear of his position, and if the loneliness now returns and you sit as a solitary ghost with all the desert world waiting upon your next decision, then join with me. Not much, say no more than a cup, or at the most two . . . Send these good dull men away to chew on what you have already said and let me this night once more be your companion."

The chair cried out when Silva pushed himself to his feet. And immediately all of the others rose expectantly. As Silva surveyed them he thought, How splendid to the eye they are, how grand and soldierly and imposing of mien! All true Romans, brave and devoted—and not a full brain among them.

"Let us sleep upon all of this," Silva said quietly. "May the gods inspire you." He raised his hand carelessly in reply to their farewell salutes and even before they had all managed to slip out of the tent he sat down heavily in the U-shaped chair. He saw his hand reach out to encircle an invisible cup and he immediately clenched it into a tight fist. Then for some moments he sweated profusely and though he made not the slightest movement, his breathing rapidly increased until he was panting. To distract his thoughts he bit his lips until he tasted blood and for a time the flavor of wine left him so that he could slump in his chair and close his good eye and call upon a lifetime of discipline to transport his mind afar. Yes ... he was at last succeeding. There was the post to think about, not this one but a post of long ago received in Gaul. There was that certain letter from Livia which he could recite to this very day. To repeat it seized the mind. To linger over its every word and phrase, so much Livia, so like her very voice, held up a shield to weakness.

MY BELOVED HUSBAND:

For the past month I have been debating ceaselessly within myself, and as long as I dare, on how to write this letter. It has always been the last wish of your wife to distress you in any way, yet I believe it better to explain now rather than have you return to find me gone and then spend the rest of your own life secretly wondering why.

Dear one, my reward will be if you always pronounce the name Livia with affection.

I have this day made sacrifice to Minerva in your behalf and to Poseidon in my own. I write these last words to you because even if you were here within the touch of my hand I am now incapable of telling you what my heart demands.

You will remember the increasing huskiness in my voice which once, before you left for the north and we were having one of our very special very privately gay evenings, you laughed so tolerantly about, saying, "Indeed it is a wonder to me *all* women do not suffer some loss of voice considering how they belabor the instrument." How true, dear one, and I was as guilty as any other of our circle.

On your return you may inquire of the physicians concerning my affliction even though I doubt you will learn very much. The more honest ones confess to be mystified, the others burn incense and roll their eyes and chatter away interminably about cacoëthes and this or that potion to effect a cure. The only matter they all seem to agree upon is that the lesions in my throat will soon prevent me from ever making an intelligible sound again and that I may soon join my ancestors. It is as if the gods so envied our mutual joy in each other they sought revenge and have by this cunning device managed to strike us apart forever.

Dear one, I wish to leave you this side of death

while we both breathe and sense the life of the other, while even our thoughts are in harmony though you be far away. Forgive me for being such a child, but the other side of death holds no promise for me— I have never met anyone who makes the slightest sense on the subject. Of one thing only am I now certain other than my everlasting love for you. I am not going to let death come to me. I will go to it.

I beg you not to deduce from this that I have lost my sanity, for such is not the case. On the contrary, during these past few weeks I seem to have new perceptions on almost everything, a clarity of thought and value that often astounds me. I see the leaves of the acacia tree in our garden in a different way than ever before. They dance in the slightest breeze, twirling as no human performers may ever do, and tell me over and over again how the beauty of life is so short we must never spill a moment of it. I see light where I never saw light before, in the fringes of summer clouds, in the shimmer of a dewdrop that must also after a short span of life vanish forever.

And why not, dear one? Is it not better for me to leave the feast now while my face and silhouette are still alluring to you? Oh, it is very well for people to say, "Let us grow old together," or worse, "What a lovely old couple!" Lovely? Not for your Livia. And now, even if I desired I could hardly be classified as a "comfort" to any man in his later years.

You have often told me that as a soldier it would be most fitting if you died in battle. So it is with me.

Funerals to honor a great man for his deeds are morbid enough, but for a woman who has done nothing else in this world but love her husband, not even the giving to him of a child, there is no excuse for the tears of mourners. While I must confess my wretched femininity by hoping you will grieve at least for a time, there is certainly no honest cause for you to brood over my ashes or otherwise mark my twenty-five years of earthly citizenship with cold monuments. So it is my intention to spare you and my family those punishing though obligatory rites.

Tomorrow I will journey to Neapolis, where I have arranged to take a vessel for Capri. I have specified the passage must be made at night. It is my determina-

tion to look down at the stars reflected in the sea and
join them.

Dear one, may the gods protect you. Farewell.

Silva rose slowly from his chair. He raised his two fists
toward the top of the tent as if it were the sky and held
them there, his whole body trembling. "Ah Mars, my
patron god, rescue me from this perpetual night! Defeat
me or give me victory, but do not leave me wandering in
the wilderness so alone!"

He lowered his fists and went to the table. There he
poured himself a full flagon of wine.

❖ ❖ ❖

VALERIUS VALENS, a Legionary of the first maniple of the second century, sat in his tent that was designed to accommodate ten men but was now crowded with more than fifteen of his comrades who had also just been relieved of guard duty along the circumvallation. They were gathered around the single oil lamp listening mostly to Marcus Fronto, a grizzled Decurion of the first cohort. Though Fronto dominated the group there were times when one of the other of Valens's uninvited guests would speak their minds, and what they had to say made him extremely uncomfortable. It was suffocatingly hot in the tent with so many bodies and so airless the flame of the little oil lamp frequently appeared to have lost its struggle for life.

Even with a watchful guard posted outside the tent to warn of the overly curious, or the approach of an officer, Valerius Valens was nervous. The Tenth Legion had been his life, so much so that he had memorialized its passage wherever he had marched with it by carving "LEG X FRET" on anything from a tree to a stone. It was a habit common to many Legionaries, who found it an economical way to pass the inevitable waiting time known to all soldiers. It cost money to play at dice but nothing to carve, so they vied with each other for artistic grace in the lettering. "LEG" was the customary abbreviation for Legion, X the Roman symbol for ten, and "FRET" was particular to the Tenth, meaning Fretensis and signifying the Straits of Messina, where they had long been garrisoned prior to Palestine duty. Thus the marchings of many of the Legions across a land were often recorded and sometimes a soldier in Britain or Africa would hope to advise others of his fate and transfer by carving his name, unit, and date on anything at hand.

Now Valerius Valens found relief from the tension

100

surrounding him by scratching in the soft stone bench on which he sat. He employed a broken dart for the purpose and somewhat to his surprise discovered that he was again carving the familiar old "LEG X FRET."

"You heard the Jew," Fronto the Decurion was saying to the others, "you heard what the old man said about the heat. And you have heard me who has served in Africa from one end to the other and knows what heat can do. Now let us listen to Plinius Severns here, who knows all there is to know about Jews."

A tall thin Legionary asked dryly, "Even more than Silva knows these days?" But no one laughed.

Plinius Severns was small for a Legionary, yet wiry and able to write his full name, and he had fought well at Jerusalem, so he was respected by the others. He was a garrulous man and his peculiarly discordant voice was known throughout his cohort. Now he rasped, "Well, first he said his name was Ezra and then he asked my name, and he didn't talk like a Jew at all but more like a human being, and he said all that we've already heard about and how we are below the level of the sea and all that and how we're all going to melt pretty soon, and he asked how could we fight for a General who was drunk all the time and—"

"We heard that too. Get to the *important* part!" Fronto insisted. Plinius Severns hesitated because he wanted to savor his sense of importance. Never before had he commanded such an attentive audience. Finally he said, "The thing you have to understand is that most Jews have a gift. They can see what is going to happen, and this man Ezra said he saw our blood boiling thirty-five days from today."

"Why don't you have yourself circumcised?" asked Vespillo, a stolid Legionary from the third cohort. "Next you'll be telling us you believe in a god that can't be seen."

Silius Proculus, who was also from the third cohort, laughed and said, "Severns, you don't know anything at all about Jews. I tell you they wouldn't direct a thirsty man to a spring. I tell you they are a race of lepers and I know for a fact they have secret laws that tell every tribe they can fatten and slaughter one gentile a year. They eat his entrails and take an oath to hate anyone who refuses to worship their invisible god. You want me to believe such a wild and mysterious people knows what will happen next month?"

Terentius, who was a cavalryman and thus considered an outsider, said, "We should have more pay for being here. After I finish paying for hay, my own ration, my boots, leggings, and the camp Saturnalia fund, I am docked a hundred and twenty denarii. Then another fifty goes to my account—which I may not live to use. I say we should have something extra!"

"We are getting away from the point of this meeting," Fronto countered. And now Valerius Valens began to carve more industriously because he sensed that he was about to play host to the very subject he feared.

"Whether you believe the old Jew or not we should decide what we are going to do if the heat comes down like he claims it will. In other words, are we willing to dig our own graves right here in this putrefying desert and not even make a protest?"

"Such as . . . ?" Proculus asked cautiously.

There was a moment of heavy silence. Fronto examined the anxious, sweating faces leaning toward him in the feeble light. "We are men," he said softly, "and we are not unarmed. Do you suppose that Silva could oppose us if he stood alone?"

"The day when a putrefying Decurion commands the Tenth is the day I desert," said Silius Proculus. "I have memories of times when you couldn't handle ten men."

"I am not suggesting myself," Fronto replied as if hurt by the inference. "I am thinking of a high Roman who could explain our actions in words that would be understood at home. Many of you saw him this morning. He impressed me."

"I saw him wiping shit off his face and I was not impressed," said Valens.

"And he is not a General," Plinius Severns croaked. "That putrefying Falco is a split-ass politician. If you walk slowly by his tent he'll reach out and rape you."

Valerius Valens decided he had heard enough without having his say so he stopped scratching at the stone and spoke with great seriousness. "I don't want to die in this putrefying desert any more than the rest of you, but the heat has already got to your brains. We are less than twenty-odd in this tent and if we do some careful talking maybe we can bring another thousand men to our way of thinking. Then what? You forget that if Silva doesn't hear of us before we are ready, there are another four thousand men in the Tenth who never heard of us. And I will remind you there are many men who will die for Silva."

"I suppose you are next going to say it is for the glory of Rome that we must stay here and defeat these putrefying Jews?" Proculus sneered.

"I care not what happens to the putrefying Jews. They can have this putrefying land. I care what happens to me, and I can feel something worse than the heat if this talk continues—and that is Silva's red-hot iron reaming out my ass."

"Easy now," Fronto said soothingly. "We are not going to hurry this. We must organize very carefully and keep our final intention strictly to ourselves. We will simply tell the others what the Jew said, how we will all soon be dead if they do not join us. My friends, you must remember that all such matters are originated and finally controlled by small groups. The fact that we are only fifteen is the very best thing."

Paternus and Severns stood looking down at her, and when at first she opened her eyes and saw their faces in the torchlight she thought they had come alive from her nightmare. She had seen their thick-lipped, sweating, Roman-nosed faces in her dreams so many times, but now Severns clearly said, "He wants you."

Paternus bent down to shake her and said just as clearly, "Make haste about it."

They waited impatiently, yet she took her time combing her hair and touching her body with the last of her precious supply of Alexandrian perfume. She wanted time to compose herself and understand why she was actually eager to see Flavius Silva again. Was it only because of the sleeping bodies scattered about the tent like fallen leaves? Those bundles of dusty cloth were her family, the not-so-proud remnants of a tribe said to have wandered the Sinai desert with Moses. They were, she thought suddenly, the near-dead, having lost themselves in scheming for their own protection and yet they objected to the only act that now preserved their skins. They squatted all day in the shade of this tent cursing Silva with monotonous regularity and though they were within sight of their blood brothers laboring at what might be their own lot, they constantly complained of their treatment. They slept and ate in plenty and their hands were becoming even softer than when they came to Judea and all the while they lamented her surrender to that Roman.

"I would rather die than know my daughter slept with Romans."

"You may very well die if I do not. And I sleep with only one Roman."

"He threw you to the whole third cohort."

"It was a gesture. I did not believe it—nor did he."

104

"Your willingness is impossible to understand. A reasonable person would say it will disgrace our family for ten generations."

"Why not eleven?"

"What possible good can you see in him?"

"None. But he is a lonely man."

"So is Satan."

"And I learn much from him."

"How to kill Jews?"

"Must I remind you that I am saving certain Jews?"

"You are a harlot, and according to the laws of our forefathers—"

"Our forefathers did not have the Tenth Legion on their necks!"

So they would all argue relentlessly until she yawned in their faces. Now, walking toward Silva's tent, she was puzzled at her urge to defend him before her family. Why should she favor a man who commanded her presence in the middle of the night and assured it by sending two guards? It would be more admirable to kill him. This night. While he sleeps. No other Jew in the world had such opportunity.

When at last she stood within his tent and they were alone she studied Silva's face intently. She saw that his bad eye was nearly closed with weariness and she allowed herself a moment of compassion for the haggard figure slouched in the chair. Then she saw the flagon of wine within his reach and decided he was drunk.

"So? The great General has such a skinful of wine he wants to see the Jewess he has thrown away?"

Silva waggled a finger at the couch, then ignoring her, turned to drink deeply of the wine. She moved toward him very slowly.

"Is the General's brain so petrified he cannot hear an old Hebrew story? Or perhaps I should save it for the next time I am sent away to become mascot of the third cohort?"

"You were not harmed. A friend of yours countermanded the order."

She smiled and approached a step closer. "Thank you, great General, for saving my vagina."

"Stop calling me 'great General.' "

"I do it now to remind myself that you are supposed to

be one, for the more I watch you the more I think of Noah and Satan."

"I thought you people had only one god."

"True, but Satan is his adversary, and if you haven't heard of Noah I despair of you."

"I know all about Noah. A sailor fellow."

"One day, after the flood, he decided to plant a vineyard—"

"Very intelligent man," Silva said waggling his finger again.

"And Satan came to him and said wine gladdens the heart, but I have some ideas to improve it. All you need is to kill four animals and pour their blood upon the vineyard. Then you will see how marvelous wine can be."

She paused, watching him carefully. General, she thought, I must reach out to you tonight or lose the chance of capture. But he was looking away from her, at the top of the tent. He took a sip of wine and seemed to have forgotten her.

"Are you interested in what kind of animals Satan chose to enrich the vineyard?"

"Go on."

"A lamb, a lion, and then a pig, and finally a monkey."

"So?"

"Ever since, the first sips of wine leave a man as a lamb, then a little more and he is like a lion—who dare challenge him? Then at last he becomes a pig, squirming in the mire, and finally he becomes a monkey, screeching and swinging from limb to limb and jumping about and not knowing what he is doing."

Silva chuckled and she was strangely pleased at his reaction. Somehow she had never thought Romans capable of inner amusement. The common soldiers she had seen both in Egypt and Judea brayed like donkeys when they were drunk, but their officers were invariably solemn as priests. They wanted the world to know the weight of it was on their shoulders. Not this man, she thought. In spite of his wounds and air of detachment there was a jauntiness about him she found intriguing. It was a quality no Jewish man she had ever known seemed to possess.

She moved cautiously until she stood directly in front of him, then praying that her hand would remain steady, she reached out very slowly and took the cup from him. I am taking a bone from a lion, she thought. Her tension eased when she saw he was still smiling. Encouraged, she bent forward to place the cup on the table as far from him as she could reach. And she was aware that during the movement her breasts were most naturally displayed to him, so she moved even more slowly.

Her fears returned when he failed to reach for her. Instead he glanced at the wine cup and then looked coldly into her eyes.

"Would you by chance have in mind matching the record of your countrywoman, Bernice?" he asked.

"I do not understand you, Sire."

"Bernice, the woman who first took her brother as a lover, then spun off two husbands, then Vespasian, and now has Titus locked between her legs."

So, she thought, he has been brooding about Bernice. The woman should be drowned like the alley cat she is.

"What is your opinion of such a woman?" he asked.

"She must be a very clever and enchanting lady to have captured such great Romans." Never in the presence of a man, she remembered, speak anything but praise of another woman—particularly if she is beautiful. And if possible change the subject lest the absent image of the other appear the more attractive by comparison.

"You seem weary," she said reaching out to pass her fingers gently across his brow. After a moment he pushed her hand away and said, "I have never met Bernice, but I would gamble you are even more artful than she is."

"Obviously not. I seem only to anger you."

"You are in quite a different temper than when I last slept with you."

"I have had time to think, Sire. My family and I are content to wait."

"So? You talked this all over with your relatives and they advised you?" He cocked his head and looked at her quizzically. "I am rather surprised—and disappointed in you. I had thought you had a mind and will of your own."

"My wish to please you is entirely my own persuasion."

She reached for his brow again and this time he closed his good eye as her fingers passed. And he muttered, "I am not sure I trust a female with claws so suddenly withdrawn."

"I ask for nothing but my freedom."

"Ah? Then you are asking for death. It is the only true freedom."

He became silent for a time, and she cautiously moved around him until she stood at his back. As she continued to caress his brow and eyes she was surprised to find herself lulled by her own manipulations. Who was this man beneath her fingers? She must remind herself ever more firmly that he was a hated Roman and this very night she should do all Jews the favor of killing him. It would be so easy now. He was utterly relaxed and his eyes were closed. There was his short sword on the table within easy reach. Soothe him more and then reach for it quickly. Plunge it down hard into the back of his neck—so bare and vulnerable, it seemed to be waiting.

Her fingers strayed to the curls on his head and he said, "If I am weary it is because I waste my energies trying to understand you Jews. When we were at Jerusalem, Titus twice offered to spare the city if you would surrender. We could not understand why you refused, why you burned down the very temple you implored us to spare."

"Perhaps I can help you to understand us," she said softly. Careful now, she thought. Keep his attention, but do not allow him to become alert. The sword was in its leather scabbard. She must keep the easy rhythm of her moving hands and yet extract it silently. Then suddenly she decided it was impossible.

"You will understand Jews better if you realize we can live on hope."

"Hope?" Silva muttered his words and drifted from Greek to Latin. "You must have something to hope for, something tangible unless you are insane. We outnumbered you at Jerusalem and you could not possibly hope any ally would join you in preference to us. Physical strength? You must know the powerful Germans are our slaves. Wily Generals? Could you forget how we took Carthage, or were your leaders so busy arguing among themselves they forgot? Even the walls of Jerusalem could not be used as an excuse for hope if you consider the sea as a bulwark and admit our conquest of Britain. Now here at Masada we meet the same stubbornness and I do not understand it."

As he spoke he tipped his head back until it rested between her breasts. It was more than a hope, yes, it was a prayer, she thought, that he would not sense her new and mounting excitement. She had moved only slightly but it had been enough to reveal a dagger lying on the table. It had been obscured by a roll of parchment and it was not in a scabbard. So easy—

"Close your eyes and forget about us, forget about everything, my General, pretend you are home in your cool garden, pacing slowly back and forth, smelling the fresh Roman air . . ."

"Worrying about how I am going to pay for the plumbing . . ."

"Being brought cool drinks by your slaves . . ."

"Wondering if I was cheated outrageously when I purchased that murrhine glass . . . No. Change the scene. There are times when I believe I am better off here."

"But you *will* go home, great General, when you have conquered the Jews?"

"You are already conquered," he grunted. "Vespasian has minted a coin to prove it."

Although she could not see his face she thought he might be smiling. She passed her fingers gently across his eyes and found them closed. Then while she continued to stroke his brow with one hand she cautiously reached for the dagger. It was as if an invisible force guided her free hand.

His voice became ever more drowsy and his Latin slurred as he muttered, "Why should I go home, ever? There is nothing there except stone walls, and walking in a garden alone is for philosophers. I have not the brain for meditation, nor declamation. It is hard to believe I have studied Quintilian and Cicero for style and inspiration and still cannot match words with a Hebrew fisherman. Why do you suppose this is so, Sheva? Tell me and I shall reward you—"

She raised the dagger behind his neck and brought her free hand slowly around the side of his head.

"You have stopped breathing, Sheva. What is the matter?"

He caught her moving hand and brought it back to his lips. He kissed her hand gently and said, "Does it surprise you, dear Sheva, that I have considered taking you to Rome with me, not as a captive but as the hostess of my house? And I have even thought that if we could live in harmony and you could cease despising all those with whom you would come in contact, then, if it were agreeable to you in every way, I would hope that you might become my wife. I will admit there would be certain social difficulties for a time, but none insurmountable by a woman of wit and grace, as witness Bernice. I assure you there are many Jews in Rome. They live quietly and in a modest way, it is true, but since the days of Augustus they have been allowed every freedom including the practice of their religious rites. Does the prospect please you at all, Sheva? Sheva, answer me."

Help me, my God, she prayed. Make me bring the knife down now. She glanced at her upraised hand commanding it to move, but it remained fixed in air. Her mind cried out to the glittering blade, but it would not move. She heard him say as if he spoke from the edge of the world, "Sheva, put the knife down. It was given me by my dear friend Gallus, who would not want it soiled with my own blood."

He had not moved even slightly, and when she instinctively passed her hand across his eyes she found them still closed. And suddenly she dropped the knife and threw her arms around him, kissing his neck and his ears and the side of his face and murmuring over and over again, "O my dear, my dear brave General, I am a traitor, a harlot traitor—I would be deliriously happy if I could soak my hands in your blood, but I cannot, I cannot . . ."

He turned and took her in his arms and pulled her down to him until he could hold her quivering body in his arms, and when she sobbed he covered her lips with his own.

At last when she quieted he wiped tenderly at her tears and whispered, "I am a monumental fool to trust my neck to a Jewish slut, but Gallus will be pleased to learn you passed his test."

"I will always loathe you—"

"Then why do you hold to me so tightly?"

He rose carefully to his feet, still holding her in his arms. He carried her to his couch and as he set her down gently, she thought, Now everything said about me is confirmed. I am this Roman's complete slave and I will know only ecstasy from the moment he enters me. My people should burn me.

She waited for his hand to linger upon her breasts. Then, she knew, he would slip down to caress all of her and she would soon enough be aroused and from then until they both lay panting and exhausted there would be no Romans or Jews in all this world or any other beings so alive.

But he made no movement toward her now. Instead he sat down on the couch beside her and became as remote as when she first entered the tent. She heard him say, "The matter of your going to Rome can wait. Who knows, I may never make the journey myself. I will tell you now that I am deeply troubled about what you have told me about Jews and hope. It confirms my very first impression of Masada. Those people are not going to surrender, because Eleazar in one way or another gives them hope. Do you realize what that means?"

"I would have at least some pride in myself if I were with them."

"Not for long, because you would soon be dead, and I have never seen a proud corpse. All the thousands I have seen killed in battle bear a dumbfounded look, as if something or someone had betrayed them at the very last instant. I do not know why this is so. It goes against my earlier belief that a soldier's death is a glorious one. . . . I suppose it really is time that I go home."

His voice trailed away and to her surprise he reached for her hand and kissed it again. But he did not look at her and the gesture was preoccupied as if such passing physical contact with another only served to sustain his thoughts. He stared at the candelabrum of bronze, marble and glass that stood beside the couch and all of the wounds about his face became deeper.

"I am not thinking of the Jews on Masada," he went on hesitantly. "By the gods, they have given me trouble enough, but I do not want them to pass on the narcotic of hope to the rest of Judea. Martyrs are always dangerous. Nor do I like losing the thousand-odd Legionaries my staff has predicted we will lose in the final attack. Yet it is coming . . . any day now . . . and I am quite certain that if I falter even slightly our friend Falco will have my head in a basket."

"It is of no interest to me," she said as evenly as she could manage, "which Roman head falls first."

"If your concern for your people is genuine you should take a very great interest in my personal welfare, for I assure you Falco's mercy is as thin as the paint on his eyes."

He rose from the couch and went to the flagon of wine

on the table. He raised it to his lips and drained it and still with his back to her he said, "I have been wondering what I can do that might be different enough to tempt Eleazar away from his doom—because if the truth were known, I admire the man. He would have made a fine Roman soldier. Lately I have been wondering if perhaps you might not be the key."

He slammed the flagon down and returned to the couch. He stood unsteadily, looking down upon her.

"What do you suppose the Jews on Masada would do to you if you suddenly arrived in their midst?"

"They would kill me."

"Not if I know my adversary. If you bore a personal and secret message from me, then how could he resist listening to you? And once he listened, would he not be honor-bound to assure your safe return?"

"I thought your opinion of Jews did not include honor."

"A Roman habit of speech. Perhaps I should have said he would be obligated to send you back safely."

"Your speech is thickening, great General. Have more wine so you will become unintelligible. I prefer you that way."

"Any General can win battles with force. I have a desire to win this one in a new way. Would you do what I ask?"

"Do what?"

"Take a message from me to Eleazar. It is something you would have to do of your own free will."

"Free? You really are drunk again."

"Of late I have rarely been as sober. I cannot force you to do this or the idea will come to naught. I realize there is some chance you will never return, but if we succeed— and you will notice that I say *we*—then it could mean the true end of the war in Judea. And we could seriously consider that journey to Rome together."

She looked up at his face trying to estimate the degree of his drunkenness. No, he was not as far gone as she had at first supposed. He was at the lion stage, bold enough with the wine to have deliberately risked his life, yet still very much in command of himself. And somehow the weariness seemed to have left his face so that he appeared much younger. If your hand had obeyed, she thought, he would now be dead.

She heard him saying, "This could be very important to

your people. You would be telling Eleazar that you are free and so would they all be if they surrender now. You would be my living word there would be no reprisals—"

"Why should he believe me?"

"Because he has nothing to lose if he does. You would only ask him to meet with me alone, at a halfway point on the serpent path. You will tell him I will await him while the desert sleeps, two hours before dawn, and I will climb the path alone."

"You will forget all this when the sun boils the wine in your brain. But I suppose I must humor the great General. When would you dare do such a thing?"

"I will arrange your escape tomorrow night. It is of the utmost importance that no one except ourselves is aware of the meeting."

"He will see in it only some sort of trap."

"Every advantage will be his. He is descending while I must climb. It is I who may be trapped."

After a moment she reached out her hand and brought him down to her. And she thought, Here on this couch I will submit to a monster who crucifies my people—a drunkard, an alien master who would risk my life to ease his conquests, a broken man, or nearly so, whom I have come to love. "Great General," she said softly, "come to me. You are so very tired."

Four

BENEATH ORION . . .

ELEAZAR BEN YAIR stood in the synagogue that was oriented toward Jerusalem according to the law and there he listened to the melodious bass voice of Hillel the priest chanting the Psalms of David. As many men as were free of their duties along the ramparts had crowded into the synagogue for the Sabbath service, and those who could not find a place waited attentively outside, where, like their women, they could at least hear the voice of Hillel and the responses. And though Eleazar ben Yair stood a head taller than almost all the others, he was conspicuous more for his stance than height. He could have been on the deck of a rolling vessel, so wide were his feet spread, and he did not rock back and forth like all the others. He held his head high and appeared to be demanding some reply to his thoughts from beyond the walls of the synagogue, and his eyes further marked his separation from the multitude because they were distant and preoccupied and there was no sign of humility in them.

He had been standing so for a long time, since the sun had gone down over the western hills of Judea and the Roman torches far below had once again covered the desert like phosphorescent particles swimming a night sea. He flexed his great hands covertly, making fist after fist to

115

soothe his impatience with the priest, whom he could only think of as a man who was still collecting shekels from the people of Masada to support a temple that no longer existed.

Yet Eleazar sensed that it was imperative for him to be in the synagogue now, for the departure of Zidon and his relatives and Ezra had wrought great mischief among the people of Masada. Now those who remained could look down upon Zidon and Ezra and all the others and see that in spite of their confinement they were very much alive. Eleazar knew the temptation to join the defectors was powerful—after all, there might be at least *some* kind of future with the Romans. Whereas here?

"I must live ever more closely with my people," Eleazar had warned himself. "I must breathe with them and touch them constantly. I must worship with them and believe with them lest they cease to believe in me."

So on this evening he had forced himself to attend the synagogue, as earlier he had accepted a ritual bath in the *mikveh*. The ancient code proclaimed how the purification of his body must be done, and Hillel and his fellow priests had gone to enormous trouble to preserve rainwater for nearly a year so that the spirit of the law could be observed. Better, Eleazar thought secretly, the same effort should be devoted to thwarting the Roman's oncoming attack. Or would it be? Here at least was something his people could cling to in their desperation. Almighty God! he thought, how blessed are those who can believe so utterly. Drive the doubts from my mind and let me hide behind your strength! Let me believe like the Essenes, who will even forgo defecating on this purest of days. Let me also rejoice that on this ancient occasion the priests are wearing their finest ceremonial garments, with breeches to cover their thighs and long blue robes with ornamental golden bells signifying thunder and dangling pomegranates which are supposed to make me think of lightning. Let me believe it is necessary for Hillel to adorn himself with an ephod when he might better wear a breastplate in the same place, and let me marvel that his ephod is mostly of gold and engraved with the names of the Jewish tribes. Give me some proof that silly thing on Hillel's head is more than a linen miter encircled with a crown of gold. I can read the Hebrew symbols inscribed around the crown. Jehovah! Does this childish display do you honor? Or would you prefer that we who are the most recent arrivals on earth show more modesty?

Now Eleazar remembered how angry he had been when Hillel and his fellow priests had insisted on bringing all of this paraphernalia with them across the desert. When they should all have been traveling fast and light they had burdened themselves with scarves, mantels, chalices, incense burners, scrolls, and eight-branched candlesticks. Well, well, perhaps he had been wrong in his displeasure. Perhaps the blind faith of so many had its own usable value.

As if to match his anxiety he now heard Hillel intoning how it had been one thousand five hundred and fifty-six years from the creation of Adam to the deluge, and another eight hundred and ninety-two years to the birth of Abraham—and then five hundred and twenty-five years to the death of Moses. And it was six hundred and twelve years from the exodus to the building of the temple in Jerusalem, and though the temple was destroyed Hillel was proclaiming it would be built again.

So, Eleazar at last decided, if these gaudy trinkets and fixed ways of my people have lasted for so long, if we are forever moaning about long-ago calamities, how am I going to make my people concentrate on the dangerous present?

He raised his eyes and shook his head. Jehovah! You had better hand down a solution soon!

His impatience continued to mount during the priest's prolonged recital and he sighed so mightily a number of times several heads turned toward him in disapproval, and Alexas, who stood next to him, whispered, "Quiet. It can't last forever."

"It already has."

"Pull at your beard. It will distract you."

"By the time Hillel is finished with the Mishna there will not be a hair left on my face."

Through the western windows of the synagogue Eleazar could see the constellation of Orion, and as always he found comfort in seeing it hover above the black line of Judean mountains. Greetings, Rigel, Betelgeuse, and my affections to you, Castor and Pollux. You are all solace to my eyes!

At last Hillel lifted his hands to his shoulders and gave the benediction. When he had finished and the synagogue was nearly empty Eleazar went to him and gave him grudging praise. "You do well to make me listen when my ears hear only the sounds of Romans building," he lied. Now of course, he thought, here I have borne false witness to the high priest himself, but I must have advice and comfort against the dark new thoughts which stalk my mind. "Hillel," he said, "I have insulted God by making your place among us difficult. I am sorry and hope you will forgive me."

"Judeans say Galileans hate the Torah. There are times when I wonder if they are not right," Hillel said coldly.

Eleazar placed his huge hands on the priest's shoulders and shook him gently. And he was careful to smile when he said, "I know my ways are rough, Hillel. O, I know that and far it is too late in life to scrape the barnacles off my manners. But my heart is with you even when my words may seem otherwise."

"It is difficult to keep God uppermost in the minds of our people when our leader seems to dismiss him as unnecessary."

"I will mend my ways." Eleazar paused and dropped his hands to his side. Then he watched patiently while Hillel unwound the phylactery from his left arm—seven turns according to the law. Then he asked casually, "All of you priests are schooled in medicine, is that not so, my friend?"

"It is so."

"Then perhaps you would reveal something that has long puzzled me. We will not seethe a kid in its mother's milk nor eat any kind of carrion because, I am told, the animals will have died in pain. Now I know how to kill for I have had much practice at it, but I have never tried to kill man or beast without causing pain. If you know how that may be done, will you, as a matter of interest, tell this ignorant fisherman?"

"The method is simple enough. You must be sure to employ a sharp knife, then cut once quickly and surely across the jugular vein and carotid artery. Death will be painless. Are you planning to make your own sacrifice?"

"No," Eleazar murmured, "I was just wondering . . ."

He turned away without saying more to Hillel and walked thoughtfully toward his quarters. Be on your guard, he told himself. Allow some time to pass before you greet Miriam and Reuben or they will sense the cloud which drapes so heavily across your spirits. For their sake pretend the noise of the Romans building means no more than the surging of the sea.

Now Rigel had vanished behind the mountains and Sirius also, and in his loneliness he thought it was like losing two friends. He forced himself to think of livelier matters—of a bracing winter day in what seemed like another life when he had stood at the joining of the Jordan with the Dead Sea, and he remembered how he had been able to see the hot luxury of Jericho and then look northward up the long valley to observe Mount Tabor crowned in snow. And he remembered how the thought of killing another man had not then ever entering his head.

"I have fought too long," he whispered to the stars, and then suddenly he remembered Abigail. O my overburdened head, he thought. I have too long neglected the best friend I have on Masada!

He half ran to the western casemates, kicked off his sandals and, stooping low, entered a smoke-filled apartment no bigger than a box. A single lamp flickered on the ground and hunched over it was a woman of such frailty she seemed transparent. She was Abigail, daughter of that Hezekiah who had first taught Eleazar to number, the legendary Abigail who had fought the Romans since the first outbreaks at Caesarea.

"Woman whom I have known all my life," he began, "may I say that you grow more beautiful every day?"

Abigail made a dry sound which came from the depths of her throat and was intended to simulate vomit. Her huge black eyes rolled upward and she shook her tiny falconlike head violently. All the wattles about her neck shook with the gesture and then disappeared when she blew out her cheeks and stared at him.

"Hadtha beitak—this is your house."

"And your mustache becomes ever more luxuriant," he continued in the special voice he had always reserved for Abigail.

"You are mellowing, boy," she grunted, "but that does not necessarily mean you are any more honest with yourself than a donkey who thinks he is a horse."

"And may I say your dignity and quiet charm are befitting to a much older woman, let us say three or four hundred years old?"

"So I am," she said and then spat in the sand between her bare feet. "I am so old I do not believe I have time remaining to tolerate your company for much longer. You are in trouble. You are in trouble or you would not bother to come see this woman who saw you drain your mother's tits. Now, out with it while Abigail still keeps her sweet nature."

Eleazar sighed. It was like coming home to be with Abigail. He said, "The trouble is not of my own making. I cannot seem to push any idea through the council. No matter what I say there is always at least one objector, and if I tell him to close his mouth at least until I have finished, I am called a tyrant. As a consequence very many important things are never done."

"If you had studied your lessons when you were a child instead of chasing every young female in Galilee you would have learned the old Greeks called your problem democracy."

"How can I solve this trouble? I care not what they call me, but the word 'tyrant' or even the thought gives the council such a fit everything halts."

"Die."

"I do not understand your bastardized Hebrew."

"I speak Hebrew such as may be set to music, but only when there are cultivated ears to listen. You are barely a fart on the great winds of Hebrew culture and your death will mean nothing unless you arrange to be a martyr. Then people will say you were right all the time even though at best you guessed right half the time."

"So—I just sit back and let everything we have fought for go to pieces? I smile when they argue until dawn and say, 'Well, what will be will be,' and I accept some sly jackal's word as just as good as mine, or believe this unfortunate idiot, whose mind is encased in the mud of self-esteem, knows as well as I do how to kill Romans? I am to do this, old hag, and weep silently while Romans cheer?"

"Drop your diphthongs in my bowl and I will eat them for breakfast. What kind of a God contributed to your magnificent stupidity? You are our leader here—no one else. If you are not ready to become a martyr then I recommend you keep your own counsel. Smile while the others flay their gums. Agree. Praise their wisdom. And agree. Delegate important-sounding duties to the most obstreperous. Separate those who would unite on a single point and lead them into arguments on various points. Agree. Be grateful for the wisdom of others while you employ your own. Leaders are not an accident—although in the case of yourself I may name it a disaster. Proceed with whatever inspires you regardless of the council. Great leaders will do anything to win."

"You are suggesting I act first and later ask the council for approval?"

"Since when have you developed a conscience?" The hoods closed over Abigail's great eyes and she spread her hands and shrugged. "If the Romans take Masada, who else is going to take the blame but you? Your perplexities do not rot my heart because I recognize them as only mouthings of your passing thoughts. Having said them, you feel free to proceed as unscrupulously as you please— like any other leader. Now get out of here, and come back when your blood is stronger than goat's milk."

Later he walked beneath the desert heavens to the western gate and found there Asshur, son of Joktan, who was responsible for that section of the rampart. It was the most important post on Masada and yet the most frustrating. For here, where Herod had once taken in supplies and had himself carried to the summit, the Romans now aimed their great ramp. And well devised, Eleazar admitted, for by concentrating on one point Silva had rendered most of Masada's defense useless. All around the ramparts they had nothing to do but stare at the empty sky or down at the Romans, and their weapons were never drawn. The great stones that had been so laboriously placed to roll down on the heads of any invaders had not since been moved. Supplies of javelins and arrows dried untouched in the sun and children played quite safely all along the eastern and southern defenses.

Here at the western gate where Asshur stood peering through a crellis in the rampart the situation was exactly the opposite. Any man who exposed himself for more than an instant was likely to find a Roman arrow in his skull, or if he lingered a trifle longer he might hear the thump of a Roman catapult an instant before he was crushed by a fifty-pound stone.

"Let me see how the locusts are progressing," Eleazar asked.

Asshur stepped away from the crellis and said, "They

have risen more than the width of my hand since sunset."
Even in the darkness Eleazar sensed that he was afraid.

He looked through the crellis and watched the now all
too familiar scene. Moving through the light of innumerable torches were some of the thousands of Jews laboring
for Silva. They were separated into groups of ten to fifty,
depending upon the size of stone they dragged up the
ramp. Once the stone was in position they would remove
the hauling ropes and then gather on one side of it to
push. Shouting in unison to multiply their will and
strength, they would shove until the great rock tumbled
down against the high wooden barricades which swarms of
other Jews were constructing on each side of the ramp.

Eleazar was puzzled at the inactivity of the overseers.
They all wore Legionaries' armor, the usual helmet, flex-
ible breastplate and apron of leather flaps over their
tunics. But their curved shields were stacked halfway
down the ramp. Apparently they were now content to rely
entirely upon the protection of their Syrian archers, who
stood silhouetted against the highest line of torches. They
held their bows at the ready and, ignoring the tumult
about them, kept their attention on the heights of Masada. It seemed to Eleazar that one archer had spotted him,
for he stared directly up at the crellis for a long time, then
raised and drew his bow with the arrow aimed directly at
Eleazar's eyes. Yet he seemed indecisive, as if he were
uncertain whether he had sighted a true target or not.

Eleazar was relieved when the Syrian finally lowered his
bow and resumed his conversation with the man next in
line. They were so close Eleazar imagined he could almost
hear their conversation above the all-pervading noise and
it infuriated him to observe how at ease they seemed. And
why not? Silva had this very day guaranteed their safety
by the most basic device. For every arrow and every stone
sent down from Masada, regardless of its effect, the Jew
nearest the point of impact would be slain immediately.
Two Jews would die if a Roman was actually hit. There
was no danger of Silva reducing his work force. All of
Palestine was his to draw upon. Thus since early afternoon
the sting of Masada had been removed, and Eleazar though
the mountain waited like a great beached porpoise for the
rising tide.

Now, watching the inexorable rise of the Romans into
assault position, he pounded the wall with his fist in

frustration. All afternoon long he had pleaded with the council, "I warn you if the Romans are not stopped now they will be upon us in a week! Let us roll the great stones down on their heads. We must kill every man on the ramp whether he be Roman or Jew!"

Esau the Sicarius had agreed with him and so had Alexas but Ezra was no longer available to sway the timid. The decision had been made by the majority, who had once more moaned and whined and lamented that it would be blasphemous to kill other Jews so helpless, or so and so had an uncle or a sister down there and certainly it was not meant to be they should die by an act of family.

Now Eleazar noticed how the overseers rarely bothered to uncoil their whips. There was obviously no need since their captives seemed to be working willingly enough, as if they were anxious to complete the ramp and have an end to Masada. Eleazar wondered if Silva had persuaded his captive Jews that their brothers on Masada were merely troublemakers. Had he promised relief for all once the outcasts on Masada had been conquered? Zidon and his Pharisees were down there. They would tell the Romans anything to save their skins.

Eleazar became aware they had been joined in the darkness by a third man. He turned, recognized young Shem, son of Ishmael, and gave him greeting. He knew that he would have just descended from his post in the tower and he saw that now his eyes were cheerless, which was unusual with him.

"Eleazar!" he said bitterly. "What kind of craziness is this? First I cannot kill Jews who will destroy us just because they are Jews. Now I am forbidden to kill Romans. Are we all supposed to die like my father? If so I say you old men have become old women!"

Eleazar smiled. "You are a thief of my thoughts, friend Shem. And you are right, except that I forbid you to call me an old man until I have at least twenty more years. I do not alone make the rules on Masada, and I cannot persuade the council their precious relatives must die."

"Then why trouble with the council?"

"That is the way things are. You would not like it if I were the only voice to be heard."

"I for one would prefer it so," said Asshur.

"And so would I," Shem said. "Give me leave, and from this very place I can kill ten Romans. Easily." In the reflected light from the torches Eleazar saw him caress his double convex bow as if it were a living thing.

"Are you willing to watch twenty Jews drop beside them?"

"Why not?"

"You are hard, Shem. I could use a thousand of you."

"Give me leave!" Shem urged. "They have never been so close."

Eleazar looked steadily into the youth's eyes and he thought of Shem's father and how those same eyes must have reflected the flames which had consumed his father, as now they reflected the Roman torches. He scratched at his beard and wondered how far he dared commit himself. Silva's threat had not been tested, so why not? . . . Ah, how easy it is to persuade thyself into an action already desired! "Tomorrow they will be closer," he said uncertainly.

"And the day after tomorrow they will be at our throats. Do you have to ask the council every time you want to piss?"

"I suppose I should if I were not a tyrant at heart."

Eleazar hesitated only long enough to consider how old Ezra would now advise him if he also stood in the case-mate with two such young-old men. Then he said, "Very well, we will not discuss this further. The council has ordered us to do nothing but watch—until they think of something, which they will never do. I am only the voice of the council and so I now say to you: *no*. You are not to throw so much as a pebble at our enemy. I also say to you that it has been a trying day and I am very weary. I long to spend a few moments with my wife and boy before they fall asleep, so I will leave you now. And what you may do when I am gone is unknown to me, because even if I had eyes in the back of my head I cannot observe what occurs in a place I have not really been or join a discussion that never really took place." He saw the change in their eyes and was satisfied, so he said, "We Jews are prone to imagine many things and then believe them—such as my presence here. We dream of impossible things if we doze off for only a moment. . . ."

Shem smiled and went quickly toward the steps leading to his tower. Asshur followed him. Eleazar paused momentarily, started out of the casemate, then changed his mind. He leaped up the steps after the others.

Eleazar stood at Shem's left while Asshur stood at his right, and they watched him draw his bow carefully. Eleazar heard Shem suck in his breath as the tip of the arrow reached his knuckle and he held it until his entire body seemed to have been turned to stone. Then his fingers parted and the arrow hissed away into the darkness. There was no sign of its swift passage across the stars or its descent into the light pools of torches, but almost immediately Eleazar saw a Legionary spin about with an arrow in his forearm. The man shouted an oath, yet before his voice had died away another arrow whirred from Shem's bow and then another and another. Each one found a mark in the neck or mouth or bare arms of a Legionary, and pandemonium took over the ramp.

The curses of the Legionaries mingled with the frightened screams of the Jews, who ran everywhere among the flickering torches. And Eleazar saw some of them caught and run through on the spot by raging Legionaries, but most of them seemed to have successfully vanished into the darkness beyond the torches and he could count no more than eight bundles of quivering cloth on the ground against twelve armed Romans.

All had transpired within a man's twenty-odd breaths, a single youth moving with the precision of a machine— draw, set, release, draw, set, release, one bolt after the other slipping with such speed through the night they were invisible until they struck their mark.

The Syrian archers held their ground long enough to send off a long thicket of arrows in the general direction of the ramparts. But they had no definite target and were obviously confused and soon they also broke ranks and ran down the ramp until they were out of range.

And then suddenly there was no visible movement on the barren ramp. The torches illuminated the great stones which threw elongated shadows and in their depths Eleazar saw a few Romans trying to squirm away. And he saw a Jew who was himself staggering through his own blood throw himself upon one of the Romans. Immediately the two were locked in terrible, silent combat until very suddenly both lay still and rigid like a single body.

Now, for the first time in weeks a heavy silence fell upon Masada. It was a silence Eleazar knew would be heard all over the summit—children would wake and ask about it and in a few moments all of the people of the

mountain would rush to the ramparts and inquire why it
was that the perpetual grinding and pounding had ceased
so suddenly.

It is a wonderful, thick silence, Eleazar thought. There
would be no more work on the ramp tonight. And not,
he believed, in the morning, until the Romans reorga-
nized. Now, in only a few moments his arguments had
been proven. One youth with a bow and a practiced eye
had done more to refute the supposed wisdom of the
council than all his own pleadings.

He spread his long arms outward so that he embraced
both Asshur, son of Joktan, and Shem, son of Ishmael.
With one great heave he lifted them both, and he laughed
so fiercely his voice echoed all across the abyss below
and seemed to roll triumphantly down the ramp. "God is
with us," he cried out and hugged his companions again
and again.

"God is with us at last!" And he inhaled deeply of the
night, for on his left cheek he had felt the first hot breath
of south wind since Silva had marched into the desert. By
the morning, he knew, the Romans would discover the
true torment of Masada.

Sometimes as he paced his tent with furious energy Pomponius Falco would come to a sudden halt and probing about the region of his heart exclaim that such pounding was a warning signal of his grievous mental distress. And he repeatedly questioned the wisdom of taking a sedative. "An opiate or a purge—I know not which—to rescue my analytical powers! They are torn to shreds by this abominable wind! Who can think in this?"

It was as if the desert itself had chosen to reflect his mood, for the wind that had risen during the night had increased with every hour until now even the morning sun was lost in blowing sand. His tent shuddered in spasms of compliance to the wind and the sound within was an all-pervading thrumming which Falco announced would soon drive him mad.

"It is absurd enough to be awakened every morning by a rhapsody on Silva's ridiculous trumpets," he whined, "but now the gods must conspire to add the beating of a thousand drums! I am now thoroughly convinced the Roman army cannot do the slightest thing without tooting on their childish tubas whenever something begins, and then tooting again whenever it supposedly ends. Little wonder our soldiers are such tedious bores!"

Falco addressed his immediate resentment to Albinus who crouched warily near the tent entrance, and to Cornelius Tertullus who was poised on Falco's couch, belly down and feet in the air. Occasionally, when Falco's eyes fell upon him, he would move his legs slowly back and forth as if he were swimming under water. The movement was approximately as Falco had prescribed. Cornelius was being punished for his table manners.

"You naughty boy!" Falco had said earlier. "I will teach you to break wind while *I* am breaking my fast! For the

127

rest of this entire morning you will be a mermaid!" Falco had then boxed Cornelius's ears until he wept, and now if he stopped swimming for long he would kick him with enough force to make him gasp in pain.

Now four days after his arrival at Masada Falco was beginning to question the wisdom of his coming. What a wretched experience! Only a reward of great treasure could equate the situation, he thought, only an honor so great he hardly dared dream about it could compensate him for the danger, discomfort, and embarrassment he had known since leaving Rome. Pomponius Falco named by his Emperor, Vir Clarissimus—most illustrious man!

This morning with the whole world become a howling bowl of hot wind and stinging sand, Falco found a masochistic pleasure in reviewing certain unpleasantries which had befallen him since he had first conceived the idea of coming to Palestine. There had been first of all his failure to establish a profitable relationship with Caenis, Vespasian's iron-willed concubine. It had been doubly disappointing because working through women had hitherto always been easy. I have, he had often reminded himself, a very great and natural talent for it. We are sympathetic. The girls trust me, the little dears. They find me refreshing after the apes they are obliged to take as lovers. They do not care that I was born beneath the tiles—they recognize ability and legitimate ambition because they observe it every day in their very own mirrors. Thus had Bernice been approached originally and enlisted as an influential friend, and many others. Unfortunately not even Bernice held an approximation of Caenis's power. After all, who in the entire Roman Empire was closer to the Emperor?

Now Falco remembered how Caenis had been cold and uninterested and had even cut their meeting short when he had complimented her taste in maternity gowns. Indeed! Nero had known what he was doing. All pregnant women should be kicked in the stomach—as he had so wisely done to his dear Poppaea!

Suddenly Falco began to tiptoe about the tent, holding a finger vertically above his head and eyeing Albinus and Cornelius with elaborate invitation. "All women are brood cows. I bid you remember that. They are thus little trouble if kept constantly with child. But in time this reproductive action becomes a bore to the initiating man, so he takes his penis elsewhere. The truly enlightened, of course, discover the ecstasies of sodomy, and once persuaded, purify themselves forever by forsaking all relations with loathsome females!"

Falco clasped his hands as he waited for the impact of his words to dissipate. When neither Cornelius nor Albinus displayed the slightest reaction he forgot what he had said and became lost in brooding upon the indifferent attitude and deliberate slights imposed on him by Flavius Silva.

The beast! he thought bitterly. That disfigured, crippled mastiff! That drunken, whoring, bastard, son of Mars had not as yet had the courtesy to invite his official guest to sup with him! His reply to your plea for provisions since your own were now exhausted had been to send down the standard Roman army fare—a disgusting porridge made of pulse, soup, bread, lard, a hint of vinegar and some scrawny bits of vegetable to thicken the mess. It was uneatable, and the wine he had sent from what he had claimed was his personal supply was a perfect match.

"It makes me fart just to look at it," Cornelius had complained, which had only caused Falco to strike him again. Ah, how he longed for a respectable meal!

To ease his gastronomic distress and divert his thoughts at least temporarily from the wind, Falco reviewed a banquet he had once attended at the home of a Senator, a true commisator, who also appreciated pretty boys. It had been intimate and deliciously obscene, with only nine honored guests. This was in the height of fashion, being neither less than the number of graces nor more than the number of muses.

The first of the twenty courses served on the lemon-wood table proved to be ram's testicles temptingly hung from candles shaped like a phallus. There followed such a profusion of delicacies Falco could now only remember a few. There were piles of the celebrated Lucrine oysters encircled by wings of tiny thrushes. Then for contrast, bear paws from Germany marinated in a pepper sauce, followed by pigeon eggs artistically set in the gelatine which adheres to the upper shell of the turtle. Then followed a course of trout from Ciss-Alpine Gaul exhibited to the guests, prior to cooking, in their traveling habit of still-frozen glacial ice. And while the cooking of the trout proceeded, there were plates of crisp seawife and mushrooms to nibble on along with great bowls of beer to stimulate the kidneys. Eventually, when the trout had been consumed, there arrived sausages inserted into the wombs of young sows to bridge the highly emotional gap betwixt fish and meat.

Then there had come the wine, an exquisite Caecuban that would have pleased even Horace had he been alive to test its flavor. And at last a gigantic flaming pie was carried into the midst of the couches by nine beautiful boys, each of whom laughingly chose a guest as his partner for the evening and from then on served him as if the poor man had lost the use of his hands. Out of the pie the boys plucked deer hearts from Spain and roebuck from Gaul, boar tongues from the marshes of Belgica, and succulent strips of gazelle from Africa.

Falco tried to recall further exotic treats that had graced the pie, but he could only be sure there had been some badger hams said to have been sent down from England and some wafers of lion liver, rationed one to each guest. Vivamus, dum licet esse bene! Alas! It now seemed so long ago.

He paused in his pacing and looked down at Cornelius, who was stiff affecting a swimming movement. But his eyes were closed as if he were trying to absent himself from the tent.

Falco puckered his lips and then kicked him. "There, Miss Mermaid," he said, "you just struck a rock. I suggest you keep your eyes open for the rest of your voyage." And looking beyond him 'he saw Albinus wince, which pleased him. What dull young men! If either of them would fight back at least they might be more interesting. Of course they would never dare with that bevy of Usipats and Batavians on guard outside. At least Titus had provided an escort which was impressive! They might not be cannibals, but they certainly looked it, and even most of the Legionaries gave them a wide berth in passing. But then they stank like hyenas, so no one cared to make their close acquaintance.

"Now hear me, both of you bitches," Falco began in a high voice to compete with the drumming wind. "My nerves are very much on edge this morning. Wind always upsets me, and I will not be teased though you festoon your groins with flowers. I am concerned only with the fact that we are at least temporarily at the mercy of that relic of all wars, that hostile, one-eyed, stumble-marching oaf ... General Flavius Silva. Now I will tell you this. I did not come this far simply to inhale the desert atmosphere, much less be driven nearly out of my wits by a Hebrew wind. Nor do I fancy being insulted by military minds, or worse, ignored. I embarked on this enterprise with the intention of making some history and that I still propose to do."

Falco strode to the tent entrance and pulled back the flaps just far enough to admit a blast of sand. He closed the gap instantly and grunted his disgust.

"I shall begin by personally exercising the rite of Damnatio Memoriae on our friend Silva. By the time I have washed my hands of him Vespasian will, at best, request him to fall on his own sword, or send him off to the farthest wilds of Britain for the rest of his marching days. Nothing he has ever done will be remembered and his name will invoke no recognition whatever."

Falco strode over to Cornelius and said, "You may stop swimming now. I find it distracting."

"Can I sit up?"

"Yes. But if you commit any further vulgarities I shall have you permanently corked."

Falco resumed his pacing, trying to organize his thoughts against the persistent assaults of the wind. All successful actions are the result of meticulous attention to detail, he reminded himself, and now was the time for an examination of present opportunities. Alertness, ability to shift quickly to the latest development, was the true mark of an expert in political life. Opportunity—where were the new and perhaps unrecognized opportunities here? Silva? How can that wretch be forced to serve the aims of Pomponious Falco? Answer? First return to the basics and review exactly what had originally inspired this particular expedition.

It had appeared simple enough when viewed from afar. You, Pomponius Falco, were clever enough to perceive how Roman blood was being diluted in the hybrid ocean of her new subjects. Vespasian alone had added enormous areas to the Empire and the administration of those provinces was delegated to an ever-thinning supply of the educated and capable. The numerical strength of the aristocratic Roman families was constantly diminishing and had been for years, while the slaves and all their ilk were becoming ever more fertile. Who then but a blind man would fail to see how they were becoming masters in fact if not in name and would soon take over their sterile superiors' powers as they had already bastardized his culture? There were many blind men in Rome. It seemed to be a deliberately acquired escape of the high-born and influential.

And where did this all leave such a one as Pomponius Falco, who was not blind to events and trends and who in former times might at best hope for some obscure appointment in a government agency? In a very special position, thank you. It had only been necessary to move discreetly when in public and be careful about taking on airs long considered the privilege of the equestrian class. Roman knights were competition for the time being, but they were anachronisms, whether they knew it or not. So tolerate them a little longer as you might an ailing relative still undecided about an heir. Their arrogance now makes little difference because you, Pomponius Falco, will one day sit in judgment on them and remind them of their behavior—how they had never seen fit to suggest a certain former occupant of an attic in Ravenna join their circle no matter how assiduously he had applied himself toward achieving an education. Any Roman, great or little, knew that it took a man of exceptional talent and energy to change his status during a lifetime. So? It had already been accomplished. After all, Vespasian himself has declared in writing you are known at court, but what that darling of manhood who looks more like a bath attendant does *not* realize is how very much further you intend to go. Nor does his son Titus—that mentally defective pretty boy with a perpetual erection.

"Did it ever occur to you, Albinus, that Vespasian could be seriously constipated? He has the faraway look."

"I have never seen the Emperor."

"Nor has he ever seen me, my dear Albinus! And I would not depend on Titus recognizing me without a strong assist from an aide. *That* is the genius of females when employed as prods to the mighty. Without spilling a drop of blood or spending a sesterce they can cause a man to authorize actions he would not otherwise dream of permitting. We have merely ventured a first step. Within a year, I guarantee you, both Vespasian and Titus will have cause to recognize me."

"Why?" asked Cornelius accusingly, but Falco was too far lost in speculation to notice his pouting tone.

"Because, my dear, I intend to earn his attention by being the first to arrive in Rome with an eyewitness report of ultimate victory in Judea. Silva will be so occupied cleaning up the mess he has made, it will be weeks before he can even start for home. I am even now preparing for my reception at court with my letters to a female. She, being privy to a forthcoming event, will be unable to contain the secret. Hence, with proper timing, everyone will be waiting breathlessly for my arrival. News, the *first* news made palatable, is the key—"

"To what?" asked Cornelius. "You make up a lot of lies and they listen and perhaps reward you a few thousand sesterces and out the door you go. My stepfather is one of those people and I know how they behave."

Falco wheeled on Cornelius and raised his hand threateningly. "Stop pouting, you little bitch! I know what I am doing. I have no intention of bowing out the door with a mere 'Thank you.' Heroes are the first to arrive home from wars. All others who dribble back even a few weeks later may have been as brave as lions, but they are ignored. I intend to make a specific request of Vespasian, after appealing to his passion for economy. He has recently created new provinces—Achia, Licia and Rhodes, to name a few. There are also Bysantium and Samalus, dreary places I suppose, but potential treasures for a Roman governor with a sense of financial acumen."

Falco picked up a mirror and thoughtfully began to preen his locks. He made faces in the mirror, pursing his lips and elevating his eyebrows as he talked. "Each of these new provinces will require a governor. For one of them the ideal choice—is myself."

"Suppose by the time we return to Rome governors have already been appointed?" Cornelius asked.

"Then I will accept some higher station in the Imperial Bureau and soon enough find cause to replace one of the appointees."

For a moment his thoughts drifted far from ambition. Wetting and working his lips and studying his image in the mirror he suddenly found himself wondering what it would be like to make love with a circumcised Jew. Dear, dear! What a mad idea! This wind is making you an eccentric.

"Only one matter need concern us at the moment," he continued. "General Silva, who has so taxed my patience.

Every man has his measure of sophism and our dear General can be no exception. Yet my intuition tells me we would be pursuing a false spoor if we accept the obvious and suppose that wine is his major temptation."

Still lost in the mirror, Falco pressed gingerly at the skin eruptions scattered across his cheeks. "Let us better suppose that Silva is as illogical as most men who are cursed with an overabundance of masculinity. As a consequence he joins the ranks of innumerable foolish men who are susceptible to even sillier females—and in the process become as vulnerable as mating doves. Silva himself has drawn the picture for us by consorting with this Jewess Sheva, and since he did not discard her after first lust— indeed we know he has seen her repeatedly—we must acknowledge she has some influence upon him—how much or how little must still be determined. It therefore behooves us to concentrate upon her for the time being, discover what *she* wants from Silva, since all women want something in return for their odoriferous carcasses. If we cannot better or sooner fulfill that desire, then we must explore other means to make her our friend. We must know her future plans and present movements about this camp. When we are sufficiently informed as to her background, and particularly her relations with Silva, then I will find cause to invite her to this tent . . . and from the moment of her arrival you may be sure Silva will no longer be his own master."

Albinus, seeking favor, said, "I know the tent where her family lives. I heard them speaking Greek so perhaps I could become acquainted."

Falco snapped his fingers and smiled at Albinus. "Go, my dear boy, go. Wrap your face carefully lest the sand blemish your skin."

THE GALE SWEPT northward from the parched Nabatean
hills, gathering heat from the wilderness of Zin and force
from the Gulf of Aqaba. It scorched all that lay before it
in the long Wadi Araba, creating a chain of vast dust
devils as it spewed into the Valley of Salt. Soon this great
wind became pinched between the rusted iron mountains
of Moab on the east of the Dead Sea and the wild Judean
hills to the west, so that in the region of Masada it
became a tempest. It sucked at the breath of men, both
Jew and Roman alike, until the desert itself seemed to
quiver beneath their feet. The sun which had ever been a
merciless white became an orb of cinnabar, and along the
exposed flanks of Masada even the shale rattled in the
heavier gusts. Occasionally torn rags of clouds combined
with racing blankets of dust to obscure the sun entirely,
and then all men moved through a lurid twilight which
some believed heralded the end of the world.

Silva thought it fitting that his mount should bear the
name *Fury*—certainly it matched the temper of this
morning. He had bought the horse in Libya, home of the
only good mounts in the Empire with the possible exception of Sicily. Fury was of splendid conformation, a typical Libyan bay with the white star on his forehead, but
somewhere in his training a mistake had been made. While
the beast behaved with admirable courage during actual
combat, he would in peaceful surroundings shy at a passing butterfly. As a consequence, Silva had himself initiated
some good-natured ribbing when the subject of his horse
arose. Fury, he had often said to his officers, should have
been a mare, since his behavior bore no relation whatever
to his name and he was as frivolous and undependable as
a very young girl. There had been many times when Silva
had resolved to be rid of Fury and yet, as if the beast

135

sensed his intention, he would then behave as if Silva were his only god and his sole mission on earth was to please his master.

Now on this terrible morning Fury proceeded warily through the camps, head down against the wind, snorting fiercely as if to call Silva's attention to how bravely he was meeting the ordeal.

At Silva's side rode the Centurion Rosianus Geminus, who as Prefect of the Camp was duty-bound to do what he could to alleviate the wind's devastation. Because of the storm Silva had excused the balance of his staff from this morning's tour and instead of walking, as was his custom, had ordered Fury brought to his tent. Now he questioned the wisdom of his choice for he worried about the effect of the stinging sand on the horse's eyes.

Silva had covered his own face with a band of silk which he had cut from a toga Livia had bought for him long ago and which he had flatly refused to wear in public. "Am I a peacock?" he had asked her. "Must I strut about in this gaudy flimsy just to be in fashion? Supposing a wind comes up and lifts it on high? Then will Romans observe not the splendor of a peacock's fan but the blushing butt of a very embarrassed General!"

This morning, at least, a piece of the toga was serving some useful purpose after being packed around for years, and he thought ruefully that if Livia were alive this morning and asked him to wear the toga he would have agreed instantly.

So much for regrets, he warned himself. There were enough discouragements at hand without reviving old ones. Half of the tents in the camp were collapsed and some had been blown completely over the wall and disappeared into the dust haze. Morning drill and reports had all been canceled, as the Legionaries were told to seek what shelter they could find. Final work on the assault machinery had stopped and the now-abandoned mobile catapults looked like the skeletons of primeval monsters rising out of the haze. Work on the main assault tower had also been stopped. It swayed and creaked so in response to the heavier gusts, Silva wondered if the whole structure would be blown over. Everywhere there was great confusion and the few men Silva saw actually moving about passed like invalid ghosts through eerie spumes of sand.

They had progressed very slowly because at times they could see no farther than their horses' ears. Masada itself had been obliterated since before dawn and they found their way to the base of the ramp only by plodding straight into the wind. Silva's crimson cloak stood straight out behind him, the collar choking his neck. His mouth and nostrils were dry with dust despite the silk mask, and the hissing of the sand against his helmet seemed to constantly remind him that Masada must be conquered very soon or perhaps it might never be done.

At last they came into the northern lee of the ramp, where they found the Tribune Gallus more morose and detached than ever. Though his lips were cracked and his face caked with sweat and dust and his eyes tormented, Silva was not in the least surprised to find Gallus at his post. Gallus was going to build his ramp regardless of the gods' indisposition. It was *his* ramp and it might be blown away today, but if so he would commence rebuilding tomorrow.

"Hail, good Gallus!" Silva began. "How is your liver this bright and bracing morning? Have you forgotten I promised you fresh cool air and maidens two days after you give me a ramp?"

"I have trouble, Sire. I have had trouble since last night when the Jews decided to kill their own."

"I was informed of the skirmish. You lost nine Jews and four of your own men?"

"I believe one more Legionary will die before the day has passed."

"When he has expired and the weather is clear enough to see from Masada, kill two Jews. Be sure the execution is witnessed from the summit."

Gallus wiped at his watering eyes. "I need every man, Sire. I need hands to build, not to die. Even my best Decurions cannot make the Jews work productively in this wind."

"Have you told them they have never been safer? Nothing can be seen from Masada, even if an arrow could fly across this wind."

"The basic trouble is more serious, Sire. Since last night's killings I have almost five hundred men who refuse duty on the ramp."

"You are speaking of Jews?"

"No, Sire. Legionaries."

Silva was puzzled. For a moment he thought the wind had tricked his hearing. He asked incredulously, "Your Centurions have ordered Legionaries to work—and they have refused?"

"They complain they have had enough of Masada and the desert. They say we will all soon die of the heat and they see no reason for it. If it had not been for the coming of this wind I believe there would be more than a thousand now. The word goes quickly from tent to tent."

"No word travels unless some man carries it. Who is the ringleader?"

"Apparently there are several, but I know of only two: a Decurion whose name is Fronto—I remember him as a troublemaker in Africa—and there is a Valens, who is a Hastatus of the second century. I believe there are many more."

"If I know of but one, that is enough. I'll geld the lot of them!"

"My information is they were inspired by one Ezra, one of the Jews who came down to us."

Silva turned to Rosianus Geminus. "Bring the men to my tent within the hour. And bring the Jew."

As Geminus rode off, Silva remounted. He said to Gallus, "Carry on as best you can, my friend, as if nothing was awry. I suspect this thing has been brewing for some time and did not just blossom with the opportune arrival of a persuasive Jew. We are drawing too many of our Legionaries through levy. You say to a seventeen-year-old, 'You are drafted,' and fail to tell him why, and at once you have the seeds of mutiny."

"It is not the boys, Sire. They serve well enough, for the most part. They send us too many foreigners these days, and most of them have never been to Italy, let alone seen Rome." Gallus looked away and grumbled. "I have never liked the use of mercenaries. They brought the downfall of our republic—"

Silva deliberately cut him short. "You are very outspoken this morning, friend Gallus. Some of our princes dead or alive might take exception to your views."

"I care not, Sire. Mercenaries bring more mischief than they are worth. They always have and they always will."

For a moment Silva thought to ease his sense of having been subtly chided by putting Gallus in his place. He had suddenly presumed a great deal upon their friendship.

How dare an engineer, in this case a man who was a civilian at heart, presume to even hint at criticism of the Roman military? Was a man of Gallus's intelligence unaware of the dangers to the Empire—of the savages to be found in every direction from Rome waiting to pounce upon the only home of civilized man? Suddenly his resentment subsided. In the first place, there was no little truth in what Gallus had said. And second, he could see no farther than his ramp or whatever he was building at the moment, for which devotion any dependent commander should be grateful.

Silva bent down to the neck of his horse so that his face was nearly level with Gallus's. "Good Gallus, your spirit is sore from lack of rest. Take this miserable day when so little can be accomplished in spite of your will and make a journey. Then tomorrow return refreshed to your obsession."

"You know it is impossible for me to leave."

"Is it? Come to my tent and I will lend you some Seneca—or do you prefer something lighter? I would then recommend a rather strange book called *Satyricon*, if you have not already seen it. Very good tongue-in-cheek Petronius. While I approve of neither author, I will admit both men are capable of instantly transporting one from Judea."

"You're kind, Sire. I am grateful."

"Or if you insist on improving your mind, I have Ptolemaeus on astronomy and Frontinus on aqueducts—which I refuse to show you lest you become diverted from your present work and try to bring water to the desert. I have all the poets from Ovid to Lucan, you have simply to name your choice."

The sudden vision of Gallus's dolorous countenance absorbed in Ovid, with his great nose sweeping back and forth along the lines, delighted Silva. How he longed for the close companionship of a man such as Gallus! Perhaps some day when Judea was only a memory he would visit the house in Praeneste.

"I will come as soon as I am certain all things are in order, Sire."

And that will be never, thought Silva. He touched his helmet, pulled the silk up to his eyes, and turned away. Well, he had tried.

Now with the wind at his back Silva found the return

ride to the camp comfortable enough to concentrate upon new problems. As for possible mutineers, he found he was more dismayed than chagrined that there might be serious discontent in his command. If it proved to be serious then he would know how to handle it. Regulations of the Roman army actually left a commander little choice.

More disturbing was this storm which was not only delaying the ramp but must also postpone the project that had suddenly become his own obsession. The more he considered it the more he became convinced that a meeting with Eleazar ben Yair just might result in a complete capitulation of the Jews. May the gods encourage it! Yet Sheva cannot climb the mountain in this wind, no matter how easy her escape is made to be.

And now what was to be done about Sheva? Perhaps I should try some of the old cures my father told me about. How did one go? Wear a crown of herbs adorned with the rind of the linden tree to avoid intoxication. Make a sacrifice to the god Fascinus to ward off feminine enchantment. Simple enough, although the Legionaries might have some cause to mutiny if they observed their General wandering about camp wearing a crown of herbs. Well then? What are you, Flavius Silva, General of the Armies, Governor of Judea and friend of Titus, last of the Cornelli, master of an empty, half-finished house in Praeneste—what are you going to do about this recalcitrant Jewess? And will you now be so bold as to envision your relationship ten years hence? Consider the Ides of May and the Festival of Lemuria when in ancient times they used to throw thirty old men into the Tiber from the Sublican Bridge. Now, of course, they only throw images made of rushes, but the implication is still there. Ten years, twenty years hence? Would Sheva secretly wish to push you into the Tiber every thirteenth of May?

Silva passed a group of Legionaries huddled in the lee of the camp forum where a low earthwork had been laid to better serve as a marketplace. They were playing knucklebones and Silva was reassured to see among them Calpurnius Cilix, the soldier he had so often accused of plotting to own the Tenth Legion. Cilix would gamble on anything should the odds be attractive, even to the possibility of the sun not rising, and here, even with the elements screeching around them, he and his comrades managed to indulge their true passion. Although Cilix ranked only as a Decurion he was still a very privileged soldier since he was also an Evocatus, one of the select class of hardy campaigners who had long ago served out their time yet had chosen to re-enlist. Therefore there were no drudge duties for Calpurnius Cilix. Even if his proven loyalty to the imperial standard were not enough excuse, his resourcefulness would have found a way out of any unpleasant assignment.

When Silva beckoned to him he immediately dropped the jacks and came jogging to Fury's side.

"Well now, cunning Cilix, how fares the richest man in the Roman army?"

Cilix returned his smile of appreciation by revealing the broken files of his surviving teeth, the majority having been lost in some long-ago affray. He glanced back over his shoulder and said in his lilting Calabrian accent, "Those who are born fools, Sire, are not worth the trouble to instruct."

"Ah? And the fact that you are plucking those innocent pigeons, who are also your comrades in arms, never leaves you with bad dreams?"

"Nightmares are for losers, Sire."

"I am trying to build a house," Silva said dryly. "The government is now lending money to qualified Romans at twelve per cent. That is more than I can afford and I have been wondering if I might do better business with you?"

"For Generals I have a special rate, Sire. How does eleven and one-half per cent strike you?"

Both men, enjoying the exchange, burst into laughter. Then Silva bent to rest his arm on Fury's neck. Careful now, he thought. Cilix has never known anything but the army, yet he is still a peasant. Twice a day he eats his porridge and drinks his posca with men of his own kind. His first loyalty is to them.

The heartiness had left Silva's voice when he said, "I hear there are fools other than clumsy gamblers in our camp." Their eyes met and Silva knew Cilix exactly understood him.

"There are some who would listen to Jews, Sire."

"Would one bear the name Fronto and perhaps another, Valens?"

"You know more than I do, Sire."

Silva believed him. He asked, "What is their discontent?"

Cilix hesitated then seemed to reach a reluctant decision. "You, Sire. It is the same old story. If the weather is bad, blame the General."

"How many are involved?"

"I do not know, Sire." Cilix bit his lips and seemed to find something of great interest on the ground.

Looking down at the top of his helmet, Silva saw it shake almost imperceptibly. His voice became firmer. "Make a guess, old comrade, and it had better be a fairly accurate guess or you will soon find yourself in farthest Armenia gaming with auxiliaries who I understand have no money at all." Silva reached out and knocked sharply on Cilix's helmet as if it were a door. "Come now, is your brain clearing?"

"The trouble is mostly in the third cohort, Sire ... then some too in the second ... and a maniple here and there in the first ... altogether I would guess there might be a thousand men."

"You will be pleased to know, Cilix, that your usual arithmetical accuracy has been confirmed by another. Now return to your jacks, and if you are questioned about our conversation by your friends I advise you for your own sake to say we were discussing the ratio of water to vinegar in your posca."

Silva rode away and passed between the lines of rattling tents that bordered the Principia. He came to the Tribunal where normally he would administer rewards and punishments. It was obviously impossible to hold any sort of audience on the exposed platform in such weather and for a moment he debated postponing his inquiry until the morrow. Then he decided against any delay. The disease is already in our veins, he thought, and if I give it another day and a night to nurse on our infections the result may be fatal.

He reined Fury to a stop and looked down the slope that supported the lower half of the camp. Most of the leather tents were lost in the blowing sand and not a single Legionary was to be seen. He knew the tents of the cavalry stood in the middle of the murk and on both sides of the mounted troops would be the tents of the Triarii, the Principes, and Hastati, then beyond them, almost invisible, would be the tents of the Syrian and Arab bowmen, auxiliaries deliberately separated from the Legionaries lest their often characteristic disloyalties infect good Romans. In each tent lived ten men with their petty officer, and this morning, he thought, they are hiding from more than just the wind.

Shielding his good eye with the palm of his hand, Silva looked up at the whirling wall of sand that totally obscured Masada. And he muttered aloud, "Jew, you have won this day and perhaps you will win again tomorrow. But the next day must be mine."

❖ ❖ ❖

As ALWAYS, the Centurion Rosianus Geminus had done his job with speed and diligence. He had brought the Jew called Ezra to Silva's tent and a Pharisee known as Zidon, who claimed to be the leader of those descended from Masada. As Praefectus Castorum, Geminus had called upon Silva's own Praetorian guards for assistance and had also brought the five Legionaries said to have sparked the fire of mutiny among their comrades. Now, with their wrists bound in heavy thongs, they stood just inside the entrance to the tent. Behind them were twice the number of Praetorians and in front of them, appearing perplexed and very out of place, stood the Jews.

As befits the occasion, Silva thought. Looking over the assembly he suddenly realized how every man in the tent shared a common appearance. They were all powdered with the gray sand-dust of the desert.

Silva lounged at ease in his ivory and mahogany chair. Epos has brought a stool for his bad leg and he moved his foot slowly back and forth as the Greek surgeon had directed. While he exercised his limb he deliberately ignored all those who had entered his tent. Finally impatience combined with pain made him raise his eyes and acknowledge the presence of others. He summoned Ezra and Zidon to approach him and when they obeyed he surveyed them in silence, as if they were a species of human entirely new to him.

Keeping his eyes fixed on Ezra he reached down to massage his leg and asked, "Do you speak Latin or Greek?"

"Both."

"So? Then you are a Jew of some education?"

Ezra bowed his head for a moment and appeared lost in meditation.

144

"If you are debating whether to answer any of my questions instantly," Silva growled, "I recommend you reach an affirmative decision now. Otherwise my annoyance with you may result in your instant and permanent silence."

Ezra folded his hands behind him and looked up at the peak of the tent. "You have a gap in your tent, General. Just at the pole—"

"I know that! You are trying my patience, Jew!" Silva was as angry with himself as with Ezra. He had completely forgotten to tell Geminus about the careless rigging of his tent. How could he have the soldier responsible whipped when the word would soon be out that a Jew had discovered it?

"I am not deliberately avoiding your question, General, only seeking a true answer. You ask me if I am educated. Who knows what an educated man is? My brain has been enriched with the logic of Aristotle, yet I know not how to milk a goat. I am acquainted with the science of Euclid, yet I cannot find a well or sail a vessel. I am familiar with Platonic philosophy, but I cannot build anything durable. Obviously I am an ignorant man."

"You sound like a man whose head is his belly and has eaten too much," Silva interrupted.

"I have also studied rhetoric under the famous Nicetes Sacerdos of Smyrna—"

Silva smiled in recognition and interrupted again. "Who should have quoted one of your better Hebrew recommendations. As I remember, it proclaims the most dangerous of organs is the tongue, which is the reason it is hidden behind a double wall—first the teeth and then the cheeks. It is an admonition you seem to have forgotten."

"The General has also been a student." Ezra nodded and the two men stared at each other in silence.

"And your companion?" Silva asked at last. "Is he also too clever for his own welfare? Can he speak except to make trouble?"

"I have made no trouble, Sire," Zidon said in a voice that was barely audible above the rumble of the wind. "I am a man of peace and my people are dedicated to peace. We have come down of our own desire to ask your mercy."

"In other words, you want to live?" Silva said.

He sighed and for a moment became fascinated watching the tic working on the side of Zidon's face. It must be a nuisance, he thought, because at one moment it would subside and then unpredictably become violently active again. The Jew must be constantly waiting for the next spasm.

Silva had already decided Zidon was a born conniver. Look at him now, he thought, see how his eyes are alert to your every movement and expression—terror draining the very blood from his face. In contrast, observe the other Jew, the one called Ezra. He stands there as if he owned the very earth beneath his feet which of course in a sense he does, but he is still standing in my tent. Watch him. There is a worthy man, and a wise one—and a brave one.

"It would seem," Silva said easily, "that one or both of you have been abusing our hospitality."

"I do not understand you, Sire," Zidon said.

"You have been fathering a multitude of lies."

Silva glanced over his shoulder at Epos, his Numidian. He signaled him to kneel beside the chair. Then he grasped Epos's head and turned his face toward the Jews. He pulled open his mouth to expose the stump of his tongue and said evenly, "Who knows? At one time this man might have also have been eloquent. I bought him after he had made a mistake. He used his tongue to make trouble for a Roman. Do you think you deserve any better treatment?"

Silva released Epos with an affectionate slap on his bare back. "He is a good man and now he always tells the truth. I urge you to do the same. I am informed how you have abused our tolerance by spreading false rumors among your guards, and they being ignorant of your true intentions have passed this nonsense on to their comrades. As so often happens when rumors are cunningly sweetened, some soldiers will swallow the bait and turn lies in fact. Five of my Legionaries who will soon regret their gullibility stand behind you. I want you to tell me now exactly what you told them."

Ezra answered quickly. Too much so for my pleasure, Silva mused. The man has come prepared.

Ezra said, "I have told no lies, General. But I have made certain prophecies and they will transpire."

"Assuming you are a qualified soothsayer, in all of whom, including our Roman variety, I have little faith—what were these words of such import?"

"If you do not wish to believe we Jews are endowed with special powers, I will ask the general to remember Vespasian and a certain Rabbi ben Zakkai. I believe the General was present at Jerusalem when the rabbi prophesied Vespasian would soon be Emperor? And it was so, was it not? And Vespasian himself recognized the rabbi's powers and remembered his promise to allow him an academy of learning. And that school is this very day functioning in the town of Jabneh. It stands as a monument of proof that when a Jew makes a prophecy it is well to believe it."

Vespasian, Silva thought, would believe anything. It seemed that every time he paused for breath in a foreign land some native found opportunity to predict he would soon be wearing the purple. "Prophets are more likely to be perceptive than endowed," Silva said. "I recall some Jewish sage prophesying Jerusalem would fall. He made his prediction after we had besieged it for three years and even a blind donkey could see what would happen. As for prophets, there was one yelling from every housetop in Judea before we came, and each one led you into more trouble. Are you then just another messiah?"

"No, General," Ezra said quietly. "But I am a believer in God."

"*God?* Who is he? The Ethiopians make their gods black and broad-nosed. The Thracians like theirs with red hair and blue eyes." Silva found he was beginning to enjoy himself. It was a day lost to the storm and he might as well pass the time teasing Jews before he decided their fate. "Show me his picture. Show me his statue. Show me your God."

"The laws will not permit his image to be carved or drawn."

"What laws? Roman laws? We are a tolerant people and have never forbidden you to have your God. But we do not intend you to use him as an excuse for insurrection. What is the matter with you Jews? On the one hand you appear to be intelligent and on the other hopelessly stupid. What is so wrong about Jupiter, or Apollo—the perfect symbol of youth and beauty? What is unworthy about Venus, or Cybele, or Diana, or even Bacchus?"

"And there is also Mars," Ezra said.

"Some divinity is required for war."

"The God of the Jews does not believe in war."

"Ho!" Silva shouted and slapped the arm of his chair. "You people have been warring among yourselves since the beginning of time! I have made some study of your innumerable sects and I find the easiest way to tell one from another is to realize you all disagree in what you believe. You who are Sadducees oppose the Pharisees, and you who are Essenes have a different opinion entirely. You are all specialists in anarchy and I can prove it. Tell me," he asked while pointing his finger at Ezra, "of what sect are you?"

"I am a Sadducee."

"And you with the sniveling manner—what is your name again?"

"Zidon."

"And your sect?"

"I am a Pharisee."

"Very well then, I will pose you both a question. Do you believe in immortality?"

"Of course. God has willed it," said Zidon. The uncertainty in his voice convinced Silva the man would betray anything or anyone to save his skin. Here was no Essene or Christian such as he had seen under similar circumstances. *They* were tough as buzzards.

"And you there, Ezra? Do you believe the same?" Ezra hesitated, then answered so softly he could barely be heard. "No, General, I do not."

Silva smacked the palms of his hands together. "There you are! Even on the most basic matters you Jews cannot agree. How can you deny your people need our guidance?"

"God is our guide," Ezra said.

"Indeed? This mysterious God who chooses to remain invisible, dictates his will from no one seems to know where, and you obey like sheep, and you cannot tell me a single thing that he has done to your benefit? Oh I know of you Jews, better than you may think! You slay a ram to ridicule Hammon, and because the Egyptians worship the ox you choose it for sacrifice. All of you were at one time leprous, a gift of your generous God as reward for your innumerable mischiefs, but you blamed some poor pig for the curse and have abstained from the taste of swine ever since. How childlike, and yet how subtle you are! To indulge your natural laziness you take a rest every seventh day, proclaiming it variously as a time of worship or, I am informed, when that excuse fails to convince, you mumble something about the flight of the god Idaei, or when that explanation of your indolence collapses, you pretend to celebrate the movements of the planets said to be in multiples of seven! Really! How even your glib tongues can persuade others to swallow such preposterous drivel is past my understanding. I pity you, and all who may fall under your scheming influence. Looking at you now reminds me of another confused Jew who was an admitted troublemaker. I cannot remember his Jewish name, but he took the Roman name of Paul, and he was also a soothsayer of sorts and forever raving about one Joshua, or Christus, who seemed to have usurped the power from your previous God. Neither one seemed to help this fellow Paul very much at his execution—which I happened to witness."

Silva was surprised to notice a hint of a smile playing about Ezra's mouth when he heard him say, "The man you are speaking of, General, was known to Jews as Saul of Tarsus. May I remind you that he also had a bad eye and a bad leg?"

Silva rose from his chair and took a menacing step toward Ezra. He could feel the blood pounding to his face and his hand reached instinctively toward Ezra. This smirking Jew who had dared so casually to mention the infirmities of his master! His voice became an agonized groan when he finally said, "Jew—I will crucify you head down!"

For a moment his heavy breathing was audible even above the rumbling of the wind. Ezra did not move nor did his eyes show the slightest fear, nor did he for an instant shift them from Silva's face. Finally he said as if commenting on a possible change of weather, "It is of little concern to me which barbarous way you choose to kill me, General. The result will be the same and will only once again prove the constancy of Roman mercy. Yet before you silence this voice forever I will promise you this. Even if you exterminate every Jew in this desert and every Jew in Palestine, Judaism will survive long after you yourself are dust. You may cut the flowers, but you will never destroy the vine."

Silva stood feet apart, motionless, his good eye fixed on Ezra. Now instead of his animallike panting he seemed not to breathe at all. A multitude of sweat globules had formed across his brow and several joined together to become a droplet which fell to his cheek and slid slowly around beneath his chin. He found that he was trembling, yet when he made an effort at control, he discovered that his hands were perfectly steady. Then he realized the trembling was inside. The sensation combined with a knotting of his intestines had suddenly become so painful he instinctively bent forward. And suddenly he thought, It is I who am the accused! The eyes of this Jew are killing me. He is not afraid.

Silva moved backward, very slowly, until he felt the chair behind him. And he was grateful for it because now a dizziness had come upon him, and he vowed that he would never again so give way to anger. He heard Ezra say as if he stood at a great distance, "There is an old Hebrew proverb, General, which states that the best way to know a man is to join him in a drink, or do business with him, or watch him when he is angry."

And then Silva heard him ask if he was married and unbelievably he heard himself answer that he was not, and Ezra's voice then echoed his own tone when he replied that he was in that case very sorry for the General, since all Jews, whatever their sect, believed marriage and the family were the basic foundations of life. "If you depart this life without fathering a son then you die, if you have one, then you only fall asleep."

It was as if Ezra's voice came from a very great distance, so remote that Silva tipped back his head and closed his eyes and reviewed those doubts that had so long haunted him. In the twilight behind his tightly closed lids he saw himself attending the worship of Cybele and he heard again the high wailing voices of the eunuch priests. He remembered how he had enjoyed the pageantry, but had left the service without any sense of satisfaction. The same had been true of his attendance upon the god Mithras, who particularly favored soldiers. He had submitted to a bath in the blood of a freshly killed bull which the Mithraic priests claimed would guarantee his being reborn—but he had not believed them. At Livia's request he had even experimented with the fashionable god Isis, but found the white-robed Egyptian priests with their tinkling sistrums too artificial for his taste. And besides, he had never like Egyptians.

Ezra's voice was still remote, but steady and assured, ". . . the world is sustained by three things, by the law, by worship, and by charity . . ."

Silva opened his eyes, the bad one as far as he could manage, and he stared at Ezra. By all the gods, Roman or otherwise, he thought, I must go home soon, for every day I am slipping further into the depths of disbelief in everything! I listen to the droning voice of this fanatic as if he were a true oracle. I let him go on and on spinning his lies without restraint or even objection, and now he is interweaving talk of his God with prophecies of our death from the heat, telling me in his impeccable Greek how our bones will melt ten days hence—and all of this, even I am half believing!

Silva held out his hand to still Ezra's melodious voice.

"Enough, Jew," he said. "You drown me in words, and apparently to put an end to them I must put an end to you."

Zidon said quickly, "But the promise of Vespasian? We were promised amnesty—"

"Those who came down with you will enjoy it. As for you—" Silva reached for the sand glass on the table and turned it over. "You, Ezra, and you, Zidon, both of you of Jewish birth, are accused of treachery against and interference with the lawful government of Judea. The penalty is death. When the sand has exchanged itself in this glass your execution will proceed."

He saw Zidon twist his hands together and begin to sob, but he could not detect the slightest change about Ezra. He seemed to be merely preoccupied.

"Did you hear me, you who are called Ezra?"

"Yes, General, I heard you."

Silva found himself wishing Ezra would beg for mercy, or if nothing else, defy him. How could a man accept his death so carelessly?

"I suppose your God will look after you?" Silva asked impulsively. He had been right the first time. The man was not only a fanatic but quite mad.

"I was not conferring with God, General. Past experience with Roman reasonableness persuaded me to make all my devotions before I entered this tent. Actually I was thinking of Sulla, the charioteer, and wondering if I should meet him in eternity how I would best phrase my compliments on his skill and daring. There was a time when I lived in Rome and I made a tidy fortune wagering on Sulla and I have always felt that I owe him a great deal—not only financially but as an inspiring example of total contempt for catastrophe. Did you ever see him race, General?"

As well ask a flame if it had ever seen a lamp, Silva thought. Did a leper ever hear a bell? If there was one single thing he regretted about all his years of campaigning it was missing the races. He had groaned audibly when he had learned the Circus had been destroyed in the Neronian fire of 64, for it meant he would be denied the special sense of guilt only to be found in using the imperial post to transmit his wagers. After careful consideration of all factors involved he would solemnly dispatch his instructions to a former Legionary who occupied a stall adjacent to the Circus and dealt in such matters. "Bet a thousand sesterces on the white if Paulinus is the driver, make it two thousand sesterces on the red if Clemens holds the reins. . . ." As for the controversial Sulla, he was ever the favorite of those tempted by the long chance. He drove every race as if he were racing against time rather than other men. Though he might be far in the lead he would continue to urge his horses at wild speeds all the way to the finish. Other drivers, more concerned for their lives than for hysterical applause, often held back, waiting for Sulla to kill himself on the final seventh circuit, which one day he succeeded in doing. Somehow there had been formed a mysterious bond among those who risked their money on his daring—perhaps, thought Silva, because they were labeled fools by so many others. Until his death there was no known cure for "Sulla fever," and ever since coming to Palestine Silva had been unhappily aware that Sulla's name meant nothing to his officers. There was not a true devotee among them and their pretense of interest only revealed their ignorance. It was, he had long ago decided, so discouraging he had not spoken of racing in over a year.

Now here was a Jew, and a condemned criminal at that, who had suffered the same exhilarating affliction.

Silva yearned to question Ezra further. Had he been present the day Sulla was so hopelessly boxed behind two drivers who had vowed to thwart him, and had Ezra appreciated how he had conserved the strength of his horses until the seventh circuit and had then maneuvered to the extreme *outside* of the course, thrown the reins in the air, and oblivious to speed on the turns, whipped his frenzied mounts to victory? Did you see *that*, old Jew? Was there ever a sight like it? And were you also witness to Sulla's win against the vaunted Greek, Cassander? Remember Sulla was only a week recovered from a spectacular crash, and his horses were much the inferior beasts? Yet when he saw a victory pending for Cassander, do you remember how he had deliberately smashed his chariot against the Greek's? And how once again he had been carried from the track?

How, Silva found himself wondering, can I execute a man who also believed in Sulla?

"You are indeed an unscrupulous liar if you claim to have made money on Sulla," he muttered.

"Not always, General—that is true. But always in my heart I received more than fair value."

"Hm-m-m . . ." Silva hummed briefly because he could find no other way to express his mixed emotions. All anger had left him as suddenly as it had come and now he was lost in memories of the Circus. How he longed to review those tense moments of crisis and triumph still so brilliant in his mind—with another man who truly understood.

The Jew is right, he thought. I too received more than a fair return.

Silva rose and thoughtfully circled his chair. He placed his hands on the back of it and let it bear his weight for a moment. The chair squeaked and he could almost feel Zidon's frightened eyes watching him. The man was a nuisance and should be gotten rid of, yet how to justify killing one Jew and sparing the other, who was probably the guiltier of the pair?

He left the chair and limped toward Ezra. He halted directly in front of him and looked into his quiet eyes where he saw resignation yet still no fear, and he thought, If I kill this man then a little piece of myself will die because here in all Judea are perhaps the only eyes other than my own that have actually seen and appreciated Sulla.

"I have changed my mind," Silva said slowly. "Since you predict we are all going to die anyway I see no reason to trouble my soldiers with your disposal."

He beckoned to Rosianus Geminus, who came quickly to stand before him. "Take these Jews to the ramp and remove all of their followers from their present comfortable area. All are to be treated the same, both men and women. See that they are put to work in the same manner as the other Jews."

He turned his back on Ezra before the temptation to discuss Sulla and the races in general became irresistible. What kind of authority is this? he thought. I cannot even discuss the races with the only other man in Palestine who knew them well.

He listened to the wind, taking time to compose himself, for now he must face quite different eyes and there must be no second softening of his judgment.

Finally he turned to look at the five Legionaries who had been brought forward to stand where the Jews had been. He recognized only two of their faces and knew the surname of but one—Vespillo, a soldier of the third cohort. They were all obviously very worried, ironically, Silva thought, far more so than Ezra the Jew. They had been stripped of their weapons and armor and their hands were bound behind them.

"Which one of you is Fronto?" he snapped.

Fronto kept his eyes on the rug beneath his feet. "I, Sire," he murmured.

"You are a Decurion—or were?"

Fronto nodded but kept his silence.

"Then you know the penalty for your offense and you should have informed the others—or did you bother?"

Fronto pressed his lips tightly together. After a moment Valerius Valens said, "I did not ask him to come to my tent, Sire. I tried to discourage—"

Silva cut him short. His rising voice became strident. "It will not save your precious skin to pawn your betrayal of the Tenth! You have each taken an oath on your birthdays and the kalends of January. You have vowed to serve the Emperor and the standard of the Legion and by rejecting those promises you have disgraced us all!"

Silva was well aware that his own Praetorians were watching him and listening to his every word. Very good. He wanted their full attention so they would recount his reactions to the rest of the camp, and by the gods, they were going to have some harsh reports to bear. He could, if he pleased, exact the ultimate punishment for mutiny by choosing Decimatio for each cohort in which these scum served. Every tenth man, regardless of his involvement, would be put to death. Yet times were changing, and while Decimatio may have succeeded in putting down mutinies in the past, it would not do here if only because the situation here was so unique. Where else had the enemy been able to look down upon every move of a Roman army unit as if they were watching a perpetual show? How delighted Eleazar ben Yair would be at the spectacle of Romans killing at least fifty-five of their comrades.

Silva wiped the moisture from his upper lip with the back of his hand and said, "I should have you flayed and then beheaded with your own swords. But such punishment is too good for you. It denotes a military death, and some relative of yours may twist the facts to please his honor and relate how you died in battle. So I shall make very certain your status is understood by every true soldier at Masada. As soon as this wind has passed, you are to be stripped naked, taken to the gates of this camp and turned into the desert without food or water. Before you are set free you will be circumcised. Perhaps then, if you meet any Jews in the wilderness, they will be merciful enough to kill you."

Five

WITH JUPITER AT THE ZENITH . . .

ELEAZAR BEN YAIR sat on the still-warm steps of the court-yard that had once been a place of relaxation for Herod's officers. It was a breathless night—it seemed as if the great wind had swept away all the air in the desert and consequently all sounds, however feeble, were magnified until the politely muffled cough of a neighbor became a rude barking and even the padding of bare feet became a heavy sound. Looking up at the stars Eleazar thought it would be like this when at last the world emitted a final sob and died. It would be as now, he decided, although the awesome tranquility would not belong to the Romans or be of their creation. Twice a day they fed the Jews laboring on the ramp and so twice a day this great silence enwrapped the mountain and prevailed until the simple meal was finished—whereupon the monstrous all-prevading noise would commence again.

On this day another attempt to stop the noise had failed. While the fierce wind was still blowing Eleazar had appeared before the council and after a long session of pleading and cajoling he had finally obtained permission to roll the great stones down upon their own people. There had been tears and prayers, and more than once he had been called a murderer.

His plan had been to strike quickly, then recoil to some protection while observing the effect, then strike again and again according to the degree of disorganization on the ramp. Ah, if the plans of a man would only behave!

He had foreseen that a breach in the wall would be necessary since it would be impossible to lift the lethal-sized stones over the top. And so an opening had been cleared just before dawn and when the first stones rolled down the ramp all was as he had predicted it would be. Both workers and overseers panicked. Only the whimpering of those still alive on the ramp broke the great silence which followed. And on Masada there was hope again.

Yet soon it seemed as if Flavius Silva had been waiting for such an opportunity. His reply had been disciplined and terribly efficient. Before the sun climbed above Masada he concentrated all the fire of his ballistas, catapults, and Arab bowmen on the narrow target presented by the breach in the rampart. Five men of Masada had been killed before the effort had been abandoned as hopeless. Adonoi! Work on the ramp had been delayed but half the morning.

Now in the night Eleazar was grateful for the consideration of the council and the relatives of the slain. They had reproached only with their eyes. So, good friends— you know that I die inside.

Reuben sat beside him watching the stars, with his head tipped back and his mouth open in wonder. Miriam also squatted beside him, her strong arms hunkered forward over her knees, her skirt pulled up and her thighs spread wide to receive the cooling night air. Reuben pointed to a star and asked its name and Eleazar told him it was Mizar, but when he was asked the name of several other stars he confessed that he did not know them, and then immediately, to preserve Reuben's faith in his knowing everything, he explained that the twin stars directly in line with his son's nose were Castor and Pollux, the guardians of storm-beset sailors, and in the future Reuben could identify them for himself if he would remember they were on the left hand of Orion's belt.

The future? For Reuben? Eleazar sighed. Reuben's future would all have to be lived within the next few days.

"Why don't the stars make a noise when they move?" Reuben asked.

"Maybe they do," Eleazar answered, and for an instant

he caught and cherished a look of amusement about
Miriam's mouth and eyes because it encouraged him to
imagine this was the step in front of his hut by the Sea of
Galilee. This might be an evening when neighbors came to
speak of the mullet and where they had been caught that
day and later Miriam would sing for their guests. He
could still so easily hear her high clear voice trembling
against the stillness of the evening, echoing out and away
across the gentle lapping of the sea. Then each guest
would demand his favorite, "The Song of Deborah," "The
Song of Hannah," and he would protest that Miriam
would be singing all night if she tried to satisfy them all.

"Do we come from the same star as the Romans?"
Reuben asked suddenly.

He heard Miriam chuckle. Then she said, "O magician
with words, I wait impatiently for thy answer to that
one."

Eleazar cleared his throat with great deliberation. Trad-
ing insults with a Roman General was easy compared to
the challenge of complete innocence.

"One cannot exactly say we came from a star," he
began uncertainly. "We were, well, we have always been
right here."

"People have to start somewhere. Did we start in Judea?"

"We are all the sons of Jacob."

"Mother is not the son of anyone," Reuben said flatly.

Over Miriam's soft laughter he told how the twelve sons
of Jacob had become fathers themselves and how their
families had multiplied until they became tribes that had
inherited both Israel and the promises made to Abraham
and thus became the people of God.

He paused and wondered if he should tell Reuben it had
all come to pass exactly as the prophets had foretold. He
decided against it. My son, he thought, has the right to
resolve for himself if he believes such things, and now
every word from my lips becomes the truth.

Thank you, my son. You who are a little old man, who
have already seen more people killed than you have years
on earth, who in spite of our calamities are still able to
regard the stars as living things, accept my secret gratitude
for your faith.

"Supposing you could buy one of those stars," he asked
Reuben. "Which one would you choose?"

Reuben pointed without hesitation at Procyon. "That

one." Then he pointed at Regulus. "That one I will buy for Shimeon."

"Shimeon?" For a moment Eleazar knew again the fierce bond between small boys, for long ago he had also had a friend named Shimeon and he remembered there had been times when he would have died for him. Suddenly all of his dark thoughts were in retreat and he yearned to prolong this moment. "And if you and Shimeon were to journey to that star to examine it before you bought it—is there anyone else you would take with you?"

"No. Shimeon and I are enough people for a whole world. Well, maybe Hodiah could go."

"Hodiah!" Eleazar slapped his leg and appeared to be astounded. "Hodiah is a girl!"

"Yes, but she can run as fast as most boys and she could cook for us."

"Man's first beast of burden," Miriam said quickly. She reached for Reuben's hand and pulled him to his feet. "If you sit up with your father much longer, dawn will take your star. Come to sleep."

She stood on her toes to kiss Eleazar and smiled when he held her silently in his arms. At last when he released her she turned away into the starlight with Reuben still clutching her hand. And as they vanished into the black shadow which marked the entrance to their quarters Eleazar thought how this night's leave-taking of his wife and son had been as in the long ago. He must be careful. Miriam had sensed his despair and made a show of concern for the boy's sleep when she must suspect he might soon sleep forever.

THERE was a certain place outside the low eastern wall of the camp which had become very dear to Cornelius and Albinus. It was situated almost directly opposite the eastern gate of Silva's own camp and near a promontory where the circumvallation met a sheer cliff and terminated. Here they could look up at the dark outline of Masada, or almost straight down into the wadi below, or back toward the camp itself and Falco's tent. Because of the impossibility of anyone's scaling the cliff there were no guards patrolling the vicinity, nor was it likely anyone would pass this way since all normal paths were at some distance from it. Thus once arrived there, both Cornelius and Albinus enjoyed a sense of privacy they had never known since being impressed into Falco's service. Here, beneath the stars with their master unable to summon them at his every whim, they gave themselves utterly to each other. Here, toying and teasing, sometimes even pretending indifference or acting in pique at some imagined slight, they declared their mutual adoration and postponed their physical climaxes with ever-increasing skill.

It was Cornelius, having spent himself, who opened his eyes and saw what suddenly caused his body to again become rigid. He gently pushed Albinus away from him and whispered, "Look—see who else likes to be alone."

Albinus rose and wiped at his lips and saw the two figures moving beneath the stars. He saw how they walked rapidly and with apparent purpose toward Masada and he was perplexed because they were inside the circumvallation and one appeared to be a woman. Ahead of her a soldier's helmet glinted in the starlight. The soldier turned his face to glance back at her, then both sank from view as they entered a narrow wadi.

"It is the Jewess—I'm sure!" Cornelius said.

161

"And a common soldier? Why?"

"Who knows where a bitch in heat may choose to rut?"

"It doesn't make sense. Silva would bury her alive if he knew."

After a moment Cornelius pressed his hand gently against Albinus's cheek and said, "Exactly!"

He moved quickly to the edge of the cliff and then lay down on his belly. Albinus joined him and they inched their way forward until they could look straight down upon the wadi below. "Why should they go so far?" he asked in disappointment.

"He is no common soldier, I believe. I could swear I recognized him as the Centurion Geminus. He is not risking his life just for a sniff—" Suddenly Cornelius pointed down at the very bottom of the cliff. Again there was the momentary reflection of a star on polished metal and almost immediately they were able to define two figures moving downward along the course of the wadi. They watched in silent fascination until the figure turned around the northern extremity of Masada, vanished momentarily in a depression and then reappeared walking east.

"So?" Cornelius grunted. "There is more here than a horny female and a willing soldier. And I would be even less surprised if Pomponius Falco might not greatly value such information."

"We had better not give him cause to know we were here together."

"Of course not. I will go back to the camp and the vicinity of the Jewess's family, where I have been vigilantly observing as usual. I will say I saw her leave the tent alone. You were simply taking a stroll, out for the cool air. And by chance you saw this. Because of our love for our master we decided he might like to put our observations together. We accomplish several things. We divert his thoughts from our own meeting here, if he has any, we prove our devotion to duty—and who knows what he may do with such information? It may even be possible he will commend us—in which event our next meeting here will be that much easier to arrange."

For a time Eleazar stood listening to the revival of activity on the ramp and he wondered at the dulled anxieties of those on Masada who were already asleep. In the direction of the eastern casemates he heard the voice of a man he was certain must be an Essene. He was reading aloud, ". . . in thee, O Lord, do I put my trust . . . let me never be ashamed . . . deliver me in thy righteousness . . . bow down thine ear to me . . . deliver me speedily . . . be thou my strong rock, for a house of defense to save me. For thou art my rock and my fortress . . ."

O, all very well, Eleazar thought. If the man will gather strength for himself from that source then the rock which is actually beneath his feet will not die quite so soon. But if we lean too heavily on the Scriptures then the rock of Masada is certainly lost.

He left the courtyard and strode toward his favorite place along the eastern rampart. The wall was built along a vertical precipice which would be impossible to scale, so no sentries patrolled the area. There according to his custom he could look out across the Dead Sea toward the rumpled hills of Moab and each night keep his solitary vigil.

When he reached the rampart he stood for a moment gazing down upon the eastern camps of the Romans and the faint outline of the circumvallation. And he sighed heavily. A rabbi had once told him that a man who lived entirely by the Scriptures was a fool. Likewise then, would not he who relied on the timely arrival of miracles simply because the Scriptures told of them also be a fool?

He spread his big hands above his head and addressed the stars in a hoarse whisper. And the words he found were comfortable for him although he knew they would not be approved by Hillel or any other priest. They would insist on the orthodox prayer, the impersonal and pompous praise of God which began with the salutation, "Our Father who art in heaven" and continued with a series of requests. It was like the Shema, a prayer so long ground beneath the millstones of endless and exact repetition he now found it more annoying than inspiring. Lately he had been given to choosing his own words, expressing his worship more directly with his head unbowed and his eyes wide open to appreciate the heavens. "Almighty God," he began, "thank you for my sight. Thank you for my hearing, for my senses of smell and touch, thank you for the morning dew and the bounty of the sea. Thank you for the temporary privilege to breathe this desert night. Thank you for life, almighty God. May I deserve it. When I do not—take it away!"

He stepped down from the rampart and walked slowly across the gently rolling terrain of Masada. He walked with his hands folded behind him, so deep in meditation he failed to notice a commotion near the eastern gate. My little red stone island, he mused. Thou art flinty and hard and ugly in the extreme, the last morsel of Israel to be devoured by the lion. And we who inhabit your iron crust are doomed with you unless a miracle actually does occur.

His concentration was so intense he strayed from the usual worn pathway. He stumbled in the darkness, and as he turned quickly to avoid falling, his shin struck a large rock. When he recognized it as one of the hundreds hurled by the catapults of the Romans he groaned in chagrin. Hashem! How could a poor stumbling human being, a clumsy sailor who could not find his way in the dark, honestly expect to cause a very necessary miracle? Ridiculous.

He was massaging his shin and reflecting on how the Romans had finally managed to humble Eleazar, the fierce Zealot, bringing him to his knees in fact, when he heard a woman's raging scream. Then from the vicinity of the eastern gate he heard the profane shouts of several men. He forgot his pain and moved quickly toward the voices.

In the deeper shadows near the gate he found a cluster of men surrounding a solitary woman. He could not recognize her, although as she cursed her audience in Hebrew, Greek, and Aramaic, he was immediately impressed with her vocabulary. She was crouched like a cornered animal, whirling quickly to avoid surprise and keeping one arm outstretched. Then Eleazar saw a knife in her hand and he asked the man next to him who the woman was. Tempers were often short on Masada. O yes! How well I know my passionate people, he thought, but women usually limited physical attacks to their teeth and fingernails.

"A cactus has sprung from the desert in the form of a woman," the man answered. Then, recognizing Eleazar, he added, "O, believe me that her skin bristles with spikes!" When he held out his fist Eleazar saw it was covered with blood.

Each time a part of the circle began to close in on her the woman would leap toward the nearest offender and make a violent sweep with her blade. Her defiance caused the men to taunt each other. Who would be the first to capture this waspish female and tame her? "You, Ananias! There is a prize for a lucky bachelor! Imagine what it would be like to bury your snook in her! Now is the chance to prove your quickness. Josiah! Ten shekels you will not take the blade from her. Eliah! Provoke her next time she turns, with a pinch in the butt!"

"Whose woman is she?" Eleazar asked.

"She came up the snake path. Chaim caught her at the gate, but she slipped away. She's quick and mean and undoubtedly a spy."

Eleazar heard a man on the opposite side of the circle call out, "Now the Romans are sending us their whores!"

Another man hooted, "The bitch claims to be a Jewess! O, what a fine lady she must be, flat on her back with her legs spread wide to receive the eagle's beak!"

"Throw her back where she came from and watch the Romans fornicate with a bag of bones!"

For a moment there was silence as the circle became smaller. It was broken only by the woman, who said she had come to see Eleazar ben Yair and no other.

Eleazar stepped into the circle and stood looking down at her. She started to lunge at him with the knife. He moved quickly aside and as the blade flashed past he caught her wrist. He held her at arm's length while he twisted her hand until the blade fell to the ground, and he thought he had been very lucky indeed to disarm her so quickly, there being no adversary so cunning and so cruel as a furious woman.

Holding her firmly he told her his name and saw her temper suddenly ease.

"Yes," she said, searching his face in the starlight. "I believe you. I would know that voice anywhere. Use it to call off this pack of hyenas."

"Listen to her give orders!" a man behind Eleazar said. "The whore has become a queen."

She whirled on the man, almost breaking Eleazar's hold. "If you scum are Jews I would have been better born an Egyptian! I can be sure from the stink of your breath your mother slept with a dromedary."

"Where did you come from?" Eleazar demanded.

"I escaped from below. I have much to tell you of the Romans."

"Say it, then." He closed his great hand more tightly about her wrist.

"I will tell it to you alone."

Other men, attracted by the unusual activity near the eastern gate, were joining the circle. And a few women, roused, were approaching from the casemate dwellings. Soon, Eleazar knew, the whole of Masada would arrive, including the council. Intense curiosity was part of the constant fear which had gradually infected every person on Masada. Trifling events became matters of grave importance. Everyone concerned himself mightily with a family fight, or a broken wine jar, or a minute change in the ration of pressed figs. Eleazar knew that if even one of the council members saw this woman he would feel obliged to notify the others lest they label him secretive, and anything worthwhile the woman might have to say would be buried in endless accusations and arguments. The council was like a boat without a keel, he thought, heeling to one side or the other at the slightest breeze, making as much leeway as headway.

He stepped to her side as if seeking better light from the stars. He regarded her quizzically and raised his voice so that all those about them would hear. "I know you," he said. "You are Jedidah, sister of Tarshish. We are related."

He was relieved to see her hesitate only an instant, then she quickly kissed his hand.

"I regret your reception," he said with a forced show of apology. "We are all irritable here."

He put his arm around her protectively and added that he would take her to his wife. Then before too many questions were asked he escorted her through the circle of curious faces. Once they were free he quickened his pace, and though she was still breathing heavily from her exertions, he was gratified to see her follow him without protest.

Soon they came to the courtyard of his quarters. Just inside the gate he turned into the deepest shadows. When they had melted into the darkness he took her firmly by the arms and held her before him. He caught the scent of perfume and somehow it made him angry. He passed his fingers across the palms of her hands, and finding them smooth, put down an urge to strike her. "My friends were

right," he said coldly. "Why should the Romans send me
their toys?"

"My escape was arranged by Silva himself—"

"Stop lying. Who would choose to escape up here?"

She told him how Silva wanted to meet with him in
secret and had sent her to bear the message because he
believed a man would be killed before he could deliver it.

"So—while other women of Israel have plunged knives
into their vaginas rather than accept a Roman, you have
made a very good thing of it. While other women die on
the ramp—"

"I did not climb a mountain to be preached at. If you
will meet with Silva I may save more Jews than your
stupid pride has killed."

Again he resisted the temptation to strike her. "The
Roman need only raise his voice if he would speak with
me."

"You have both tried that without the least success. He
wants to meet you alone."

"I have nothing to gain by listening to Roman lies."

"You might even have something to lose. If peace came
to Masada—then where would you be? Just another Jew.
And you would not like that, would you, Eleazar ben
Yair? Your power would be gone and your great voice
would no longer capture your little private army or irri-
tate the Romans. You would not be a hero any longer,
and that is more than a man like you can bear. I will tell
you that for a time even I was impressed by your words.
But now you are a disappointment. If a great Roman
General can curb his pride and climb to you—"

"He will climb here alone?" Where was the hidden
trick, he wondered. Why should Silva take the slightest
chance on his personal safety when he must certainly
believe victory was near?

"He has given his right hand he will be alone," she said.

Eleazar thought, as he had so many times before, how
unpredictable the Romans invariably proved to be. Their
crimes could not be repaid until the stars fell out of the
heavens and yet in almost seven long years of warring
against them he had never heard of a Roman commander
betraying the oath of his right hand. And a miracle?
Perhaps there might be one in the offing even if it had to
be contrived by Eleazar ben Yair.

He glanced up at the stars. "Go to your Roman," he

said finally. "Tell him when Jupiter is at the zenith . . . to begin his climb."

Flavius Silva could not remember when his mind had been so disordered. It seemed as if his thoughts had gone to war against each other, and with each new development of this extraordinarily eventful night he became alternately elated and dejected. He chided himself. "I am fretting like some Syrian usurer caught with a risky investment."

What a roll call of conflicting contingencies! And innocent of all, Epos had placed the flask of wine temptingly in its usual place on the table. Yet not a drop must moisten your lips this night. If you would climb Masada and meet face to face with such an eloquent scoundrel as Eleazar ben Yair, then all of your wits had best be drawn up in the most formidable line of battle, with the Hastati of verbs and nouns where they belonged in the front line, the Principes of insults in the second rank, and the Triarii of patience in the third. This was a military adventure so rare and unpredictable of result there had been no point in discussing it with staff. They would only wonder what possible advantage could come of your meeting alone with a verminous Jew. And well they might inquire—which was precisely why their opinions had not been sought. All the more reason to remember that military innovations are considered disastrous if they do not succeed brilliantly, and other better-known causes are subscribed to the success if they do. Only if an innovation *fails* is it recognized as being responsible for the resulting calamity, and the innovator himself may soon find himself hanging by his testicles. Hence no wine. Tonight the enemy in the flask is more dangerous than the one on the mountain.

Apparently something has already gone wrong, for where is Sheva? Rosianus Geminus had escorted her to the perimeter of the eastern camp and after a show of struggle let her slip away. He had reported all had gone smoothly and even the guards posted along the eastern circumvallation had been convinced a Jewish woman prisoner had escaped. Later Geminus had proceeded to the northeastern camp and had there explained to the sentries how a woman would eventually appear bearing the correct password for the night "Venus Genetrix." It was the same wording inscribed on the Tessera which had been carried through the camp at twilight by their own Centurions.

Well enough, but then why was Sheva so long overdue? Certainly Eleazar ben Yair would not harm one of his own kind. He had only to tell her yes or no and send her on her way. Yet, a Jew? Who knew what a Jew would do?

To divert his increasing concern Silva had tried reading *The History of the World,* by Nicholas of Damascus, but he had found it a poor distraction from the magnetic power of the wine flask. Away, grape! There are other excitements this night. Here is an interminable history of ancient Rome by one Dionysius of Halicarnassus, who must be the world's greatest bore. Here is Strabo's geography of the Empire. Who cares? I am making geography. Here is a volume on dreams by Artemidorus. If a man manages to sleep in this wretched desert, does he need help with his nightmares?

"Sheva," he said aloud. "You are overdue. . . ."

He reached for the wine flask, hesitated, then placed it carefully under the table. Then he paced for a while and attempted to concentrate upon his house in Praeneste. Supposing, he thought, I do marry the woman? There must then be structural changes in the house, at the very least an addition to the Cubicula, since the present sleeping apartment is not really designed for two. It had indeed, he remembered with pleased astonishment, been planned by a man who had despaired of ever again being capable of copulation, much less once again giving service to the Greek god Hymen. Marriage would bring alterations to life which would be pleasant, but also alterations to an almost completed house. Every true friend had warned, "Do not change a stone once it has been put in place. Resist all temptation to have constructional second thoughts or you will certainly go bankrupt!" Now if a black-eyed Jewess deigns to consent, the plumbing will have to be rerouted, additional window openings fitted into the general scheme and more expensive Lapis Specularis must be mined and polished to cover those openings. And in the hands of that prime idiot, that mentally retarded Antoninus Mamilianus, who had the presumption to call himself an architect, the total expense might well fulfill the dire predictions of your gloomiest friends. The bank of Maxinus and Proculus was not in the business of philanthropy. They knew to the last *as* what was already invested in the house and they were equally aware of your sixty-thousand-sesterce salary as Procurator of Judea. Without changing the expression in their eyes or moving their lips in the slightest, without any real knowledge of the territory involved, those coin-jingling buzzards could estimate how meager the loot might be for any General who followed after Titus, and they would balance that equation against the 5 per cent inheritance tax if their military client was regrettably killed in line of duty, and divide it by the 5 per cent tax on the additional slaves he would need if he survived. And they would say this man suffers delusions of grandeur which in our language means a poor business risk, and let us not only refuse to lend him more but increase the pressure on him to pay off what is outstanding. The firm of Maxinus and Proculus was not even remotely interested in the kind of numbers which enabled them to do business in such high-handed fashion. They cared not that Roman Legionaries under the leadership of certain indebted Roman Generals regularly marched twenty miles in five hours, or twenty-four at quick time, and while they were about it carried an incredible sixty pounds of gear in addition to their weapons. Such soldiers kept the teeth of the world's barbarians from the soft throats of Maxinus and Proculus and all their kind, a fact which failed utterly to alter their rate of interest. So?

The whole idea was impossible to begin with, and who indeed do you think you are to even speculate on marrying a Jewess? Do you of all men have to be told by some minor bureaucrat that no Roman citizen may marry a noncitizen without the consent of the Senate *and* the Emperor? Or would you prefer to be told in his pithy manner by Vespasian himself that any intelligent man past the age of thirty should follow his own example and take a concubine rather than bind himself in the nuisance of marriage? The gossips claimed Titus had pleaded with his father to authorize his own marriage to the Jewess Bernice—and had been refused. If a prince could not succeed, what hope for you? And it would be boorish in the extreme to ask good friend Titus to confer Roman citizenship on Sheva and thus clear the way when he would not so honor his Bernice. Nor had he thus far made any citizenship arrangement for Tiberius Alexander, the Jew who had not only been formerly Governor of Alexandria but had actually served as Titus's chief of staff during the siege of Jerusalem! Oh no! You might put spittle on your seal ring so the wax would not stick, but you did so discreetly. And the very great had a way of *not* always being flattered by imitation.

The very great. Of the hundreds of Roman Generals scattered across the world who else had such a close relationship with Titus? It was a bond forged in danger, hammered into shape by mutual admiration and devotion. It was as true as your sword of Spanish iron, as incomparable—and precious—as that mineral to any other.

He changed the pattern of his pacing from a direct traverse of his tent to an egg-shaped circuit of the table. I should sit down, he thought, or I will be dragging my leg up the mountain, but I cannot while the woman I suddenly regard as treasure walks alone through a battlefield. Have I been deserted by all the gods? Where in the name of each and every one of you is Sheva?

Ordinarily the most exciting event of the entire week would have been the letter from Titus that had been brought by special courier earlier in the evening. Sheva had not been gone long on her mission then—actually, he remembered, she could not have as yet arrived at the summit of Masada. Consequently the letter had come at a time of waiting and he had been able to give it his full attention.

It had been mostly a chatty letter, such as brothers who were fond of each other might enjoy. Except for the very last part it was not a communication from a prince to a soldier but a sharing of views, exactly as it had been when you were young Tribunes together in Germany.

Here a prince had begun with a most memorable salutation. "Greetings to my esteemed comrade-at-arms . . ." What soldier could ask for more?

Next came an apology for not writing "my dear friend Flavius Silva more often, but the press of affairs in the capital has been extraordinary and Father has been turning more and more matters over to me."

Dear friend, you cannot imagine the problems both amusing and tragic which result from the wild explosion of population this city now enjoys—or should I say suffers? Besides ourselves who really are too few (and I hope all the others never count our noses and discover how few we are), there have come more Greeks, Syrians, Jews, and Egyptians, all of whom barely tolerate each other. In addition there have arrived untold numbers of Armenians, Ethiopians, and Arabs, with a seasoning of Bithynians, Cappadocians, and Parthians. Most of these elements are now gathered into colonies as exclusive of the rest of the city as their national origins. Even more noxious and restless is a sort of floating population who eat wherever they can squat and sleep wherever they can find space to lie down. They seem to come and go and it is impossible to keep track of these people with the aim of putting them to good purpose. They are mostly barbarians from Dalmatia, Thrace, and Germany, and the occasional savage from Britain, who exhibit their tattoos as if they were medals. Lately there has been a virtual invasion of Gauls stalking about the streets as if they owned them and twisting their disgusting mustachios as if they were flags of pride.

How can we ever hope to unite such a variety of peoples? I am personally of the opinion we are overly generous in opening our gates to the rest of the world, particularly when so very many of our visitors or self-adopted residents have not the faintest notion of appropriate sanitation. They urinate or defecate wherever or whenever the mood inspires them, and the situation is not improved by Vespasian's new tax on use of our public facilities. Knowing Father, you may smile when you learn that upon my objecting to the recently imposed tax on public urinals he held a coin before my nostrils and inquired if I found the smell objectionable. . . .

Silva tried to smile as he had during his first reading of the incident, but he found it impossible now. Titus was being a bit harsh on his father. *Someone* had to rescue the insolvent Roman treasury and there was the final conquest of Britain to be financed. Alas, if Vespasian could only say a few sharp words to one Antoninus Mamilianus, the world's most extravagant architect!

His bad leg was beginning to throb so he sat down at the table. As if by plan his foot struck the wine flask, but instead of reaching for it as his desire begged him, he deliberately reached for Titus's letter.

By the by, one of my Centurions brought me this jewel of graffiti dedicated to our goddess of sewers:

> Fair Cloacina, goddess of this place,
> Daily resort of all ye human race,
> Graciously grant my offerings may flow
> Nor rudely swift—not obstinately slow.

The Centurion had copied it on a paper which I recommended he anoint with a juice of cedar to preserve it forever from moths and rottenness.

Dear friend, I pass on to you these trivialities because I know full well what it is like to campaign far from home and particularly in that barren land where duty now holds you. In some respects it is worse than exile because you cannot nurse your natural longings of either resentment or revenge.

Among other chores Father has thrown my way (please do not think public sanitation is my principal responsibility, although from the foregoing you might well have reason to believe so) is command of the Praetorian Guard, which is in healthy morale, and the civil courts, which are in an incredible mess. You will recall that during the civil wars a great deal of property was appropriated on one excuse or another and naturally the abused are suing for retribution. There are now so many cases and the court calendars are so far behind, many of the litigants will never reach trial in their lifetimes unless we find some way to circumnavigate the regular legal proceedings which are so ponderous. I am doing my best to alleviate this unfortunate impasse, and while involved in it will try to correct another injustice which has also been too long a part of the Roman legal scene. I believe it should be unlawful for any person, citizen or freedman, to be tried under several laws for the same offense. Such a procedure places a person in double jeopardy (or more), and it seems that only the most influential or cunning scoundrels can escape such a net, while too often the innocent or half-guilty are convicted.

Silva paused in his reading and listened. Some time ago he had been aware of a cessation in the sounds of the ramp. He recognized it as the audible measurement of mealtime. Now, of course, the predominating sound had resumed and become an eternal presence, only to be noticed when it ceased again. In his reply to Titus he must include his opinion that this was most certainly the noisiest camp ever to be maintained in the history of the Roman armies. Why not describe how, after long exposure to this perpetual turmoil, it was possible to select sounds? For example, just now there are the voices of the guards outside. It is possible to sense the tone of their voices if not the actual substance of their words. No? Their sudden speech had *not* been caused by the approach of Geminus escorting Sheva. Would it be an exaggeration to report that those who actually stood duty at the ramp had developed such acute powers of hearing sounds other than those produced by their laborious environment, they could actually detect the approach of arrows? Nonsense. Yet so they claimed. Should you recommend to Titus, not altogether facetiously, that if ever new forms of torture were required for obstinate criminals, he might well consider prolonged exposure to massive noise? Or silence . . . such as now seems to have possessed your guards. Were they all asleep? Could they not at least engage in some trivial chatter to pass the time?

He read again what he had already thrice reviewed:

So much building is in progress you would not know Rome. Father is on a building spree, which leads me to believe the many caustic remarks about his parsimony may have finally gored his pride! Among other structures he is proceeding with his Temple of Peace, of which more later. Then, I am rather embarrassed to report, he is building an arch in my name which will eventually be embellished with carvings depicting our capture of Jerusalem. Last week I viewed some of the preliminary work—the city burning, which I thought very well done and most accurate, and another panel representing myself driving a chariot, with which my daughter found most grievous fault. She exclaimed the figure standing so proudly did not resemble her father in the slightest because he was much too beautiful. Ah, the young!

While on the subject of construction I must tell you that I had occasion to pass through Praeneste not long ago and there paused to explore your new villa which had been pointed out to me. Hearty congratulations! It will one day be a place of well-earned repose for a citizen and a soldier who has served the Empire well. I look forward to the day when in our advanced years I may come to visit you there and we can reminisce of times when our young heads concentrated for long only on the same subject as the heads of our penises.

Perhaps you have already attended to the matter, but I would like to make one suggestion concerning your villa. Do, by all means, engage a talented muralist. Our architecture is essentially rather cold of line and I find the present extensive employment of murals most refreshing.

Do you, now, dear friend Titus? I also find well-done murals contribute greatly to the charm of a house, but is there anything more annoying and inescapable than a *badly* done mural? And good painters charge fortunes, my dear rich prince who will never have to consider such details. But never mind. Stay you, and I will stay I. For what was it Epicurus said, "I shall give you a rule by which to measure yourself and your development; in that day you will come into your own when you realize that the successful are of all men most miserable."

A drop of sweat left his chin and splattered on the letter. He flicked it from the surface of the paper with a sense of satisfaction. *There!* Man's talent for acclimation to his environment is once more proven! In spite of the continuous roar outside my tent I actually heard the droplet splat. Now, how can we focus this same wondrous ability on ignoring heat? How can we overcome the natural advantage of the Jews, whose blood has had a hundred generations beneath this sun?

. . . it will please you to know Father has also devoted himself to improving the medical situation. He has instituted a campaign to be rid of the quacks who have so long infested Rome and he has opened auditoriums for instruction in the art of medicine. The professors are paid by the state and the graduate doctors will be the only men legally authorized to practice. Father himself is still suffering from the foot wound he took at Jopata which was repaired by a clumsy-fingered charlatan who has since perished of his own remedies. There are times during depressive weather when Father limps rather badly, which misery, shared with you, may partially account for his sympathy and great fondness for you.

He paused and wiped the sweat from his face lest another drop stain the letter. If my bad leg holds the affection of Vespasian then it is more than worth it, for he has never been known to forsake those who somehow come to his favor. Ha! Here it is again! Now Titus leads gently into the true meat of the letter. After thrice reading, the message seems unmistakable:

. . . actually Father has not been of good cheer since he closed the gate to the Temple of Janus almost three years ago. When the spoils from Jerusalem were all assembled even he was impressed with the golden table, the candelabra, et cetera, and he commanded these should be deposited in his new Temple of Peace along with the innumerable other treasures gathered from all over the world. In a sense this is *his* temple, signifying to history and to the world that his only desire is for peace and it is Vespasian who has brought peace. . . .

Here, in the middle of the letter, there had obviously and intentionally been left a blank space. Across it Titus had inscribed a message in his own hand. How like him to revive the old cipher we once shared when communicating the amorous talents of certain Roman ladies! Simply remember the phrasing key, "Puipus flaprr attuh ipsetuv uhm dhcuhvlw," which became "Primus clamor atque impetus rem decrevit," if you simply substituted the preceding third and legitimate letter for every letter that caused a word to become gibberish.

Titus had written: "As your friend, must warn you arrival Pomponius Falco. Handle extreme caution. Do not know why Father employed him, but assure dangerous."

Dear princely friend, you are a trifle late, but I do appreciate your confirmation of my own opinion!

And the balance of the letter needs no interpretation. Its words clang:

On the receipt of this it is of the utmost importance you take Masada *immediately*. Losses of our Legionaries are to be disregarded and you will only be held to account if victory is delayed. The Emperor and I are deeply concerned over this pocket of resistance, this taunting of our claim to universal peace. We are embarrassed by this situation at home and cannot cover it longer. Worse, we have a very real fear that if those on Masada are able to hold out even a short while longer they may inspire new uprisings throughout Palestine. Salutes, old comrade. I need hardly remind you that you bear not only the dignity and pride of Rome with your standards but the honor of Vespasian himself.

Silva's good eye roved once more across the paper and then focused upon his Spanish sword. With the words of Titus still thundering across his mind he saw once more a march he had known in the sweet memory of long ago.

It was now difficult to believe there had not been so much as a scratch on the blade that morning when you shared an isolated rise in the land with another youth called Titus Flavius Vespasianus. The hump projected like a monstrous tit from the floor of the Rhone valley and from it you watched the passage of a fresh army bound to restrain the German tribes.

It was indeed a morning to hold forever in the mind's eye. There were alpine snows glittering against the sky and the blue-green fields of the valley spread out like a lush carpet for the parade. Even the river itself, rumbling and thrashing under the driving night of fast-melting snows, seemed exhilarated by the morning.

The two of you, the rawest of youthful Tribunes, leaned on the necks of your horses and critically observed the style of the first lightly armed auxiliaries who served as scouts before the main body. And you had agreed they exposed themselves overmuch. Next in line were two cohorts of regularly armed footmen flanked by horsemen. You approved. A good formation. Then came the engineers carrying their arms, but with their tools behind them in carriages, dull fellows all, you agreed, and then the veteran General Vespasian himself, followed by his elite corps of footmen, horsemen and pikemen. So passed the vanguard, their javelin heads and pike tips glistening in the morning sun.

Ah, those were better days and better climes for two young soldiers who thought they knew everything.

He wiped the sweat from his eyes and thought how marvelously the mind of youth could store an impression. Here, though I melt in Judea, I can still hear the rhythmic chink of equipment echoing across a distant valley. I can hear a shouted order, a complaint, or even laughter of those long-gone ghosts.

Who would ever have thought on such a bracing morning, with Nero on the throne, that Vespasian would one day take his place?

Once again he could see the line of march as clearly as he could hear the gushing Rhone.

There was a gap in the column and then came a troop of more than a hundred cavalry. They were followed by a packtrain of mules carrying the needed gear for siege in the wilderness of Gaul or Germany, and then finally the two legions marked at their heads by eagle ensigns representing dominion. They were followed by the trumpeters, so young they were treated by some as children, and then the main column with six men in ranks.

On that morning it had been inconceivable any people could long withstand the might of Rome. And as it transpired the tribesmen were not overly difficult when they could be brought to direct battle. The Ampsivarii, the Tencteri, the Usipii and the Tubantes, the Chatti and the Cherusci and the Hermunduri—all met in one circumstance or another during that first campaign. What a stink! Arabs and the Jews were as jasmine by comparison.

He pushed the letter aside and concluded that he must be aging faster than his years deserved if he found such pleasure in reviewing the past. By the gods, there was no time for such useless reflections now! The orders were unmistakable and it was typical of distant princes to ignore the very real obstacles in the local field. Attack at once! Press on until victory and disregard losses. On the plains or even in the forests of Germany compliance would be simple enough. But here? Sheer determination and courage could not immediately bridge the physical gap between sword and enemy. It would be another week at least until the ramp would be done, and then who could be sure how many assaults would be necessary? Who knew what the heat would do to soldiers already near the limit of tolerance?

Then all the more important this meeting with Eleazar. And where was his answer, not to mention the woman who supposedly bore it?

He was about to send an inquiry to Geminus when he again heard the voices of his guards outside the tent. He restrained himself from rushing to the entrance, but he rose from his chair and stood easily, as if impatience were unknown to him.

He saw a movement of the leather entrance flaps, then the stolid faces of Paternus and Severns, and moving just behind them was not Geminus with Sheva, as he had presumed, but Pomponius Falco, who stepped quickly around the guards and, with a confident air Silva found infuriating, crossed the carpet toward him.

"What are you doing here?" he grunted. "Or has my tent become a thoroughfare for the sleepless?"

"Since this is only my second call upon my Judean host, I thought he might be more hospitable," Falco replied with a forced yawn. "I must say I really do not sleep very soundly in your nasty desert—and perhaps it is just as well, since the essence of duplicity seems to be everywhere about."

"You talk in circles, Pomponius Falco. State your business and be gone. I have a busy night scheduled."

How he reeks of perfume, Silva thought. I would as leave sniff the scalp of a German tribesman.

"Indeed you have, General. And may I be the first to congratulate your cunning. I beg your forgiveness for previously underestimating you, and perhaps now that I humble myself you will appoint me to take him back to Rome? After all, the purpose of my visit will have been accomplished and there will be no reason to further impose upon your good—"

"What are you raving on about?"

"Eleazar ben Yair, of course."

Heed the bastard's way of insinuating he knows much more than he possibly could, Silva thought. Suddenly we are partners. Is this overconfident fraud implying he may put in an invaluable word for me at home? Following his thoughts is like chasing a butterfly through the forest.

"Falco, the longer I am in Judea, the shorter my patience—and I have been here too long. Now quickly, what exactly is your supplication?"

"There you are, classifying me as a supplicant again, when I warned you of my refusal to tolerate—"

Silva slammed his fist on the table. "And I now warn you to give me a sensible reason for your midnight invasion of this tent immediately or you are going back to your own in chains!"

"Temper, temper, General!" Falco cocked his head to one side and held up an admonishing finger. "How unwise of you to confine me when I hold the key to your whole career—perhaps your future happiness, perhaps your very life."

"You're drunk."

"Somehow that sounds odd coming from you, although no one could deny your qualifications for recognizing fuddlement in the brilliant." Falco paused and with the tip of his little finger touched delicately at the paint on his eyelids. "My only wish is to congratulate you, Sire, on this master stroke of strategy whereby you intend to seize the leader of the Jews and forever silence his skillful tongue. Masada will fall at once, and assuredly I will applaud your campaign to the most influential of Roman ears."

To cover his surprise Silva muttered sourly that he could get along very well without the help of meddlesome opportunists, but now he sensed a challenge in Falco's manner which went far beyond his customary insolence.

"For reasons I confess mystify me," Falco said easily, "Eleazar has literally thrown himself into your omnipresent chains. He has agreed to meet you halfway up the snake path tonight, when Jupiter is at the zenith. He will not be armed and he will be alone."

"Who put those words in your mouth?"

"Need you ask, since you chose the messenger and sent her? And very clever of you to think of using a woman. They have a way of allaying certain elemental fears in a man, thus blinding him to the unexpected."

"Where is she?" Silva glanced at his sword and barely resisted an urge to sink it in Falco's groin.

"Presently she is my guest, as I am yours—although she does not have to bear the insults you have directed toward me, which, by the by, I do not propose to endure any longer. I find your opinions vary between the boring and the annoying and suggest from this time on you demonstrate how even a dull soldier may improve his manners—"

"I am going to kill you," Silva said, fighting to keep his voice calm.

Falco smiled and said, "I doubt if you will be so impetuous, since your Jewess is presently with my Usipats, and may I remind you of their rather brutish nature as well as their reputation for absolute obedience to whomever they serve? If I do not appear before them by noon tomorrow unharmed, they have instructions—"

"Your head will decorate a pike beside my personal standard. Now where is the woman, and be quick about it!"

Falco smiled tolerantly. "Come now; General. May I recommend you be as sensible as your precious Jewess, who hesitated hardly a breath when given the choice between voluntarily explaining her mysterious descent from Masada or suffering certain ugly forms of encouragement to speech. She is as wise as she is clever and could not understand why one Roman might wish to withhold information from another when both are engaged in the same enterprise."

Falco shook his head as if in pity and appeared to be so completely at ease Silva decided he at last understood how he had risen so rapidly in Vespasian's court. Without really listening, he heard Falco saying, "*You*, my military stud, are the romantic! In contrast, your Jewess surveys the practical future. And she has asked herself if it would please her General to retrieve a mutilated body. She is, in the way of all females, a pragmatist—and therefore knows that one day you will forget the whole affair, particularly if she is near to please you. Come now, my dear brave General, would you deny she has used her intelligence? Here is a woman who has cast aside sentiment and reached for life. Would you prefer some stupid female enamored with a vision of herself as the silent heroine? Would you deny it is a greater pleasure to lie with an intelligent female rather than with some noble and imbecilic slut? You must admit the conquest of a woman's thoughts, providing she has any, can be far more exciting than merely slathering about her pubes. There is no substitute for brains, dear dull-witted warrior, and even you may now realize how those of a man and a woman grinding together may sometimes produce the powder of

imagination. Thus it is possible for even the most mediocre of individuals to become passionate mates—"

Falco paused to examine the two jeweled rings on his
little fingers. He held them before him momentarily, com-
paring them. "I bought these from a merchant in Rhodes
intending them as a gift to you. However, soon after we
sailed I discovered the stones were fake and the rings
nearly worthless, so I have kept them to remind myself
what a poor man of business I am. I shall now demonstrate that I have actually learned nothing by offering to
return your Jewess intact, at a very modest price. Indeed,
you need not even open your purse. All I ask is that you
provide sufficient horses and provisions to keep my party
comfortably for, say, ten days. And because of your open
regard for me and your natural generosity I will be
pleased to deliver both Jew and Jewess to Rome—the man
Eleazar, to represent the gift of Masada from yourself to
Vespasian, and the woman for your later pleasures."

Silva rose very slowly from the table. He avoided Falco's eyes and pretended to concentrate on the task of
rerolling Titus's letter. He was pleased that his fingers
remained so steady as he manipulated the paper. Where
was Geminus? How had this nauseating peacock managed
to intercept Sheva when he could not possibly have known
of her departure?

When he had finished with the letter he placed it carefully in a bronze bowl. Then he walked slowly around the
table, casually, as if he had lost all interest in the conversation. Finally he halted before Falco, facing him with his
hands tightly clutched at his back, and he thought, I must
be very careful for the next few minutes, then it will not
matter. He spoke slowly and with particular solemnity, as
if he had carefully considered a project and found it
worthy. "You are the one with imagination, Pomponius
Falco. Yes, I do agree Eleazar ben Yair could represent
more than a mere man and no doubt he should be ex-
ploited at home. Furthermore I see no reason why you
should not be appointed my envoy to deliver him as you
suggest—providing, of course, no harm has come to the
woman."

"I assure you, Sire—"

"Since she has not been long gone from the camp, she
cannot be far away. Where is she?"

"If I told you, it would be the end of your Jewess. The

Usipats will release her only to Pomponius Falco and he must appear before them in his present excellent state of health. If you will reflect a moment perhaps you will understand how anxious I am she be returned to you without blemish. I am far more interested in what may happen on my return to Rome than I am in satisfying your sensual hungers, but I am fully aware one may not be favorably accomplished without the other. It is Eleazar that I prize."

"I have given my right hand no harm will come to Eleazar."

"How silly of you! So you larded your stuffy honor with the anachronism of your right hand. All of you soldiers are living in a world long gone. No one of any sophistication believes in gloria patria any longer—we have risen above such adolescence. You may be sure the Jew will kill you if he has the chance. Wait—"

Falco bent forward and peered into Silva's eyes. He pouted his lips for a moment, then slowly sucked in his breath. *"Wait!* Is it possible our dear General is even more clever than I supposed? Could it be he is simply going to have a chat with the Jew, and scoundrel though he may be, allow him to run back to his fortress? Well, well! There is something about this whole affair that is beginning to smell quite differently—perhaps this tent is merely a scab covering a pustule of treason!"

Falco tapped his head with his long forefinger. "How blind I have been! How naïve! I failed to ask myself *why* our great and brave General should behave in this way . . . unless the Jew holds some great treasure he would secretly trade for his personal safety—"

Silva felt his hands close on Falco's neck before he realized his arms had moved. He dug his thumbs into his throat and pressed until Falco sank to his knees.

Falco gagged, his mouth fell open, and his words of protest were drowned in phlegm. And still Silva pressed relentlessly until he saw Falco's eyes slide upward beneath the lids and felt his body become limp. Only then did he relinquish his grip and let him slip to the carpet.

He clapped his hands for Paternus and Severns, and when they stood looking at the slowly writhing figure on the carpet he said, "Our friend suffers from too much sun. Remove him to his tent and post six men to keep him there. Tell the Centurion Clemens to make up some chains so he will not be tempted to overexpose himself again."

As they heaved Falco to his feet Silva was relieved to see that he was breathing and a hint of color had returned to his face. For a while, the thought, even Pomponius Falco will not feel like being a nuisance. Poor fellow. Like so many of the hangers-on at court, his ambitions exceeded his training and capabilities. He had not even learned a most primary lesson in military tactics: Never *personally* inform the enemy you hold something he values.

He buckled on his sword and took his helmet from its stand. So I am an innocent, Pomponius Falco? Perhaps. Yet after nearly a lifetime in the field my standard is still flying. And for the moment Sheva is as safe in your care as she would be on the mountain. By morning you will order your Usipats to deposit her most gently back in her own tent—and by next week, who knows? She may well be on her way to Praeneste.

ELEAZAR BEN YAIR had hesitated only a moment when he encountered the sentries posted at the eastern gate. He agreed with them on the relative coolness of the night, and stood back while they opened the heavy door. Fortunately they were a different group than those who had been standing guard when he had sent the woman back to the Romans. Because they stood in the deep shadows of the casemate he could not see their faces, yet he sensed their curiosity as plainly as if they had expressed it. Has Eleazar lost his wits? What possible business could their leader have on the serpent's path at this hour alone, and since they could not see the knife in his tunic, apparently unarmed? He had debated asking them not to discuss his departure and had then decided the request would only add mystery to an already intriguing event. Romans could order. Jews could not. And to hope his departure would be kept even a temporary secret was asking an impossible restraint of Semitic nature. Of course they would discuss it, hopefully at such length he would be back on the summit before word reached the council. When they learned of his action they would most certainly demand an explanation as to why they had not been consulted. How had he dared consort with the most vicious murderer of Jews since Florus? And if there was any hope in such a meeting, then he should have taken one of the council along to approve or disapprove. And so on. O yes! The politicians will accuse thee of conniving and the priests will accuse thee of sinning. And so on and on. Shalom! What are you? Peace was not to be found either inside or outside of Masada!

And now be honest with yourself. Admit your consent to meet with Silva had very little to do with the people of Masada. You agreed because a wild-eyed female accused

185

you of false pride and dared say you thirsted for power.
You agreed because you have secretly nursed an almost
overwhelming desire to meet face-to-face with Flavius
Silva. No matter how you might explain this need to the
council they would not comprehend how he had become
an invisible presence within you, an ogre marching
through the hours of even your troubled sleep. Flavius
Silva is all Romans. He is as much the symbol of Roman
rule as his own glittering standards. Now that the chance
has come you must see into his eyes and discover this lord
of evil to be a lesser man than your fears have created.
You must find him as weak and as susceptible to fear as
any other human being . . . or you are lost. The risk you
take this night is for yourself and you must continue to be
honest with yourself. Dedicate these next hours to Eleazar
ben Yair.

As he picked his way cautiously down the twisting path
he wondered how he would behave if Silva proved to be a
disappointment. O, *there* was a perplexity! The diminutive
figure you have observed from the heights of Masada is an
unreal toy soldier possessed of certain offensive character-
istics with which you have endowed him. You, who do not
know whether he is a big man or a small one. You, who
have no idea how he will appear standing alone. How will
his manner be, and will the man who climbs the path
actually be Flavius Silva or a substitute of near likeness
who might be a sacrifice to some wholly new plan of
attack?

"I *know*, I will know," he whispered. "I will know the
man."

Glancing at the sky he also reassured himself Jupiter
was still ascending and thus he was well ahead of time. He
intended to be, for at approximately the halfway point the
path made a double twist. There the shale base was so
loose passage across it could only be accomplished slowly
and with the greatest caution. Here, just above that place,
he would wait and observe Silva's climb.

There was not even a remote possibility of his being
surprised, for the entire eastern base of Masada lay before
him in the starlight, and Jupiter now stood like a beacon
overhead. Near him he could easily distinguish the tortured features of the mountain's sheer face and beyond
the wadi at the bottom he could make out details on the
circumvallation.

He glanced upward and was astounded at Masada's apparent union with the heavens. It had been almost three long years since he had achieved such a view and he had forgotten how different every aspect of the desert appeared from this low altitude. Masada itself was much more imposing, but then so were the towers projecting from the Roman circumvallation. Also the wall itself seemed considerably higher.

He positioned himself so he could observe not only the very bottom of the path but also oversee its wandering course through the brush to the Roman wall.

When he was satisfied with the solitude he sat down on a rock to wait.

The Centurion Rosianus Geminus had faulted, and his highly polished military instinct reminded him Silva was more likely to smile upon a man who openly confessed his mistake rather than sought ways to excuse it. As they approached the eastern circumvallation he presented the facts to Silva as they had actually occurred, hoping by such frankness to avoid painful inquiry. Seizing this moment of obvious preoccupation for his General, he hoped he might not even be heard, or his punishment would at least be postponed. "I should have been more curious, Sire. But I detest talking to men who would be women and so I ignored their presence when I should have wondered why they would come so far from their own quarters. Later when the Germans appeared I thought it strange, but I hesitated to leave the wall and make inquiries because I was alone, and the woman was already overdue. . . ."

Because Silva remained silent, Geminus became increasingly uneasy. He scratched at his great black beard and debated the wisdom of complimenting Silva's ability to quickly cover ground in spite of his limp. "As you ordered, Sire, I sent away the regular guards on this section, and they were very glad to be relieved . . . and . . . as soon as they were out of sight the females with balls came along and began to taunt me until finally they got to my temper and I had after them—"

"How far from your assigned post did you chase them?"

"Not at all, Sire. I would not leave a post unless I was carried away dead. I was always in the area, but they were quick as deer and dodging among the rocks and saying things to aggravate a man past his patience—and I thought to teach them respect for their betters—"

"There were Falco's two boys, and how many Germans?"

"I was never sure, Sire, because they kept their distance from the wall."

"How, in the dark, could you be so sure they were Germans?"

"Sire?" Seeing that Silva was still more preoccupied than angry, he ventured a note of humor. "My nose could be quite sure."

"When did you realize you had been duped?"

"Not until much later, Sire. I remember chasing one of them just over there behind those rocks—it is not far, as you can see. Then I returned to the wall and waited, looking up the path for some sign of the Jewess. The female boys continued to harass me for a while, then suddenly they were gone and I saw the Germans had also disappeared. I could see the path all the way to the top of Masada and there was no movement on it. I knew then something had gone wrong."

"You were the something. However, I may be influenced in adjusting your punishment by the outcome of this night's events. Now listen carefully and have a care you do not fault these orders."

Silva removed his helmet and unbuckled his sword. He handed them both to Geminus.

"Sire?" Geminus shook his head in bewilderment.

"You are to remain here at the wall. Regardless of any further distractions you will keep your eyes on Masada. At the slightest sign of any unusual movement along the summit you are to call out a warning to me. At the sound of your voice you will be joined immediately by two maniples of the first cohort who are now waiting just beyond the rise. You will lead them with all speed to the base of Masada and up the path, where I hope you will find me still very much alive. If all remains quiet as now you will wait here for my return though it may not be until dawn. Do I make myself clear, Geminus?"

"But Sire, you are practically naked." He fingered the sword and helmet unhappily.

"I find it a rather pleasant sensation. I feel curiously light."

They moved along the wall to the place where Silva had

ordered temporary steps constructed to ease Sheva's original journey. They mounted the wall, and as Silva started
down the opposite side, Geminus held out his sword.

"Sire, if you will not take me—whatever business you
have with the Jews, it will cut better with this."

Silva pushed the hilt aside, then quickly stepped down
the steps. In the starlight Geminus was able to follow his
limping figure until the path dipped into a wadi. Then he
was gone.

As he climbed, the path became increasingly steep of
incline and the footing less sure. By the gods, he thought,
little wonder Eleazar ben Yair had agreed to the meeting.
If this was the only way to him, any sort of formal attack
was hopeless.

He negotiated a double turn in the path and paused to
ease his breathing.

It is curious, he thought—here on the side of a mountain in Judea you remember something Titus said long ago
when he was told construction had started on the house in
Praeneste. "By all means make provisions for a tennis
court, my friend. I know of no physical endeavor which
will keep you so vital." And you had persuaded yourself
soldiering was enough to keep any man fit—yet perhaps it
is not, if mountain climbing is any criterion.

He looked down at the void below and instantly looked
up at the stars again. A place for goats. If I look down
again I shall vomit.

Just after the shale he had disturbed ceased rattling he
heard an answering slide above him. He looked up quickly, expecting to see a man silhouetted against the stars.
But there was nothing.

He waited and though he could now hear his own heart
pounding he managed to keep his voice casual when he
said in Latin, "Show yourself, Jew. I will climb no farther."

He was startled to hear a voice address him in Greek.
It was Eleazar ben Yair's voice, close behind him. He
whirled about and raised his arms defensively. Then he
saw a man standing in the turn of the path he had just
passed. He was saying, "Experience has convinced me it is
safer to let a Roman pass and make sure what his splendid
façade is hiding."

"I have come unarmed."

"So I assured myself. At first I thought you were wearing a helmet. Then I saw that what I thought a helmet was only an illusion created by your fair hair."

Eleazar's voice faded as he moved closer to Silva. He muttered in Hebrew, "What kind of a monster hast thou created in the shape of this man?"

They stood in silence only a few paces apart. Eleazar was nearly a head taller than Silva, yet the incline of the path made them seem to be of equal height. Examining Silva he saw his breastplate embossed with crouching lions, trumpeters, and rearing horses. And he saw that when he decided to use the knife the target would be easy, for Silva's entire neck was exposed.

"You are a younger man than I had supposed," Eleazar said.

"And you are larger than I thought," Silva answered. "I hope your wisdom matches your bulk."

"If you live on a mountain, the view is broad. It is the people who live in valleys who have difficulty comprehending what lies beyond."

There was silence again until Silva moved his foot. The sound of his sandal brushing against the loose shale caused both men to tense, and for a time they stood like two fearful animals poised for attack. Then gradually their quick breathing subsided.

"Do you have a family?" Silva demanded.

"There is no reason to raise your voice, General. I am neither your slave nor one of your poor Legionaries. But since you have made inquiry with as much politeness as I suppose any Roman is capable, I will tell you we are all one family on Masada. I will also remind you Judea is our given home—now unfortunately crowded with boorish visitors."

"You may save your speeches for the public ear. I have not made this climb to hear such stuff or more of the fatuous declarations of which you are so fond. Apparently you believe words serve you as both shield and weapon. Perhaps they do, but now you are burdened with them."

Silva paused, then suddenly all he had wanted to say for so long came rushing to his thoughts. It was as if he had nurtured the words for years and had at last found audience for them, as if their final release also freed Flavius Silva of all doubt. And strangely, his voice seemed to accuse himself as well as Eleazar ben Yair.

"You have stood before your people and promised them victory, being careful to ignore the power of numerals and deliberately vague about the date of victory. There is nothing new in such leadership. The kind of lies you so glibly serve have been told to the near-vanquished since the first battle was fought. You declare you are winning which you know very well is a lie, since you know it cannot happen, so you declare some mysterious force will arrive at the last minute to defeat your enemies. These lies were told a thousand times before Masada and I suppose will be told long after we are gone. You tell these lies because you are clever enough to know that if you admit the truth your followers will lay down their arms and make the best of life they can. I will confess we Romans are experts at such persuasions."

Silva paused and sighed. He seemed to be a man removed from the scene, as if he were talking to himself.

"The curious thing about this ancient device is that you often convince yourself as well as your followers—and there, unless the numerals are in your favor, lies disaster. Now I have come to you tonight because I suspect you are not a fool but may be a victim of your own eloquence. Perhaps in spite of your lofty view you have managed to blindfold yourself. Certainly you have not considered honestly the numerals, or you would have surrendered by now. I have come to you as one soldier to another in the hope you will at last be realistic and save your people. I have come to offer you life."

It was so quiet Silva could hear Eleazar's heavy breathing. Only by listening carefully could he detect the sounds from the ramp on the opposite side of Masada. For once he wished they could be louder.

"I am not a soldier," Eleazar was saying. "I am a son of God, who will protect us from your numerals."

"Nonsense—and you know it. Even your God must understand you have less than five hundred fighting men and I have more than five thousand. It is as simple as that."

"And I have the Hebrew sun which will soon melt your armor."

Silva sighed. Without a doubt, Jews were the most unreasonable people in all the world. "You do not seem to comprehend," he said patiently. "Within two days, three at the most, my ramp will be at your western gate. No matter what you do or what your God decides, our machines will be pounding on your wall and in a matter of hours we will be inside. It will be too late then. Once they are on top I cannot hold my Legionaries, much less the auxiliaries. I cannot say to them you have fought hard to get here—now desist. Even if I tried, they would not listen. In a sense I am burdened with the same sort of declarations you are. I have told my officers and men to endure the heat and discomfort only a little longer and victory will be ours. I have told them we will go to better surroundings then. I have come to tell you in private what I cannot admit before an audience of twenty thousand people. Now that so much energy and expense have been involved, I cannot possibly admit that I think your deaths will be meaningless to Rome and the few Legionaries I will lose in the final assault will be good men wasted. We have brought peace to Palestine for the first time in many years. No matter what happens here in the desert we will continue to rebuild it and make it prosper. I am trying to convince you that your continued resistance is not only hopeless but utterly worthless—and if you refuse to recognize this as the true situation, then the vaunted Jewish intelligence is overrated. We cannot but lie to each other with our followers heeding our every word. We are leaders, so we must, whether we will or not, boast and threaten and constantly parade our pride. Here, alone, I hope we meet as human beings. So I say again to you, Jew—I have come to offer you life."

After a moment Eleazar said softly in Hebrew, "I have seen the wicked in great power, and spreading himself like a green bay tree."

"What was that you said?" Silva asked. "My Hebrew is limited."

"Just something that occurred to me, a phrase, which really belongs to our priests." He paused, then moved slightly to one side so the light from Jupiter would better shine on Silva's face. "You are a curious soldier," he began, "and a curious Roman. I have listened to you in wonder, for since when does the butcher suddenly turn away his knife and say to the sheep, 'Run along now before I change my mind'? You offer us *life*? Are the Jews laboring on your ramp alive? Are those alive who work your mines, and build your canals, move your galleys, and furnish sport in your arenas? *Alive?* Even the privilege of

dying when they choose is denied them. It comes only
when *you* choose. If you are offering us complete amnesty,
and if you guarantee we will be allowed to return to normally fruitful lives, then I suppose it would be my duty
to at least present your new policy to my council of elders.
Do you make such an offer?"

"You know that is impossible."

"Of course I do. Therefore I wonder why we stand here
any longer. My curiosity is satisfied. I know what you look
like and it is reassuring to find that my information about
your bad eye and leg was accurate. There are many other
things we know about you, your trials and plans—"

"You are bluffing. There is nothing to know other than
what I have already laid before you."

"So? What about the five mutineers you sent to their
deaths this morning? What about your devotion to the
grape? What about the woman Sheva? You may be sure
there is nothing occurring in any of your camps about
which we are not informed. This very night a messenger
arrived from Rome with a dispatch for you. Unfortunately
our system is not so thorough as to reveal its contents, yet
by splicing two broken ropes together we can usually
make one whole, and I would guess your arrival here and
the message are not unrelated. You are quite right about
the numerals, and may I remind you, all Jewish children
learn to count at a very early age. But you are not nearly
so perceptive in your estimation of Masada's power. We
have weapons and supplies and water enough to fight
another ten years. You are in trouble because of Masada,
and because of you Rome is in trouble. The only solution
you can see is to knock us off the mountain or talk us into
becoming your slaves. We will not submit to your exploi-
tation of our people any more than we applaud your
colonial obsessions."

"You are still making speeches. The rabble you call
your family are the dregs of Jerusalem, with a few half-
wits and cripples picked up along the way. Not one in ten
of them would know what you are talking about when you
object to Roman rule. Of *course* we are colonialists! And
the finest. This very night thousands upon thousands of
Jews sleep peacefully under the protection of Roman
arms. Do you have any notion what we have done for the
entire world?"

"My teachers were careful to explain what you have

done to it, but could find very little to say about what you have done for it. Even so, because we are a peace-loving people we are willing to forsake vengeance and compromise."

Silva shook his head in disbelief. "I envy your ability to act the victor when you are as good as condemned."

"If you will remove your troops from the desert we will remain here and not interfere with your actions in the rest of Palestine."

"You are mad. I cannot even consider such a proposal."

"Of course not. Because with typical Roman arrogance you are convinced only might wins. In some ways I pity you, Flavius Silva—particularly on the day when you discover it is not true."

Eleazar reached into his tunic and pulled out his knife. He held the blade so the starlight would reflect on it as he turned it slowly around. "I brought this along because I have no cause to trust any Roman. Had I not found you were at least somewhat different I might have decided to kill you."

He tossed the knife carelessly away. It was still clattering down the mountain when he said, "But you are a poor man who does not believe, a wretched man who doubts the use of might or you would not have come here. Soon enough, I believe, you will kill yourself."

Eleazar deliberately turned his back on Silva and started slowly toward the stars.

Later, still breatiing heavily from the exertion of his climb, he lowered himself to the pallet beside Miriam. And at once he knew her eyes were open in the darkness, so he said, "Go to sleep."

And she replied, "Where have you been so late?"

"Is there a wife in the world who has never asked that question? I have been talking with a Roman."

"I am having a nightmare."

"Flavius Silva."

"Of course you have. How silly of me not to realize it. Eleazar, I do not mind your fancy words, but when you start lying to your wife——"

"I found him a very interesting man. He is somewhat shorter than I supposed."

"What a disappointment. Let me tell you, dear Eleazar, that I love you, as I have told you ten thousand times. I know you are a great man, far greater than any other on this mountain, and I know you must sometimes stretch the truth for the sake of our people, but I wish you would not bring those half-truths to this little home and ask me who know and love you so well to believe your every word."

"It often takes a great deal of imagination to believe the truth. I will not disturb you with further facts if you will go to sleep."

There was a moment's silence between them, then she whispered, "How can I sleep when our world is coming to an end?"

"It is not yet the end. There is still much we can do."

"I beg you be truthful with me. What will happen to Reuben?"

"I do not know. Let us first control what happens to ourselves. Then we can best plan for him."

"I am not interested in myself."

"Very noble of you."

"You set the tone with thy noble speeches. But words do not drive away Romans."

"You are right upon right, dear wife. They only seem to bring them."

He rolled over on his side away from her and for a long time in the darkness he tried to drive his thoughts away from envisioning Flavius Silva and himself as the two loneliest men in the world.

❖ ❖ ❖

WASH me . . . wash me carefully, dear Cornelius," Falco whimpered. "Wash the filthy hands of that monster from my throat . . . and my face, here too, where he touched me . . ."

Pomponius Falco lay outstretched on his couch, his hands manacled behind his back, his ankles fitted with heavy bronze clasps and connected with such a short length of chain he found it difficult to move more than a few paces. In his despair he had sought his couch, hoping its familiarity would ease his newborn fears, but his helplessness was only emphasized when he was obliged to ask Albinus if he would assist him in urinating.

"One does not realize how inaccurate one's aim is," he said looking down at the wetted carpet, "when one's hands are behind one's back. You know how fastidious I am about these things? Hold the pot higher, dear boy. There," he sighed. "Now wash me."

Earlier he had submitted with cold dignity to the muttered requests of the armorer, who asked him to move his arms and legs so he could fix the chains. He saw the shock of incredulity in the eyes of Cornelius and Albinus as they stood watching the process, and hoping to reassure them, said, "I am glad you can bear witness to this monstrous insult which, believe me, will be repaid a thousand times in the almost immediate future. You will soon have further entertainment. You will see a certain Roman General enter this tent on his knees—*literally* on his *knees*—and you will hear him plead with me not to breathe a word of this in Rome. You will witness him lament how it was all a dreadfully stupid mistake on his part—and you will hear him drown us in apologies. This I promise you!"

While the armorer worked silently about his ankles and wrists each blow of his hammer seemed to excite Falco

196

the more, until his whole body trembled and his voice
broke repeatedly as he addressed Cornelius and Albinus.

"Silva is *mad,* do you understand? *Mad!* Have you
noticed his eyes—or eye, one should say? His brain needs
an enema! Deranged! Hopelessly insane! Look what he is
doing to a friend of the Emperor! If you knew what *I*
know, then you could join me in anticipating the scene
when this same muscular oaf who now secures these
chains—have you noticed how well made he is, by the
way?—when this same man sweats to take them off again,
with Silva himself standing where you are and urging him
to hurry—*that* will be a show I assure you! An hour from
now, two hours at the most, and you will behold the
spectacle of a famous General literally dribbling spittle in
his anxiety to free me. Because he will want to know
where his Jewess is, and I am the only person in all
Palestine who knows! Our barely tamed Usipats who
presently keep her company have neither the wit nor the
language to communicate their whereabouts to anyone—
if, indeed, they had the slightest desire to do anything but
spend their time picking lice from each other. *I* alone
know where Silva's precious Jewess is! And I will now
express my gratitude to you, dear boys, for providing me
with such a sharp weapon. I shall not forget that it was
you who put what you saw and heard together—and you
particularly, dear Albinus—you knew something was un-
natural. You are to be complimented upon your powers of
deduction as well as observation. Then, let us recognize
the proper use of such information is one of my special
talents. And see the result? Ah? You may well inquire
how it is that I am being put in chains by this beautiful
oaf if I have employed my knowledge wisely? The truth is
our General is in a state of shock—thus his violent reactions, which he will so deeply regret. The madman in him
has become all the more irrational because of his lust for
this Oriental woman. Who but a maniac would choose a
female whelped in an Egyptian ghetto?

"Yet, never mind. You will soon have the extraordinary
pleasure of seeing him humiliated far more abjectly than
these simple chains can affect me. I have not yet devoted
my full imagination to his repayment for this absurd
situation. I have deliberately refrained from it, as one
might postpone the most delectable morsel on one's plate,
or an orgasm with a new-found boy. Yes, I will tease him

for a while, even seeming to forgive him if it suits my mood—toy with him until we can hear him panting in his anxiety. No matter how he denies it, I am the key to his life! I am the only person in the world who can rescue Silva's future and he knows it. I alone suspect his treachery, and I need only wait to prove it. But I will not think further on how he may best be rewarded until I can lie down in these chains and let their harsh surface torment the body you both so love—I will let them remind me how General Flavius Silva is a traitor to Rome."

When the armorer had finished and had taken his leave, Falco commanded Cornelius to oil his face and neck. He considered weeping to better impress Cornelius and Albinus with his suffering, but soon decided against it as contrary to his role as an ultimate victor. Now as he relaxed, his voice became increasingly melodious, and as he eyed his two attendants his smile became winsome and he seemed to purr.

"Dear Cornelius, dear Albinus, I cannot suitably express my appreciation of your love. We have been through so much together—perhaps I have been severe with you occasionally, but never have I thought to dismiss you from my household. Yes, Albinus. When we return to Rome and are received with approbation and honor, then we will do something specific about your bondage. I will make the necessary arrangements and within a reasonable time you will be free. Cornelius, dear boy, perhaps we should give a party to celebrate Albinus's manumission. Whom shall we invite? Perhaps we should already make plans for what we will serve, and what we should do for entertainment. It must be a party that will be the talk of Rome for years to come."

Cornelius ceased his rubbing away of the oil and stood back expectantly. He cocked his head curiously as Falco continued speaking, and soon, as if he wished to form an audience, Albinus came to stand beside him.

"Shall we have ram's vetches again? Shall we have goose liver and snails? Do you remember your Greek fables, how Tereus raped Procne's sister, Philomela, and cut out her tongue so she wouldn't tattle, but she wove the whole story into a tapestry? This gives me an idea. Why not teach Silva's slave, Epos, to draw—and let him in that fashion tell of his master's iniquities before a suitable assembly in Rome, and thus refute any claims of diligence

Silva might make? But let us not dwell on our mad General. Let us return to thoughts of our party. Shall we roast a tender Ambracian kid and mix the drippings into some exquisite sauce of our own invention? Shall we arrange to have some oysters brought down from Britain instead of the Lucrines, which are of course superb but which *everyone* seems to be offering these days? Perhaps we should call in some play actors, or perhaps watch a pantomime? No? Doesn't appeal to either of you? You are both so quiet. Jaded, I should say, and frightfully spoiled. Come now! I cannot stage a circus to rouse your enthusiasm, but wait—I know! I *know! This* might excite your horny little minds. Supposing we attempt something quite different for the occasion. Suppose we invite a woman, preferably one of high social rank, which should be no great problem since her husband would hardly suspect us—and let us previously inform this grand lady she has long been secretly adored by a famous man who will await introduction to her in our midst. Nothing, I assure you, appeals to females quite like clandestine yet safe romance. Now, after hints and suggestions to arouse her erotic desires, we will confide that her illustrious friend has concealed himself in the little room which is just off the dining area. Then we have two things working for us—a secret, which all women regardless of class cannot resist solving, and curiosity, which gets them into trouble from the time they are little girls. During these preparations we will fill her with wine until she is fit to burst, then send her off to her tryst.

"Now! We have been careful to describe her celebrated lover as somewhat hirsute. True enough—because he is an ape we will hire for the ocasion and whose potency we will guarantee by filling *him* with the most effective aphrodisiacal solution on the market. Now: it is dark in the room. Time passes as they wonder at each other's silence. Inevitably she must squat to relieve herself, and instantly— ho, ho—you know what the ape will do. And when she comes out of the room—picture her face! It is not even something she will dare tell her husband! Of course, who knows about women? She might enjoy herself—in which case the joke is on us."

Falco paused. His contemplation of future pleasures had allowed his thoughts to drift from the very immediate discomfort of his chains. He turned slightly on the couch and regarded Cornelius and Albinus with new interest. They had been so strangely silent, standing there staring at him, unmoving. They seemed almost removed from the tent, as if, he thought, they stood on a street in Rome watching the flow of traffic.

"What is the matter with you two?" he asked irritably. "Can't you see I am most uncomfortable? If I have the grace to divert our thoughts temporarily the least you could do is join in. Don't you want a party? Don't you understand what I have been saying about Silva and his need for me?"

He studied their faces, outlined against the dark top of the tent. They were looking down upon him, their eyes expressionless. In the yellow light their heads seemed to be carved of wax.

"What *is* ailing you two?" he insisted. "You look like a pair of statues. Are you by chance trying to imitate Damon and Pythias?"

Neither Cornelius nor Albinus replied. They simply glanced at each other and moved closer together.

Falco said, "I must look dreadful to you. Hold the mirror for me."

Albinus obeyed instinctively. In a moment he was kneeling before Falco, dutifully holding his mirror. Falco squirmed on the couch, trying for a more erect position to view his face. The lamp struck his head at such an angle it exaggerated the coarse surface of his cheeks and emphasized the new outbreaks of heat rash which had joined the older imperfections to create large unified blemishes. "Oh! . . ." he moaned. "Agh."

Albinus moved the mirror slightly. Falco strained to keep his image within view. "Hold still, you idiot!" He studied his face reflectively then bared his teeth and ran his tongue along his lips. "Cornelius. Bring the bowl, dear boy."

Like Albinus, Cornelius seemed to move in a trance. He went to the corner of the tent where they kept their immediate supplies and took up the heavy bowl that was filled with ass's milk and that now gave off such an odor he was obliged to hold his breathing. It was a wide-mouthed bowl of bronze, designed for facial bathing rather than as a container for the transport of liquid. Thus Cornelius moved very slowly and cautiously lest his progress across the tent cause the milk to slop in rhythm with his steps and spill over the lip of the bowl.

When he arrived at the couch without accident Falco smiled up at him. "Admirable! I shall not have to chastise you for clumsiness like the last few times you brought the milk, will I, dear boy? All of which proves that a lash well placed is well remembered."

He looked up at Cornelius and with his eyes bade him kneel. Normally he would have administered the milk to his face himself, but now he shook his head sadly. He glanced in the mirror to be certain his expression was sufficiently woeful and said, "Tonight it is you who will apply the milk, dear Cornelius. I am obviously quite unable at the moment, so I caution you to brush it on gently, particularly on those places where the skin appears most raw . . . I am very sensitive you know. Now bring the bowl closer to my face. My dear boy, don't you realize I can barely move?"

Cornelius bent down and held the bowl just below the level of Falco's chin. Then he lowered it slightly, and as if by silent agreement Albinus lowered the mirror.

"Now, dear boy, proceed. And mind you, gently."

Cornelius glanced at Albinus questioningly and seemed to find confirmation in his eyes. So he braced the bowl firmly against his leg and with his free hand seized Falco's hair. Then he pushed his head deep into the bowl and almost simultaneously Albinus swung down with his free hand and caught the back of Falco's neck. Together they held him until his violent struggles subsided and finally ceased. And all the time they were silent, for their eyes, meeting across the head bent between them, spoke of all they had to say.

At last, when they were convinced Pomponius Falco would never draw breath again, they washed the milk from his face and from those places where his struggling had caused it to spatter on his tunic and on the carpet. Then they stretched him on the couch in an attitude of repose and closed the lids of his eyes. Cornelius returned the bowl of milk to its usual place and Albinus removed the water and towels.

Together they studied Falco's face and were reassured suffocation left no marks. Then Albinus blew out one lamp and Cornelius pulled down the wick of the other until it was only a bead of light. He took Albinus's hand

and together they moved to their pallets near the entrance. They disrobed and lay down as they normally did as if to sleep, but their eyes were wide open when they reached for each other and they trembled with rapture when their mouths and bodies joined.

Six

INDICTIVUM
(AD QUOD PER PRAECONEM HOMINES EVOCABANTUR)

THE climb and descent of Masada and the long trek twice around its northern base had brought continuous shooting pain to Silva's bad leg. So to distract his thought he brooded upon what the Jew had said to him. "What you have done *to* the world . . . a wretched man who doubts the use of might . . ." It was absurd rubbish of course, but he had spoken with the same conviction displayed by the older Jew called Ezra. Then they really must believe what they were saying. And if so, Sheva was right. There was just not going to be any way her iron-headed people could be rescued from disaster.

Silva reluctantly decided the expedition had been a failure. By the gods it served a man right for trying to deal with an essentially barbaric people in a civilized fashion. Yet, think of Sheva. Perhaps that very barbaric influence was a part of her magic. There was ever a hoyden quality about her, as might be seen among the street urchins of Rome, who were so often also little savages. Because they fought for everything in life? She had the same limitless energy, her eyes took on the same luster when she pleased and she could put on a mask of

203

complete innocence or remove it as easily as a garment. You must constantly remind yourself Sheva is an Oriental —as much so as Eleazar ben Yair. There are depths within them you will never understand and you should waste no more time trying. Take Eleazar ben Yair as your antagonist and defeat him. Take Sheva as your woman and stop concerning yourself about the legal niceties of the union. Fill Praeneste with her and all she means to you. Lay in a cask or so of fruity Albanum for those ladies who must come to inspect her—if they drink enough of the stuff they will believe she is a vestal virgin. Sit back and thank the gods for sending you a Jewess named Sheva and be content you have once again found a woman you can love.

The mountains of Moab were fringed with scarlet and the whole of the eastern sky had become a soft coverlet of mauve when Silva and Geminus passed through the Praetorian gate.

Silva said, "I am weary. I cannot march like a soldier any more."

He wanted to say he was exhausted and his leg was giving him excruciating pain, but he could not bring himself to such a confession before Geminus. A Roman of the equestrian class is accursed, he reminded himself. He can never indulge in the balm of crying. "But we cannot rest as yet, Geminus. We have some nuisance business with Pomponius Falco. Go to his tent and bring him to me."

Geminus turned away and Silva continued up the street as the day crept up behind him. Just as he entered his tent the full sun struck the faces of his guards, seeming to cast their features in polished bronze. It was almost dark within the tent and it was a moment before his eyes adjusted to the feeble light. Then he saw waiting for him Timoleon the surgeon, and Albinus and Cornelius—and instantly he sensed something had gone wrong.

Timoleon bowed and mumbled his greeting. He is the only Greek I have ever known, Silva thought, whose Greek I find nearly incomprehensible. "Sire, I must bring sad news, he said. Your guest, Pomponius Falco, is dead. I was called to his tent at mid-watch and found him stricken beyond recall. A great Roman . . ."

Silva walked slowly to his chair and sat down heavily. He forced himself to concentrate on Timoleon's peculiarly difficult Greek while at the same time his mind churned with the need for immediate action. There was Falco's threat about rejoining his Germans by noon . . .

"When I arrived, Sire, partial rigor mortis had already set in and my first impression was that he might have suffered an attack of hydrophobia. I learned, however, the deceased had no record of the affliction, his worst being recurrent attacks of impetigo, some evidence of which was still apparent. For such troubles I normally prescribe a mixture of saffron, Lycium, verdigris, myrrh, and charcoal in equal proportions, boiled in raisin wine—"

"Come to the point, Timoleon. Why did he die?" Silva's voice was flat and hollow. His whole attention had turned to Albinus and Cornelius.

"I beg you, Sire, not to conclude I have lost my wits. Yet it is my diagnosis the man drowned."

"In the desert? You *are* mad."

"I use the term loosely, Sire. In this case suffocation is perhaps a more exact term. Under certain admittedly rare conditions it is possible for a person to suffocate, or drown, in his own phlegm. Perhaps that is what happened. I could be certain if permitted to make an autopsy—"

"Permission denied." Greek surgeons were always wanting to experiment. "Are you certain he was not murdered?"

"I am positive, Sire. There are no marks of violence about his body and no evidence of any struggle within the tent. However, I was puzzled at his being in chains."

"What about these two?" Silva frowned at Albinus and Cornelius.

"Since the deceased was restrained, he had requested they be alert to assist him during the night. They expected to be summoned, but after some hours no summons came, so they decided to investigate. On discovering the situation they found me out at once and begged me to make all haste, which I did. Even so, it was obvious the deceased had left this life some hours previously."

Now Silva turned on Albinus and Cornelius. His voice was tense with anxiety. "Tell me one thing, for your lives. Where are the Usipats and the woman?"

There was a long silence, then Cornelius ventured to speak. "We were not told, Sire. That is the truth."

"Would a hot iron make you see the truth more clearly?" Silva watched their faces carefully. If Falco's threat was to be believed, there was not time to squander on such business—and usually information obtained under use of the iron was the truth of convenience. Here, even the time to prove a lie was not to be spared, for there remained little more than five hours until noon. "Tell me," he said as quietly as he could manage. "Tell me all you know at once and you will be rewarded by a quick and safe trip home. Otherwise you will never reach it."

He saw Albinus glance fearfully at Cornelius, then he said, "We were not told, Sire. We were advised to pack in anticipation of leaving this morning. I would suppose our escort might be somewhere along the road waiting for us. Believe me, Sire, I beg you. That is *all* we know."

Silva rubbed at his weary eyes. *Think,* he warned himself. Think, though your mind begs for rest. Consider this as you would a military situation. Falco would have been in haste to reach the more comfortable climates of Jerusalem and then the seacoast. Certainly, then, he would not have departed to the south along a difficult route which led only through interminable desert to the Arabian Gulf. Therefore somewhere in the wilderness to the north were a handful of savages—and Sheva. In that region there were innumerable places of concealment. No time to explore them all. Therefore somehow the quarry must be made to show themselves.

For a long moment he stared thoughtfully at Albinus and Cornelius. Then suddenly he raised his voice and shouted for Attius, his aide. The young Tribune appeared almost instantly.

"Attius, you will do the following with the utmost dispatch. Call Rubrius Gallus from his ramp. I have an urgent engineering problem for him. Tell him to hurry here. Have the Centurion Lupercus Clemens find a Jew who at least vaguely resembles Eleazar ben Yair and put him in mobile chains. Advise the Centurion Geminus he may redeem himself by killing some Germans. And now send someone to take these two fawns out of my sight."

He nodded in acknowledgment of Attius's salute, then turned to Timoleon. "Doctor, you stay here. We may require certain technical advice. And while you wait try to think of some potion that will restore my energies."

Soon after the trumpet notes announced the beginning of another Hebrew day Eleazar ben Yair broke his fast with a single meal cake and a handful of dried figs. As usual he regretted his inability to wash properly, and he thought ruefully how many mornings it had been since anyone on Masada had seen soap. All attempts to discover some substitute form of mineral alkali had failed. Washing in plain water did little to remove the red dust stains of Masada.

He went directly to the synagogue where the council was assembling according to now-long-established custom. It had also become custom, although not a requirement, for each man to mount the parapet at the western end of the synagogue, from which vantage point they could look almost directly down upon the Romans. By raising their eyes slightly they could also observe the activities about Silva's personal camp. Instinctively, on viewing the progress of the ramp and the ever-impressive military spectacle below, each man would thoughtfully stroke his beard and make his own estimation of future events. They remained fascinated spectators while they automatically wrapped phylacteries about their left arms in the direction of their hearts and waited for Hillel to call them to prayer.

Eleazar viewed most synagogue ceremonies with impatience. If most of the able-bodied men on Masada were going to stand about and commune with God for so long each day, then why not devote more attention to the prayers created by the Hebrew poets? What greater beauty would be found in any language! Yet since the siege of Masada began he had never been able to give his complete ear to them. Always there was the grating distraction of the ramp building, a constant and harsh offense to the verbal magic of the prayers. Always there was his preoccupation with an enemy who never seemed to sleep, and Hillel's constant hammering at morals and the law. As he pointed behind his pulpit at the "Ark" where the rolls of the law were deposited, his eyes took on the same flaming intensity as the ever-burning lamp. "O, I say to you, five things Canaan taught his descendants! Love one another, love robbery, love licentiousness, hate your master, and do not speak the truth!"

The priests live in their own world, Eleazar thought. They refuse to recognize we are marooned in the desert, losing the fight for our lives.

On this morning he became more than ever impatient with Hillel's lengthy prayer because he knew the time had come at last when a terrible choice must be made. Now, for the first time, he was actually grateful for the existence of the council. At least now the choice would not be his alone. The men with whom he had argued so frequently and had as often cursed for obstinacy or refusal to accept his dictates without question seemed on this morning to be good men, trying as best they could to surmount the impossible and govern the unmanageable. Two were absent, the irreplaceable Ezra and the flabby Zidon. But Alexas was still present, although strangely subdued. The "slippery one," with his highly developed instincts of self-preservation, must sense the final encounter was near. And there was the normally fierce Esau, who had rushed through his marriage to the Essene girl and had ever since seemed in a trance. Hopefully he would recover in time to face the Romans as he always had. There were still the stalwarts, Javan and Kittim, sons of Tema, there was huge Asshur, son of Joktan, and scrawny, buck-toothed Nimrod, son of Abram. And there was Heth, son of Ezra, a strikingly handsome man who had been appointed in his father's place. Another replacement elected to the council over Eleazar's strong objections was Matthias, son of Jeshua. He had been appointed to take Zidon's place and unfortunately not only resembled him physically, being weak of eye and spirit, but was also possessed of Zidon's whining manner and fearful approach to all matters.

Now, with the morning sun shafting through the entrance and splashing on their backs, these men were led by Hillel in praise of God. And because it was one of the days decreed by Ezra and Nehemiah for special devotions, he read from the Torah. Afterward the Mishna was spoken by Shimeon ben Yoezer, a gaunt black-skinned Idumaean whose posturing and hollow profundities exasperated Eleazar.

He tried to persuade himself all of this was good for the spirits of those on Masada, but another voice persisted in reminding him that soldiers of the Tenth Legion had not troubled to read the five books of Moses.

At last when religious tradition had been satisfied Eleazar was able to stand before the assembly and tell them of his meeting with Flavius Silva. "What we desperately require now," he warned them, "is a Joshua—a man who can command the sun to stop. Yet perhaps a near-miracle is at hand, if I have not the perception to recognize it. You must understand Silva made no promises. If we go down to the Romans we will be their slaves, and it is as simple as that. Is that a miracle?"

Alexas's deep voice rumbled from far in the rear of the synagogue. "If we tell our people of Silva's offer then we will stand alone upon Masada."

Nimrod said quietly, "We must tell them. To keep such a matter to ourselves would be unforgivable."

Esau challenged him. "Why? Once the people know there is a hope for life they will say it is better to breathe a foul odor rather than not to breathe at all. We will never stop them."

"Perhaps," interrupted Matthias, "we should now seriously consider going down to Silva, but make it an action led by us for the benefit of all—"

"If we were not in the synagogue I would give thee the word for such drivel," Esau snarled.

"I say, tell them nothing!" Asshur shouted.

Javan stood beside him and said, "The Romans are not here yet. I am going to fight them if I have to stay here alone!"

Eleazar held up his hands, clapping them above his head to gain attention. It was always so, he remembered. If ten Jews convened for any purpose whatever, there were ten different opinions each much cherished by its originator. "By tomorrow morning the Romans will be knocking at our gate. We must make a choice. We may keep Silva's visit our secret and hope none of us talks in our sleep. Or we may lie to our people and say the Romans have sworn to kill every man, woman and child regardless of his usefulness. With nothing to lose then

perhaps they will put up a fight. Or we may deceive our
people deliberately, hoping to arouse their fighting spirit.
We can promise them that if they throw back the Romans
the way will be open for our escape to easier lands beyond
Judea."

Eleazar hesitated. He had thought on this morning to
expose his darkest thoughts before the council. He would
lay them out one by one, pulling them from his tortured
brain like knives long impaled, and he would say, "Here
are the thoughts which have haunted me and which so far
I have not found the courage to announce. Help me to
emerge from this lonely darkness, help me, for you are my
brothers."

On this morning with the sounds from the ramp crashing upon his thoughts, he could not bring the words he
wanted to his lips. He saw only a sea of questioning eyes
before him—Alexas, the slippery one, Esau the Sicarius,
Javan and Kittim, glowering Asshur, uncertain Nimrod,
and Heth and Matthias and Hillel also. Their eyes were
saying, "Lead us!" and he was faltering while the morning
sun spewed radiance all through the synagogue. And he
was suddenly dumb for the first time in his life, he who
had ever before been in such complete command of his
tongue. He who was Eleazar ben Yair of Galilee was
barely able to make a sound.

"Tell us what *you* think we should do," Heth was
saying, and he could only shake his head instead of reply-
ing, and when Hillel said, "We must put our trust in God
our savior," he could not even find words to object. Just at
this moment, with the voices of the council echoing all
about him, he could only visualize the faces of Miriam
and Reuben and how their eyes might appeal to him if he
did what he thought was right.

He saw their eyes and he saw the wrinkled, pock-
marked face of old Abigail.

After his morning inspection of the casemates and towers, he made his way to Abigail although he was not at all
sure he was prepared to withstand an inspection by her
black eyes.

He found her squatting as usual in her black robe, and
the smoke from her oven so enveloped her figure she
seemed to be perched on a blue cloud. "Why have you
come to me, great man?" she rasped. "Why, suddenly, do

you bother coming to see this old crone you remember only at your convenience? Your conscience is troubling you? Or have you simply decided to peek in and see if the old spider is dead and if so how does the carcass smell?

"Eleazar, the great one!" she cackled. "What a fine trap you have fashioned for your people! Moses led us out of the wilderness and you lead us into it! And more cleverly, you have placed us on top of a mountain from which there is no escape. Tell me, great one, you who are a fisherman with the arrogance of a king—and I know you were a better fisherman than a soldier or you would long ago have starved to death—tell me, you who are so clumsy at guile, tell this old woman how many shekels the Romans paid you to bring us here. Tell me this so that at least when I die it will not be from curiosity."

Eleazar smiled and squatted beside her. "My ears inform me you are in fine spirit for an old hag this morning, but my eyes reveal nothing through this wall of smoke. You are not cooking. Why not douse the fire?"

"It warms my bones, boy, bones that have caged the passions of better men than you will ever be."

"There is no need to recite your record of copulations. It is as legendary as your sweet and gentle nature. And I am so struck by your ravishing beauty on this morning it is difficult for me to believe you are only ninety-eight years old."

"I have also been insulted by better men than you will ever be. I have not yet reached seventy, and under the protection of such as yourself, never expect to. I sit here all day and ask myself whatever happened to the *brave* Jews? Were they all lost at Jerusalem? Are those still sucking on their mother's tits inheriting your meekness? Bah! The Jewish men are all dead. You baboons who have survived are Egyptians in disguise. Now, what have you come here to cry about?"

Eleazar coughed and fanned the smoke away from his face. "I am in grave trouble, Abigail."

"Humph! This is new?" She spat at the sand between her feet. "I am not your mother, so stay out of my womb."

"I will now tell you, although I dare not admit it elsewhere: I do not believe we can defeat the Romans."

"A man who locks defeat in his thoughts by night is doomed by morning."

"If he is a leader, does he have any right to admit his despair to his people? Or is it his duty? Should he stand down from his office and make way for a more resolute man even when he knows the situation is hopeless, or should he carry on to the very end? I came here to seek your opinions on these matters, worthless though they might be. I came here because I have nothing else to do and wished to give company to the aged, lewd old hags though they may be. I came for no other reason, but I would not object if I heard your silken voice soothing my worries and removing these thorns from my conscience."

"What you name your conscience is more likely your foolish pride. What benefit would there be if you told our people the truth? They neither expect nor appreciate truth from leaders. Does it do any good to tell a man who is going to die that he is going to die? If he already knows it he is only embarrassed watching you suffer in the telling, and if he does not know it then you are the robber of all his final joys and the murderer of his hopes."

"If I tell them then they will go down to the Romans and survive."

"Are you sure? And if you forsake them as their leader, who would take your place? Esau? That conniving lecher would be seducing someone's daughter while the Romans stormed the gates. Alexas? He would make an exchange with Silva—the people of Masada for his own freedom. Asshur? He is even more stupid than you, and as for the rest of your confederates, they are not worth—"

She grunted and spat into the sand again and her lids descended to hood her eyes until they were nearly invisible.

"Do not pretend you are dozing, old hag. Your silence hums like a beehive."

"I am thinking of a Roman defeat and wondering if Galilean trash such as yourself could be capable of achieving it. I am meditating on the possibility of your inspiring the people of Masada to a deed far beyond the abilities of ordinary mortals. You must call upon your eloquent tongue to inspire them as never before. You must convince them that they must greet the Romans from beyond the river of silence."

Eleazar tried to smile. "I should know that if I waste my morning fishing for counsel among old women my only catch would be senile evasions."

Abigail reached out her tiny hand which was so like the

claw of a bird, and touched his arm. "The Romans thirst for our blood," she whispered. "Let us deny them. If we have remaining so much as a vial of courage, then it will be our victory."

❖ ❖ ❖

BY now the hills of Moab were wriggling in the scorching air and in places along the distant horizon the same hills were sliced through with sheets of undulating water and others floated on their summits halfway between earth and sun. Sheva watched the sun with growing concern, for the words of Pomponius Falco still rang in her ears: "I anticipate a reunion no later than noon tomorrow. Until then you are my guarantee of liberation, and when we meet in good spirits you shall have yours. You have thus far been very sensible, so I ask you to remember the men entrusted with your care are savages. Since they are rather childish I must caution you not to tease them."

Long before dawn they had come to this narrow wadi in the Judean slope which tumbled down to the Dead Sea. The broken rim of the wadi blocked all view to the south except the top half of Masada itself. But to the north it was possible to observe a continuation of an elevated mirage which she knew must reflect the oasis of Ein Gedi. Directly down the wadi, fringing the shore of the sea, was the supply route between fertile Palestine and the Roman forces at Masada. Two long caravans had already passed, bound south for the camps, and the yellow dust from the last still hung in the air.

Three of the Germans were sprawled behind a great rock which had given them protection from the earlier sun. Now with it full upon them they still slept and snored mightily. The others squatted immobile except when they moved to scratch at their hairy bodies.

She was certain they would not remain much longer in the wadi since they had brought neither food nor water, and she was convinced her own thirst must match that of one German, who reminded her of a great ape she had once seen displayed in the Alexandrian market. He had become restless and climbed to the lip of the wadi and now lay on his belly looking down upon the road. The air was so still she could hear the rattle of stones as he occasionally shifted his weight.

To ease her increasing fear she imagined herself with Flavius Silva. You unspeakable slut, he would say. It was not to save your family but your own precious skin that you consented to lie with a Roman. Were you afraid Falco would damage your Semitic beauty or your chicken heart when you betrayed the man who offered you his life? Tell me, dear General, do you seriously believe your friends in Rome would let you push me down their aristocratic throats? They would see what you refuse to see, and say not only is she a Jewess but a craven adventuress and obviously for sale. What would you do, dear General, if you sired a half-Jewish, half-Roman son? You will be known as the conqueror of Masada. Would you send your son here to see where his father killed so many Jews—and where his mother lay in your arms while thousands of her people died? Better to invent some story of a Roman mother so he may march up and down in style.

She closed her eyes and whispered, "Let him hate me, God. Make him drive me away."

She heard a rattle of stones and looked up to see the German sliding down from the crest of the wadi. He roused the others and two of them came to her. They seemed troubled when she quickly retreated from their extended hands, then pleased when she cautiously returned. They pointed anxiously down the wadi, seeming to urge her with their strange gutturals. Then she understood, for a small caravan was moving along the road bound away from Masada.

One of the Germans tried to push her forward. She swung her arm to knock him away. If Pomponius Falco had come to collect his liberation ticket, she resolved, there was no reason to make it any easier for him.

When she saw the caravan stop she slowed her descent until she actually sauntered down the wadi. As she approached, with the Germans moving protectively about her, she was shocked to recognize Eleazar ben Yair as part of the caravan. He was on foot and in chains, and she thought, Adonoi! Now I have committed the ultimate betrayal!

She saw Pomponius Falco mounted on a horse at the

head of the procession. He was supported on both sides by his two pretty boys. Was he drunk? Behind Eleazar were two cavalrymen and behind them more than a score of Jews on foot. They were harnessed to a heavy supply wagon. A single cavalryman rode at the tail of the procession.

She looked to the south toward the looming bulk of Masada. There was no dust cloud of another procession. Nothing but empty desert. So, General? You have finally decided you have had enough of your Jewess.

She lingered while the thirsty Usipats quickened their pace and drew farther ahead of her. They waved at Falco but made straight for the supply wagon.

Suddenly she halted. Thirst and the heat had certainly affected her sight. For she saw the caravan seem to scatter as if it were a great animal coming apart. The cavalrymen left the line and circled behind the approaching Usipats. Then the Jews at the wagon threw off their harnesses. She saw the flash of metal in the sunlight as they threw themselves upon the astonished Germans. Before these had a chance to draw their weapons a cluster of Legionaries leaped from the wagon itself and also fell upon them. There were a few moments of hoarse shouting mixed with the heavy sound of bodies locked in combat. Then the desert became silent again.

Finally a man came running toward her, and though he wore the garments of a Jew she recognized him as the Centurion Geminus.

He stopped, and offering his great hand growled, "I hope you are as good for him as you are trouble to me."

When he led her to the supply wagon she saw that Falco's eyes were closed and that he was supported on the horse by a cage fashioned of narrow metal bars. The structure was held together by leather thongs and supple enough for his arms to respond to the movement of the horse. Glancing up at him, Geminus said, "In my opinion he looks better dead than he did alive."

Before the Legionaries had pulled Falco from the horse and dumped his body in the wagon the buzzards had already swooped down upon the fallen Germans.

When he had been assured Sheva was safely returned to her tent Flavius Silva at last surrendered to his weariness and slept. It was evening before he awakened again and reluctantly decided against calling for the Jewess. Instead he summoned certain of his officers and, as if they were totally unaware of the fact, solemnly announced the death of Pomponius Falco. "Of course we are distressed such a distinguished Roman departed life while our guest. It therefore behooves us to honor him in a style appropriate to an envoy of Vespasian. The funeral will be at tomorrow's evening watch. I depend on each of you in your various departments to make suitable preparations."

Thus on the following day when the flaming sun had submerged behind the western hills and a soft blue twilight enwrapped the desert, Flavius Silva stood bareheaded watching the smoke rise from an enormous funeral pyre. All of his staff wore their finest armor and were assmbled behind him. On his left hand stood his lictors with their fasces wreathed in laurels and on his right his standard bearers.

Silva was pleased with the preparations and had so expressed himself to those officers responsible. Special couriers had been dispatched to bring flowers from the oasis of Ein Gedi and a cavalryman on the fastest horse had ridden night and day to bring a traditional sprig of cypress from Joppa. Suitable wood for the pyre had been a problem until Rubrius Gallus, who had appeared dutifully surprised to learn of Falco's passing, suggested breaking up the ballistas which could not be used against Masada. Ordinarily those torsion machines would have been employed along with the rest of the Tenth's material quota to shower the enemy with short javelins and bolts, but the desert atmosphere had somehow caused their specially treated ropes to deteriorate and lose all elasticity. Attempts had been made to substitute horsehair, and even the sinews of animals, without success. The Legion's normal battery of sixty had been reduced to only twenty-four serviceable machines. Silva had agreed to their destruction, commenting only that he was glad they were not fighting on a Gaullic plain or British moor, where ballistas were indispensable.

Lack of perfumes and spices to sweeten the funeral fire had also presented a vexing problem, but the ever-resourceful Ummidus Fabatus, after a great deal of sighing, had finally discovered a small supply of incense, myrrh and cassia available among the Nabatean tradesmen.

All of this had been carefully recorded by Silva's scribe, who had also been instructed to report meticulously on the ensuing ceremonies. The completed history was to be presented to all who remained of Falco's party, Cornelius Tertullus and the slave known as Albinus. They were to deliver the manuscript to Rome along with their firsthand account of how the Usipats had been ambushed by a marauding band of Jews.

Silva had looked Rubrius Gallus straight in the eye and said his melancholy was such at the loss of his distinguished guest he did not feel up to delivering a eulogy. Would good friend Gallus mind? Gallus had declined with equal solemnity, explaining that he had been so preoccupied with the ramp he had been unable to become better acquainted with Vespasian's envoy and feared to do his ghost injustice. It was therefore agreed to dispense with a eulogy and instead Silva would personally place a coin on Falco's lips for Charon. He chose a shekel depicting the head of Vespasian on the face and Judea conquered on the reverse.

All of this was recorded.

As the flames crackled upward along the pyre and began to lick at the splendid couch which supported Falco's body, Silva was pleased to see the ceremonies commence according to the law of the Twelve Tables.

There were the prescribed number of flute players in attendance, no mean feat, Silva mused, since there were not enough flute players in the entire Legion to make up the required complement of ten. His orders had been, "Let those who are the musicians make the noise. Find other men to stand there with flutes to their mouths and have them go through the motions."

Tradition also demanded that everything that had been agreeable to the deceased should be provided and cremated with him for use in the next world. Silva had gravely inquired if either Albinus or Cornelius would care to join the ghost on the pyre. And he had pretended to be surprised when they declined.

Watching now as darkness slipped over the desert he glanced over his shoulder and saw that even the Jews were impressed with such a grand funeral. Good. The cessation of work on the ramp would not be entirely time wasted. Now, in accordance with his orders, two cohorts were parading the regulation three times around the pyre from right to left with their ensigns inverted and striking their weapons against each other—all as if Pomponius Falco had been a most illustrious commander.

For a moment Silva was intrigued with the brief panto-mime occurring a few paces down the slope from him. There Cornelius Tertullus and Albinus stood side by side. As the flames rose and obscured the couch he saw they were holding hands. He found it difficult to hold back a smile when he suddenly remembered something Falco had said about duplicity being everywhere about.

When finally the parade had finished he raised his hand in salute to the pyre. And he whispered in Latin, "Fare-well P. F. As you also quite recently remarked, no one of any sophistication believes in gloria patria any longer."

Once again Flavius Silva lay watching the dawn present itself in the form of a crescent at the peak of his tent. He would not have the gap taken up now, for he had become strangely fond of it as if the imperfection was a needed factor in this marvelous and private world into which he had again retreated. Here was Sheva at his side, and for the first time he was convinced she had given herself to him without even a hint of reserve. Now with the first of day he yearned to make some offering to the gods for the gift of this woman. I have merely to consider touching her, he thought, and I am roused. But she is more than that—without words her lips confide more love and life to me than I have ever known. Even lying side by side with all our passion spent we are still as one. We are life, and I have been so long in the business of death I am even a little afraid of this that is between us. Is it too fragile to survive? Am I capable of handling it without breaking it? Little Jewess of the marvelously smooth and amber body, little Jewess who could not kill this troubled soldier, help me to comprehend your magic so I can give myself utterly to our future. You must not want for one thing in this world within my power to give you.

He heard her moan gently, then stretch, and though her eyes were still closed he heard her ask, "What are you staring at, General?"

"How do you know I am looking at anything? Your eyes are closed."

She was silent, then she said very slowly, "I see you

from within me. Sometimes I think I would know what you were doing though you were a mile away."

"I am staring at the gap over our heads. I am not going to have it fixed as I first intended."

"Why not?"

"I do not know why not. I just like it. It announces the arrival of a new day quite as silently but just as forcefully as my conviction we must spend the rest of our lives together. To do otherwise would be a criminal insult to the gods."

"God."

"As you please."

"What was the name of your wife? I have forgotten."

"How can you possibly change from one subject to another so instantaneously?"

"I am a woman."

"Is that an excuse or an explanation? Her name was Livia."

"Were you in love with her?"

"Yes. Profoundly . . . but it was not the same."

"The same as now?"

"Yes. There has never been anyone like you in my life. I cannot conceive of duplicating this sense of perfect union with any other woman. It is—"

"Liar."

He raised himself on one elbow so he could look down at her. "Just what prompts you to say that?"

"All Romans are liars. In your sleep you called out the name Ummidia. Who was she?"

Silva hesitated. He was amused at the ease with which she had accused him and more so at his own pleasure in acceptance. The time has come at last, he thought. I am obviously ready to be domesticated.

"Ummidia was my concubine—unfortunately not a very happy one."

"Why?"

"I do not care to discuss the why. I only wish she could see me now."

"Did you not love her as you did your wife?"

"No."

"Then what was wrong with Ummidia?"

"Nothing was really wrong with Ummidia. She tried and I tried. The fact we were drawn to each other made no difference. Now let us discuss other matters."

"I do not care to discuss other matters. I want to discuss what was wrong with Ummidia."

"Why, suddenly, should she be so important?"

"Because Ummidia and Livia and Sheva are all related. If I should bear your child they would be aunts."

"Your reasoning leaves me utterly confused. Livia was of a patrician family, very Roman, very quiet and studious. Ummidia was rather plump, a devoted gourmet, and of an exceedingly understanding and mellow nature. The contrast between all three of you is indescribable. Where could there be any possible relation?"

He saw the corners of her mouth quiver in the beginning of a smile and her eyes became mischievous. "Right here," she said, reaching for him. "Here is our Uncle Flavius—uncircumcised but still charming."

Laughing, he rolled upon her and silenced her mouth with his own.

The gap at the peak had become a white-hot crescent of light when they lay quietly again. And Sheva said to him, her breathing still hurried, "Beloved liar, you exhaust me. I have no longer the strength to hate you."

"Then Rome progresses."

"Do you still propose to take me there? I am afraid of it. I am afraid I will not transplant well. Once you are surrounded by all that is familiar to you, I will not look the same."

"If you insist on staying in Palestine, I suppose it could be arranged. I will speak to the Procurator—an acquaintance of mine named Silva. He's rather a clod in many ways, but he tries to be reasonable."

"What is he going to do to the Jews on Masada?"

He noticed a distinct change in her voice and she seemed to draw away from him without actually moving.

"I do not know what he is going to do with them since they stubbornly refuse any compromise. I am afraid the matter is out of his hands now."

"Why? Has he lost his command?"

"He most certainly will if he fails to take Masada. And it is now plain the Jews are not going to give it to him."

"So those on the mountain must die."

"We are not there yet."

"How can I live with myself, how can I live with you after—"

"May I point out that you are not solely and personally

responsible for the woes of the Jews? Nor am I charged with the major policies of the Roman Empire. We are two people . . . nothing more. Everything is right for us. This is the month of April so we are under the protection of Venus. Some people even make sacrifice to the Isis of Pharus, which is in your very own Alexandria. We should accept what the gods give us. We can argue about whether it was too much or too little when we are dead."

"Eleazar ben Yair was right. He said I was a disgrace to the Jewish nation."

"As usual, he twists the facts. There is no Jewish nation."

Suddenly he stiffened and half-rose on the couch. Here was the all-pervading quiet again and it was not the meal hour. Work on the ramp had ceased.

He waited, cocking his head as if to hear better. And still there was no resumption of the general noise. He glanced up at the gap in the tent and then at the entrance. He listened alertly. The guards were engaged in an argument, apparently with a stranger. He heard one of them insisting the General was not to be disturbed.

He sat up in bed and called out to them, "What is all that racket out there? Hold it down!"

Then he heard the familiar voice of Paternus. "Sire! A messenger has come from the Tribune Rubrius Gallus. He wishes to report the ramp is ready!"

Seven

MARS, RAMPANT . . .

THE tribune Metilius Nepos was the first officer to be summoned to Silva's tent. He arrived at midmorning to report all weapons and machines ready to move. Nepos had hardly expected to find his General still lingering over his bath, but he noticed at once how markedly his zest for all things seemed to have been restored.

"You have enjoyed a good night's sleep for a change, Sire?"

"Splendid, thank you, Nepos. I could easily delude myself I am a youth again."

Later Nepos was pleased to confide in his fellow officers how their General had indeed returned to high spirits and intended to consult the auspices this very noon. And knowing of the Jewess, all of them were secretly grateful to her.

Word of impending action passed swiftly through all the camps and was confirmed when Silva appeared in full battle regalia and marched briskly along the Principia to the Tribunal, where the priests and his staff had been advised to wait upon him. While most Generals normally took the auspices in the relative privacy of the Praetorium, where the ceremonies were witnessed only by their officers and personal guards, Silva believed in opening the ceremonies to all ranks, thus partly compensating for his refusal to make a formal harangue before battle.

As he strode resolutely along the broad Principia, Silva sensed a renewal of himself. It came in part, he thought, from this new sense of completeness which last night with Sheva had created. Now it was augmented by the continuously rising acclaim of his Legionaries. As he passed before them their voices were at first very few and the men seemed to call his name without enthusiasm, but by the time he approached the Tribunal the hoarse cries of greeting and pleas for immediate action became an overwhelming confirmation of his original popularity.

He heard his name shouted thousands of times, the very repetition of it serving as a mighty cadence for his steps. "Sil*va!* Sil*va!* Sil*va!*" Always the last syllable was heavily accented so that it could be sharply terminated and the tempo increased.

Word of Silva's solitary parade spread quickly through the camp and at the sight of his trim figure arrayed in his finest battle armor, and with the swing of his scarlet-lined cape seeming to emphasize his limp, few men could resist cheering. Here in the hottest part of the day, when a man's breath was like sucking fire, marched their commander, as splendid and as full of vigor as if he were advancing on Rome itself. The tilt of his head spoke of great events about to unfold and the confident way he raised his hand again and again to greet nearly every face turned his way left few Legionaries unmoved. They picked up their shields and beat upon them with the hilts of their swords, falling into a steady rhythm to match their gruff shouts and singing.

As the uproar increased so did Silva's sense of fulfillment. Now, he thought, *now* was the time for successful conquest no matter what the auspices foretold! Thunder on the left is a good omen? Very well, here is thunder to shake the wall of the desert, and it can always be kept on the left if a man simply turns to his right.

The great noise from the Legionaries rolled down the incline, splashed over the eastern wall of the camp, fell down into the wadi, and rose to explode like a series of waves against the awesome façade of Masada. Here amid the shouting, Silva thought, was the ultimate right. Here once more was might and right. Here, in spite of arguments voiced by a wretched Jew, was Rome civilizing the world.

Silva paused before the steps of the Tribunal and made a show of staring up at the mountain. Then to the delight of all who could observe him, he smiled and raised his fist toward the ramparts. The gesture released a tremendous shout as he mounted the Tribunal.

Silva studied the faces of his officers and became all the more certain this was a moment of triumph. And why not, he reasoned. Here was veteran soldier Flavius Silva, Roman patrician and General of the Armies, returned to the fold. Here was home. Here were men who knew his family history and his personal history. Here were comrades in arms who would follow him to the ends of the earth.

He handed his helmet to Attius and greeted each officer with a separate display of affection. "Arvianus . . . is all ready in communications? Liberalius . . . have the other camps been notified? Dear Rubrius Gallus . . . what will you do with yourself now your ramp is complete? Read a few of my books, perhaps? Clemens . . . I venture to say your disciplinary problems will cease as of this night. . . . Fabatus, dear fretting friend, how will you account for our abundance once we take over what the Jews have hoarded?"

He greeted the priests with less spirit. There were five of them, now wearing their embroidered tunics bound with brazen belts and their high conical caps. These were the priests dedicated to Mars, so each wore a ceremonial sword, held a short spear in his right hand, a shield in his left. Silva had always been ill at ease when priests were officiating. They sense my doubts, he thought. They are endowed with one power and that is to see inside a man, and looking through me they discover a skeptic. I make some priests lose their appetites, which is the most grievous wound they will ever suffer.

Silva was amused because for once it was the priests who seemed uncomfortable as he watched their anxious preparations. Apparently word of the ramp's completion and his decision to take the auspices had been late in reaching them, or some other factor had gone awry. The high priest, an unfortunate man in Silva's opinion because he was afflicted with a stutter as well as a lisp, now became nearly unintelligible as he ordered the brazen tripod which was sacred to Apollo placed at a certain distance from the altar. He fussed about frantically when his aides could not succeed in promptly lighting the fire, and finally the ancient goat chosen for sacrifice refused to mount the Tribunal of his own will, which was in itself a bad omen. During the confusion Silva held animated conversations with his officers and frequently smiled and waved at the ever-increasing number of Legionaries gathered to witness the ceremony. Watching the priests struggle with the goat, Silva confided to Rubrius Gallus, "The priests may consider it a bad omen, but I consider that fellow simply a smart draft-evader. He has not the slightest desire to do his bit for a Roman victory." Silva exuded so much confidence both officers and those Legionaries who had pressed close enough to hear him laughed easily.

At last when all was reasonably satisfactory to the high priest he began to sing the verses called *Axamento* in a style of Latin so archaic no one could understand him. "I doubt if he understands it himself," Silva muttered. He was ready for battle now. He knew he would conquer, and all of this was simply marking time.

When he had done with his vocalizing the high priest recommended the Auguratorium be opened. It was a huge wooden cage which had been transported across the desert, Silva remembered, at considerable cost and effort.

Within the cage were some half a hundred birds collected from whatever sources the priests had been able to discover in Palestine and were of every variety from swallow to sea gull. Silva had known commanders who, believing everything the priests said, had been either vastly encouraged or hopelessly depressed by the behavior of the birds after their release. If the priests proclaimed the birds should fly south and they flew north, then the auguries were unfavorable.

"Woe to him who defies the auguries!" the priest cried as they opened the cage.

To Silva's open amusement the birds flew in all directions and some even refused to leave the cage. One squealing sea gull knocked off a priest's cap in passing and Silva clapped his hand over his mouth to hide his laughter. This is very *good,* he thought. This time before battle I became more alive than at any other time! No, it is not the same now. I am not as much alive as I am with Sheva at my side.

In spite of the birds' erratic behavior the high priest advised Silva that he was pleased. He called attention to the goat, which was standing before the altar without restraint, and he pronounced his submission as a very good omen. When Silva nodded and told him to proceed with the Libatio, the priest crumbled a salted bran cake above the goat's head, and after tasting a mixture of frankincense and wine himself, poured it between the animal's horns. Next he plucked the highest hairs between the horns and threw them into the fire with a gesture Silva considered altogether too grandiose for the occasion. At once another priest struck the goat with a heavy maul and asked, "Agone?"

And the high priest answered, "Hoc age." Then all the priests stabbed the beast with their knives and caught the blood in goblets. They poured the blood on the altar and since the goat was obviously not fit to eat, Silva readily agreed to their proceeding with Holocaustum so the entire carcass could be consumed by the fire.

Only the liver was saved, and Silva stood patiently while the priests made a great business of examining it. They cut the liver into two parts, the Familiaris, which would indicate forthcoming events for the Legion, and the Hostilis, which would denote the destiny of the enemy. Silva watched while they sought the protuberances at the ends of the blood vessels called Caputs, and he knew that a liver in which such lobes might not be observed could be a very bad omen.

While he waited for the verdict Silva raised his head and watched a buzzard circling against the blazing sky. There, he thought, is an omen I can understand and believe.

Staring at the ramp Silva found it difficult to believe he had been responsible for its creation. Now, cleared of workers, machinery, animals and tools, it appeared of much vaster proportions, the total effect being so stunning it seemed a capricious outgrowth of nature rather than a purposeful creation of man. It rose as an enormous shoulder supporting the body of Masada. It stood as a blinding white monument in the sun, and Silva found it necessary to openly express his awe. "Our friend Gallus," he solemnly told his staff, "has dared to affix his own nose to the face of the earth."

Even as he had earlier regarded a buzzard, Silva now watched the sun, for its rate of descent during the afternoon was of the utmost importance, and he was pleased to see it coincide with his program as exactly as if he had command of it.

Since every detail of the final assault had been discussed for months there had been no need for a formal staff meeting after the priests had finished their rites. Silva had simply looked away from the buzzard and declared, "We will now take the mountain from the Jew"—and that had been the end of it.

At once all of Roman order came into evidence as the carefully groomed military machine bestirred itself. In a matter of minutes mounted couriers' were sent off to the eastern camps and to the southernmost camp with orders to send their previously established quotas of Legionaries and auxiliaries. Guards were doubled all around the circumvallation lest any Jews attempt to escape during the coming turmoil. Every cohort in the Tenth Legion was ordered to make a light meal and stand in fully armed readiness for combat. Silva believed the peculiarities of this engagement would place the greatest demands on the engineers, so he assigned them two cohorts, the third and the fifth, as supplementary strength. All of this had been long ago arranged, and as a consequence the Legionaries went about their tasks as if they were still at drill.

The main assault tower had been moved to the base of the ramp even before final work had been completed. Now the engineers, under the watchful eyes of Rubrius Gallus, made the last inspection of their winches, ropes and tackles. The ramp was very steep and the tower of tremendous weight. It must not fail to arrive at its destination intact and on schedule.

The great battering ram rested on a separate car which would be hauled up the ramp after the tower. It was the longest and the heaviest ram any Legionary had ever seen, but lacked the traditional ram's head on the pounding end. There were no smithies capable of such metal work in all Palestine, so the engineers had substituted a simple iron cap to protect the wood. Silva secretly marveled at Rubrius Gallus's confidence in claiming the great beam would swing with ease. Yet Gallus had explained in his heavy engineer's voice, "Once the ram's center of moment is known we will adjust the slings accordingly, Sire. After that a small child could establish momentum simply by pushing rhythmically. Give us the protection and we will knock down your wall."

And he would too, Silva thought. Rubrius Gallus was the kind of man who had built the pyramids and if he was commanded to knock down Masada itself he would find a way.

He would have protection. Indeed, Silva thought, because of some foresight on the part of his General, Gallus would have a most formidable friend in the sky. At last the torture the sun had inflicted on Romans would be repaid, because it would be shining directly into the eyes of the Jews during the assault. And while it blinded it would also brilliantly illuminate every target daring to show itself behind the wall.

Fifty of the most expert Arab bowmen had been selected to ride in the armored top of the tower. If Gallus's figures were correct, and Silva had never known them to be otherwise, the tower should be approximately halfway up the ramp two hours after it began to move. At that location the bowmen would be within range of the ramparts with the sun at their backs. And as the tower rose so would the sun descend. Thus if all went as planned the Jews would have the sun almost directly in their eyes for the latter half of the tower's ascent—the critical time, in Silva's opinion, when they might offer the most serious defense.

Now Silva remembered how he had stood with Gallus so long ago, when the Tenth had first come to the desert. And he had then suggested that as long as such an enormous effort must be made to conquer Masada, perhaps they should steal an advantage from nature. The month of April offered thirteen and a half hours of day and ten and a half of night. Since they must attack from the west, why not angle the proposed ramp to take full advantage of the western sun? Gallus had grumbled unhappily about complications, but he had gone away and calculated the azimuths and the altitudes of the sun at the time he claimed the ramp would be completed, and he had found that a slight angling toward the north would bring the sun directly up the center. Thus even before the ramp was begun both men knew the assault must be at this time of day and approximately on this date. It was a secret they shared only with each other, and now with all in readiness, including the sun, they were compelled to celebrate. "I thank you, good Gallus!" Silva said. He embraced his Tribune and pounded affectionately on his heavy shoulders. "The master of time, the master of mountains," he laughed, "—the master of the sun!" And for the first time since he had known him he saw Rubrius Gallus actually smile.

Behind the assault tower and already poised at the base of the ramp were two testudos. Under each turtlelike structure there was a catapult manned by Legionaries of the fifth cohort. Ammunition for their future use had been carried up the ramp by Jews and stacked near the two platforms built out on each side of the ramp at a carefully calculated distance below the assault tower. The position was considered to be sufficiently far down the ramp to escape direct fire from above and yet still close enough to provide flanking protection for the all-important tower. The testudos were defended by Balearic slingers, who would be obliged to fight in the open. Silva did not expect many of them to survive the day.

Now he found himself astonished at the vast number of people his simple order to attack had brought together. If there was not a light wind to blow the dust away, he thought, at least half of them would be lost to view. Great clouds of the stuff rose from the baking desert floor and drifted across the moving spectacle in a series of grimy curtains. Sometimes Silva could see black clusters of the more than fifteen thousand Jews who he knew had been assembled along the ramp and would soon be hauling at the tackles. Most of them were lying down in the dust or were propped against the larger stones, apparently dozing. Legionaries, with their whips coiled in a loop, stood at intervals near the Jews and for the moment seemed to take less interest in their charges than a shepherd in his sheep.

Silva estimated there must be twenty thousand human beings waiting on or near the ramp for his final word of command. Titus, he remembered, had seemed able to take this sort of thing with ease when he stood before Jerusalem. But I cannot, which I must assume is the difference between princes and ordinary generals. I cannot accustom myself to the fact that with a nod of my head twenty thousand human beings will engage themselves either directly or indirectly in slaying less than one thousand. And I must confess to myself now, while I still dare think, that I shall not only remember this afternoon for the rest of my life but also that some animal instinct is causing my mind and body to tingle with anticipation. I am deeply in love and dream of tranquility in Praeneste and yet I must acknowledge to myself these are the moments for which I was born and trained. I do not hate any Jews, much less Eleazar ben Yair and his pitiful little tribe of troublemakers. I do not even believe the world will benefit from their deaths, as I might believe if they were Gauls or Germans. But die they must. Those are my orders.

Silva saw the hills to the west were speckled with groups of camp followers seeking the very best vantage points to observe the assault. It would be a better deed to eliminate those leeches, he thought, but unfortunately they were not mentioned in my orders.

He took a deep breath and held it for a moment as if wishing to absorb and retain within him every element of the scene. And he looked quickly to his left and right, and to the sun, and behind him, shifting his weight jauntily from one leg to the other, smiling, and trembling with excitement, for everywhere about him were the shouted orders, the curses and cheers, and the great metallic dissonance of war.

Again he glanced at the sun. It was almost time. He folded his arms and thought how very long he had waited for this moment. He was standing on a promontory near the base of the ramp with Rubrius Gallus at his side in recognition of his importance to the moment, and the balance of his staff waiting expectantly behind him.

Their immediate position was surrounded by the bearers of Silva's personal standards, his lictors, and those who carried the wild-boar and eagle emblems of the Tenth Legion. Five maniples of Silva's Praetorian Guard had been deployed about the command area by the Centurion Geminus. A matter of custom, Silva thought, rather than any real need to protect the Tenth's commander. Geminus was all soldier and this had been the way his men had been disposed in Gaul and in Germany, hence this was the way it would be done in Judea regardless of the impossibility of an attack from the rear. Commendable, thought

Silva. There were so many foolish mistakes and unforeseen snags befouling any battle. The major factor preventing total chaos was ironbound devotion to form. Form had built the Roman army—form would hold it together. Form had prescribed he remove the crest from his helmet in anticipation of combat, and he noticed with satisfaction how the ritual had been repeated by all his officers.

He studied the behavior and disposition of his troops, whose numbers were lost in the distant clouds of dust. Many of them were wearing the new laminated loricas, which were now of brass rather than leather. As protection for a man's chest they were superior, but the Legionaries complained bitterly of the increased weight. He noticed with open disapproval that some of the men who passed nearby had discarded their spiked caligulas, evidently preferring the comfort of Palestinian sandals. So did an army start going native, he thought, when it had served too long in a foreign land.

Now it seemed a pity the majority of these fine troops had been brought all the way to the desert simply to stand about and swat at flies while they watched a distant battle, yet there was room for just so many men on the ramp. Two cohorts, the second and the fourth, had been designated as first through the breach. They had been drilling every day against units of the cavalry that had been deliberately dismounted for the project. The results had often been almost too realistic, and one cavalryman had been killed in the resulting melees. Silva chuckled. Everyone in the Roman army knew how the average Legionary and cavalryman loved each other. Take the cavalryman's horse away and stand back while the foot soldier delighted in teaching him some humility.

The sun—the sun! Move! Are you waiting for our tubas to sound the attack? The second and fourth cohorts were moving into position now, already formed into their fighting units, with the Hastati at the fore, the Principes in second place, and the Triarii in third. Silva watched them carefully and could find no fault with their discipline. Good enough. Form and discipline built soldiers, and these fellows would not charge wildly through the wall the moment they spied an opening—and most certainly be overwhelmed as a result. Discipline. The maniples would not unite directly behind each other and simply run for the enemy. They would take position obliquely in the form

called quincunx which would separate them by such intervals each man would have a space of at least three feet
about him. Thus he had room to fight and his unit would
not present an easy mass target to the enemy.

Sun? Are you mired in the sky? I do not intend to seem
impatient, but you have not descended the width of a
finger in the past hour.

He wiped at the sweat rivering down his cheeks. His
helmet irked him. It was suddenly much too tight. Then
why wear it, when there was not the slightest chance any
missile sent from Masada could reach him? Custom, form,
discipline. Of course. I am a soldier in the Roman army.

He was pleased to notice the twenty-four Greek surgeons, the total complement of the Legion, had set up shop
at some distance to his right. Fear of what further damage
the Greeks might do made an already wounded Legionary
extremely wary of the surgeons, but Silva had chosen the
best men he could find and had long ago initiated a
campaign to encourage greater belief in their ministra-
tions. But still they were known as "the butchers."

Suddenly he realized his preoccupation with the sun had
been so consuming he had not once bothered to look up at
Masada. Now he turned to study the ramparts. No sign of
activity. He touched the arm of Gallus and said in an
undertone, "The Jews are too quiet. I will confess to you,
dear friend, they are strangely capable of giving me moments of doubt."

But Gallus was himself preoccupied, for he had been
watching an engineer who stood in exact line with the
ramp, yet at a considerable distance from it. For some
time he had been bent over a transit and now he had
turned to face Gallus. He raised both arms slowly and
clasped them over his head. Gallus waved his hand casually in recognition of the signal and said, "We may proceed
now, Sire. The sun has become our ally."

✧ ✧ ✧

Shem, son of Ishmael, stood in the tower which had so long been his home. It rose from the ramparts like a spike and was the most important tower of all since it was adjacent to the imperiled western gate. Shem knew only too well he had been given the responsibility for such a vantage only because of his extraordinary skill with the bow, so with all the determination of his sixteen years he had resolved to deserve his reputation.

Now he was a nervous host to Eleazar ben Yair, and to Heth, son of Ezra, and to Esau the Sicarius. He knew them to be the three greatest men in the world. O, most certainly! And here they were being as easy with him and speaking in the familiar with him as if he were their equal in age and honor. O yes! This time was worth all the months of loneliness and watching Romans who remained so tantalizingly just out of range of his arrows. He had shown them the intricate decorations he had scribed on his arm guard of hide, and while flexing it, praised his double convex bow. Such a weapon gave the maximum distance, and with the grip so close to the spring, the highest velocity.

Yet as he enthused, Shem was puzzled by the faces of these three men, known to all as the most veteran fighters on Masada. For most of the afternoon they had been watching the ponderous approach of the Roman tower and still they had not displayed the slightest elation. Here, at last, were the Romans deliberately coming within range. And neither Eleazar ben Yair, nor Heth, nor even Esau, seemed excited.

Shem had boasted how he would soon avenge his father fifty times, for such was the number of arrows in his store, and Eleazar ben Yair on hearing him had simply laid his hand on his shoulder and said nothing. He had

234

shown them the arrows, caressing them and delicately
adjusting their feathers to assure true flight, and he had
vowed every one of them would penetrate the flesh of a
Roman. He showed them how he had painted on each one
the Hebrew letters שם בן ישמעאל for Shem, son of
Ishmael.

He tried not to show his disappointment that not one of
his guests had so much as said they were depending on his
marksmanship, or cautioned him about the south wind
that had come, or even wished him luck. They seemed
hypnotized by the actions of the approaching Romans and
simply stared down at the ramp in silence.

At last Esau spoke in a voice so low Shem could hardly
understand him. "At Jotapata we boiled fenugreek and
managed to pour some on their gangways. It was so
slippery they fell down, and it worked for a while. . . ."

"We do not have any fenugreek," Heth said.

And Eleazar, who had hardly bothered to look at the
arrows even when they were held all shining before him,
said, "We are going to have the sun in our eyes."

And Shem, who worshipped Eleazar ben Yair not only
because he had always treated him as a man but because
he had in addition actually known and fought with his
father, thought he had never seen his idol so forlorn.

Zidon, the Pharisee, was bent like a blade of grass
before a tempest and all the other Jews along the thick
rope were hunched in the same fashion. There were on
this same rope more than one thousand Jews, including
those men who had come down the mountain with Zidon
and given themselves to the Romans. Ezra, the Sadducee,
was not among them. He had been crushed by one of the
first great rocks rolled down from the heights of Masada.

There were on the opposite side of the ramp another
thousand Jews and these also were bent backwards with
their bleeding heels dug into the flinty surface of the
ramp. And they too pulled on a great rope which was as
thick as a man's forearm. As these two columns of force
inched down the ramp so did the heavy assault tower
creep upward, for the ropes over which they grunted and
sighed and cried out in exhausted pain were led through a
system of blocks and tackles which the Tribune Gallus had
ordered set in place during the preceding night. Thus the

combined strength of two thousand Jews was transmitted through the rope to the tower itself, and even Zidon, whose eyes were stinging with his sweat, could occasionally raise his head and see the tower moving.

There were times when the massive cart which supported the tower sank into the surface of the ramp or lodged against a half-buried stone. Then the Roman engineers who were following closely behind the tower would investigate the cause, and soon the order would come down for greater effort. The Jews would cry out to the sky and to each other while they tried to summon more energy from their weariness, for unless they did succeed in again starting the tower on its way the Legionaries would certainly lay on with their whips.

The Tribune Gallus being experienced in human endurance, had recommended the ropes be secured and the Jews allowed an interval for breath four times each hour, and this was done. This was a time of whimpering for them all and agonized sobbing for a few. And it was a time when the Legionaries passed down the line and removed those who were already dead from exhaustion, or dying. They heaved the bodies off to each steep side of the ramp and watched them bounce and tumble off the rocks until finally they lay crumpled in the wadi below. Then the Legionaries sent word down to the base of the ramp giving the number of replacements they required. These numbers increased at each halt until as many as a hundred Jews were replaced each time.

The car which supported the great ram was now close behind the tower. It was also set in motion through a series of tackles, but since it was of much less weight than the tower, only two hundred Jews on each rope were required. They were positioned inside the lines of the other Jews and knew that if any part of the system at the top of the ramp gave way they would certainly be crushed. Yet they did not have to pull quite so hard as the others and very few of them died of their exertions.

Behind the ram were the two key catapults which would later be joined by others. These machines were on sledges and were hauled upward directly by the strength of twenty Jews straining along the five ropes leading from each sledge. Thus there were one hundred Jews pulling each catapult and they suffered terribly until the Tribune Gallus saw they were not enough, and rather than let

them fall too far behind in the procession sent fifty Jews
to push on the ends of each sledge.

By late afternoon when the sun was yellowing, the
assault tower was very nearly in place. And all of the
other elements were also moving upward according to the
Tribune Gallus's original schedule.

The south wind which had risen so suddenly rendered
Silva's original command post untenable. He had called for
his horse Fury and had ridden to windward of the tremendous column of dust which rose from the ramp. By late
afternoon it ascended nearly to the height of Masada itself
and was swept northward on the wind until it obscured
the horizon.

All of Silva's staff except Rubrius Gallus had followed
him and were now also mounted. He turned to them and
declared, "I trust so much dust will not dim the enthusiasm of our friend the sun!"

Instantly he regretted uttering the words. What a stiff
comment, he thought. Prebattle babble obviously spoken
in the rather wistful hope an opportunist will quote you
when historians get around to recording your name, if
indeed they ever do. What a pompous fellow you have
become, Flavius Silva—so suddenly the almighty phrase-
making, world-conquering Roman General! I puke at your
new pose and call upon a great and realistic woman called
Sheva to laugh at your boundless conceit.

Then quickly he said to the others, "Of course our
infallible Gallus had undoubtedly taken the dust factor
into his considerations. And I suppose if the sun is not in
the right place, he will move it."

Here on the windward side of the ramp it was possible
to observe the progress of the tower since there was no
dust preceding it. But from underneath the tower a continuous cloud of white dust blossomed and formed a long tail
which compounded itself and enveloped the entire length
of the ramp. Somewhere in the murk Silva knew there
were thousands of Jews and twenty cohorts of Legionaries, but he could see only small groups when the wind
pleased.

"This wind may give us trouble," he said to the Tribune
Arvianus, "but we may be confident Gallus will turn it off
when he no longer desires it."

Arvianus, who was overly stimulated by his commander's high spirits and attention, laughed and said, "Poor Gallus! It's all his commotion. Now he's eating his own dust."

"By the gods, Arvianus," Silva growled, "I may appoint you to bathe our good Gallus with the utmost reverence when this day is done. Meanwhile you will acquire a speck or two of grime yourself. You will take yourself to the ramp at once and discover why the catapults have not yet fired, and—"

Silva's words were lost in a shout from his staff and the surrounding Praetorians. For they had seen the first stones loft upward from the dust, arc, and descend behind the western gate of Masada. They heard the strong arms of the catapults thump against the crossbars again and then again.

And Arvianus sighed with relief.

In all of his life, even before his battles with other men had begun, even in the ancient history of his days when peril descended upon him only from the natural will of God, had Eleazar ben Yair ever known such anxiety. For at last, after an eternity of waiting his people were joined with the Romans and it was not at all as he had anticipated. The enemy were mostly invisible, either concealed behind the iron plates of the great tower which was still moving inexorably toward the western gate, or hidden in the white dust which foamed across the ramp like the sea exploding against a reef.

He had expected some harassment from the Roman catapults, but nothing like the destruction they had already wrought. Esau and Heth, both having previously experienced such attacks, had agreed that if a man simply stayed alert and heeded the warnings of approaching stones, the hazard was more dangerous to the spirit than the body. A number of the weaker men, including some of the infirm, had been posted along the ramparts to sing out the imminent arrival of Roman stones.

Eleazar watched the collapse of the system with dismay. Somewhere in the clouds of dust the catapults were set and triggered. There were few targets visible to Shem or any of the other archers Eleazar had spaced along the ramparts. The great fifty-pound stones came out of the blinding sun, and by the time they were seen by the observer they had arrived.

As soon as he realized the Romans had no need to aim their catapults at specific targets but were content to pound the area about the gate, Eleazar had sent every man to a safer post. Yet by the time the transfer had been completed and confusion dispelled, nine of his best men were dead, including Jacob, son of Tema; and fourteen others were so grievously injured they would never fight again.

Eleazar was heartened only by the remarkable change which seemed to have come over his fellow councilmen. At last they appeared to be united in resolve, and even the sniveling Matthias had refrained from any suggestion of surrender. And the people who were his tribe were now also transformed. Adonoi! There on the most exposed section of the rampart, shouting defiance at the Romans, was old Jacob, son of Sosas, a man normally afraid of the dark. Near him, waving a sword menacingly, was Meirus, son of Belgas, who was not only a thief by trade but had often boasted that he was the laziest man on Masada. There was Ardalus, and Lud, Aram, Uzul, Onam, Kedar, Cush and Ham, all with a new and determined look about them. All of them had hitherto been the most voluble and recalcitrant of sea lawyers, forecasters of doom, and complainers about rations. They were those well known to have schemed they way out of Jerusalem, but were now at last willing to fight Romans.

Eleazar had met with the council on the roof of Herod's old palace. It was built mostly of wood and was in serious disrepair, but from this vantage they could watch the ominous progress of the tower and still remain out of the line of catapult fire. By turning away from the sun they could also look down upon the entirety of Masada itself. And what Eleazar ben Yair saw within the citadel troubled him deeply.

For he observed how all of the women and their children had gathered near the crumbling building which had once enclosed a small bathing pool. All through the siege this area had been an oasis of lightness for the people of Masada. The delighted screams of children splashing in the water and the perpetual undertone of gossiping mothers had created an air of normality never to be seen elsewhere on Masada. Now the women huddled together in silence and their children pressed against them in terror. They stood transfixed as if already dead, and they stared at the western gate and at the great stones which came thumping down behind it with eyes that refused to believe.

Eleazar thought, Those eyes will haunt me forever! Just as Silva had foreseen, the owners of those eyes had chosen to interpret all he had ever said as unassailable truth. The Romans would never come. Had not Eleazar defied them? The Romans would melt in the sun because Eleazar ben Yair said they would melt in the sun. Those Romans who did not die of disease or melt in the sun would have no energies left to attack the mountain which had become their world. Eleazar ben Yair had said it would be so. And here, almost at the gate, were the Romans.

Eleazar looked away because he could no longer bear inspection by such eyes. If they would only reproach him it would be so much easier, but they would not forsake their trust in him. They were asking salvation, and worse, expecting it. Abigail had spoken the truth when she said even God had deserted the people of Masada. Now he suddenly remembered how after cursing the indifference of Jehovah she had taken to muttering mysteriously about her own private plans for their future.

The Tribune Rubrius Gallus had never known such satisfaction. All of his secret doubts concerning the conquest of Masada were now dissolved one after the other until it seemed he could do no wrong. The ramp had not only been completed on schedule but was also of the precise incline he had planned half a year ago. All along he had known an error of even two degrees in grade would cause an infinite number of problems, some of which might prove unsolvable. A steeper grade would have squared and perhaps even cubed the apparent weight of the assault tower. A softness of the surface could have created the same effect. In either event the ratio of Jews required for hauling would be correspondingly increased and it was now obvious the ramp simply could not have accommodated more bodies. Likewise the circumference of the hauling ropes and the blocks to guide and multiply the power of the Jews would be inadequate. And where in all the world were bigger ropes and tackles to be found?

Rubrius Gallus found he still had qualms when he reviewed all the factors which could have gone wrong.

Yet all was well. The entire operation had gone so smoothly he was compelled to immerse himself in it as completely as he had during the days of building, as if he had created a great beast and feared to unleash it without his closest supervision. As the assault tower moved upward, Gallus followed behind, choking in the dust, wiping constantly at his irritated eyes, and moving constantly from one concern to another. There were times when he could hardly see the length of his arm, and his engineers along with the assault Legionaries and even the Jews marveled at a Roman Tribune who would suddenly appear out of the murk and share their misery.

He constantly inspected the rope on both sides. He crawled underneath the tower to assure himself the engineers were applying enough fat to the axles. He exposed himself to possible fire from Masada by personally inspecting the hauling blocks which were fixed to the upper side of the tower. He climbed into the tower and stood on one of the great cross members listening anxiously to the continuous groans and squaks emanating from the tremendous structure as it crept upward. He nearly suffocated before he satisfied himself the occasional rocking motion was not causing excessive strains in the basic design.

Later he climbed to the armored tower where the Arab bowmen waited out the ascent. Once above the thicker dust he found he could survey the whole of the ramp, the ten thousand-odd Jews waiting in reserve along the hillsides, and the complete attack force of the Tenth Legion. On a rise behind this multitude he saw the cluster of Silva's fasces and standards. He noticed with relief that Silva's command post was already in shadow, so the timing was still exactly as he had planned.

As the distance to go decreased, Gallus saw a corresponding restlessness among the Arab bowmen. He looked through one of the slits to assure himself the uppermost tackles were running smoothly, then he descended from the tower and emerged into the smothering dust. Now he must see if the all-important ram was coming along properly.

He was troubled to find the distance between ram and tower had increased, so he stood quietly in the maelstrom of dust while he considered whether it would be more expeditious to augment the number of Jews on the ropes or drive those already laboring much harder. He decided on a third possibility and sent for a hundred Jews to push on the cart itself. Then he went back to the tower, which had become like a magnet to him. Never in his career had he been so proud of anything.

Gallus made his way back up the column of Jews on the south side of the ramp until he passed the last hauler and came to the bare rope. He watched it inch past him for a time and clamped his hand over his nose in a desperate attempt to filter the dust. A variation in the wind momentarily cleared the area and he instinctively turned his sore eyes toward Masada. Almost instantly an arrow pinned his hand to his mouth. As Rubrius Gallus fell, most of the shaft protruded from the back of his neck. On it was painted the Hebrew letters for Shem, son of Ishmael.

THE molten sun seemed to be burning a wound in the western hills as Eleazar ben Yair drove his people to exertions he had never thought possible. The great tower approached inexorably; like some primeval giant it screeched and groaned as if in agony, but always it moved upward, and it was already obvious nothing would prevent its union with the western gate. When he paused to estimate the ever-decreasing distance between the tower and the rampart Eleazar could catch an occasional glimpse of eyes behind the tower's iron plating. And he saw these were the Arab bowmen who had already killed many of his people.

From Shem's lookout just south of the ramp Eleazar could now see a part of the car which was being hauled behind the tower. He saw that it supported a great ram and he understood how once the tower was in place the car would be drawn in through its backside and the man swinging the ram would be perfectly protected. He was satisfied the Romans had also been hurt, for when the occasional breeze cleared the curtains of dust he saw the ramp was strewn with dead Legionaries. While he watched, hoping to more exactly estimate the time remaining before the tower was in position, he saw Shem pick off three more Legionaries who had only momentarily exposed them-selves. "Ah, Shem," he said, embracing him fiercely, "if only we had a thousand of you!"

When the tower was within javelin distance of the western gate he left Shem and ran down to the shelter of the ramparts where the people had collected. There was no use manning the eastern or southern walls any longer. Here at the western gate the battle would be fought.

When he arrived among those who remained of his fighting force he found them even more defiant than he

243

had hoped. They intended to stand and fight. They were saying to each other how they yearned for Roman blood on their blades and they also insisted they were ready for them. All fine talk, Eleazar thought, and he noticed that those who had previously fought Romans were saying the least.

He decided against reminding them of Roman efficiency at slaughter. Not while the will to resist was still so hot within them. There was still much to be done. There had been vessels which would not have gone to the bottom of the sea if their crews had not despaired. Who knew? Storms had been known to subside without any reasonable explanation, and was the thumping of catapults any more ominous than the crashing of waves?

Suddenly Abigail appeared to be everywhere he looked. She came blinking toward him out of the scarlet sunset and her rheumy eyes called out to him. She even managed to catch his arm once and shake it urgently. *"Now!"* she cried. "Have I wasted my precious breath trying to dignify a hyena? If you wait long I will sing when the rats are feasting on your face. Call all the people to you and tell them *now* how to grasp victory!"

He pushed her aside and ran to the wall of the western palace where most of those who were not actually posted on the ramparts had gathered. He first asked them if they were satisfied to die where they were, and when they answered they were not, he told them to rouse themselves by any means and follow Asshur, son of Joktan, who stood beside him, and do all he bade them do. They were to tear down the very wall which now protected them and pull away particularly the great timbers which were the framework of the palace.

"We will build a wall within our wall!" he announced in a voice he was careful to keep as confident as ever. "And we will build it in such a way no Roman ram or any other device can knock it down!" Then he told them how they would take the great beams of the palace and drag them to the area behind the western gate and lay them down parallel to each other and staggered end to end so they would in combination become like a great lattice. And he explained that as they were doing this he would send all the women except those who were pregnant or nursing the very youngest children, and they would carry earth to be dumped between the timbers. He raised his right hand and pounded his fist against the open fingers of his left, allowing them to yield, and thus demonstrated how the longer and harder a ram struck such a wall the more compact it would become.

"Masada is ours! There is no power on earth able to drive us off this mountain. I promise you it will remain ours—forever and ever!"

Soon after they set to work the great tower crept within a spear's length of the western gate. Then it paused for a time as if exhausted from the climb, and then once more, marshaling all of its creaks and groans, crawled through a final veil of dust until it crunched heavily against the gate.

When a courier brought the news of Rubrius Gallus's death, Silva was so distressed he went at once to the field hospital where the body had been carried. He had always loathed visiting army hospitals where it so often seemed more blood flowed than on the field itself. But Gallus had been a fine officer and deserved a farewell salute from his commander. More importantly, Gallus had been a friend, which made the visit all the more abhorrent. There was something about the sight of a friend killed in action which always shook him more than one lost to natural causes. The timbre of a friend's voice was still to be captured because it had been heard only so short a time before, and familiar gestures were too easily remembered though the friend's body lay still.

Timoleon the Greek insisted on explaining why his fellow surgeons were not busier. He waved his hands across carefully prepared displays of lancets, forceps, cauteries, and trephines. He cited Dioscorides as his mentor for the plants he had available with pharmaceutical properties. "Opium, for example," he proclaimed, holding a pinch before Silva's eyes. "We find it more effective than mandrake."

As he continued describing in clinical detail how the extraordinary marksmanship of the Jews had left far more dead than wounded, Silva found his elaborate Greek and feline purr more annoying than ever. He only half heard Timoleon's oration on gangrene and erysipelas, for he was looking down at Gallus's craggy face, wondering how he would phrase the obligatory letter to his family. "Our dear brave comrade charged into a horde of the enemy ... fearless of their numbers. . . . Our most valued friend and great officer fought the enemy hand to hand. . . . He led his soldiers through the wall. . . . He was ambushed by a horde of Jews. . . . Our gallant Tribune and dear friend perished with your names and that of Rome upon his lips . . . I feel confident our great Vespasian will award him—"

Silva sighed. It would be something like that. Certainly it would not do to say that Gallus had been so obsessed with a pile of sun-baked stones he had needlessly exposed himself to enemy fire. Or that he was apparently blowing his great nose at that fateful instant the enemy took advantage of his foolhardiness and removed such a valuable officer from the Roman military roles.

Because he was a Tribune and known to be a confidant of Silva's the arrow had been removed from Gallus's mouth, his face had been cleaned, and his torn hand placed in a reasonably natural position. While Timoleon hummed on in his labyrinthine Greek describing the efforts he had made to save Gallus and unctuously explained how the arrow had successively pierced his hand, the tongue, the pharynx, the common carotid, and finally the jugular vein, and how the wounds had been treated with dittany and other analgesics just as if there had been any hope of life, Silva could only think how Gallus's nose appeared to be more monumental than ever and his brow much less troubled. Good Gallus, he thought, you are at last engaged upon that adventure for which I had hoped to buy you a ticket. Even my most intriguing books cannot match what you are seeing now, nor can the ramp which you built here compare with your present endeavors. That is, I *think* so, dear friend Gallus, and I wish there were some way you could reassure me that it *is* so. I am melancholy enough about losing your company in this desert of deserts, but I should be all the more desolate if I discovered a man of your talents had suddenly become no better than the next man. I would say then that all we have done as Romans has been a total waste of time and effort. Do you agree to that, dear Gallus? Have you now supplemented your already extensive wisdom and perhaps reached the conclusion that among other things we are all fools—Jew and Roman alike?

As twilight came to the desert Silva rode slowly back toward his command post. On his own right hand he now wore the golden ring which had been Gallus's privilege as a Tribune. He would send it to his family along with the letter of condolence, and he thought it ironic this would be the only time in his life he would willingly wear a ring.

Attius, his aide, rode with him, and both men kept their eyes on Masada which still caught the very last of the sun. Silva could not detect any movement along the ramparts and he was surprised to see so little activity along the ramp itself. Everything seemed to be waiting. The catapults were inactive and the helmets of the Legionaries as static as cobblestones. He suddenly realized the continuous heavy concussions which had pounded the desert air most of the afternoon had ceased.

Near the base of the ramp he intercepted a messenger who was so breathless from his long run he could barely speak his mission. He said he had come from the Tribune Sextus Cerealius and that the wall of the Jews had been breached.

"Then what are they waiting for?"

"The Jews have built another wall within the first. I am to tell you the ram will do nothing against it."

Ah, good Gallus! Why could you not have survived the day? A wall which could not be breached by such a ram must be a very unique wall indeed!

Silva dismounted and turned Fury over to Attius. It was a long climb up the ramp and he would have preferred to ride, but man and horse would present too attractive a target for the Jews. He told Attius to transfer the command post to the base of the ramp and wait with the staff for further orders. "Advise them something has gone wrong and we may be all night about this. Fabatus should make provisions to feed the cohorts who will actually engage with the Jews. Those in reserve can wait. Advise Arvianus I will have the cavalry brought to the ramp, where they are to stand by. They should be ready to come up the ramp immediately on signal. Advise Liberalius he should personally assure himself all of his sentries are doubly alert by nightfall, particularly along the eastern circumvallation. There is something very odd about these new developments. I would not be surprised if the Jews were planning a breakout."

Silva handed his cloak to Attius and started up the ramp. Before he had taken a hundred steps the pain in his bad leg became excruciating.

He reached the assault tower in the very last of the light. There, nervously awaiting instructions, he found the

Tribune Sextus Cerealius, son of that rash man who had commanded the Fifth Legion at Jerusalem. Nepotism, Silva thought, has once more conquered good sense, for Cerealius the younger was anything but a reproduction of his incautious father. Instead he was a shy and studious boy Silva had long considered might make a much better poet than soldier. Only the tolerant Rubrius Gallus would have agreed to take him under his wing and hope to make a man of him. And Gallus, of course, as an engineering officer, was not expected to be killed.

Now, Silva realized, the whole assault had waited over an hour while this child stood about gnawing at his nails. And he reminded himself to speak with Titus concerning the selection of Tribunes—particularly the younger ones who might by ill chance be left with important decisions. There were three veteran Centurions fuming in silence behind young Cerealius and he was certain any one of them would have conquered the problem had he but had the authority.

Escorted by Cerealius and the three Centurions Silva climbed to the armored tower. An Arab bowman was ordered back from his slit so Silva could look out upon the broken wall of Masada. He had rather expected to see some movement, perhaps even a face, but he could not perceive the slightest sign of life. The silence was eerie yet he had been warned that if a man exposed himself even momentarily an arrow would find his flesh.

He saw how the ram head had passed the crumpled masonry of the original wall and appeared to be jammed against a newly constructed barrier. Ignoring Cerealius, he turned to question the Centurions. "Would it help to move the tower closer? We can set the Jews to hauling again."

"No, Sire. We have not the proper support beneath the tower, and the angle would change. The problem is the wall itself. It is built mostly of wood and gives before the ram."

Silva went back to the slit and saw how costly it would be to attempt storming the new wall. The Jews would have every advantage and might even succeed in destroying the striking force of the Tenth Legion since they would be taking them on only a few at a time. There was simply no room for more than two or three assault ladders.

He turned away from the slit. "We have a south wind,"

he said thoughtfully. "If we can't knock it down we'll burn it down."

His suggestion met with less enthusiasm than he had hoped for. The Centurion Lupus, who was the senior of the three and whom Silva knew to be a nearly fearless man, cleared his throat unhappily.

"Well? Well now, Lupus?" Silva asked. "Shyness ill becomes you. What is it that vexes you?"

"The wind here is fickle as a whore, Sire. If we set fire to the wall and it shifts, we stand to lose this tower."

Here, Silva recognized, was the age-old dilemma of any commander. Lupus of course was absolutely right, and it was all too easy to envision how flames might jump the narrow gap if the wind reversed itself, and equally easy to picture the tempers of both Vespasian and Titus when they were informed that regrettably, due to an "unfortunate error in judgment" of their esteemed commander in Judea, the conquest of Masada would take at least another three months—if indeed it could be attempted at all this summer. And Lupus, he knew, was sincere in his desire to win this battle, but at the same time he was protecting himself and his immediate group with the armor of caution. Before witnesses he had made a statement which would clear him of all blame if things went wrong.

Silva reminded himself that the cautious rarely won battles.

"Set fire to it!" he snapped.

When Eleazar ben Yair saw the first flaming arrows streak across the stars he called Hillel the priest to him and said, "Now raise thy voice to Jehovah and beg him for a shift in the wind. He is obviously weary of listening to me."

As he stood watching the blossoming fires along the new barricade he soon realized the flames were spreading so rapidly it could not last through the night. The south wind blew the flames across all of the area where any further defenses might be built, and the heat and noise was that of a monstrous furnace. All of the western part of Masada was now bright with the fire and sometimes Eleazar could see the eyes of the watching Romans through the slits in the armored top of the tower. Below and behind the tower he saw the glittering helmets of the assembled cohorts and he knew they were waiting only for the fire to diminish.

All of his leaders were now about him, not only the council but also Simon, son of Judas, Ebal, son of Ludim, and Tarshish, son of Elam, all of them heads of large Sicarii families and dependable fighters. There was no man or woman or child upon Masada who was not in some way under the influence of these men, and with many of them Eleazar had shared other battles. Never had he seen their faces so uncertain.

He said to them, "O, hear me! I want to hear *you!* Now is the time. We have need of each other's minds as much as the support of our hands."

Alexas, the slippery one, raised his hand for attention. "While the Romans are so busy on our west, why not escape to the east? We can fight our way through the eastern camps. They are nearly deserted."

Josiah, whom Eleazar had always considered a better baker than a fighter, suddenly became hysterical. "What would we do with our women and children? We can't drag them into an open battle!" He began to weep and moan that they had all been betrayed by Eleazar ben Yair.

Eleazar sensed an undercurrent of rebellion, the more dangerous and unpredictable because no one made any attempt to quiet Josiah. Their tone was desperate and their eyes spoke of their seething desire to vindicate themselves. He spoke to them very slowly, trying to calm what was already too calm. "Even if some of us managed to fight our way through and escape beyond the camps, even if the Roman cavalry did not pursue us—where would we be but in the open desert? At this time of year without water, I fear—"

"Once in the Negeb I nearly perished of thirst," Ham said, "and I tell you all now I would as soon feel a Roman blade in my belly. At least I might take the Roman with me."

"O, I say we could carry enough water to reach Ein Gedi, or even Herodium! The Jews there would look after us—"

"Ludim thinks like a child! He is thinking of times gone by!" Esau yelled. "All the Jews who would defy the Romans are here on Masada! The others would not dare give us so much as a greeting!"

Tarshish cleared his throat mightily and spat, which was

his usual way of begging attention. He was a shy man in spite of his long record of Roman assassinations from Caesarea to Jerusalem. And he so rarely spoke in a meeting, his attempt now, Eleazar thought, only proved his fears. Something must happen soon to unite or the only rule would be anarchy.

Tarshish was saying, "O, I remind you the Romans will do anything for money. Why not gather all we have and scatter it across the breach? Then when they stop to pick it up we can jump them!"

"We have not enough coins to hold three men," Javan growled.

"We have been all over these things a hundred times,'" Eleazar said. "And we are right back to the same old choices. Do we stand and fight or try some means of escape? And I have yet to hear any scheme for escape worth trying."

Then a high thin voice called out, "You got us into this! You must get us out!" It was Uzul, who had wanted to go down to the Romans with Zidon. "Why did you refuse Silva's offer?"

"I told you his only offer was slavery. And wasting breath accusing me of things past is not going to help us now."

"O, I say once more you should go down to Silva and tell him anything he wants to hear! Make him change his mind."

"I am not God."

"You act like him!"

Eleazar advanced on Uzul. He raised his hand to strike him, then suddenly lowered it. "You are right, Uzul," he sighed. "But I am only a little man—like you. It is not a very pleasant discovery, is it?"

There fell upon all of them now a long silence and the words of Eleazar's admission seemed to be echoed and re-echoed by the roar of the flames. Then very suddenly, as if the power of his despair had somehow affected the natural deserts, he felt a change of the wind on his cheek. Unbelieving he touched his face, looked about him, and then ran to the brink of the rampart where he could look toward the place where the western gate had been, and he was amazed to see how the wind had swung about until now it blew from the north and carried the flames toward the Roman tower. Even as he watched, the Romans began abandoning the upper works of the tower and those below retreated from the intensity of the flames.

"Hillel!" Eleazar called out triumphantly. "God has answered you! Send him our gratitude!"

Now at last Eleazar knew they would have the full night to do all that must be done to achieve victory.

The Arab bowmen in the top of the tower were the first to flee the intolerable heat. They scrambled down the ladder and even their Roman Centurions conceded they had been nearly baked alive.

The flames did not reach the lower decks of the tower, nor did the fire more than warm the night air about the Legionaries on the ramp. Yet the moment the wind changed, Silva knew he would not take Masada on this night.

"It must be that miserable goat!" he complained to the Tribune Metilius Nepos. He was trying to make light of the setback, more for his own sake than for any effect his levity might have on Nepos. He could not recall ever having known the fortunes of war to be so capricious. "That flea-bitten goat did not want to be sacrificed . . . so he fouled the auspices. I thought all through the ceremony he looked like a Semite."

When Silva called the Tribune Cerealius and his Centurions to him, he asked if the ropes should be slacked and the tower allowed to slip down the ramp away from the fire. Cerealius looked up at the flames and said nothing, as Silva knew he would. But Lupus the Centurion was also studying the flames and at last he said, "In my opinion, Sire, we stand more chance of losing the tower if we slack the ropes than from the risk of fire. Our tackle is not designed for descent. An instant of overload, a sudden slip, and our fixed blocks could be torn right out of the earth. And I now doubt the flames will do much except heat the iron plates. See how the air is rising above the fire in spite of the wind."

Silva turned away from the fire and looked down at the long columns of Legionaries deployed along the ramp. They had been waiting since early afternoon and he knew exactly the trend of their spirits. By now, sullen with inaction, they would have transferred all their hostility from the Jews to more familiar aggravations. What was the delay? The stupid engineers had never been able to do anything right, much less on schedule. And undoubtedly, Silva thought, his own name would be mentioned in combination with many colorful adjectives.

He looked back at the illuminated escarpments of Masada. The Jews were certainly not going to come down, he decided, and because of the flames they could not construct another wall in the same area.

He pulled off his helmet and beckoned to Attius. He wiped at the accumulation of sweat, dust and soot on his face and said, "Sound withdrawal. Pass the word we will take Masada in the morning."

When he had returned to his tent Silva found he was exhausted. Then even after Epos had bathed him he found he could not sleep, so in time he rose and poured himself a full goblet of Falernum. He stared at the liquid shimmering in the candlelight then suddenly threw the goblet across the tent and sat down at his table.

He sat for a long time blinking sleepily at the single oil lamp and trying to discipline his unmanageable thoughts. Should he spare the Jews on Masada when it was taken tomorrow, as a gift to Sheva the Alexandrian? If so, how? The Legionaries had not endured all these months to meet the Jews and coddle them! And they were a miserable stew of people anyway. You are a sentimental idiot. Sheva is a practical woman. She understands that being Procurator of Judea is your duty and your business and she is realistic enough to know you will have perplexities enough without the rabble on Masada mixing with the present population and infecting them with new dreams of revolt. How little these seditious people appreciate what is being done for them—and *could* be done! Ah, Sheva! How did you deserve the misfortune of being born a Jew?

Now then: If somehow Eleazar ben Yair could be taken without serious wounds, was it worth sending him back home as a sort of souvenir? Falco's idea, and a bad one, because it suggested the war was not over when it was said to have been long ago. The appearance of a Jewish leader in Rome at this late date was precisely what Vespasian was trying to avoid. He just wanted to hear confidentially that the last stubborn Jew was dead.

Silva slumped far down in his chair and forced his thoughts away from Sheva by composing the draft of a letter he would sent to Vespasian:

Flavius Silva to Vespasian. Our esteemed Emperor . . .

None of the familiar, as you would begin a second letter to Titus. Next, of course, the letter S for *Salutem. During the morning of this day I had the honor of commanding the Tenth Legion during the capture of Masada*—Clumsy and patronizing. You imply that Vespasian does not know the Tenth is here, which he most certainly does, and you employ the word "during" twice in the same sentence.

During the morning of this day I had the honor of commanding our forces in the Judean desert and I am pleased to report—Pompous in the extreme—and no man is more quick to be annoyed by pomposity than Vespasian.

On this morning, at such and such a time, we took Masada. There, that was better.

Silva closed his eyes and dozed. As he drifted through a limbo of half-wakefulness and dreams he saw himself returned to Praeneste. He was standing on the terrace with Sheva and she was smiling. Then Antoninus Mamilianus appeared and presented a bill for the construction of a supping tower. While Mamilianus enthused about the incomparable view to be enjoyed during meals Silva heard himself explaining, "If you pay one *as* monthly for the use of a hundred, my dear fellow, in a hundred months the interest will equal the capital. In other words, at twelve per cent per annum I cannot afford the tower, much less the food to be consumed therein. Cancel everything."

Then Sheva appeared in the tower and announced she was not the daughter of an Alexandrian shipper but of Vibo, his banker, and the interest on all that had been built at Praeneste was canceled.

He was awakened by the voice of Rosianus Geminus who stood before him, his bulk so strangely exaggerated by the candlelight he seemed a giant.

"Sire," he growled. "The wind has swung about again and the Jews have set fire to everything on Masada."

Eight

THE HOLOCAUST

ALL about him the conflagration raged and the stars were
lost in the heavy smoke which rolled and tumbled across
the top of Masada. The flames, excited by the south wind,
extended from the southern citadel all along both the
eastern and the western sides of the casemates where the
Sicarii, Pharisees, Essenes, and Sadducees had lived. The
priests themselves set fire to the ritual bath and to the
wooden parts of the synagogue. The small palaces were
already burning, as was the apartment structure in which
most of the council had lived. Flames were just beginning
to appear in the vicinity of the storehouses while what
remained of the Western Palace collapsed in bloated
columns of smoke. Undulating rivers of sparks shot across
Masada, carried on the wind which gathered storm velocity as the fires increased.

It was all as Eleazar ben Yair had urged: "Let us not
leave one whole bit of wood for the Romans! Let us
destroy all that may seem precious to us and show our
contempt for all possessions. Let us throw what money we
may have upon the ground, scattering it as we would the
seeds of a poisonous weed. Let us burn all of our weapons, knowing the metal parts remaining will be evidence
enough we had them in plenty. Let us burn our

255

storerooms, all except for a part of one, leaving it full of oil and meal and figs to prove we never despaired for food. Let us leave this place such a charred desert for the Romans the one below will seem like a refreshing oasis. Let us do all of these things while we are still masters of Masada!"

Miriam watched impassively as the first fires were lit about the building which had been her home for almost three years. She stood with her neighbors, Atarah, the wife of Alexas, Jerioth, the wife of Heth, who had been one of the first to die beneath a catapulted stone, Sheba, wife to Javan, and Keturah, wife to Asshur.

As the flames illuminated the courtyard Miriam deliberately ignored their frightened eyes and their weeping, and when she saw how rapidly the flames were advancing she left Reuben with them and entered her apartment, taking care to walk without haste. She soon reappeared carrying her cosmetics which she casually arranged on the steps of the courtyard.

Eleazar had said she must set an example. Very well, my beloved husband, you who have said so many things to me with only your heart and eyes. Thy wish is mine to fulfill. More than any other time in our lives together I hope you will look upon me now and see only beauty and devotion. I want you to believe for all time we are as one.

And so while her neighbors watched. Miram propped the mirror against a step and squatted down until she could see her face in a flaming light. She picked up her broad wooden comb and looking up at her friends began to stroke her hair. She managed to smile and said she was perfectly aware that all they had known together was being destroyed and soon all they had loved individually would be lost. "Like you," she said firmly, "I am screaming inside—but no Roman ears will ever hear me."

When she was satisfied with her hair she glanced at the approaching flames, then reached for her eye-shadow stick. She carefully touched the spatula end to the palette, which held a mixture of antimony, zinc, and oil in its depressions. She waited until she could be certain her fingers would not tremble as she worked the blue and green colors together or when she meticulously applied the paint to her eyelids. The wife of Eleazar ben Yair must not falter now. She studied her face thoughtfully, concerned that in the fluctuating light she might have been too lavish with the paint.

Jerioth, the wife of Heth, began a wild sobbing as the flames were sucked into the quarters which had been hers. She raised her fists to the black sky and cried out, "Thou art only an evil God and I spit at you!"

Miriam hesitated only an instant then continued with her ritual. She had set two small perfume vials beside the mirror. Now she picked up the one which was shaped like a cylinder and tested the scent. She rejected it in favor of the myrrh which was in the bulbous vial. She touched a drop of the liquid behind each ear, then to her cheekbones, and finally to her lips.

She rose unhurriedly and picked up the comb and the mirror, the vials, palette and stick. Then she walked toward the door of her own quarters and casually tossed all she carried into the flames. She beckoned Reuben to her side, then stretching out her arms to her friends said "Let us go to the men who have loved us."

Everywhere about the top of Masada there was great activity. Men who had never known what was in the storerooms were now within destroying the contents. They broke down the doors and made clubs of the pieces. Then they methodically passed down the rows upon rows of clay vessels and shattered every one, allowing the grain to spill on the floors until they were ankle-deep in it. They smashed the jars of figs and pulse and fruit wherever they came upon them. They broke open the vessels of wine and drank as much as they pleased, yet their zeal to destroy was such only a few paused long enough to become drunk. After they had opened many jars of oil and poured the contents over everything that was of wood they set fire to the mess.

Before the blazing ruins of the Western Palace other men were throwing great piles of weapons and scale armor and arrows into the flames.

Hillel the priest had deliberately turned his back on the crumbling synagogue. He preferred to watch the increasing flames about the building he had shared with Eleazar ben Yair and the families of the council. Beneath the floor of the small room which had been his, he had buried all of the silver shekels and half shekels which he had collected during his time on Masada. The money had been intended for the sometime rebuilding of the temple in Jerusalem, and since coins were not combustible he was fearful they would fall into the hands of the Romans. Now he was satisfied. The money was hidden forever.

Everywhere along the casemates there were people setting fire to the makeshift quarters which had been their homes.

In the eastern casemate, north of the gate to the snake path, old Shimeon, who was an Essene, fingered the white leather scroll which was the only thing left to him in life he loved. It was the Book of Psalms, and he held it up to the fireglow so he could view the script for the last time. He had intended to burn the scroll along with his sleeping mat and the two woven baskets which were his principal possessions, but now found he could not bring himself to even think of such words turned to ashes. So he fell to his knees and began digging frantically into the dirt floor with his fingers. He was panting with exertion and his fingers were bleeding before he had made a depression deep enough to satisfy him. When he saw the advancing fire was nearly upon him, Shimeon kissed the scroll and tenderly deposited it in the earth. Then he covered his treasure and left the casemate.

They came to Eleazar ben Yair as entire families, and in groups which had formed without regard to sect. They came to him as leaves drifting before a wind, sometimes half running and then suddenly pausing to look about the summit they knew so well, as if to convince themselves they were still on Masada. Their progress was marked by a continuous undercurrent of human sounds, their lamenting foaming up from them in a fountain of anguish and then subsiding until only the name Eleazar dominated all sounds. Some said Eleazar ben Yair would now cause a miracle and deliver them, and some said once the fires had started he had thrown himself from the ramparts.

They were drawn to the place where Eleazar ben Yair had last been seen, and they were hungering for reassurance. They came carrying their weeping children, who were more terrified of their parents' despair than of the fires.

The few aged who had survived on Masada appeared out of the rolling smoke and made their way to Eleazar ben Yair as if he had immediate need of them. They came bearing nothing except their sticks to support them, nor did any of the other eight hundred and two survivors of

Jerusalem and Masada carry anything with them. They wanted Eleazar and each other to see how utterly they had rid themselves of possessions.

When they saw Eleazar ben Yair a silence fell upon them and even the whimpering of the children was hushed. For a time there was only the rumbling noise of the great fires.

Eleazar instinctively returned to a rise in the ground which was nearly in the middle of Masada, between the Western Palace and the gate to the snake path. Here there was not so much smoke and the heat from the fires was tolerable. Miriam stood close beside him, and about him were nine men he had chosen with the utmost care. There were Kittim and Esau, Javan and Asshur, Nimrod, Josia, Alexas and Ham and Abram. Each of these men was armed with a sword, as was Eleazar ben Yair.

When the people had gathered around him and while some were still joining the fringes of the multitude, Eleazar began to talk with them, very quietly at first, as if inspired by nothing more than reaction to the day's events. He expressed his sympathies to the more than one hundred families who had lost their men during the Roman attack and he praised those who had in one way or another distinguished themselves. When he saw that all who could walk were within the sound of his voice he raised his hands and begged them to listen. His face was smeared with soot and sweat and his powerful body bent in weariness, yet his eyes flashed in the firelight as he called to many of his audience by name. "You, Tema, and Elam, and Atarah, and Dodamin, and Put, and Ludim, and Sheba, and Keturah, and Tarshish, and all of you whom I have brought to this mountain must understand how there is still a chance for victory!"

He took Miriam's hand and pressing it he thought, Give me of your vast courage, woman! I am within an instant of yielding to the idea I am a maniac leading the insane, because here is the wild and unbelievable truth again. Yet my guts curdle when I must ask others to believe.

"We are all the servants of God!" he began. "We swore long ago we would never be slaves of the Romans! Now we must prove God alone is our master and will be forever. Many of us were among the very first to defy the Romans' might. You can see that some time tomorrow they will overwhelm us."

He paused to study the filthy and exhausted faces turned up to him and he sought without success for some comfort among them. What he was about to tell them had been Abigail's plan for victory, and for an instant he wondered if she might be a devil's witch who had cunningly deceived him.

His deep voice cut through the roaring of the fire. "God has given us the chance to die bravely and achieve the only possible victory over the Romans! Now you may be sure Silva wants to take us alive if he can. Our men are of a certain use to him according to his fancy. You strong ones will be tormented until your spirit is utterly broken and you become mere shadows of men. You will be beaten as you labor and as you rest, and you will soon die building something for Rome. Most of us know how the weak are employed for as long as they last. You will furnish sport for the Romans who will take extreme pleasure in matching you against wild beasts. All of this, I assure you, is the truth!"

"How do you know so much?" a voice asked from the crowd. "There are other Jews working for the Romans and they are not all dead!" The accusing voice came from Hadad, son of Jetur, and for a moment Eleazar could think of no way to answer him.

"You forget we are not like the other Jews. Before we came to Masada the Romans invited us to accept them as our masters and we refused. Now we have defied them for almost three years. Do any of you believe they will treat us mercifully? Do you really believe they will forget the trouble we have been to them? They will enter here over the bodies of their own dead and I say to you they will avenge themselves far beyond our most terrible fears. They will be eager to capture as many men alive as they can so they can torture the son before his father. Your children will be raised high on their spears because they are the children of extraordinarily stubborn Jews whose seed must never be allowed to flower again. As for you women, the wives and daughters of our friends. I need hardly remind you Silva's army has been in the desert a long time. Every woman on Masada will be raped until her body is torn apart and then she will be dumped in a heap with the dead and near-dead. Do any of you really believe the Romans will come laden with sweet gifts for the Jews of Masada? If so then I say you are insane, and we who refuse to be put on the rack or tortured with fire and whippings, or devoured by beasts, we are the people who are sane!"

Eleazar paused because he suddenly remembered something he had intended to say when he began and he now wanted to be very certain of his words. He became suddenly aware that he was standing in an island of silence and for a moment the realization unnerved him. He sensed that over eight hundred souls were awaiting his next words and he saw how even the children and those most likely to speak out against him were quiet. He glanced at Miriam and their eyes exchanged more in an instant than they could have said of their love in days. He pressed her hand tightly and whispered, "Thou art my strength."

He dropped her hand and took the sword from Javan, who stood next to him. He held it toward the island of silence until he saw all eyes were upon it. Then he said, "Death is a part of life! God prepares us for it in his own way, from the very moment we are born. The fear of death is instinctive because it so often approaches in an instant. Yet those who have time to contemplate death do not react in the same way at all. Invariably a strange peace comes upon them if they know their passing is a certainty, as if they already knew the secrets hidden beyond life.

"Let us during these last hours take advantage of our privilege. Let us rob the Romans of their victory. Let us deny pleasure to their swords by using our own—let us go out of the world in a state of freedom!"

Eleazar lowered the sword and with it his voice. Now he spoke as though he had joined by chance with a few trusted friends and wished to explain to them a difficult problem.

"The men behind me are well known to you. We have drawn lots to determine who will take the life of the other and who will be the last alive. He is Asshur, son of Joktan, who has no intention of greeting the Romans in the morning except in his own way. Those of you who naturally hesitate because of love for your family may desire assistance. We will give it to you. We have kept a sufficient supply of weapons from the fire to provide every man his need. If the man of a family is dead, then the woman may come and choose a weapon, or if she prefers, one of us will strike the blows. Let us commence now because the morning is not far off. Let us accomplish this with the purpose of victory, with the name of God upon our lips and only love and freedom in our thoughts."

Even as the people of Masada started to move away, Abigail appeared out of the roiling storms of smoke. She moved very quietly amid the confusion until one by one she found five small children who were only a little way from the attention of their mothers. And she spoke to them softly saying to them sweet and enticing things and she invited them to take her hand and steal away with her to a place of marvels. She told them they would be gone only momentarily, and those who believed her were Tamar, Ezra's granddaughter, Laban, son of Gideon, and Hodiah, daughter of Kedar, Ishmael, son of Magadatus, and Reuben, son of Eleazar. None of them had more than five years of life when they vanished in the smoke.

❖ ❖ ❖

FLAVIUS SILVA rose with the very first light. In spite of his fitful sleep he was refreshed, mainly, he decided, because he knew this would be the day when the nuisance of Masada would finally be eliminated.

He smacked his hands together, and when Epos appeared, signaled him to bring his toilet bowl. After he had defecated he stepped into his bath and sent for the Tribune Larcus Liberalius.

As he relaxed in the lukewarm scented water he found considerable pleasure in assessing his powers of recuperation. Ah, yes! How remarkable the effect of a single female—a certain female! Driven away now were those terrible fears of impotence, perished forever in this desert the numbing sense of loneliness which no amount or variety of company had been able to disperse. Now at last, because of a little Jewess, Rome could have back her completely dedicated Flavius Silva. Rome had her Vespasian and her Titus as heir apparent, but she had need of her Silvas too.

Ergo. Under Flavius Silva and his native wife, Judea might become the most flourishing colony of all.

When Liberalius arrived Silva greeted him warmly and said, "Yesterday my spirits were up, today they soar. I am eager as a young Tribune before his first battle. And I had a rotten night's sleep. How do you account for that?"

"I think we all sense victory on this day, Sire. Need I remind you who have experienced so many, how very stimulating it can be?"

"This one has been so long in materializing, I suppose it means more to me."

"The combination of circumstances has been extraordinary, Sire."

"Exactly. And I am going to make very sure they never

263

combine again—which is why I have called you here. Perhaps a part of our troubles has been created because we have not always convinced the Jews we really mean what we say. Perhaps we have not been firm enough and the benefits we are bringing have been misinterpreted. Who knows? They may think we are afraid of them. Now, during my restless night I conceived a ploy which might do us some lasting good, but I hesitate to make it an official order until I have heard another's opinion. You know your Jews as well as any man, so what do you think of this? The assault will proceed as originally planned, but we will add a third cohort to follow close on the heels of the first two. This cohort will not be intended to fight, indeed they will be ordered to refrain. However, each man in that cohort will serve as an escort to one of our laboring Jews and he is to be charged with getting him there in good enough health so that he can see what happens. Then when everything is secured and our business up there finished, those Jews are to form the burial parties. When they are done with that mess you will have a surprise for them."

Silva pushed himself to his feet and stood impatiently while Epos rubbed him with a towel. "You will announce to those Jews they are free to go back to wherever they came from, and each of them will be issued sufficient water and rations to last them until they are out of the desert. How does that strike you, Liberalius?"

"I'm afraid I do not follow you, Sire. Most of the Jews we have here are little better than criminals or have been involved in opposition to us one way or another. I fail to see how their release would contribute to tranquility in Palestine."

Liberalius hesitated uncertainly and Silva saw at once that he thought he had spoken too openly. "Well, well . . . now come along, Liberalius, I have deliberately sought your opinion, not your approval. What else were you going to say?"

"Well, Sire, I would be willing to wager a thousand sesterces that over half the beggars will kill each other before they get out of the desert."

"You're probably right. Then double their number. What I am after is a hundred-odd emissaries carrying a significant message to the population of Palestine. I want them to tell their brothers and their sisters what happened

on top of Masada when the Tenth Legion finally demonstrated that a Roman means what he says."

"I understand. Very good, Sire. After today we will be
feeding far more Jews than our actual requirements, so I
suppose the more we lose the better."

"One more thing. A personal matter. You are aware of
my special interest in a certain Jewish family?"

"I would be negligent in my duty if I were not, Sire."

"I prefer not to have them in the vicinity during the
events of this day. You will provide them with all the
necessities for a comfortable caravan to Caesarea. They
may be told that those who wish may there take ship for
Alexandria. You will make every provision for their comfort and provide an escort of two maniples for their
safety. They are to leave as soon as your preparations are
done, preferably within the hour."

"It will be done, Sire."

"*She* will not accompany her relatives. You will request—and I repeat *request*, Liberalius—*that at her convenience* she come to this tent and here await my return
from the mountain. Any questions?"

"One, Sire. What do I do if she does not want to
come?"

Silva hesitated. Then he took a deep breath and said
firmly, "Tell her . . . my life depends upon it."

The pale ivory sky was smudged with smoke from
Masada. But only above the mountain itself did it subdue
the brilliance of the morning sun while in no way diminishing its heat. When he first left his tent Silva was stunned
by the oppressive power of the sun. Its sheer physical
force seemed to press him into the flinty earth and skewer
his eyes with its reflections from every piece of armor. A
cloud of flies stormed about his face and in moments his
entire body was glistening with sweat. By the gods, he
thought, we are departing this desert just in time!

Silva had hoped to speed the assault, but it was
midmorning before all the units had assembled, the bewil-
dered Jews who were to be witnesses properly stationed,
and the ammunition supply for the catapults replenished.
And it was just as well, Silva mused, for there was little
wisdom in using the sun one day and ignoring it the next.

He waited until the sun was high enough to deny the

Jews any advantage and then gave the order for the
catapults to commence their opening barrage.

The ramp was an airless oven when the catapults
grunted and the first stones sailed upward. The stones
disappeared in the smoke beyond the blackened breach
and in the echoing silence of the desert the Romans could
actually hear the stones hit. There was no answering fire
from the ramparts, but then Silva had not expected any.
Eleazar, he knew, would be saving his arrows and his
fighters for the critical time when the first assault ladders
were raised.

Silva had now taken direct command of the forces on
the ramp. There must be no unforeseen delays this time.
How he missed Rubrius Gallus! Young Cerealius had
reported the smoke-blackened tower was undamaged and
cool enough for bowmen. Very good. At least the young
man was alert to its need.

While he waited for the sun to break over the ramparts
Silva passed among the men of the second and fourth
cohorts, who would be the first up the ladders. He touched
the helmet of those whom he recognized as a signal of his
affection and he made an effort to wish well those whom
he did not know. Postponing the attack had been a wise
decision, he decided. In spite of the heat his Legionaries
were now obviously fresher and in better spirits. Even
when they moved a step or two they seemed to swagger,
and that was as it should be. His own spirits soared as he
viewed the healthy Roman faces beneath so many polished
helmets, and even his limp did not mar his air of jauntiness as he strode up the ramp. The Centurion Rosianus
Geminus was at his side and he said to him, "Give me a
hundred of that sort and I can make the world turn from
east to west."

When at last the sun had climbed high enough so that it
could not blind the Arab bowmen in the tower, Silva
called for the assault ladders. They were brought from
behind the tower at a run and had no sooner touched the
face of Masada than they were solid with climbing
Legionaries who shouted encouragement to each other
and cursed and called out defiance to the mountain itself.

Inside the tower Silva waited for Eleazar's certain retal-
iation. He was flanked on both sides by Arabs poised to
cover the mounting Legionaries. Anything that moved was
to be their target, and yet not one had loosed an arrow.

Silva watched unbelievingly as the first Legionary, a man known as "the Chamoix" because of his agility as a climber, disappeared into the thin curtain of smoke.

Silva turned smiling to Geminus. "Brave fellow! Let us not forget to award the Chamoix his Corona Muralis."

A second man from the same ladder vanished into the smoke and then those from the other two ladders surged over behind them. Soon an entire cohort had passed over the rampart and through the smoke. When Silva saw the bowmen had still not found a single target he hastily descended from the tower. Something was very wrong. The Jew had set a trap and there was obviously no time for rear-rank analysis.

With Geminus trotting behind him and protesting the risk, Silva ran to the base of the ladders as fast as his limp would permit. "You would make an old woman or one of Falco's boys of me!" he shouted at Geminus. Then he pulled a Legionary aside and took his place in the mounting column of men.

When Silva emerged from the smoke he was accompanied by Geminus and three Legionaries, who were so astonished to find their General among them they barely remembered to draw their swords. Following him, they ran only a few steps before they halted and stood aghast. For whatever had been the splendor of Masada was now only a stifling furnace which stank and crackled in the heat of the morning.

Silva could not believe his eyes. All about him he saw his veteran Legionaries, men he had never known to flinch during the bloodiest campaigns. Now they stood, still breathing heavily from their climb and anticipation of mortal combat, yet their jaws had gone slack and their eyes were fixed on some distant object which they seemed not to see at all. Some of the men had pulled off their helmets and others had sheathed their swords. They sighed and glanced furtively at each other and scratched at their whiskers in bewilderment. All about them was death they could not comprehend.

Silva moved through them warily, looking everywhere about the summit for a possible source of ambuscade. There *must* come a sudden attack. Of course—there had always been one, no matter where in the world or who the enemy. What kind of Oriental trickery was this for the Jews so long to expose themselves to an invading force when they had so little left to hide behind? Where were the fighting Jews?

Silva ordered the Legionaries to put their helmets back on their heads and be prepared for immediate attack from any quarter. They began to march very slowly across Masada, moving cautiously, a few steps at a time their eyes darting about them. Sometimes they turned completely around to reassure themselves, but they saw only more and more Legionaries emerge from the smoke. They said almost nothing to each other, seeming to fear speech lest they break the spell and so bring the Jews back to life. For they discovered the Jews were not in any one place but everywhere—near this smoking ruin a man, a woman and two children lying neatly side by side. Here on the open side of a hillock were the bodies of four families as carefully arranged as if they were on parade. Here was an elderly man and a woman alone, and then side by side, two old men.

"They've murdered each other," Silva whispered, "and not one of them appears to have resisted." He caught his breath, for even the sound of his whispered words seemed to shake the mountain.

Silva's staff, having learned of their General's recklessly early ascent, made haste to join him on the summit. They followed him in silence while he examined a storehouse which had not been burned and they saw how it was filled with grain and wine and oil in plenty. They imitated Silva's brooding pace and paused with him when he stopped to look down upon a family, or a man and his woman locked forever in each other's arms. And these, they noticed, most affected Flavius Silva.

The sun was directly overhead and the profile of Masada shimmering in the heat when they came upon a strongly built woman of remarkably fair complexion. Beside her was sprawled a powerful man who had apparently thrown himself on his own knife. Somehow he had reached out and caught the face of the woman and turned it toward his own. Silva accused his imagination of being under the influence of necromancy, because after staring at the woman's face for a time he could have sworn she was smiling.

He stepped around the couple for a better look at the man and he said in a troubled voice, "This man was Eleazar ben Yair." And suddenly, as if some vital fiber of his discipline had snapped, he whirled on his officers and shouted, "I have had enough of this ghoulishness! We have won nothing but a rock! *Leave* me!"

Shocked, they turned about, and only the occasional clink of their armor marked their departure.

WHEN the heavy pounding of the catapults ceased she forced her thoughts away from Masada. There was need for this little time to be sure of herself. This was his house and for these stolen moments she would be its contented mistress. Here on the table were his books by which he set so much value, and here the neatly stacked rolls of communications from his land which was so far away and so strange there was no true comprehension of it. Here, near the scrolls, were his writing materials and the ceremonial dagger he had said had been given him by his friend Rubrius Gallus, the same dagger which refused to descend upon its owner's neck.

Here was his goblet and his flask of Falernum which he said was the finest wine in the world and which had nearly possessed him. Will you forgive me, dear Flavius, if I now make a confession? I do not like your Falernum. It is too bold for an Oriental. It is like so many other things, a multitude in which we would always differ, for my people prefer greater subtlety in all things. And we are as you say, sometimes overly capricious. I lack the solidity of a Roman. I would too often disgrace you, dear General, and all of Rome would laugh themselves silly at my attempts to be a matron.

But I love you, my Flavius. It is something I am as powerless to remedy as I would be to successfully imitate a Roman lady. My God proclaims your gods do not exist. So it is with us. We cannot. If we try to exist together we will destroy each other.

I would like to forget you are the enemy of my people, but I will never manage it. It would come to me at odd times, the wrong times probably, and since there would be nothing gained by my repeatedly calling you names, you would be puzzled at my sullen behavior and start blaming my Jewish blood. Then more and more little faults would appear which you would also assign to my blood, and in time all of the joy you find in me now would have rotted away.

And I too must be influenced by your every word and gesture. The most genuine humility could become Roman arrogance to my eyes. You might ask me to sit down or stand up, or eat this or not eat that, and I would find a way to transform the request into a Roman military order. You might say here is a jewel for you, and eventually my reaction would be that you are showing off or displaying typical Roman ostentation. In a place such as Praeneste must be, you might find it necessary to discipline a slave for some minor offense, and no matter how mild your punishment I would interpret it as outrageous Roman cruelty. All of these things make it impossible. Ah, dear great General, how the arguments boil within me! How I justify and condemn. How I try to fashion the beautiful from the grotesque. I should this very moment run away from your influence by joining the caravan for Caesarea. They cannot have gone far. But will I? I am so weak with my love for you I will stay right here—thy obedient slave. I will accept your Romanness and cherish it, even while I revile it. Hail, victorious Flavius Silva. You have totally conquered this unhappy Jewess.

Now she heard the approach of many heavy voices outside the tent and from their Latin inflections and occasional phrases in Greek she judged they must be Silva's officers. And she wondered why they were returning so soon.

She listened anxiously, though the voices still melted together and distinct words were lost in the chinking of metal equipment and crunching of spiked sandals on the hard-packed street. Then as the voices passed the entrance she was able to separate them until they became individuals. She held her breath lest she miss a word.

"I think I will take to the hills and be alone for a time."

"Did you see Silva's face? He looked like a whipped dog."

"More like a pole-axed ox."

One of the men laughed as they passed on, and she changed her mind about showing herself outside the tent. The new voices approached and passed.

"I feel like a bath."

"I intend to get drunk."

"I thought I had seen everything in this world."

"Once, in Britain—"

"I cannot understand how a man can kill his entire family."

"And they all did it—not one of them weaseled on the bargain."

"Did you mark how the rats and buzzards were already having breakfast?"

She covered her ears as the voices passed on, and for a moment heard only the cadence of her own pounding heart. Then she forced herself to listen again as new voices passed.

"I cannot believe we took the place without a fight."

"We didn't take it. They gave it to us along with the backs of their hands."

"I am wondering how Silva is going to report the deliberate suicide of our entire enemy force, including their families."

"It will make interesting reading—but no one in the Tenth will get a medal."

"It's a slap in the face for all Romans."

"Who expected a welcome kiss?"

"Who could kiss a putrefying Jew under any circumstances?"

"Our noble General, for one."

Again there was laughter, then she heard another voice saying the sight of so many Jews laid out neatly side by side was something he would not soon forget.

Yet another voice responded with the firm opinion that all Jews were crazy, and another, objecting, said they could never be accused of lacking pure courage. Finally all the voices were gone and in a moment even the hard war sounds of their owners' movements faded into silence.

She closed her eyes, and covering her lips with her fingers whispered, "Flavius . . . Flavius . . ." And with the name still ringing through her mind she began to sob uncontrollably.

At last when her anguish was spent she yearned to touch and hold something that belonged to him. She walked as in a dream to his table, circled it slowly, then reached out to caress its surface.

You asked me to await you, Flavius Silva, and that I intend to do. But I know now it must be in my own way.

You have been very un-Roman to leave me a choice, and so unfeeling, so very very Roman to assume our life together could continue now that so many of my people have cursed it with their blood.

She halted near the rolls of parchment and her hand moved steadily across the table until it stopped upon his ceremonial dagger. She fingered it a moment, then pulled it from the scabbard. She turned the blade over several times and finally looked up at the gap in the tent. Without lowering her eyes she quickly punctured the veins of both wrists. Then she walked carefully to the couch and lay down.

For a time Silva stood alone in the drumming heat. My mind, he thought, has been drained of all order. I alone on this mountain knew my antagonist, but that is not what brings anarchy to my senses. It is no great surprise to me that a leader chooses death before defeat. But the rest of them? If it was so important to win this pathetic victory against us, I can only believe they were all inspired by a power unknown to ordinary men.

Ordinary men? Like you, Flavius Silva, crumpled General of the Armies? You, who are shaken to your very marrow. How are you going to explain to a mighty Emperor there is an ultimate limit to power?

Because he had so long admired the lofty perch of Herod's villa from below, he now found himself drawn toward the northern end of Masada. He walked very slowly, so lost in reflection he nearly collided with Rosianus Geminus, who stood waiting for him near the smoking remains of a gate.

"May I disturb you, Sire?" Geminus said cautiously.

"You already have."

"We have some prisoners."

Silva's face changed instantly. His back straightened, his eyebrows rose, and a relieved smile spread over his face. "Have you, now! Well then, my belief in the frailty of the human race is at last restored!"

"This way, Sire." Geminus turned and led him past the charred embers of what appeared to have been a bathhouse. He turned sharply, entered an arched door and started down the narrow stairway leading to Herod's palace-villa.

Soon they emerged upon a circular terrace which Silva

saw must have once supported a lovely pavilion. Here he
had once envisioned bringing Sheva, here together he had
hoped they would celebrate when Masada was truly conquered.

Now he saw the terrace was occupied by two of his
Praetorians, an old woman, and five awed children.

"*These* are your prisoners?"

"There are no more, Sire. These were hiding in a small
cistern in the next level down."

Silva shook his head. He looked into the eyes of the old
woman and the children and saw they were unafraid.
Almost defiant, he thought. They seem to be daring me to
kill them.

He passed his hand across his eyes and then made a
small uncertain gesture as if he were seeking something in
the air about him. He started to say something in Greek
to the old woman and then changed his mind.

His voice became unnaturally harsh when he spoke to
Geminus. "I am going to get out of this place. Bring these
children and the old woman with us."

He turned, started back up the steps, then halted momentarily. As Geminus and the Praetorians began to herd
the children and finally Abigail after him he said, "Cover
their eyes until they are well down the mountain. If they
see what is on top they will never see anything else for the
rest of their lives."

Silva held his nose as the little procession passed
through the ruins and finally came to the smoking barrier
at the western gate. And he was vastly relieved when they
descended through the assault tower and at last emerged
on the ramp. He took a deep breath of the comparatively
cool air and wanted to tell Geminus how very close he
had come to anointing Masada with his vomit. Instead he
told him to take the children and the old woman to the
Nabatean camp followers.

"Find the best family you can. Advise them my personal purse will provide a hundred shekels toward their
care."

He watched as they left him and made their way down
the ramp. He watched until even Geminus was very small,
then he took off his helmet and looked back at Masada.
Now it stood in silence, baking in the heat, and above it
he saw a squadron of buzzards wheeling past the sun. As
he took off his buckler and draped it along with his sword

across his arm he wondered idly if the buzzards would ever learn the difference between victors and vanquished.

He shuddered and warned himself he must not hold the gruesome image of Masada any longer in his mind. Now to new and more admirable things. Sheva would be waiting. There were worlds to conquer in her company, worlds without flies and stink and bodies dripping blood as they rotted in the sun, worlds for a soldier who now wanted only peace.

He began to walk very slowly down the ramp. How unsatisfying. He had risked his career in building this great incline and yet there would never be any reason for him to climb it again. Away with such brooding. Now only Sheva mattered and plans, *plans!* Dear woman, we can now actually make plans!

His pace quickened as he considered the essential matters which must first claim his attention. A few weeks more in Palestine to assure all was calm, then by ship to Ostia. Strange, he had never inquired if the sea made her ill. Then to Rome for a few days, of course—it would be necessary and might even be productive. Perhaps Sheva's peculiar charm might help Titus melt down a regulation or two. It was not really important. The important thing, the exciting prospect, was that within less than a week of arriving on Roman soil you would lift her up in your arms and carry her across the threshold of Praeneste!

Imagine! After waiting all these years, both love and honors!

He smiled, and when he discovered he was half running down his ramp, he began to laugh softly at his youthful eagerness.

SIGNET Bestsellers

☐ **LISTEN TO THE SILENCE by David W. Elliott.** A total and unique experience—gripping, poignant, most often, shattering. A fourteen-year-old boy narrates the chronicle of events that lead him into, through, and out of an insane asylum. "Each page has the ring of unmistakable truth . . . a well-written tour de force, another **Snake Pit . . ."—The New York Times Book Review.**
(#Q4513—95¢)

☐ **THE SUMMIT by Stephen Marlowe.** Intrigue, blackmail, treachery and romance, THE SUMMIT is a wire-taut novel as devious as LeCarre, as fast moving as Ambler or Greene—chosen by **The New York Times Book Review** as one of The Year's Best Criminals at Large, 1970 . . . "A shining example of the political extrapolation that pumped new lifeblood into the espionage novel in 1970." (#Y4632—$1.25)

☐ **SANCTUARY V by Budd Schulberg.** A gripping study of men and women under the most extreme kinds of pressure in a Cuban political haven. Writing with power, compassion, and with a rare gift for characterization, Budd Schulberg reconfirms with SANCTUARY V his position as one of America's master storytellers.
(#Y4511—$1.25)

☐ **THE STUD by Jackie Collins.** A novel about the ambitious, fast living—and loving—people among the swinging "in-crowd" of London's discotheque scene . . . and Tony Burg, ex-waiter, ex-nothing—now elevated to the rank of superstud. (#Q4609—95¢)

SIGNET Bestsellers

☐ **BLACK STAR by Morton Cooper.** A scorching new novel by the author of **The King.** As timely as today's headlines, BLACK STAR is the story of Robin Hamilton, a beautiful, seductive and greatly talented black girl who seeks love and identity in the world of bigtime show business. (#Y4333—$1.25)

☐ **SNOW GODS by Frederic Morton.** A dazzling triumph about the money built world and honey-sweet pleasures of the International Set at their leisure in the luxurious Alps. "Power is the great theme . . . Frederic Morton builds his power skillfully."—New York Times
(#Y4025—$1.25)

☐ **THE PRETENDERS by Gwen Davis.** The exciting bestseller about the jet-setters is a masterful portrait of their loves, lives and fears. (#Y4260—$1.25)

☐ **OR I'LL DRESS YOU IN MOURNING by Larry Collins and Dominique Lapierre.** The penetrating story of the rise of "El Cordobes," the greatest living matador today, and the changing face of Spain. (#Y3949—$1.25)

SIGNET Bestsellers

SIGNET Bestsellers

Watch for these Bestsellers from SIGNET

☐ **THE GOVERNOR by Edward R. F. Sheehan.** A novel of politics and passion and Emmet Shannon who rode into the Governor's mansion on the strength of his physical charm, his Irish-American background, the support of an earthy Boston Archbishop and the backing of a boss who knew and controlled every inch of the Massachusetts political jungle. (#Y4818—$1.25)

☐ **MAKING LOVE by Norman Bogner.** From the author of Seventh Avenue comes a crackling and bittersweet account of an unlikely affair between a rich and jaded blonde and a has-been professional football player. (#Y4815—$1.25)

☐ **THE WALTER SYNDROME by Richard Neely.** A psychopathic rapist who calls himself the Executioner terrorizes all New York, as one after another violated and grotesquely mutilated female corpses are found. You are invited to discover the strange and terrible secret of his identity—if your nerves and stomach can take it! "An eerie thriller . . . even the most hardened reader will feel its impact."—The New York Times (#Y4766—$1.25)

☐ **THE MARRIAGE OF A YOUNG STOCKBROKER by Charles Webb.** A wonderful novel . . . a saga that picks up where THE GRADUATE left off, these are the bittersweet misadventures of a young man bugged by success, baffled by marriage, and obsessed by the wildest compulsion this side of 42nd St. A 20th Century-Fox film starring Richard Benjamin. (#Y4714—$1.25)
